THE ANGEL OF MERCY SERIES

FAR ABOVE RUBIES

BOOK TEN

AL LACY

Multnomah® Publishers *Sisters, Oregon*

FAR ABOVE RUBIES
published by Multnomah Publishers, Inc.

© 2000 by ALJO Productions, Inc.
International Standard Book Number: 1-57673-499-4

Cover illustration by Vittorio Dangelico
Design by David Uttley Design

Scripture quotations are from: *The Holy Bible,* King James Version

Multnomah is a trademark of Multnomah Publishers, Inc., and is registered in the U.S. Patent and Trademark Office.

The colophon is a trademark of Multnomah Publishers, Inc.

Printed in the United States of America

For information:
MULTNOMAH PUBLISHERS, INC.
POST OFFICE BOX 1720
SISTERS, OREGON 97759

Library of Congress Cataloging-in-Publication Data:
Lacy, Al.
    Far above rubies/Al Lacy.
        p.cm.–(The angel of mercy series; bk. 10)   ISBN 1-57673-499-4 (alk. paper)
    1. Frontier and pioneer life–Missouri–Fiction. 2. Women pioneers–Missiouri– Fiction.
    3. Outlaws–Missouri–Fiction. I. Title
PS3562.A256 F37 20000   813'.54–dc21   99-056051

00 01 02 03 04 05 — 10 9 8 7 6 5 4 3 2 1 0

To Blair Jacobson, a faithful fan who reads all of my novels,
and according to his dad,
sometimes reads two at the same time.

Who can find a virtuous woman?
for her price is far above rubies.
PROVERBS 31:10

PROLOGUE

THE HISTORY OF THE TAMING of the Wild West is a story of contrasts. There were the good men and the bad men. The good men were the early explorers, trappers, fur traders, and settlers such as Jim Bridger, Jedediah Smith, Kit Carson, Meriwether Lewis, William Clark, Zebulon Pike, William Sublette, and David Jackson. And of course, there were the lawmen—Bat Masterson, Bill Tilghman, Charlie Siringo, "Bear River" Tom Smith, James Butler "Wild Bill" Hickok, Pat Garrett, and Teddy Roosevelt, who had a brief but successful tenure as deputy sheriff of Stark County, Dakota Territory, prior to entering politics.

And then there were the bad men—Frank Reno; Bob and Grat Dalton; Cole, Bob, Jim, and John Younger; Jesse and Frank James, and their infamous gang members such as Jim Reed, Bill Chadwell, Charlie Pitts, and Clell Miller; Sam Bass; William "Billy the Kid" Bonney; Sam Starr; and Butch Cassidy and Harry "The Sundance Kid" Longbaugh. The contrasts do not stop there, however.

There were the good women and the bad women, although the scarcity of women in the Old West means there are not as many names written on the pages of history. Still, there were some who made their mark.

Some of the unnamed good women were strong, resourceful farm and ranch wives, women who operated their own stores in the towns that dotted the hills, mountains, and plains; women who served as nurses in a violent land, and those who served as schoolmarms. Others were simply the wives and mothers who gallantly faced the hardships, trials, and dangers that came with taming the West.

Many of the good women have left their names on the pages of history—Eliza Spalding and Narcissa Whitman, who blazed a gospel trail riding sidesaddle from Independence, Missouri, all the way to Oregon. There was Frances Grummond, an army officer's wife who followed her husband to the wilds of Wyoming, lived the rugged life at Fort Phil Kearney, and had her heart broken when her husband was killed in the Fetterman massacre.

There was Julia Bulette of Virginia City, Nevada, who brought her eastern culture to the West and helped young women learn how to be ladies in a rugged man's world. There was Janette Riker, who was traveling through Montana in a covered wagon with her father and two brothers as the winter of 1849 came on. As soon as they set up camp, the men went out to hunt buffalo. They never returned. Alone, Janette endured the hard Montana winter in the covered wagon and was rescued by Indians in the spring. She showed the true grit and courage of a woman of the West.

There was Susan Magoffin, one of the first women to travel the Santa Fe Trail, who was a pillar of strength to many of the other women in the wagon train. And let us not forget gallant Esther Morris, a dignified lady in her midfifties, whose famous tea party in South Pass City, Wyoming, set the wheels in motion that in 1869 brought women the right to vote for the first time anywhere in this country.

There were also the bad women. In spite of the fact that womanhood was respected and admired in the Old West, some women chose to pass all bounds of respectability in the brothels and gambling halls, while others became full-scale, gun-toting outlaws. Among the female outlaws, there were "Cattle" Annie McDougal, Pearl Hart, Belle Reed Starr—who began her outlaw career with the James-Younger gang—Jennie "Little Britches" Stevens, Genie Carter, Rose of the Cimarron Dunn, Ella "Cattle Kate" Watson—who was lynched by angry cattlemen— "Bloody" Flo Quick, Fannie Porter, Laura Bullion, Annie Rogers, and Etta Place, who rode as an outlaw, a reward offered for her capture with Butch Cassidy and the Sundance Kid.

It was the decent and respectable women who caused men to maintain the Western tradition of protective chivalry over them. In Miles City, Montana, in 1883, businessman Charles Brown used his gun barrel to crack the skull of foulmouthed Bill Rigney for insulting the respectable wife and daughter of one of the town's leading citizens.

Rigney, who lay bleeding on the ground and was supposedly dying, was hastily lynched by townsmen intent on avoiding the embarrassment of trying Charles Brown for manslaughter. The townsmen, feeling strongly about virtuous, respectable women being insulted, regarded Brown's act as justifiable homicide, necessitated by the Western code of chivalry.

In His Word, the God of heaven has much to say about good women and bad women. It is pleasant to find in the book of Proverbs that God devotes most of the last chapter to the virtuous woman who fears the Lord, and says she shall be praised.

Her children arise up and call her blessed,
her husband also, and he praiseth her. (Proverbs 31:28)

In the same chapter God says in verse 10:

Who can find a virtuous woman?
for her price is far above rubies.

Let's get into our story and learn of young outlaw Ginny Grayson, who finds that through the grace of God she can become one whose price is far above rubies.

IT WAS AN HOUR AFTER DARK when Clell Miller rode his bay gelding at a steady trot toward Kansas City. He traveled north beneath the star-bedecked vault of sky, holding a lead rope that kept the saddled but riderless chestnut mare trotting along behind.

A three-quarter moon hung above him, clear-edged and cold. It was mid-February, 1866, and winter had come to Missouri, bringing its raw winds. The breaths of the horses puffed out in steamy clouds on the icy air.

To Miller, the rolling hills stretching into the distance looked like mounds of cold silver bordered in black. Soon the dim lights of the town winked in the night, and Miller slowed the horses to a walk as they turned onto a shadowed street dotted with hanging lanterns swinging in the wind.

When the railroad station came into view, Miller could make out the dark shapes of horses, buggies, and wagons in the parking lot. A few figures moved across the lot and filed through the doors of the depot. He found a spot at the hitching rail near the door and tied both animals to it. Above him, telegraph wires moaned a lonely song in the wind.

When he stepped inside the depot office, people were milling about and he could hear a telegraph instrument clicking faintly.

He ran his gaze slowly around the depot for any sign of a lawman, but saw none.

Miller's attention was drawn to a large blackboard near the ticket window. A message written with chalk in bold letters announced that the train from Chicago would be thirty minutes to an hour late.

Miller sighed and thought of Jesse and Cole and the rest of the gang waiting for him and Charlie back at the Younger farm. But there was nothing he could do about the delay. Just as soon as the train arrived, he and Charlie would head for Lee's Summit.

He went to the waiting area and spotted a bench at the rear that was still unoccupied. As he threaded his way past the people sitting on benches, he pulled off his gloves and slipped out of his coat. As soon as he sat down, he stretched his legs out and slid down a bit on the bench, tilting his hat over his face.

The conversations around him became a low drone in his ears, and Miller thought about that cold day a little more than a month ago when he and the gang first laid eyes on Charlie Pitts. Miller was one of the men positioned outside the door of the Missouri State Bank in Springfield. Jesse, Cole, and six other men were inside the bank, holding the tellers at gunpoint as they filled canvas money bags. Clell and three other gang members waited outside with the horses.

Some fifteen or twenty feet away, outside the bank, Frank James and Jim Reed stood close together. Clell waited with the gang's youngest member, Billy Sterling. This was Billy's first holdup as a member of the James-Younger gang.

"Settle down, Billy," said Clell, noticing young Sterling's jittery breathing.

Billy flicked a glance at him. "Shouldn't they be out here by now? What's takin' 'em so long?"

"Must be makin' a big haul. Maybe they found a huge stack of money in the vault."

"Well, I just wish they'd hurry up. Those people across the street are givin' us the evil eye and—"

Frank James pulled his revolver as he called out, "It's the sheriff!"

Greene County Sheriff Preston Martell and two deputies were a half block away, coming on the run. There were four rugged-looking townsmen with them, also carrying guns. Martell was shouting for people on the street to take cover.

Just then, Jesse James came out of the bank carrying a canvas money bag and a cocked Colt .45 revolver in his right hand. Behind him was Cole Younger and his three brothers. The rest of the gang followed. Each man carried a money bag and a cocked revolver.

"Jesse!" shouted Frank. "It's the sheriff!"

Jesse James looked down the street and lined his Colt .45 on Martell. He dropped the hammer and Martell went face down in the dusty street.

The deputies and the four townsmen returned fire. Clell Miller saw Billy Sterling take a slug in the midsection and drop to his knees, then fall dead.

More townsmen united with the deputies.

Although the gang was now outnumbered, they kept up a rapid fire of bullets. One of the men shouted to Jesse, saying they had better mount up and ride out.

Suddenly, a stranger moved in among them, gun drawn, and started firing. One of the deputies went down. Clell saw the tall, slender man fire again, dropping one of the townsmen. The stranger's face was set in firm lines and his features were deeply bronzed. It was as if he had been in this kind of gun battle before.

The stranger popped off another shot, then turned to the youngest James brother. "You're Jesse James, aren't you?"

"Sure am," said Jesse, firing another shot. "Much obliged. You ah…. must be an—"

"Outlaw?"

"Yeah. What's your name?"

Before the man could answer, Cole Younger shouted, "Jesse! Another deputy just went down! Now's the time to go! Billy's dead. We'll have to leave him."

"On your horses, boys!" Jesse ordered. "Quick! We'll go north!"

Each man popped off another shot at the townsmen before mounting up.

Jesse looked at the stranger. "The black, here, belonged to that dead kid lyin' in the dust. Get on him and come with us!"

The man hopped on the black and galloped away with the gang.

The dozen men rode hard for about ten miles, then Cole Younger shouted at Jesse that they should rest the horses. Jesse nodded and pointed at a deep ravine coming up on their right. Soon they were at the bottom of the ravine. The horses' sides were heaving as their riders dismounted, and everybody gathered around Jesse James as he smiled at the stranger and said, "Okay, my friend. Now you can tell me your name."

"Name's Charlie Pitts," the hatchet-faced man said.

Jesse stuck out his hand. "Well, Charlie, we're in your debt. You joined us and made a dent in the opposition when we needed it most."

Jesse then introduced Charlie to Cole Younger. As Charlie was shaking Cole's hand, he said, "I'm really glad to make your acquaintance. You and Jesse have sort of been heroes to me."

"Well, now you're our hero, Charlie!" Cole said.

"Never dreamed you boys would ever know my name!"

Jesse introduced Pitts to the rest of the gang. Each man thanked him as he made the rounds to shake hands. When he got to Clell Miller, he said, "I saw you take out a couple of those guys back there while they were runnin' and zig-zaggin'. You're a good shot."

Clell grinned. "That's because Jesse taught me."

"Charlie," Jesse said, "we've got to get movin' here in a few minutes. But there's time for you to tell us about yourself. Where're you from...and how did you happen to be on the street in Springfield today?"

"I come from Columbia, Missouri. I used to run with a gang headed up by Ford Kellerman."

Jesse and Frank exchanged glances, and Cole said, "Kellerman's gang was wiped out during a bank holdup over in Scott City, Kansas, about a year ago, weren't they?"

Charlie nodded. "And you're wonderin' how come I'm still alive."

Cole grinned. "Well, yeah."

"Simple. I was in the Missouri State Prison up until three days ago. Did a couple years of a five-year sentence on a robbery charge. Got out on parole for bein' a good boy in prison. I came to Springfield to see an old friend, but I found out he died while I was in prison. I'd just left his widow's house and was gonna do a little shoppin' before I left town. That's why I was on the street when the shootin' started. My horse is still at the house."

Cole nodded sharply. "Well, Charlie, I'm sure Jesse will agree with me that we should ask you to join the gang. We're short a man now. How about it?"

Charlie shook his head in wonderment. "Well, I'd sure like to, Cole. And I'd be honored to be a part of this gang. But right now I've got to head for Chicago. Little unfinished business to take care of there. But I'd sure like to join up when I'm through."

"I agree 1000 percent, Cole," said Jesse. Then he said to Charlie, "How long will your unfinished business in Chicago take?"

"Hard to say exactly. Probably four or five weeks. I'll be takin' a train from Kansas City to Chicago, and I'll come back to Kansas City when I'm done."

"How about I give you a contact in Kansas City?" Jesse said. "You can send him a wire and tell him what train you'll be on. Don't mention Cole's name or mine. Just send the telegram from Clyde Fisher. I don't want you usin' your own name either. Our contact will get the message to us."

"Clyde Fisher. Okay. Got it."

Jesse took a moment to scribble the man's name and address on a piece of paper. When he handed it to Pitts, he said, "You can go ahead and take Billy's horse if you want to."

"Okay. I will. What should I do with him when I get to Kansas City?"

"Sell him and pocket the money."

"Oh. Well, thanks."

"One more thing."

"Mm-hmm?"

Looking at Cole, Jesse said, "How about since Charlie helped save our hides back there, we give him something for his trouble?"

"It's all right with me," Cole said. "We owe him, that's for sure."

"Five hundred?"

16

"Sure."

"Five hundred!" gasped Charlie. "I'm not even part of the gang yet!"

Jesse laughed. "But you're gonna be, Charlie. And besides, we owe you that much."

Charlie was given his five hundred dollars and Billy Sterling's horse. He gave a wave and rode away.

Clell Miller's thoughts came back to the present when he heard someone say the train was coming in. He glanced at the big clock above the ticket window. Not quite thirty minutes had passed since he'd sat down on the bench.

The sound of the engine whistle filled the air, followed by the clanging of a bell. People headed for the double doors leading to the depot platform. Miller shifted his hat to its normal position and shrugged into his coat. As he walked toward the doors, he grinned to himself. It was almost 8:40, but at least Charlie was arriving on February 12, as he'd indicated in his telegram.

The big engine chugged into the station as the crowd gathered along the platform. The windows of the coaches were fogged up, but Clell could see people moving about inside as the train eased to a stop and the engine ejected a long hiss from its boiler.

It was only a few minutes until Clell spotted Charlie coming down the steps of coach number three. He watched him thread his way through the crowd.

When Charlie set his bags down and offered his hand in greeting, Clell said, "Got any more luggage?"

"Nope. Just these two pieces."

"Good. I didn't come in a wagon. Just brought a horse along for you to ride."

"Let's go, then. I'm excited about joinin' up with the gang."

"No more than we are to have you," Clell said as he led Charlie across the platform toward the parking lot. "Jesse and Cole really liked the way you handled yourself that day in Springfield. You helped save our hides, that's for sure. You'll get rich ridin' with us, I guarantee it. Everybody's waitin' to see you."

Clell led Charlie toward the horses at the hitching rail. "We've got a bed all ready for you at the hideout."

"Sounds good. How long's it take to ride there?"

"About an hour and a half this time of night. It's about two miles east of Lee's Summit. Here's the horses. The mare's yours."

They tied a piece of luggage behind each saddle, and as they mounted up, Charlie said, "I'm sure glad I joined in the fight that day. Who'd have thought Charlie Pitts would be ridin' with the famous Jesse James–Cole Younger gang!"

As they rode southwest through the cold night, Miller explained to Pitts that the gang was actually made up of two gangs of six men each. Jesse was the leader of one gang, Cole was the leader of the other, and it was working like a well-oiled machine.

"Since Billy Sterling was in the James gang, you'll be taking his place," Clell said. "Jesse and Cole like the combined gangs evened out as much as possible."

Charlie nodded. "It's best that way. Say…things were pretty hectic that day in the ravine. Tell me the names of the guys again. I know Frank is in Jesse's part of the gang, but the rest of the names I'm havin' a hard time rememberin'."

"Well, besides Jesse, Frank, myself, and you, the other James men are Jim Reed and Bill Chadwell. In the other gang, besides Cole, there are his brothers, John, Jim, and Bob. The other two are Arch Clements and Sly Chapman."

"Okay. All I have to do now is put the names and faces together."

"That'll come quickly when you're with the gang a day or two."

Pitts shook his head. "I still can't believe it, Clell. Me, a member of the James-Younger gang. Sounds too good to be true. I've been thinkin' of what I've heard about the James brothers and the Younger brothers. Did they actually meet for the first time when they were ridin' for William Quantrill?"

"Sure did. That's where I met 'em, too. I rode with Quantrill almost from the very day he put his guerrilla pack together."

"Then I suppose you were with Quantrill on that day when he sacked Lawrence, Kansas."

"Yeah."

"What was it…a hundred and fifty civilians killed, and their bodies left in the streets and their yards?"

"Yeah. I really wasn't for doin' it, but Quantrill wanted to make a statement."

"Well, I guess he got it across." Charlie was silent a few seconds, then said, "Did you guys kill children, too, as the newspapers reported?"

"Yeah."

Miller, who wore a hard exterior much of the time, said no more, and Charlie let the subject drop.

After a few silent moments, Miller said, "Charlie, you're gonna get your feet wet real quick. Jesse and Cole are plannin' to rob the Clay County Bank over in Liberty tomorrow. Know where Liberty is?"

"Sure. A little ways north of Kansas City."

"Right. Liberty's about thirty miles north of the hideout."

"Exactly what is this hideout, Clell? A house…a barn…or what?"

"Oh. I guess nobody told you. It's the old Younger farm. The old folks are dead, so Cole and his brothers took the place over."

"Hmm. That surprises me a bit."

"What do you mean?"

"Usin' the Younger place as a hideout. Certainly the law would look for 'em there."

Miller chuckled. "Cole took care of that problem. They've got a couple of neighbors on their payroll who watch out for the law. A couple of times when lawmen came, the gang was alerted soon enough to be hidden when the badge toters rode up to the house. The other neighbors are intimidated and fear for their lives if they should do anything to bring the law down on the gang's hideout."

"I see. Sounds like Cole's got things in hand."

"Yep. Of course, in the eyes of the community, the Younger brothers have brought shame on the name of their dead parents by becomin' outlaws."

Charlie didn't comment.

The two outlaws had been riding almost exactly an hour and a half when Miller pointed with his chin and said, "That's the Younger place, just up ahead."

When they turned off the road, Pitts saw two dark forms move out of a stand of cottonwood trees, carrying rifles. They moved into the path of the two riders, and one of them called out, "That's you, ain't it, Clell?"

"It's me, Ted," Miller said.

As the two riders drew rein, the pair of men moved up close.

"So this is your new man."

"That's right. Charlie Pitts, meet Ted Pack and Gene Vader…the neighbors I was tellin' you about."

When they rode up to the house, Clell and Charlie were met by two more men with rifles, who stood on the front porch. Both men called out a welcome to Charlie, and he remembered their faces from the day in Springfield.

The reunion between Charlie Pitts and the gang was enthusiastic.

Jesse offered Charlie and Clell food, and while they were eating at the big kitchen table, both Jesse and Cole sat with them. Jesse explained to Charlie how the gang always split up the loot from each robbery, with himself and Cole taking larger cuts because they were the leaders.

Twenty-two-year-old Cole was the oldest of the Younger brothers and was already balding. He set his clear gray gaze on Charlie and said, "We're all about to hit the hay for the night, but there'll be time in the morning to fill you in on the robbery details and what we expect of you."

"Fine," said Pitts. "You name it, I'll do it."

Cole looked at Jesse, who at nineteen, was dark-haired and quite slender. "I like this guy's attitude."

"Me, too," said Jesse. "He's gonna be a real asset to the gang."

The gang leaders filled Charlie in on previous robberies and the amounts of money they had taken. Charlie's excitement mounted with each story. He had always wanted to be rich, and now his opportunity had come.

When the two men finished eating, Jesse told Charlie he

would bunk in an upstairs room with Jim Reed. He called Jim from the parlor and told him Charlie was ready to hit the sack.

"Me, too," said Reed. "C'mon, Charlie. I'll take you to the room."

Charlie told everybody good night and headed up the stairs with Reed, whom he could tell was one tough hombre.

The next morning, after breakfast, Jesse and Cole gathered all the gang members in the parlor and went over the robbery plan in detail, explaining each man's role.

Cole ran his gaze over their faces and grinned, saying, "Jesse and I picked this particular bank because it will yield a large take."

"Sounds good to me, brother-boss," said Bob Younger, chuckling.

Jesse spoke up. "We'll need to leave here about ten o'clock to allow plenty of time to ride to Liberty. The bank closes at three o'clock. We want to pull the robbery at precisely 2:40."

After the robbery scheme had been planned to precision, coffee was poured by Arch Clements and Frank James. Charlie Pitts listened as the rest of the gang talked leisurely about the money they had laid their hands on just since the first of the year. When the conversation about the money diminished, and silence fell over the group, Arch Clements said, "Hey, have you guys seen Sly's new girlfriend?"

Jim Younger grinned. "You mean that little filly at the general store in Lee's Summit he's been flirtin' with?"

"Yeah," said Arch. "How old is she, Sly? Fourteen?"

"Fifteen," Chapman said quickly. "Okay, so she's a bit young. She'll grow up. I'll just keep things real friendly between us so's she'll still be interested in me when she's old enough to get married."

There was a round of laughter, then Bob Younger said, "Maybe she won't want to marry an outlaw."

"I won't be an outlaw then. When I get rich enough, I'll do just like the rest of you guys are plannin'…I'll take my little bride and head for someplace where they've never heard of Sly Chapman, the most intelligent member of the James-Younger gang!"

There was more laughter, then Jesse said, "Speaking of girl-friends, Cole, how are things going between you and Belle?"

Jim Reed shifted on his chair at the mention of Belle.

Charlie Pitts, wanting to feel a solid part of the gang as quickly as possible, winked at Jesse, and said, "Hey, Cole, I want to hear about Belle. Who is she?"

Cole's face tinted. "Aw, it ain't that serious, Charlie. I've only spent a total of maybe two hours with her, a few minutes at a time."

"Well, c'mon. Tell me about her."

Cole grinned. "Good gal."

"How old is she?"

"Eighteen."

Charlie laughed. "Well, at least she's out of the cradle. That's more than I can say for this girl Sly's been flirtin' with."

"Her name's Myra Belle Shirley," spoke up Jesse. "Her older brother, Bud, rode with the Quantrill guerrillas the same time Cole, Frank, and I did."

"Oh, I see," said Pitts.

Jesse went on. "John Shirley, Bud and Belle's father, was a Quantrill sympathizer and a strong Confederate. He was ecstatic when Bud joined up with Quantrill. It was through Bud that Cole met Belle and her parents."

"Yeah," said Cole, "then Bud had to go and get himself killed. He was cornered in June of '64 over in Sarcoxie by a small Union militia unit who were huntin' Quantrill and the men who had ridden with him. Bud resisted 'em, and they riddled him full of bullets without tryin' to take him alive."

Jesse looked at Cole. "Tell Charlie what Belle did."

Cole chuckled. "Get this Charlie. This is why I like Belle. She was sixteen at the time the militia unit killed her brother. It made her so mad she strapped on a gun, dead-set on killin' every man in the unit. Her dad had taught her when she was twelve how to use both a revolver and a rifle, and she was an excellent marksman with both. With some ingenuity, which is somethin' Belle has plenty of, she found out that the unit of men who killed Bud were part of a federal army installation camped near Carthage. Belle rode there, and without arousing an inkling of suspicion she was able to learn the names of the eight men who made up the unit."

Charlie chuckled. "Sounds like quite a gal."

"She is, I assure you. Belle told me she did some camping herself in the woods close by the army camp. Within two days she'd found four of the eight men, waited till she could get each one alone, and shot 'em dead. The army was quickly on the trail of the 'man' who had done this. Realizing they might figure her out, Belle hightailed it for home, disappointed that she hadn't been able to take out her vengeance on the other four."

Charlie popped his hands together. "She's really somethin'!"

"And when she got home, Charlie," put in Jim Reed, "both of her parents commended her for at least takin' out half of the men who killed her brother."

Cole eyed Reed. "How'd you know that, Jim?"

"Belle told me one day a few weeks ago when I ran onto her in town."

Charlie snickered. "I marvel at Belle's accomplishment, Cole. For two reasons…"

24

"Yeah? What are they?"

"Well, number one, that she's a girl. Not many men could have done what she did. And number two, that at sixteen years old she was able to take out four men who were professional soldiers."

Every man in the gang voiced his agreement, but it was Jim Reed who showed the most admiration for Belle's courage and ability with a gun.

THE GANG MEMBERS NOTICED Cole Younger watching Jim Reed as he talked about Belle.

Suddenly Jim felt the weight of Cole's eyes on him and fell silent.

Cole let a lopsided grin curve his lips and said, "Jim, ol' boy, it appears to me that you've got more than admiration for Belle. I'd say you just might have some other kind of feelin's for her."

"Well, I...uh—"

"Hey! It's all right, Jim boy! I haven't carved my name in her forehead. You've got as much right to get to know her as I do."

"I've only talked to her a couple times, Cole. I really do admire her courage, and I have to say I've sure never seen a female so good with a gun."

Cole laughed. Then he turned to Pitts and said, "Charlie, since you're new here, I should explain that Belle is livin' with her cousin Edgar Shirley and his wife, Allene, over in Strasburg."

"Strasburg... where's that?"

"'Bout five miles southeast of here. Very small town."

"Guess I never heard of it."

"Edgar and Allene were Quantrill sympathizers right up until Quantrill was killed by federal troops last June. And they're both sympathetic with the James-Younger gang."

Charlie nodded. "So Belle's cousins don't mind if she's friendly to you and Jim?"

Cole grinned as he flicked a glance at Jim Reed and said, "That's right."

Reed managed a slight smile. "It's really more than that, Charlie. The gal is good with a gun. She's proven herself valuable to the gang."

Cole laughed. "Even though she's not much to look at, Belle's smart as a whip and has a mean streak."

"She is homely," said Bob Younger, "but she sure is valuable in a robbery."

The men laughed, all except Jim Reed.

"What do you mean, Bob, 'she's valuable in a robbery'?" Charlie asked.

"We've been takin' her with us on some bank and stage-coach robberies. Belle dresses like a man and pushes her hair up under her hat. She's as tough and intimidatin' as any man in this gang."

"That's right," spoke up John Younger. "Maybe even a little tougher than some of us."

This time even Jim Reed laughed.

"Tell you what we did, Charlie," said Cole. "Twice when we planned stagecoach robberies, I sent Belle to the stage stop to board the stage as a passenger—wearin' a dress, of course. When we converged on the stages and pulled 'em over, Belle already had the passengers at gunpoint and the male passengers disarmed. So they could offer no resistance durin' the robbery."

Charlie shook his head. "Cole, you're a genius!"

"The idea was Belle's," Jim Reed said.

Cole nodded. "Sure was. I tell you, Charlie, she's quite a gal."

With that, Cole rose to his feet. "Well, boys, we'd better get done whatever needs doin' so we'll be ready to ride outta here by ten o'clock."

When Charlie entered the room he shared with Jim Reed and saw him cleaning his gun, he said, "That's exactly what I need to do."

"You can use these cloths and the cleanin' oil if you don't have your own," Jim said amiably.

"Much obliged." Charlie slid his gun out of its holster and sat down on his bunk. As he started the task of cleaning his gun, he said, "Now, Jim, if I'm stickin' my nose in where it don't belong, you just say so, and I'll shut up, okay?"

"Sure."

"Well, I kind of get the idea that you may have some tender feelin's toward Belle Shirley. Just by what went on between you and Cole. And I noticed you were the only one who didn't laugh when Cole said Belle isn't much to look at. So maybe there's somethin' between you and Belle?"

Jim kept his eyes on the gun as he used a cloth-tipped rod in the barrel. "I fell for her the first time I saw her, Charlie. I just haven't let on to Belle—or to Cole—because I thought there was romance between the two of 'em. But after what Cole said this mornin', I think maybe all he has is admiration for the way she handles herself when it comes to robbin' banks and stagecoaches. But since I'm not sure there isn't a little romance mixed with it, I'll still keep my mouth shut. I don't want to upset things with the gang."

Charlie grinned. "I see your point. Better to sort of let things develop as they will, huh?"

"That's exactly what I'm gonna do. Not push anything between Belle and myself. Just let things develop."

28

"Well, if it's meant to be, you'll end up with Belle. If it ain't, then so be it."

"Yeah. So be it."

It was precisely ten o'clock in the morning when the James-Younger gang mounted up and headed due north. They would skirt Kansas City on the east side and head directly into Liberty. A brisk wind caused them to pull their coat collars up and tug their hats tighter.

They drew near the town at 2:15 and rode down into a ravine to wait. At 2:30, they began riding into town two and three at a time. Moving slowly, the men placed themselves strategically inside and outside the bank exactly as planned.

At 2:50, Jesse and Cole bolted from inside the bank, carrying canvas money bags. The other inside men were on their heels. When every man was in his saddle, they each fired a shot at the front doors of the bank.

People on the street froze in their tracks as the bullets flew, shattering glass and splintering doors and clapboard on the wall.

On the boardwalk, a teenage boy swung his fists at the gang, shouting angrily.

Jesse James aimed his gun at the boy and fired four shots before leading the gang away.

When the riders had disappeared in a cloud of dust, the townspeople gathered around the fallen boy.

When town marshal Jared Manley skidded to a halt beside the small group surrounding the boy, a middle-aged man looked up and said, "It's Jolly Wymore, Marshal. He's dead. The varmints robbed the bank and shot Jolly as they rode away."

"It was the James-Younger gang, Marshal!" said another man. "It was Jesse James who shot Jolly because the boy was shoutin' at 'em. I know it was Jesse!"

"That's right, Fred!" a man said. "It was Jesse. I know him when I see him. He shot poor Jolly down in cold blood! Look at his body. Four bullets. All of them came from Jesse's gun!"

Jared Manley's breathing was ragged, and white splotches showed on his cheeks, contrasting with his dark eyes. "I want a posse," he said through clenched teeth. "Right now."

Immediately the men around him volunteered.

"Marshal," Manley's deputy said, "while you're collecting the rest of the posse, I'll go tell Jolly's parents what happened."

The James-Younger gang rode hard and headed south toward Lee's Summit. After a while, they stopped at a shallow creek to let the horses drink. As they waited, Jim Younger glanced in the direction they had come. "Cole, you think they'll come with a posse?"

"Wouldn't surprise me."

"Then maybe we'd better hide out somewhere besides the farm for a while. There were probably people back there who recognized some of us. That marshal will take the posse right to our door."

"I was thinking the same thing," said Frank James. "We'd best hole up somewhere else till things cool down, Cole."

Jesse hadn't spoken yet.

Cole set his gaze on him. "What do you think, Jesse?"

"I think Jim's right. We'd best find somewhere else to hide for a while. Especially since I killed that loudmouthed kid."

Frank eyed his brother. "That wasn't necessary, Jesse. He was no threat to us."

His brother's words changed the slant of Jesse's lips. Deep lines formed on his brow as he said in a level tone, "He was yapping his head off. Should've kept his mouth shut."

Frank held his brother's gaze for a long moment, then looked back at Cole and said, "Got any ideas where we might hole up?"

"There's the posse now!" Clell Miller said.

Every eye swung north to see a band of riders coming at a full gallop

"Let's ride!" shouted Cole, jerking his horse's head up with water dripping from its muzzle.

With Cole and Jesse in the lead, the gang put their horses to top speed. They galloped down the road for about half a mile, then veered across a field and raced through a thick stand of trees. They left the trees, galloped across a wide field, and entered another stand of trees. Passing through the deep shadows, they emerged into another field and came to a wide, shallow creek, termporarily out of sight of the posse.

"Let's ride the creek for a ways," Cole said. "I know a place to pull out."

They rode the sinuous creek upstream for about a mile, then Cole looked back to see if the posse was anywhere in sight before leading them up a bank covered with small rocks.

When they topped the bank, they galloped across a wide field, weaving among scattered trees, and soon were in a ravine where Cole raised a hand, signaling them to stop. He looked at his brothers John and Bob and told them to go back to the rim of the ravine on foot and see if they could see the posse.

While John and Bob did as they were told, Cole said, "I think we should go to Edgar Shirley's place to hole up for a while, Jesse. What do you think?"

Jesse nodded, then turned to Charlie Pitts. "Just to fill you in, Belle Shirley's parents moved to Scyene, Texas, a few months ago. It's a small settlement just southeast of Dallas. They asked Belle to stay with Edgar and Allene because Allene has been pretty sick. But the Shirleys will take us in and hide us."

"Helps to have friends in the right places, don't it?" Charlie said.

Cole glanced toward his brothers who were bellied down in thick brush, studying their back trail. Then he swung his gaze to Jesse and said, "If for some reason Edgar and Allene would object to our staying on their farm, I guarantee you, Belle will persuade them otherwise."

Jesse grinned. "I guess you know her well enough to come to that conclusion."

John and Bob were walking briskly toward the gang. When they drew near, Bob called out, "No sign of the posse, Cole. We lost 'em."

When the gang arrived at the Shirley farm near Strasburg, just after sundown, they indeed found a welcome. In the parlor, Edgar, Allene, and Belle were told about the bank holdup in Liberty, and Cole quickly convinced them they had thrown the posse off their trail.

Edgar, who was in his early thirties, said, "That posse is probably at the Younger farm about now and madder'n wet hornets 'cause you ain't there!"

Charlie Pitts was watching Belle and Jim Reed furtively eye each other.

Edgar, who stood behind Allene's chair, said, "Tell you what, gentlemen...there's room for half of you to sleep here in the house. The other half can sleep in the hayloft out in the barn."

"Good enough," said Jesse. "We'll switch off, so everybody sleeps in the house every other night. That all right, boys?"

Everybody agreed.

"We'll need to get some more groceries from town tomorrow," said Edgar. "While you're here, Belle and I will cook the meals."

Belle, who was slender with long dark hair, chuckled. "And if anybody complains about the cookin', his next meal will have a dash of strychnine in it!"

Charlie Pitts studied Belle covertly and told himself Cole was right. She wasn't much to look at. He wondered what Jim Reed saw in her.

Edgar moved toward the kitchen and said, "Well, cousin Belle, you and I better get busy with supper."

"And while you two are doin' that," Cole said with a grin, "we'll count our loot."

The men stood around the small table in the parlor where the canvas bags were being opened. Jesse and Frank James, and Cole and Jim Younger counted the loot. They were elated to find they had relieved the Clay County Bank of over fifty thousand in cash, plus some ten thousand in negotiable bonds and about ten thousand in gold.

When Jesse shouted out the figures so all could hear, Belle and Edgar came in from the kitchen. Allene, who sat in her chair with a blanket covering her lap, said, "Belle, you sure hooked up with the right bunch!"

Cole let out a whoop. "Tell you what, Belle...Jesse and I talked privately a few minutes ago. We agreed that since you and your cousins have taken us in, that he and I will share some of this money with the three of you from our part of it. Each of you will get five hundred dollars."

Belle moved to Cole, wrapped her arms around his neck,

and kissed his cheek. Charlie's gaze flicked to Jim Reed, whose face remained impassive.

The next day, while the gang was lounging around the Shirley farm, Jesse and Frank James told the others they were going into Strasburg. Edgar had given them a list of what he and Belle needed in order to feed the bunch for a few days.

"I appreciate you fellas goin' after the groceries," Cole said, "but don't forget your faces are on wanted posters decorating stores and shops all over Missouri. Be careful."

Jesse chuckled and elbowed his brother in the ribs. "Cole, you're an old grandma. Frank and I will be careful. Don't you worry."

"Okay, so I'm an old grandma. I just want you guys comin' back, understand?'

"We understand," Jesse said. "See you in a little while."

While Jesse and Frank were gone, the gang members sat around in the parlor, talking about what bank or stagecoach they might rob next. Having increased their bankrolls, they were a happy bunch. Belle and Allene were in the kitchen. Belle had washed Allene's hair and was putting curlers in it.

When a couple of hours passed, Cole was beginning to fidget about Jesse and Frank being gone so long. Just then, Jim Reed glanced out the parlor window. "Here they are now, Cole."

The James brothers drove the wagon alongside the house and headed for the rear.

Immediately Arch Clements and Sly Chapman were on their feet to help carry in the groceries.

Some ten minutes later, the James brothers entered the parlor, followed by Clements and Chapman. While Edgar was making Allene comfortable in a chair, Cole grinned at the James brothers and said, "I was gettin' worried about you guys."

Jesse chuckled as he and Frank sat down in straight-backed wooden chairs. "Well, ol' grandma, we made it, didn't we?"

"Yeah. You made it. But what took you so long?"

"We were gathering some vital information."

"About what?"

"Putting our hands on more easy money."

"Keep talkin'," Cole said.

Jesse leaned forward and looked Cole in the eye. "You can thank Frank for this."

Cole looked at the older James brother. "Thanks, Frank. Now, what am I thankin' you for?"

"I've got big ears, and I just happened to overhear a conversation while Jesse and I were in the general store. Two men were talking in low voices, but I picked it up. One was a Wells Fargo employee who lives in Strasburg, and the other guy was some kind of businessman in town. The Fargo employee was telling his friend about a stage out of Kansas City day after tomorrow that will be carrying a large payroll to Joplin. Seems there's a big construction company erecting some new buildings in Joplin's downtown area. The construction crew gets paid once a month, and the payroll will be on the stage that stops in Harrisonville at nine-thirty, six mornings a week."

Harrisonville was some thirteen miles southwest of Strasburg on the direct line between Kansas City and Joplin.

Cole grinned. "Sounds good. You say the payroll will be on Friday's stage?"

"That's right."

"Okay. Let's put Belle on this one as a passenger…if we can get her a seat. We'll hit the stage somewhere in the sixteen-mile stretch between Harrisonville and Adrian."

Belle left her chair and stood over Cole, smiling from ear to ear. "Let's do it, Cole! I like doin' that 'passenger' role!"

"Cole," said Jesse, "how about you and me take Belle with us and ride to Harrisonville right now. While we're picking out the spot to stop the stage, she can see if there's a seat available and buy a ticket."

"Sounds good to me," said Belle.

Cole nodded. "Let's go."

It was just after noon on Friday when Edgar and Allene Shirley watched the gang ride into the yard. The men entered the house in a merry mood and told the Shirleys that Belle had done her job perfectly. Posing as a passenger, she had disarmed four male passengers and held them at gunpoint while the rest of the gang disarmed the stage driver and shotgunner and took the cash box. The crew and passengers were relieved of their cash and valuables. All in all, the robbery had netted the gang over twelve thousand dollars.

Belle received her normal percentage, and the Shirleys were paid a sizable amount for their hospitality. Cole and Jesse agreed they would stay only a few more days then return to the Younger farm.

On Thursday, February 22, the James-Younger gang took a back road and soon were near their farm.

Jim Reed's thoughts of Belle's parting words to him were interrupted when Cole and Jesse signaled the gang to stop in front of Gene Vader's farm. Vader and neighbor Ted Pack moved out of a stand of trees.

"Howdy, Gene...Ted," Jesse said, pulling rein.

Vader and Pack returned the greeting, and Vader said, "We read about the bank in Liberty. You boys really made that Marshal Martell mad. He was by here twice with a posse, tryin' to find you. After that, an army unit came three times. We hoped you boys would hole up somewhere else till things cooled down."

"Yeah...and we're sure glad you did," Pack said, "or they would have had you."

Cole looked at Vader. "How long since the army unit was here the last time?"

"Monday. They stopped by here after they checked your place and asked if I'd seen any of you. I told them I hadn't, and the captain in charge told the rest of the men that you had probably gone to another state and wouldn't be back. So...I don't think they'll be showin' up again."

"We appreciate you looking out for us," Jesse said. "Come on over to the house after dark and we'll see that you get your usual pay."

As the weeks passed, the James-Younger gang kept a low profile.

By early April, they had several new bank and stagecoach robberies planned. To keep the law off balance, they planned the robberies to take place in Kansas, Iowa, Arkansas, and Kentucky. Each time it was just inside the borders of the states so they could quickly cross back into Missouri. As the weather grew warmer, they hid out in forests and gullies to further evade and frustrate posses and army units who were trying to track them.

It was mid-May when the gang showed up at the Shirley farm once more and spent a week with them. Because Allene was now well enough to take care of herself, Belle told Cole and Jesse that she would like to ride with the gang on a regular basis. Both Jesse and Cole were pleased at her decision, but no one was more pleased than Jim Reed.

By the first part of August, Belle and Jim had a romance going, which was no problem with Cole Younger. It had become clear by that time that his attraction for Belle was purely admiration.

When the romance became obvious, Cole and Jesse talked to the couple in private and pointed out that although they were not against the romance, the couple could not let their feelings for each other get in the way of the precision work they were doing in the robberies.

Belle and Jim assured the gang leaders they would handle their jobs as skillfully as always.

The months passed with more robberies pulled off without a hitch. The gang was so successful that they added a few more members.

In November 1866, Belle and Jim got married and parted from the gang for a while in order to visit Belle's parents in Texas. While there, Jim and Belle learned of a cattle rustling outfit and the kind of money they were making. They moved to a ranch house a few miles south of Dallas and started their own cattle rustling outfit.

Cole and Jesse received a letter from them via Gene Vader, explaining what they were doing and saying they would come back to Missouri to ride with the gang again when things got too hot for them in Texas.

✦

The James-Younger gang rode hard, plundering and killing, while losing some gang members and adding others to take the place of the fallen. They pulled off bank robberies in several states, leaving behind a wake of dead and wounded citizens and lawmen while becoming richer with each job.

In March of 1868, the gang robbed the banking house of Nimrod and Company in Russellville, Kentucky, seriously wounding the owner of the bank during the holdup. More such incidents occurred as time passed, including a raid on the Bank of Richmond in Richmond, Missouri, leaving behind several dead citizens, including the mayor of the town and his young son.

It was late in the summer of 1868 when Jesse and Frank James, and Cole and Bob Younger entered a photographer's studio in Kansas City and compelled him to take a picture of the four of them. They posed with two rifles and six revolvers in hand, grinning evilly. They held the photographer at gunpoint while he made several copies of the photograph, which Cole and Jesse mailed to the lawmen who had shown the strongest desire to capture them and hang them.

The photographs only served to instill a greater determination in the hearts of lawmen all over the Midwest to bring the gang to justice.

3

FOR TWO YEARS, JIM AND BELLE REED rustled cattle in Texas and made a good deal of money. But by early 1869, the law and angry ranchers were breathing down their necks. On a cold day in late January, the Reeds left their ranch and headed for Missouri, rejoining the James-Younger gang.

In March of 1869, the gang purchased a farm near Smithville, which they began using as an alternate hideout. One day in the first week of April, Jesse told Cole he thought they could add a lot of money to their coffers if they started robbing trains too.

Cole agreed, and the gang launched its train-robbing campaign. Belle was with them every time and once again proved herself as capable as any of the other gang members. When they robbed banks, she played the part of a man; when they robbed stagecoaches, she played the part of a lady passenger and held the other passengers at gunpoint when the gang stopped the stage.

The newspapers in six states wrote of the gang's daring holdups and soon labeled Belle Reed as the "Bandit Queen." Some writers even made it appear that Belle was actually the "gun-toting leader of the gang," and many killings were attributed to her.

One day in late April, the gang was at the Smithville farm, resting up from a strenuous train robbery in eastern Nebraska. Jim and Bob Younger had gone to Kansas City to buy ammunition. As the sun was going down, Belle was in the kitchen of the farmhouse, preparing supper, when she heard Jim and Bob come through the front door.

She heard Jesse ask if they were able to obtain enough ammunition. Bob Younger assured him they were, then said, "We've got somethin' here to show all of you. Where's Belle?"

"She's in the kitchen," came Jim Reed's voice. "I'll get her."

Belle instantly laid aside the potatoes she was peeling, wiped her hands on her apron, and headed for the front of the house. She met Jim in the hall. "I heard, honey. What is it?"

"Must be what's in some newspaper. Bob had a folded paper in his hand."

Belle nodded at Bob Younger as they entered the parlor.

"Lookee, here, Belle!" Bob said, eyes wide. He opened the newspaper in his hand. "It's this morning's issue of the *Kansas City Star*. There's a big article on page three about the gang, but it's mostly about you!"

"Me! What about me?"

He pointed at the page while the rest of the gang looked on. "It says right here that since you joined the gang back in '66, you've killed a total of thirty-four people durin' robberies! They say it's by far more than even Cole or Jesse have killed."

Belle pursed her lips and shook her head. "They ain't got it right. It's only twenty-six." She flicked a glance at the two gang leaders and said, "It's bad enough the newspapers make it look like the 'Bandit Queen' is the leader of the whole gang, but to make it look like I've shot down and killed more people than either of you is ridiculous."

Cole winked at Jim Reed and said, "Belle, honey, Jesse and I don't mind at all if the public sees you as boss of the outfit. We've talked about it of late. We really think it's good that the public sees you as even more rough and ruthless than you actually are."

"Right," said Jesse, looking around at the rest of the gang. "Don't you boys agree?"

The gang spoke their agreement.

Bob Younger flashed the page with the article about the gang and said, "This writer also tells about you two, Jesse and Frank, bein' born into a preacher's home. Says you've gone against everything your godly daddy and then your godly step-father taught you."

Charlie Pitts's eyes widened. "You fellas never mentioned this before now. Were both your pa and stepdad preachers?"

"No," Jesse said in a clipped tone. "Our stepdad, Reuben Samuel, was a doctor. But he was just as fanatical about the Bible and its teachings as Ma and our real pa were."

"Tell us more about it, fellas," said Pitts.

Jesse shot a sidelong glance at Charlie and said, "We don't want to talk about it."

"Yeah," chimed in Frank. "It isn't a subject we like to dis-cuss. So just drop it."

Charlie shrugged. "Sorry. I didn't mean to upset you."

Jesse let a slight grin slant his lips. "It's all right, Charlie. Frank and I just try not to think about it."

On Saturday, February 12, 1870, John Mimms was sitting in his buggy, about to drive away from his St. Joseph, Missouri, home. He was saying good-bye to his wife, Clare, and his pretty twenty-two-year-old daughter, Zerelda, when suddenly Zerelda looked past her father and saw a lone horseman trotting down the street.

"It's Jesse!"

John and Clare watched their daughter run up the street to meet Jesse James. When they drew abreast, he slid from the saddle and took her in his arms to kiss her.

Clare sighed. "John, I wish she would get him out of her mind."

"It's not going to happen, honey. She's very much in love with him."

"I know. To a fault. It's bad enough they're second cousins, but she's so blindly in love with him. Always faithful, never questions him, and never complains, even though they've been engaged for over four years and still there's no wedding date set. It was Christmas when he was here to see her last, yet she goes on like he worked a good job and was here to give her of his time like any normal man in love would do."

Jesse and Zerelda were holding hands as they walked slowly toward Zerelda's parents.

Leaning close to Clare, John said, "You put it best, honey. She's so blindly in love with him that he can do anything and she'll still want him. And he can go as long as he wants between visits, but she'll always be here to welcome him with open arms."

The young couple drew up beside the buggy.

Jesse smiled. "Hello, Aunt Clare…Uncle John."

John nodded, forcing a smile.

"Hello, Jesse," said Clare. "It's been a long time."

"Yes, ma'am. Christmas." He glanced at the lovely brunette beside him. "I've missed this sweet girl so much. But you understand. We've been quite busy."

"So the newspapers tell us," John said.

Jesse knew he did not have his great-uncle's warmest approval to be engaged to Zerelda. Acting as if all was well, he said, "I'm going to spend the rest of the day with Zee, Uncle John. We've got some time to make up."

John nodded silently, then turned to his wife. "I'll be home by suppertime, honey. If Jesse can stay for supper, he and I can chat then."

"I won't be able to stay quite that long, Uncle John. I'll have to head back for Smithville by about four-thirty."

"Well, see you next time then." John told Clare he loved her, then drove away.

"Come on inside, Jesse," said Clare. "You and Zee can sit in the parlor while I do some dressmaking in the sewing room."

When Jesse and Zerelda were seated in the parlor, she said, "Darling, I've missed you so much."

"I've missed you, too," said Jesse as he looked into her dark brown eyes. "But all this time I've been gone I've been putting more and more money away for our future. When I get a suffi-cient amount set aside, we'll get married and head somewhere I'm not known. Then, as Mr. and Mrs. Thomas Howard, we'll begin our new lives."

"Oh, I wish it was today," she said, sighing.

When it was time for Jesse to leave his beloved Zee, they walked out onto the porch where he kissed her tenderly then mounted his horse and rode away. When he reached the cor-ner, he drew rein and hipped around in the saddle to wave. Zee waved back and threw him a kiss, which made Jesse smile. He put the horse to a trot and disappeared around the corner.

At the same time Jesse James was riding south from St. Joseph toward Smithville, a tall, handsome man of twenty-seven was standing on the platform of the train depot in Kansas City. As he waited, he tipped his hat to young ladies who walked past him.

It wasn't long before his train rolled into the depot, its bell clanging and steam hissing from the engine. When the steel wheels came to a squeaking stop, the tall man threaded his way through the crowd to the baggage coach where a baggage handler was sliding the heavy doors open.

The tall man stepped up and said, "Hello. My name's Wesley Logan. I'm a hardware drummer. There should be a box of hardware articles addressed to me from the Cushman Hardware Company in San Francisco."

"All right, Mr. Logan," said the husky baggage handler. "If you'll wait right here, I'll give it to you just as soon as I come to it."

"Appreciate it," Logan said, smiling.

He backed away as two more baggage handlers came with a cart and joined the first man to begin the unloading process. He let his gaze roam over the crowd. His attention was drawn to a young woman stepping down from the rear platform of the car just behind the baggage coach. She was carrying a rather heavy-looking overnight bag, and it seemed to have her a bit off balance.

Logan moved that direction to offer his help, but before he could get there, she slipped from the bottom step and tumbled to the platform in a heap.

He rushed to bend over her, and with one hand he took the bag from her grasp and extended the other hand, saying, "May I help you up, ma'am?"

"Thank you, sir," she said, her face flushed with embarassment.

When Logan had her on her feet, he held onto her left hand and asked, "Are you hurt, ma'am?"

"Only my pride."

When he let go of her arm he looked down and noticed there was no ring on her left hand. In fact, she wore no jewelry at all.

She brushed imaginary dust from her well-worn but clean wool coat ands gave him a captivating smile. "Thank you for helping me up, sir. How clumsy of me."

"I wouldn't call it clumsy, miss. This bag is quite heavy. I can see why you lost your balance on those steps."

"Well, thank you for coming to my aid. You are a gentleman, indeed."

Wes Logan was fascinated and charmed by her delicate beauty. "It was my pleasure, ma'am," he replied softly, touching his hat brim. He stood grinning for a moment, overwhelmed by his attraction to her. She was petite with long auburn hair, dark blue eyes, and a face so exquisite that he told himself he had never seen a girl so strikingly beautiful.

At that instant, the husky baggage handler drew up with an oblong wooden box on his shoulder. "Here's your box, Mr. Logan."

"Oh. Thank you," said Wes, taking the box from his shoulder and placing it on his own.

When Wes turned back around, the beautiful girl with the long auburn hair was gone. His eyes scanned the milling crowd, but she was nowhere in sight.

He carried the heavy box through the railroad station, and when he moved outside, he searched in vain up and down the street. He moved to the waiting buggy he had hired and greeted the driver, placing the box beside his luggage in the back.

"Need to stop anywhere else before I take you to Wells Fargo, Mr. Logan?"

"No, the stage leaves in about twenty minutes, so I need to get there right away."

The driver veered the buggy to the side of the street as they drew up to the Wells Fargo office and reined to a stop near the stagecoach, which was being loaded by the crew. Wes hopped out and checked with the crew to be sure this was the Joplin-bound stage, then handed them his luggage and the wooden box. He turned back and paid the buggy driver, then headed for the office.

Inside, Wes saw an elderly woman sitting on a chair. A young couple was talking to her. At the counter was a middle-aged couple who were purchasing tickets. The agent looked at Logan, grinned. "Hello, Wes."

"Hello, Jerry."

"Be with you in a minute."

Wes stood behind the couple until they stepped away with their tickets in hand, then moved up to the counter.

"So, how's the hardware business?" asked Jerry Ward as he took Wes's money.

"Doing fine."

"Ever get tired of traveling?"

"Yeah. Sometimes."

Wes heard the door of the ladies' powder room open behind him and light footsteps move across the wooden floor.

"Think one day you'll take an office job with the company and stop traveling?" asked Ward.

Wes angled his head a little to the left as he said, "Probably will, but I—" His heart lurched in his chest and his skin tingled. It was her!

As she passed through the door, Jerry Ward said, "What's the matter, Wes? Never see a pretty girl before?"

"Oh…uh…I saw her at the depot. Is…is she a passenger on this stage?"

"Mm-hmm. She's goin' as far as Harrisonville."

"I see. Ah…what's her name?"

Ward looked down at his pad. "Ginny Grayson."

Taking the ticket stub from Ward's hand, Wes smiled and said, "Thanks, Jerry. See you next time."

"Sure. Next time."

Wes Logan hurried out the door in time to see the middle-aged woman being helped aboard the stage by her husband. The elderly woman was already inside the stage. Ginny Grayson was waiting to board.

Wes rushed up and was barely in time, for the middle-aged man was just offering Ginny his hand. "Excuse me, sir," Wes said in a kindly manner. "I'll help Miss Grayson aboard."

Ginny's head whipped around as the man smiled and climbed in to sit beside his wife.

"Well, we meet again!" said Ginny, warming Wes with her smile. "Are you on this stage, sir?"

"Yes, ma'am," he said, extending his hand. "Please allow me to help you aboard."

"Of course. How did you know my last name?"

"Aha! That's my secret! And I know your first name, too."

As she gave him her hand, he said, "I think Ginny fits you perfectly."

She shook her head in amazement and stepped aboard.

Wes was glad to see that there were empty seats on each side next to the door so that he and Ginny could sit opposite one another.

When the stage was rolling south out of Kansas City, the elderly woman spoke. "Well, I guess we might as well get acquainted. My name is Sophie Smith. And I'm going all the way to Joplin. I live in Carthage."

The couple introduced themselves as Ed and Stella Wiggins, on their way to Joplin, which was their home.

The auburn-haired beauty said, "My name is Ginny Grayson, and I'm only going as far as Harrisonville."

Ed Wiggins said, "Your ride won't be too long today, then, Miss Grayson. Just about thirty miles."

Ginny nodded.

All eyes turned to the tall young man.

"And I'm Wesley Logan," he said amiably. "I'm going to Joplin, too, but not today. I get off this stage at Nevada."

When the older people began talking about the Joplin-Carthage area, Wes looked at Ginny and said, "Is Harrisonville your home, Miss Grayson?"

"It's actually my new home, Mr. Logan." She went on to explain that she had just come from San Francisco to live with her aunt and uncle.

Wes noted a slight trace of sadness in Ginny's expressive blue eyes. "Were you living with your parents in San Francisco?"

Ginny hesitated for a moment and then explained that her father had died seven years ago when she was twelve, leaving her and her mother in dire poverty. Her mother was ill at the time and unable to work. Ginny had to drop out of school and find a way to provide for the two of them. She cleaned houses and took in washing to provide food, clothing, and shelter. What little money Ginny might have been able to save had gone for her mother's medical bills.

It was then that Wes noticed her well-worn coat, the thread-bare calico dress beneath it, and the faded hat on her head.

"Sounds like you've had it pretty rough, Miss Ginny. And your mother…how is she doing?"

Tears misted Ginny's eyes. "She died two weeks ago, Mr. Logan."

"Oh. I'm very sorry."

"This is why I'm coming to live with my aunt and uncle.

When Mama died, I sent a telegram to let them know. They offered to take me into their home if I would come."

"That's nice of them. I'm glad you had someone to take you in and give you a home."

Ginny took a hankie from her coat pocket and dabbed at her eyes. "Enough about me, Mr. Logan. Let's hear about you. Are you married?"

"No, ma'am. Not yet. I just haven't found the right girl."

Ginny smiled. "What do you do for a living?"

"I'm a hardware drummer. I travel all over Missouri and a small portion of Illinois selling hardware to merchants in the major cities and towns. In fact, I have a hardware store in Harrisonville that I deal with, but I won't be stopping there on this trip. I mentioned earlier that I'm headed for Joplin. I'll be stopping at a few places in between. From Joplin, I'll go east to Springfield, then on up to Jefferson City, and from there to Columbia."

Ginny slipped the hankie back in her coat pocket and said, "How long are you on the road at a time, Mr. Logan?"

"Usually from ten to twelve days. I'll be going home from Columbia."

"And home is…?"

"Kansas City. I always have a week at home between trips. My next time out will take me north to St. Joseph, then across the state to Quincy, Illinois, with several stops in between. From Quincy, I'll go south to St. Louis, then make my way back to Kansas City."

Conversation in the stage dwindled as it rocked and swayed over the road. Ed Wiggins set kind eyes on Ginny and said, "Miss Grayson, I couldn't help but overhear what you were telling Mr. Logan. Things were all right before your father died, though?"

Ginny cleared her throat. "Not really, sir. Papa had a hard time holding a job."

When the others looked at her curiously, she began talking about her growing-up years. Her voice took on a tinge of bitterness as she told them her father had been a heavy drinker and was fired on several occasions for drinking on the job.

Wes told her he hoped things would be a great deal better for her, living with her aunt and uncle. The other passengers murmured their agreement.

At Harrisonville, Walter and Carolyne Hansen left their buggy in front of the Wells Fargo office and went inside. They found agent George Hampton talking to a well-dressed young man who was taking notes as he and Hampton talked.

The agent glanced at the Hansens and said, "Excuse me, Mr. Golan."

The young man smiled. "That's all right, Mr. Hampton. I think we're finished. Thanks for the interview."

Golan was putting the pad and pencil in a small valise as Hampton said, "Walt…Carolyne…you must be pretty excited to have your niece coming to live with you."

"That we are," said Walter. "You just wait till you see her. She's an exceptionally beautiful girl and as sweet as Carolyne's sugar cookies."

Carolyne chuckled. "Of course, she gets her good looks and sweetness from her aunt!"

"Can't argue with that, sweetheart!" Walter said with a grin.

"Folks," Hampton said, "I'd like for you to meet Neal Golan of the *Kansas City Star*. Neal, this is Carolyne and Walter Hansen. They live here in town."

The Hansens greeted Golan in a friendly manner, saying

they had read many of his articles in the *Star*.

The Fargo agent then said, "Mr. Golan came in on an earlier stage this morning. He's interviewing Wells Fargo people about the stagecoach robberies taking place all over this part of the country and in the West. I was talking to him about the continual robberies by the Jesse James–Cole Younger gang all over Missouri, Kansas, Nebraska, Iowa, and even as far west as Colorado."

Walter nodded. "I've kept up with the articles about the robberies, not only in the *Star*, Mr. Golan, but in other papers, as well. One article I read in the *Harrisonville News* just last week told about how frustrated federal marshals and town marshals are because they can't catch the James-Younger boys. They've been able to hang a few of the other gang members who were wounded in robbery shoot-outs and left behind when the gang rode away. And, of course, some gang members have been killed in shoot-outs. But the frustrating thing, according to the article, is that Jesse and Frank James, and Cole Younger and his brothers have proven to be totally elusive."

"They're slick, that's for sure," Golan said.

Walter pulled at his handlebar mustache. "And the article talked about Belle Reed. She's as mean as any outlaw they've ever seen and can outshoot most men. People just expect a woman to be soft and tender. But not Belle."

Neal Golan nodded, then said, "Mr. Hansen, did you read the article I wrote a couple of weeks ago in the *Star* about the bank holdup in Ottumwa, Iowa?"

"Must've missed that one."

"Me too," said Carolyne. "Was it about the James-Younger gang?"

"Yes. When they held up the Ottumwa Bank and Trust on January 20, there was a shoot-out with the town marshal and some citizens. Belle Reed was dressed like a man, but people could tell it was her. While still inside the bank, she shot three bank employees in cold blood."

"How could she be this way?"

"Good question," said Golan. "In the shoot-out, two of the gang members, Willie Carson and Bill Chadwell, went down wounded, and the gang took off without them. They were patched up by the town doctor, jailed, and were waiting for federal marshals to take them to Kansas City for trial.

"When some of the Ottumwa men learned that Carson and Chadwell were still alive and in their jail, they formed a vigilante mob and broke into the jail while the town marshal looked on, and hanged them from a tree on Main Street."

"Oh my," said Carolyne.

"And what's more, the townspeople gathered around the hanging tree and cheered when the outlaws hit the end of their ropes."

Carolyne shuddered at the thought of it.

"The problem here in Missouri," said Walter, "is that so many people look at the James brothers and the Younger brothers as heroes. They wouldn't lift a finger to help a lawman stop them."

"That's right," said George Hampton. "It's their connection with the late William Quantrill. Those who have Confederate leanings in these parts think of Quantrill and all those who rode with him as knights in shining armor. We've got another gang around here, led by an ex-Quantrill guerilla…Dub Thaxton."

"Thaxton," said Golan as if the name tasted bitter on his tongue. "It's quite evident that he and his bloody bunch are fast becoming rivals with the James-Younger gang. Though the Thaxton gang is smaller, they're getting away with large sums of money and gold in their robberies. It's come to the place where there's bad blood between the Thaxtons and the James-Youngers."

"I've read a little about the rivalry in the *Harrisonville News*," said Walter. "One of these days there'll be a real war fought between them. Of course, when it happens, I fully expect Jesse and Cole and their bunch to come out the victors, in spite of how cold-blooded the Thaxton bunch are."

The sound of pounding hooves and rattling wheels met their ears. "Stage is coming in," George Hampton announced as he headed toward the door.

4

AS THE STAGE ROLLED IN, George Hampton called out a greeting to the driver, Leon Krebs, and shotgunner Blake Freeland.

Neal Golan watched as a tall, handsome man stepped out of the stage and helped Ginny down. Immediately, the Hansens rushed up and embraced her.

When Ginny introduced Wes Logan to her aunt and uncle, telling them about Wes's gallantry at the Kansas City depot, Walter and Carolyne expressed their appreciation. Then Walter took Ginny by the hand and led her to the Fargo agent. "George, I want you to meet our niece, Ginny Grayson."

Hampton made a slight bow and said, "Miss Grayson, it is a pleasure to meet you. However, I must say that you're even prettier than your uncle described you."

Ginny blushed. "Thank you, Mr. Hampton."

Blake Freeland took Ginny's one bag from the rack and brought it to her. "Your bag, Miss Grayson."

"I'll take that," said Walter. "Thank you."

"I believe we have one new passenger, George," said the driver.

"Yes. Mr. Neal Golan, reporter for the *Kansas City Star.*"

The driver took Golan's bags, and said, "We'll pull out in just a couple minutes, sir."

"Miss Grayson," Wes Logan said as he took a step toward Ginny, "it has been a pleasure to meet you."

"Even more for me," she said, flashing him a smile. "I sorely needed some help at the moment we met."

Wes grinned. "I hope you will be happy in this new phase of your life, ma'am."

"Thank you. I hope we meet again sometime."

"Me too."

Wes was still drinking in her flawless beauty when Walter and Carolyne moved up beside Ginny. "Mr. Logan," Walter said, "if you're ever in the area again, please feel free to come by the house."

"Yes," said Carolyne. "It would be nice to have you stop by for a visit. We live right here in town at 341 Grove Street."

"I'll do that," Wes said, swinging his gaze from Carolyne back to Ginny. "Until then, Miss Ginny, let me say again that meeting you has truly been a pleasure."

Ginny's eyes shone as Wes turned and headed toward the stagecoach and extended his hand to Neal Golan, who was about to board the stage. "Mr. Golan, I'm Wes Logan. I've read many of your articles and stories in the *Star*. You always pick the most interesting subjects."

"Thank you, sir," Golan said as he gripped Wes's hand.

When the two men were seated inside the stagecoach, Wes introduced Golan to Sophie Smith and Ed and Stella Wiggins.

When Leon Krebs snapped the reins, putting the team in motion, Wes looked out his window and waved at Ginny. Her face lit up with another lovely smile as she waved back.

Neal Golan leaned toward the window and looked out, then eased back on the seat and said, "Mr. Logan, that is one beautiful young lady."

Wes sighed. "She is absolutely the most beautiful girl I have ever seen. I hardly know her, but she seems to have the heart and soul that goes with her good looks."

Some ten miles south of Harrisonville, outlaw leader Dub Thaxton and his gang were hiding in woods near some huge boulders that made the road so narrow two vehicles could not pass at the same time. A heavy log some twelve feet long was poised on top of a boulder, ready to be dropped in front of the stage at just the right time.

Thaxton, a big, burly, bearded man in his midthirties, paced back and forth in the small clearing where his six men were seated on fallen logs and rocks. Periodically, he glanced through the trees to the north.

Dub's younger brother, Lambert, looked up at him from where he sat. "Dub, I wish this stage was carryin' some gold or a payroll or a cash box with lots of money in it."

The big man paused and set his gaze on his brother. "Who knows but what it does, Lambert? And if not, we'll still do well, just cleanin' the passengers out of their pocket money and valuables. And we'll take whatever weapons we can find."

Gang member Nate Roach said, "Dub, we've got to find out when these stages are carryin' a special load of gold or money. It's a mystery to me how Jesse James and Cole Younger seem to know; they always get away with a big haul."

"I don't know if it's some special connection they've got or just plain good luck," growled Thaxton.

"All I know is those dirty skunks get away with a whole lot more money and gold than we do," said Lambert. "I hate 'em for it."

"Yeah," spoke up Ray Dodd. "I hate 'em, too."

"I know Cole Younger is tough and all that," said Dub,

"but the real leader of that bunch is Jesse James. If Jesse was put six feet under, the gang would fall apart."

"You're right, boss," said Tom Portell. "Maybe we oughtta see if we can't find a way to make that happen."

Ernie Mills chuckled. "Sure, Tom. And just how do we get close enough to Jesse to take him out? He's always got the gang around him."

"Not always," said Dub, checking the road again. "Jesse makes a periodic ride to St. Joseph to visit his girlfriend. I've already been thinkin' about that. I'm gonna work on a plan to catch Jesse on one of those rides and shoot him dead."

The men laughed, agreeing with Dub's plan.

Frank Baldwin said, "More than anything, Dub, I'd like to do a jig on Jesse James's grave!"

"Well, if I have my way, Frank, we'll all do that jig! And what's more, we'll—uh-oh! I see a cloud of dust…the stage is comin'. C'mon, let's get ready!"

As the Wells Fargo stagecoach rolled along, Ed Wiggins looked at the man sitting directly across from him. "So where's your next stop, Mr. Golan?"

"Rich Hill."

"Another interview with a Wells Fargo agent?"

"No, the man who runs the stage stop at Rich Hill only does it on a part-time basis. I have an appointment to interview Civil War veteran, John Tidball, who was a captain in the Union Army. He displayed great heroism at Gettysburg by saving the lives of two colonels during the heat of the battle. My editor wants a firsthand account of the incident for a special series we're doing on the war."

"Sounds interesting," Wiggins said.

Wes Logan looked at Golan. "Tell Captain Tidball hello for me, will you, Mr. Golan?"

The reporter's eyebrows arched. "You know him?"

"Quite well. We fought in the same outfit until I was wounded the second time and given a medical discharge. I agree 100 percent that Captain Tidball is a genuine hero. I'll look forward to reading the article."

"You were wounded in combat twice, Mr. Logan?" said Wiggins.

"Yes, sir. Once at Wilson's Creek on August 10, 1861. But the one that took me out of the war was at Pea Ridge on March 7, 1862. I was a lieutenant in charge of a fighting unit from June of '61 until the Pea Ridge battle. That, of course, was some sixteen months before the battle at Gettysburg. I haven't seen Captain Tidball since Pea Ridge. So, please, Mr. Golan, greet him for me."

"I sure will."

Up in the box, Leon Krebs and Blake Freeland were approaching the narrow place on the road between the two massive boulders. Suddenly, a large log sailed off a boulder and landed crosswise, directly in front of the stagecoach. The horses flinched and Krebs yanked back on the reins, skidding them to a stop.

Four men charged out from the trees, guns in hand. Three more came up from the rear.

"You two in the box!" Dub Thaxton barked. "Throw down your rifles and handguns right now and get your hands in the air!"

Krebs and Freeland instantly obeyed.

On the side of the stage where Wes Logan and Neal Golan

sat, Lambert Thaxton stood a dozen feet away, waving his weapon as he called out, "Everybody inside...get out! And don't try anything funny unless you want to die! Do what I tell you and nobody'll get hurt!"

The other gang members, a few on both sides of the stage, were watching both the crew and the coach windows that gave them a partial view of the passengers.

Wes Logan set his jaw as he pulled out a .47 caliber derringer from his coat pocket. "They're not taking my money from me!" he muttered.

Neal Golan leaned toward him and said in a strained whisper, "Logan! That's Dub Thaxton out there! The whole gang are cold-blooded killers! Don't do this. They'll kill us all! It's better to let them take everything they want than to get shot dead for resisting them."

"Yes," said Ed Wiggins as he gripped his wife's trembling hand.

Wes hid the derringer next to his leg and said, "I told you, I'm not letting them have my money!"

They could hear Dub Thaxton asking the driver if he had a cash box under his seat.

"Logan, listen to me," said Golan, "there are too many of them! Our lives are worth more than your money."

"Just stay calm," Logan said. "I'll take care of the situation."

"But—"

"I was a combat leader in the war, Golan. I'll handle it! Let me go out first."

Just then, Lambert Thaxton stepped up to the door and blared, "Quit talkin' in there! Get out, like I told you! We're takin' the men's wallets, the ladies' purses, any small handbags, and all jewelry. If any of you tries to hide anything from us, you'll be shot. Now come out of there!"

Lambert jerked the door open, and Wes Logan stepped out, still concealing the derringer. He held Lambert's gaze then suddenly pretended to stumble. When he bumped into Lambert, throwing him off balance, he rammed the muzzle of the derringer under Lambert's chin, saying in a low tone, "Move a muscle and I'll blow your head off."

Lambert froze, stunned at the speed and precision of Logan's move. A tiny groan came from his throat. The other gang members looked on, motionless and wide-eyed.

Dub, who was in the process of taking the metal cash box from the hands of Leon Krebs, saw what had happened and froze in place, his eyes bulging.

Wes pushed the muzzle of the derringer even tighter against Lambert's chin and said, "Drop the gun."

Immediately Lambert let go of the weapon and let it fall to the ground.

Wes knocked Lambert's hat off and sank his finger's into the mop of straw-colored hair, rasping the words, "All of you drop your guns or this man dies! And every one of you come around here where I can see you…with your empty hands above your heads!"

The other passengers remained inside the coach, watching the scene unfold.

Dub Thaxton swallowed hard. His gun was still in his holster and he held the cash box in both hands.

There was a note of fear in Lambert's voice as he called out through clenched teeth, "Dub, this guy's a maniac! Make 'em do what he says, or he'll kill me!"

Still motionless as a statue, Dub bawled, "Do what the guy says, boys!"

Five guns hit the road. Tom Portell, Ernie Mills, Nate Roach, Ray Dodd, and Frank Baldwin moved slowly into Wes's clear view, hands raised above their heads.

When they were in place, Logan put hard eyes on the gang leader and said, "You, Thaxton! Drop the cash box, then drop your gun belt! Move real slow. Just blink or twitch the wrong way and this low-down skunk gets his head blown off!"

Dub pulled his thick lips into a thin line and dropped the cash box. It clattered when it hit the ground but didn't break open.

The stagecoach drivers watched, ready to move when Wes Logan had the situation completely in control.

"All right, Thaxton," Wes growled, "now the gun belt. Remember what I said about a twitch."

Keeping his hands at chest level, Thaxton glared at the man who held the derringer under Lambert's chin and said in a deep tone, "You won't get away with this, mister. We'll track you down and kill you an inch at a time! Let my brother go right now!"

"Trying to buffalo me won't work, pal," said Wes. "So this is your brother? Are you willing to let him die so you can make empty threats? Drop that gun belt, or you can kiss your brother good-bye!" With that, he rammed the muzzle of the derringer even tighter against the underside of Lambert's chin.

Dub Thaxton realized he was in a Mexican standoff and the tall, determined passenger had the upper hand.

Lambert could no longer speak because of the pressure against his throat, but he ejected a pitiful whine.

Dub slowly reached down and began unbuckling his gun belt.

Wes said, "Okay, Mr. Krebs, Mr. Freeland, Mr. Golan, and Mr. Wiggins…pick up their guns."

When the outlaws looked at Logan with eyes full of venom as the guns were being laid inside the stage, he said, "You bunch of no-goods lie down on the road, face down. Put your hands behind your backs."

While the outlaws obeyed, Wes said to his fellow passengers, "Gentlemen, take their belts and use them to bind their wrists together."

Neal Golan grinned at the ex-Civil War combat officer and said, "I owe you an apology, Mr. Logan. You did handle the situation, just like you said you would."

"I apologize, too, Mr. Logan," said Ed Wiggins. "I was wrong about you."

Lambert's jaw was trembling as Wes kept the pressure on, making his head tilt back in an unnatural position. Wes fixed him with steady eyes. "Uncomfortable, fella?"

"Mm-hmm," came Lambert's reply.

"Just think. If you weren't an outlaw, you wouldn't be in this position right now."

When Neal Golan saw Leon Krebs cinch up the last pair of wrists, he said, "All done, Mr. Logan."

Wes finally took the derringer from under Lambert's chin. "Now tie this one up."

While Lambert's wrists were being bound, Wes stepped to the stage and looked inside. "Are you ladies all right?"

Both women were pale but assured him they were fine.

Turning back to the crew and the other male passengers, Logan said, "Since the Cass County sheriff is back there in Harrisonville, we need to take these no-goods and put them in his hands."

"Let's do it," said Golan. "I'll be late for my interview, but it'll keep."

The gang's horses were retrieved and led to the road, then each outlaw was hoisted into his saddle. The horses' reins were tied to the rear of the stage.

While the passengers and crew boarded the stage, Wes

glanced at Dub Thaxton and said, "Don't look at me like that, Thaxton. If you hadn't stopped the stage to rob it, you wouldn't be all trussed up and headed for jail, would you?"

A white border edged Dub's lips as he said, "I'll get you for this."

Wes held Dub's gaze for a few seconds, then turned and climbed inside the stage.

Cass County Sheriff Dave Landis held his gun on drifters Louis Wertz and Clarence Quint, while his deputy, Bart DeWolfe, handcuffed them. A crowd stood on the boardwalk and the edge of the street, looking on.

Sheriff Landis turned to the proprietor of Harrisonville's general store. "I'm sorry for the trouble these two caused you, Mr. Fielder. We'll have them behind bars for a while, and when we release them, they'll be glad to get out of town."

"Okay, you two," said Deputy DeWolfe, "let's go."

The scowling drifters walked stiff-legged down the boardwalk, escorted by the two lawmen. The crowd watched them for a brief moment, then dispersed. Some drew up to Gerald Fielder to ask what the drifters had done in the store.

The lawmen and their prisoners were almost to the sheriff's office and jail when they saw the stagecoach coming into town from the south with horses and their trussed-up riders behind it.

"What do you make of that, Sheriff?" said Bart.

Landis squinted and shook his head. "I don't know. But by the looks of it, I'd say those guys on the horses attempted to rob the stage and somehow were foiled. Why else would they be tied up like that? It's the same stage that stopped here a couple of hours ago. I recognize the driver…Leon Krebs."

As the stage veered toward them, Landis said, "Bart, take

these guys in and lock them up. Better put them in the same cell. We may need the other cells for this bunch. Can't tell for sure how many are back there behind the stage, but I'd say five or more. They—"

When the sheriff stopped talking, Bart said, "What's the matter, Sheriff?"

"It's the Thaxton gang. I just recognized Dub. These people have captured the Thaxton gang!"

A wide grin spread across DeWolfe's face. "Well, whattaya know!"

"Lock these guys up and hurry back out here, Bart," said Landis.

As the deputy hurriedly ushered Wertz and Quint inside, Sheriff Landis stepped to the edge of the boardwalk.

When the stage squeaked to a halt, Leon Krebs called down, "Howdy, Sheriff, got a little present for you."

"Yeah, I see. The Thaxton gang! How did you do this?"

"Let's get them locked up," said Krebs, "then we'll tell you all about it."

Ed Wiggins stayed with his wife and Sophie Smith in the stagecoach while the crew, Golan, and Logan helped escort the outlaw gang inside the sheriff's office and down the hall into the cell block. Four of them were crowded into one cell and three in another.

After locking the cell door, Bart DeWolfe laughed gleefully and said, "Wow, Sheriff! This is great! The Thaxton gang…in our jail! Locked up and helpless."

"Yeah," Landis chuckled. "This is really good."

The gang members scowled at the lawmen, their eyes blazing with hatred.

Landis turned to the stage driver. "Okay, Leon, I want to hear about it. How'd you capture these skunks?"

"It was a one-man effort, Sheriff," said Krebs, laying a hand on Wes Logan's shoulder. "This man's effort."

While the prisoners looked on, Krebs introduced Landis and DeWolfe to the other men, pointing out that Neal Golan was a reporter for the *Kansas City Star*. He then proceeded to tell how Wes Logan had tricked Lambert Thaxton, got the advantage of him with the derringer rammed up under his chin, and disarmed the gang.

Sheriff Landis and his deputy shook hands with Logan, congratulating him.

"So what are you going to do with these low-down skunks, Sheriff?" asked shotgunner Blake Freeland.

"I'm going to wire the chief U.S. marshal in Kansas City and let him know that I've got the entire Thaxton gang locked up in my jail. No doubt he'll send some deputies to escort them to Kansas City to stand trial and be hanged."

Ernie Mills jumped off his bunk and gripped the bars, crying out in a high-pitched voice, "No! No! Not me! I haven't killed anybody! I'm the newest member of the gang and I haven't shot anyone! They can't hang me! I'm not a killer!"

"Sit down and shut up, Ernie!" snapped Dub, who was in the adjacent cell. "When you joined the gang you said you wanted to have people afraid of you like the rest of us do. You were braggin' just yesterday when we planned this stage holdup that if anybody got out of line while we were robbin' the stage, you were the guy who was gonna shoot 'em. Remember?"

Ernie licked his lips and swallowed hard. "Yeah. I remember. But I didn't shoot any of 'em today, did I?"

Tom Portell left his bunk and stood breathing down Mills's neck as he said, "How come you didn't take out this Logan dude before he got the drop on Lambert, if you're such a tough gunman?"

Mills let go of the bars and silently returned to his bunk.

"Tell you what, Ernie," said the sheriff, "it doesn't make any difference if you haven't shot and killed some innocent robbery victim yet. You run with this gang of blood-hungry killers who have murdered dozens of innocent people. You're an accessory. The noose will fit your neck, too."

Ernie's features drained of color and he turned his gaze to the floor.

"Well, Sheriff," said Krebs, "we've got to get back on the road. We're way behind schedule now."

As the men filed out of the cell block, Dub Thaxton gripped the bars, screaming, "I'll get you, Logan! Do you hear me? I'll break loose before they can put a rope on my neck, and I'm comin' after you! You're as good as dead already! Y'hear me? You're dead!"

Wes turned and gave him a bland look then quietly went out with the others.

The stage arrived in Rich Hill almost three hours late. When it rolled to a stop in front of the small building with the Wells Fargo sign over the door, Neal Golan told the ladies and Ed Wiggins good-bye, then reached across and shook Wes Logan's hand. "Thank you, again, Wes," he said, "for handling the gang, even though I tried to talk you out of it."

Wes smiled as he shook Neal's hand. "Now we both still have our money."

"Yes. And on a reporter's salary, I need every dollar."

"Will you still be able to have your interview today?"

"I don't know why not. There's still plenty of time for it. I'll be heading back to Kansas City on the early stage tomorrow morning."

Golan stepped out of the stage, then turned back and said, "Wes, you're a real hero. Maybe I should interview you for an article."

Wes blushed and shook his head. "Not me, my friend. I just did what had to be done. I'm no hero."

"Some of us would disagree with that, Mr. Logan," spoke up Stella Wiggins.

"That's for sure," said Sophie Smith.

Wes shook his head. "Good-bye, Neal. Be sure to tell John Tidball hello for me."

Golan grinned as he closed the stage door. "I'll do that for sure."

5

As THE STAGECOACH ROCKED and bounced along the road, Wes Logan let his gaze roam over the rolling hills. The Wigginses and Sophie Smith were dozing, their heads swaying as if their necks were made of rubber.

Wes's thoughts drifted to Ginny Grayson. He relived the moment when he first saw her…when she tumbled from the train and landed in a heap. He thought of her magnificent smile and how every time she flashed it to him, it made his heart leap. He closed his eyes and imagined that she was talking to him. What a lovely voice, so soft and sweet.

The coach lurched to one side, causing Wes to open his eyes. They were passing over a bridge that spanned the Little Osage River. The water level was low, which was normal for this time of year. The sound of the horses' hooves pounding the bridge and echoing inside the stage caused the other three passengers to stir for a moment. Only Stella opened her eyes, but the stage passed off the bridge onto solid ground again, and Stella was instantly back to sleep.

Wes's thoughts went to the last moment he had been with Ginny. Was that just this morning? It seemed like days had passed. He wondered if she would be happy living with her aunt and uncle. *Poor little gal. Never has had much in this life.*

Yes, that sweet girl deserves some comfort and happiness. She deserves nicer clothes than she was wearing when we met in the depot.

He thought of her face when the stage pulled away from the Wells Fargo office in Harrisonville. He envisioned her sparkling smile as she waved at him and he could still feel the strange empty feeling that settled over his heart when she passed from view.

Is there really such a thing as love at first sight? He had always said it was impossible. How could you fall in love with someone you really didn't know? But now—

"Looks like the sun's going down, Mr. Logan," said Ed Wiggins.

Wes glanced out the window toward the west. Only the last bright rays of the setting sun showed in a hazy fan shape above the distant tree-laden hills.

While the women continued to doze, Ed Wiggins talked about Wes's courageous move when Lambert Thaxton jerked the stage door open. Wes let him talk without commenting.

Time slid by. The glow in the west had turned a reddish golden color and was quickly fading. Toward the Kansas border some twenty miles away, twilight was a settling grayness on the crests of the hills and already dark in the hollows.

Leon Krebs's voice came from the box above: "Nevada…ten minutes, Mr. Logan!"

Wiggins leaned toward his window. "Sure enough. We're almost there."

Darkness was falling as Wes Logan approached the Osage Hotel with the heavy box of hardware samples on his shoulder and two bags in his free hand. A silver-haired man was coming out of the hotel as Wes drew up to the door. "Come on in, young man," he said, opening the door wide.

"Thank you, sir." Wes nodded as he passed by.

Desk clerk Eldon Avery smiled when he saw Wes. "Good evening, Mr. Logan. I assume the stage was late getting in?"

"Yes, Eldon." Logan set his luggage down and eased the wooden box onto a chair near the counter. "Little problem on the road."

"Oh. Nothing serious, I hope?"

"Not really."

Avery took a key from one of the cubbyholes behind him and laid it on the counter. "Two appointments as usual tomorrow, sir?"

"Mm-hmm. Nine o'clock at Kerman Hardware; ten-thirty at Nevada Hardware."

The desk clerk nodded and pushed the guest register toward him. Wes took the pen from its holder, dipped it in the inkwell, and signed the register.

Sliding the key toward the hardware drummer, Avery said, "Your favorite room, sir. Number 12."

Wes thanked him and started to pick up the box from the chair.

"Ah-ah-ah!" said Eldon, rushing around the end of the counter. "I'll take that for you, Mr. Logan. You get the bags."

When the desk clerk set the box down on a small table in room 12, Wes handed him a silver dollar and walked him to the door.

Avery stepped out into the hall. "Thank you, Mr. Logan."

"And thank you," Wes said, closing the door softly. Immediately he went to a desk that stood in a front corner, reached inside a side pocket of his coat and took out the derringer. He broke it open, checked the loads in the twin vertical barrels, and slid the gun back into his pocket.

He then reached to another inside pocket and drew out two white envelopes. Testing their weight, he sighed. "Sure am glad I didn't lose you guys to Thaxton and his bunch, or I'd be a dead man."

After eating a quick supper in the hotel dining room, Logan walked briskly down the street and entered the Wagon Wheel Saloon and Casino. The place was crowded.

He angled across the large room to the bar, where the bartender looked past a customer and said, "Hello, Mr. Logan."

"Evening, Reggie. Is Mr. Boswick in?"

"Yep. Up in his office."

"Thanks. Okay if I go up?"

"Be best if you let one of the bouncers take you. Turk is over there at the stairs."

Wes threaded his way among the tables toward the staircase.

Turk Kastin saw him coming and moved up to meet him. The big muscular man nodded at Logan without smiling. "You wanna see the boss?"

"Yes, Turk. Reggie said he's up in his office."

"Mm-hmm. The boss has been wantin' to see you, too."

Wes felt a slight tension at the back of his neck. "Reggie said you should take me up."

"Let's go."

As Wes Logan mounted the stairs beside Turk Kastin, his heart was fluttering and his mouth had gone dry. When they reached the second floor and headed down the hall, the big bouncer said, "I hope you've got good news for the boss, Logan. He's expectin' it."

Wes didn't reply. Kastin gave him a sidelong glance and frowned, then shrugged. "If you don't...it's your funeral."

They drew up in front of a solid door and Kastin knocked on it lightly.

"Yes?" called a voice from inside.

"It's Turk, boss. I have Wes Logan."

"Bring him in."

Turk opened the door and gestured for Logan to enter ahead of him. When Logan stepped inside the office, Turk followed and closed the door.

Dolph Boswick sat behind his desk and fixed Wes with cold, shrewd eyes. Boswick was a dark, lean-faced man of fifty, with deep pockmarks that looked even deeper in the shadows cast by the overhead lantern.

"Well, have you got it?"

Wes's hand trembled slightly as he reached inside his coat pocket and withdrew a white envelope. "I only have half of what I owe you, Mr. Boswick." He placed the envelope on the desk in front of him. "One thousand five hundred and fifty. I couldn't raise any more these past three weeks. But—"

Logan broke off when Boswick's eyes narrowed and the pupils looked like sharp black points.

"But...but by the time I come back through in another three weeks, I'll have all of it. My gambling debt will be paid in full."

Turk Kastin took hold of Logan's arm in a powerful grip. But Boswick raised a hand and shook his head. "Not yet, Turk."

Then to Wes he said, "You disappoint me, Mr. Logan. You told me last time if I gave you three weeks you'd pay me in full. You've failed to do this."

"Well, sir, I—"

"I'm going to be lenient this time, Mr. Logan. Turk can tell you that leniency toward men who owe me money and fail to pay when they've promised is seldom seen in me."

Kastin's grip on Wes's arm eased.

Wes was trying to think of the right way to phrase his appreciation when Boswick stood up, looked him square in the eye, and said coldly, "If I don't have the rest of the money in my hand by three weeks from this very night, Mr. Logan, you will be in deep trouble. I know where you live and who you work for. If you welch on me…well, let me put it plainly. I'll send a couple of my boys to find you. You will die a slow, agonizing death if the debt is not paid in full by exactly three weeks from tonight. Am I making myself clear?"

Wes licked his lips. "Yes, sir. You'll have every dollar of it, Mr. Boswick."

"Good. I'll be waiting." Then he said to the big bouncer, "Turk, you may escort Mr. Logan all the way to the front door of the casino. He's not allowed to gamble in the Wagon Wheel until his debt is paid in full."

Wes Logan's knees were still a bit weak when he entered his hotel room and removed his coat. He shuddered at the thought of how close he had come to losing Dolph Boswick's money to the Thaxton gang. Boswick meant business and would have sent his lieutenants to track him down if he hadn't shown up tonight with some of the money.

Weariness descended upon Wes as he stretched out on the bed. He thought of his moments with Boswick. The cold glare in the man's eyes gave him goose bumps. He had faced blazing guns on many a battlefield, but this situation was different. Boswick's men would get to him when he was at a disadvantage and couldn't defend himself. Somehow he must come up with the other half of the debt.

He forced his thoughts away from Boswick and thought of Ginny Grayson. He must see her again as soon as possible.

Then another thought drove itself into his mind. Tomorrow night he had to face another casino owner.

The next morning, Wes kept his appointments with the hardware store owners and then took the afternoon stage to Joplin.

The desk clerk greeted him as he entered the lobby of the Hotel Joplin. "Welcome back, Mr. Logan."

"Thank you, Dwight. It's nice to see you again."

"I have your usual room for you, sir. And I see you have a box with you. I'll help you get it up to your room."

After getting settled in his room, Logan went to the hotel's restaurant, ate a good meal, then walked down the street to the Ozark Saloon and Casino. Upon entering, he was approached by a big, thick-shouldered man who reminded him of Turk Kastin.

"Another day or two," said bouncer Monte Maxim, "and the boss would have been sendin' somebody on your trail."

"I'm right on schedule, Monte. I'm not a welcher."

"Glad to hear it. Makes it better for your health. Come on. I'll take you to the boss."

Wes Logan left Jack Wall's office and was escorted by Monte Maxim to the front door. "You'd better have the other half of what you owe Mr. Wall next time, or believe me...you'll be a dead man."

"I'll be here with the money."

As people moved past them, Maxim said in a husky whisper, "If you've had any thoughts about hightailin' it for Mexico or Canada, forget it. Mr. Wall has plenty of connections. Just last month he took care of a welcher who ran away to Bermuda. The guy's bones are tied to a couple of big rocks at the bottom of the Atlantic Ocean. The month before that, a welcher tried to hide himself in Argentina. He's six feet under. Get the message?"

"Yeah. I get it. I'll have the money in Mr. Wall's hands in three weeks."

"Good," said the big man, giving him a hard pat on the back. "Pleasant dreams."

Although the evening was cool, sweat beaded Wes's brow and chills slithered down his backbone. Soon he came to the Dusty Trail Saloon and Casino, where he owed no money. He played poker for the rest of the evening, hoping to win a sizable amount of money to go toward what he owed to Dolph Boswick, Jack Wall, and Pierce Burns. He owed the Silver Dollar Casino in Kansas City nine thousand dollars. The owner, Pierce Burns, had given him one more chance to pay the debt before fulfilling his threat to kill him.

Wesley Logan had to come up with over thirteen thousand dollars before the next three weeks had passed. Actually, the nine thousand dollars he owed Burns would be due in less than two weeks…when he returned to Kansas City from this trip.

The evening at the Dusty Trail turned out bad for Logan. When he left the place and headed for the hotel, he had barely broken even. Clenching his fists, he cursed his rotten luck. If his luck didn't change for the better, and quickly…

As he climbed the stairs toward his room, he thought about trying to hide. Maybe if he went far enough he could elude these ruthless casino owners. Africa? Russia? Japan?

No, these guys had too many connections all over the world. He would live the life of a fugitive…hounded and trailed until he was finally caught and killed.

As Wes lay in bed that night, he pushed his gambling debts aside in his mind and thought once more of lovely Ginny

Grayson. The longing to see her was stronger than it had been the night before.

The next morning, Wes left his room to keep an appointment with the first of two hardware store owners.

It was almost noon when he arrived back at Hotel Joplin. He had lunch in the restaurant, then returned to his room to wait until time for the second appointment. He sat in an overstuffed chair by the window that overlooked the street until it was time to go.

At just after two o'clock, Wes left his room with the heavy box on his shoulder, descended the stairs, and headed through the lobby toward the front door.

As he was passing the desk, he heard Dwight Kinard call out, "Well, there he is! Congratulations, hero!"

Wes paused uncertainly. "Pardon me?"

"Aw, c'mon, Mr. Logan, let's not be modest. That was really something!"

Wes moved toward the desk. "Dwight, I have no idea what you're talking about."

Dwight waved a copy of the *Kansas City Star* and pointed to the headlines. "Right here! This is the morning edition of the paper. Came in on the noon stage from Kansas City. You're quite the hero, Mr. Logan!"

The bold headlines read:

STAGECOACH ROBBERY FOILED BY CIVIL WAR HERO! THAXTON GANG IN JAIL!

Wes set his box on the counter and took the paper from the clerk's hand and scanned the front-page article written by reporter Neal Golan.

He read the details of how ex-Union army Lieutenant Wesley Logan had courageously foiled the robbery and single-handedly disarmed the feared and hated Thaxton gang who were now behind bars in the Cass County Jail at Harrisonville.

Golan had checked Civil War records with the U.S. Army in Washington, D.C., by telegram, and learned of Lieutenant Logan's impressive deeds of heroism in the war.

A bit embarrassed as he handed the paper back to the desk clerk, Logan said, "Mr. Golan sort of embellishes things, Dwight. I'm no hero. In the war I simply did what a soldier is supposed to do. And as for this robbery thing…again, I just did what a man is supposed to do."

Dwight chuckled. "Sure, Mr. Logan. But according to the article, there were two other men inside the coach—one being Golan himself—and there were two men up in the box. None of them got a hold on that Lambert Thaxton and put a gun under his chin. It was you. I say you most certainly are a hero."

"Well, you're very kind, but I'm no different than any other man." As Wes spoke, he picked up the box and set it on his shoulder. Turning toward the door, he said, "See you later."

"Yes, sir. See you later, hero!"

Ten minutes later, Wes moved through the door of Joplin Hardware and greeted the owner, Lucas Donovan, who was stocking a shelf with small boxes of wood screws.

"Hello, Wes. Welcome back." Donovan turned from the shelf and extended his hand. "I read in the *Star* what you did day before yesterday. Congratulations! That was really something. Just think of it…you got rid of the Thaxton gang! They'll hang for sure when they get to Kansas City. I think the law ought to sic you on the James-Younger gang. We'd be rid of them, too, I'm sure!"

Wes grinned as he set the wooden box on top of a nail keg.

"Neal Golan built me up too much. He's a nice fella and is trying to do the right thing, Mr. Donovan, but I'm really not the big hero he makes me out to be. I was only doing what anyone else would have done in my place."

Lucas Donovan chuckled and shook his head. "Not anyone, Wes. Most men would have played it safe, let the robbers take their money and possessions, and just be glad to be alive when the outlaws rode away."

Wes thought about it. He was sure he wouldn't have made his daring move on Lambert Thaxton if he hadn't been carrying the money to pay on his gambling debts. It was the fear of Dolph Boswick, Jack Wall, and Pierce Burns that forced him to put the gun on Lambert Thaxton and take control of the desperate situation.

At their farm near Lee's Summit, Gene and Marla Vader were eating supper when there was a knock at the back door.

Gene hastily swallowed a mouthful of mashed potatoes then shoved his chair back and went toward the back porch.

"Well, Jesse! Good to see you! Come in."

Jesse James stepped through the door and nodded at Vader's wife. "How are you, Marla?"

"Just fine, Jesse. You?"

"Fine, thanks." Then to Gene, "The boys are out in the trees behind your barn. Just wanted to find out if there have been any lawmen or army units at the Younger place of late."

"Nobody's been there."

"Good. Guess it's safe to hole up there again."

"I'd say so. We saw in the papers that you boys have been doin' some robbin' in Texas and Indian Territory for the past few weeks."

"Yep. We figured to let things cool down here for a while, so we headed south. Still gonna stay away from the Smithville place a little longer."

"Smart."

Jesse reached into his coat pocket and pulled out a wad of bills. "Here's what we owe you for watching the place. We'll see that Ted gets his pay tomorrow."

Vader closed his fingers around the fat wad and grinned at Marla.

"See you later," said Jesse. "We're a tired bunch. We're gonna hit the hay pretty early."

The next morning, the whole gang sat around the kitchen table while Cole Younger and Jesse James counted the loot from the last robbery, took their share, then handed out the rest to each gang member.

When Belle Reed received her share, she held the money close to her heart and said, "Jim, I'm dressin' up fancy, and we're goin' into town this afternoon. I want to get some more fancy clothes."

Jim Reed chuckled. "It's your money, sweetheart. You earned it. You can buy whatever you want. I'll take you to town. There are a few things I need to get, myself."

It was early afternoon when Jim Reed guided the horse and buggy to a halt at the hitching rail in front of Middleton's Clothiers. He jumped out and started toward the boardwalk, then looked back at his wife. Belle sat there, arms folded.

"What's the matter?" he asked.

"Some gentleman you are!"

"Whoops! I get so used to seein' you dressed like a man I forget that you really are a lady."

Belle laughed. "Well, you could get some arguments about the 'lady' bit from a lot of lawmen. But you have to admit that I'm dressed like a lady today, even if inside I'm only a woman."

Together, the Reeds crossed the boardwalk and entered Middleton's. As soon as Jim closed the door behind them, they saw a group of people gathered around Ralph Middleton, the store's owner. He was holding a copy of the *Kansas City Star*.

Middleton was telling the group about the way some ex-Union lieutenant-turned-hardware-drummer had outfoxed the Dub Thaxton gang who were attempting to rob the stagecoach in which he was riding. Wesley Logan, who was employed by the Cushman Hardware Company of San Francisco, had disarmed the gang, and they were now in the Cass County Jail at Harrisonville, waiting to be transported by federal marshals to Kansas City for trial.

Belle grabbed Jim's arm, and in a low tone, said, "Honey, this is great! Jesse and Cole and the rest of the gang will be thrilled to hear this!"

"You're not woofin', sweetie. Our archrivals are in jail and goin' to trial! Let's get us a copy of that paper."

Upon returning to the Younger farm, Jim and Belle gathered everybody in the parlor and showed them the front page of the *Star*.

Jesse read the entire story aloud to the rest of the gang. When he had finished, he looked at Cole and said, "You know what?"

"What?"

"We could use a guy like this Wesley Logan. He's got guts. Even if he was a Yankee soldier."

"Yankees like that I can cotton to," spoke up Charlie Pitts.

"Cole," said Jesse, "we've been talking about adding some more men to the gang. Maybe we ought to find this guy and have a talk with him."

"Sounds good to me." Cole turned to the others. "What about the rest of you?"

"If you can get him, he'd be a good one," spoke up Belle.

"Chances might be pretty good, Cole," said Clell Miller. "I don't think I ever heard of a hardware drummer makin' much money. Not nearly as much as Mr. Logan would make with us. I think you oughtta talk to him."

"He shouldn't be hard to find," said Jesse. "The paper says here that he lives in Kansas City. If we have to, we could wire his company in San Francisco and ask for his address."

6

Ginny Grayson was sitting at the small desk in her room. Before her was the *Kansas City Star* edition that told the story of Wes Logan's heroic deed.

She rubbed the front page of the newspaper with a gentle hand. "Wes—ah…Mr. Logan, you are a wonderful man. It took a lot of courage to do what you did. Of course, I didn't know you had been an army officer in the war. Wounded twice, it says. You seem to be all right now."

Ginny heard footsteps in the hall. Lifting her head, she saw her aunt standing at the open door. "I thought I heard you talking to someone, honey," said Carolyne.

"Oh, I guess I was just thinking out loud."

Carolyne stepped into the room and focused on the newspaper. "If you're not careful, you're going to read the print right off that paper," she said.

Ginny chuckled. "Now, Auntie Carolyne, that's not so."

Carolyne looked her in the eye. "You know what? I think Mr. Wesley Logan made an impression on my niece."

"Well-l-l…"

"Come on. Am I right?"

Ginny cocked her head and frowned slightly. "Let's just say that I have never met a man like him before. He's such a gentleman.

He was so swift to come to my aid when I fell on that depot platform. And now I learn that he's a very brave man. I mean…Auntie Carolyne, how many men would have the courage to do what he did when those seven outlaws had the stagecoach surrounded and were all holding guns? Oh, he's so wonderful!"

Carolyne smiled and laid a hand on Ginny's shoulder. "You're showing signs like I did when I was getting interested in your Uncle Walter. You'd better be careful, little lady, or you'll find yourself falling for Mr. Logan."

Ginny took a deep breath and let it out slowly. "I don't know how you tell love from infatuation. I barely know the man, so it must be infatuation, right?"

"I would say so. Of course there is such a thing as love at first sight, but it doesn't happen very often. You have to get to know a person before you can fall in love with him. I think you must have a dual case of admiration and infatuation."

Ginny nodded. "That must be it."

"When you really fall in love, Ginny, you'll know the difference. When the man who is meant for you comes into your life, and you fall for him, you'll know the difference for sure."

"Right away?"

"Well, it won't take too long. When you have an attraction for him, all you have to do then is get to know him well enough to fall in love with him."

Ginny looked back at the front page of the newspaper, ran her finger over one of the places where Wesley Logan's name was printed and sighed. "All I can tell you right now is that Mr. Logan is the most wonderful man I have ever met."

Carolyne squeezed her niece's shoulder. "Well, I hope this wonderful, brave young man comes back to see you…or certainly you won't be able to get to know him at all."

✦

Wes Logan stepped out of the stagecoach in front of the Wells Fargo office in Kansas City and waited for his luggage and the wooden box to be unloaded by the crew.

While he was waiting, he beckoned to the driver of a nearby buggy for hire. Wes knew just about all the hired buggy drivers in Kansas City, including this one. Leroy Drysdale smiled as he swung the buggy around in the street and pulled up close to the rear of the stagecoach.

When the shotgunner handed Wes the wooden box, Leroy jumped out, took the box from Wes, and placed it in the back of the buggy. Wes grabbed his two pieces of luggage from the boot. "Okay, Leroy," he said. "Take me home."

When they had gone several blocks without Wes saying anything, Leroy looked at him. "You're awfully quiet, Wes."

"Guess I'm not my usual talkative self. Sorry."

"Something wrong?"

"Just tired I guess. It's been a grueling trip this time."

"Well, a good night's sleep will help that."

Wes figured Leroy hadn't read about him in the *Kansas City Star,* and he was glad. He'd had enough of the "hero" talk on this trip to do him a lifetime. But that wasn't the problem. His stomach was churning and had been since he'd left Columbia. He had made some money gambling while on the road, but not nearly enough to pay his gambling debt to the Silver Dollar Casino. If he didn't pay Pierce Burns the money he owed him upon returning home this time, his life wasn't worth two cents. He was almost sick to his stomach.

Leroy pulled the buggy to a halt in front of the boarding-house where Wes lived, jumped out, and handed him his luggage. He carried the box into the room for him, then said,

"You get yourself some rest now."

Wes forced a smile and handed him a silver dollar.

When Leroy was gone, Wes paced the floor, wringing his hands. What was he going to do? How would he ever face Pierce Burns?

The pacing went on for some time, then he decided to unpack his luggage. He should be hungry, but he knew his stomach was too upset for food. Suddenly there was a knock at the door.

His first thought was that Pierce Burns had sent a couple of his hired killers to collect the debt. A pulse throbbed in his temples and his mouth went dry.

The knock came again. With a shaky hand, Wes pulled the derringer from his coat pocket. Cold sweat beaded his brow as he tiptoed to the door. He had told Pierce he would come to the casino with the money when he got home from this trip. Why would he send his thugs to his room already?

He eased up to the door and called out, "Who is it?"

A familiar voice said, "Mr. Logan, it's me, Neal Golan. You remember me. *Kansas City Star?* I have a couple of men out here who would like to talk to you."

Wes let out his pent-up breath and slipped the derringer back in his coat pocket. He pressed a smile on his lips and opened the door.

"Good to see you again, Mr. Logan," Neal Golan said, extending his right hand. He carried a small valise.

"It's good to see you, too," Wes said, meeting his grip.

Golan gestured to the two men with him. "These gentlemen are Wells Fargo executives. This is Wayne Mitchell and this is Ray Kramer."

Wes shook hands with both men, then invited them in. When they were seated comfortably in the living area of the room, Kramer said, "Mr. Logan, our company wishes to express its deep gratitude for your act of heroism when the Thaxton gang stopped our Joplin-bound stage."

"Yes," said Mitchell. "If you hadn't put a stop to it, the cash box would have been taken, which contained two thousand dollars. And the passengers—including yourself—would have lost your cash and valuables."

"It's very kind of you to come here and express your gratitude, gentlemen," said Wes.

Ray Kramer chuckled and reached inside his coat to pull out a white envelope. "We're expressing our gratitude in more than mere words, my dear sir." Extending the envelope to Logan, he said, "There is a check in here made out to you in the amount of five hundred dollars."

Accepting the envelope, Wes said, "I…I don't know what to say."

"You don't have to say anything, Mr. Logan," commented Mitchell. "Just know that what you did is very much appreciated by Wells Fargo."

"Words fail me, gentlemen, but I'll use the old standby of 'thank you.' I can really use this extra money right now."

Neal Golan grinned. "Well! Now that the Wells Fargo reward ceremony is over, the *Kansas City Star* wants me to do a personal interview with you, Mr. Logan."

Wes looked at him quizzically. "You mean for another story like the one you put on the front page last week?"

"That's it. Only this will be even better, because our readers will get to hear from the hero himself."

Wes scrubbed a hand over his eyes. "Well, if you insist."

"I insist," Golan said as he took a pencil and paper pad from his valise.

Golan asked Wes questions about his background and

pressed him for details about his army career, battlefield experiences, and the wound sustained at Pea Ridge which took him out of the army. He then asked Wes to tell about the foiling of the robbery, so the readers could learn what went on in his own mind when he faced the guns of the robbers.

When Golan was satisfied that he had sufficient material for his story, he put paper and pencil away and said, "Mr. Logan, I appreciate the interview. It will be on page 3 of the paper day after tomorrow. I'll put it in the article that you were rewarded by Wells Fargo and Company for your heroism."

When the men had gone, Wes opened the envelope and took out the check. It would help pay the gambling debt he owed Pierce Burns, but he still must come up with almost eight thousand dollars when he added his meager winnings on the road to the reward money.

He went downstairs to pick up the mail that had come while he was gone, then started up the stairs again to his room. He reminded himself that Pierce Burns only knew that he was due back this week. He didn't know which day.

Wes sat down at his small desk with the mail. Before he opened the first envelope, which was his paycheck from his employer, he made the decision that he would gamble at another Kansas City casino—the Broken Spur—for a couple of nights. Maybe his luck would change and he could win the money he needed to pay Pierce Burns.

After extracting his paycheck from the envelope, Wes quickly went through the rest of the mail, then left the boardinghouse and walked down the street to his bank. When he walked up to the teller's window, she called out to the other bank employees that the hero was back. They converged on him, congratulating him on his deed. Customers joined with them when they realized he was the man they had read about in the newspaper.

While accolades were heaped upon him, Wes deposited the paycheck in his account, keeping back a small amount of cash for his wallet. He then cashed the Wells Fargo check and stuffed the money in his coat pocket to use at the casino later.

That evening he ate supper in a cafe near the Broken Spur, then walked to the casino, hoping his luck had changed. The five hundred dollars reward from Wells Fargo made him believe that maybe it had.

Three hours after entering the casino, Wes headed home, shoulders slumped and head hanging low. In a single poker game he had lost the reward money, plus the other money he had won on his business trip. All he had on him was the small amount of cash in his wallet.

What was he going to do now? Pierce Burns would be after him in another day or so if he didn't show up at the Silver Dollar Casino with the nine thousand dollars.

He tossed and turned in bed for a while, then put his mind on something more pleasant…Ginny.

"Oh, Ginny," he whispered, "I can't go any longer without seeing you. I've got another day before I have to face Burns. Your Uncle Walter said if I'm ever in the area again, I should come by the house for a visit. Your aunt said it would be nice to have me stop by. All right then, tomorrow I will just 'happen' to be in the area. I'm coming for a visit, Ginny."

The next morning, Wes Logan rented a horse and buggy and drove down to Harrisonville, arriving about 11:30. He remembered that Carolyne Hansen said they lived on Grove Street, but he couldn't recall the number. He found the street easily enough, then stopped and asked a woman who was sweeping her front porch if she knew the Hansens. She directed him to number 341, just two blocks down.

Moments later, Wes pulled rein and tied the horse to the hitching post and hurried across the yard to the porch. He mounted the steps and knocked at the door.

He heard light footsteps inside, then the door opened to reveal a smiling Carolyne Hansen. "Well, Mr. Logan! How nice to see you! Please come in!"

As Wes entered the doorway, Carolyne turned and called toward the rear of the house, "Ginny! Walter! We have a very special guest. Come see him."

Carolyne said in a half whisper, "Ginny's going to be so glad to see you!"

Wes smiled. "I hope so."

"Take my word for it," Carolyne said, muffling a tiny giggle.

When the other two put in an appearance, Ginny rushed to Wes and took both of his hands in hers. "Hello, Mr. Hero! We read in the *Kansas City Star* what you did that day after you left Harrisonville on the stage!"

The Hansens commended him for his courageous deed. While her aunt and uncle were talking to Wes, Ginny looked at him with admiring eyes.

"Mr. Logan," Carolyne said, "it's almost lunchtime. Can you stay to eat with us?"

"I'd love to."

Carolyne looked at her niece. "Ginny, let's go fix lunch. We'll let the men talk." Then she said to Wes, "Do you like tomato soup, Mr. Logan?"

"Sure. Sounds good."

"Tell you what," spoke up Walter. "Since you're a hardware man, how would you like to see my tool shop while the ladies prepare lunch?"

"Great!" said Wes. He turned to Ginny. "See you shortly."

She flashed him one of her mesmerizing smiles. "Thirty minutes should be about right, Mr. Logan."

Wes's heart beat a little faster. "Okay. Thirty minutes."

When the half hour had passed, the foursome sat down at the kitchen table. Wes sniffed the aroma of the tomato soup and declared it smelled delicious.

As soon as Walter had sipped his first spoonful of soup, he said, "Mr. Logan, I would like to hear firsthand ab—"

"Pardon me," said Wes, cutting across Walter's words, "but it would make me real happy if all of you would call me Wes."

Walter laughed. "Good enough for me, Wes! As long as I'm Walter, my wife is Carolyne, and my niece is Ginny."

Wes looked at each of them and replied, "Then so be it, Walter, Carolyne…Ginny."

He tried to hurry through the story, but Walter Hansen cut in a few times, asking for details. Finally Wes realized that he was going to have to go over the story even as he had for Neal Golan. When he finished, Ginny said, "You really deserve some kind of an award for what you did, Wes."

Knowing that Ginny and the Hansens would no doubt read Neal Golan's newest article on the subject and learn of the Wells Fargo reward, Wes told them about it without revealing the amount.

"I think it's wonderful," said Ginny. "The Wells Fargo people know a genuinely heroic deed when they see one."

"Let me ask you something," said Carolyne.

"Yes, ma'am?"

"When you climbed on the next stagecoach, did you have any feelings like you might be faced with the same task again?"

Wes laughed. "No. It didn't even cross my mind."

Lunch was almost over when Walter said, "Wes, I've got a little story to tell you about a stagecoach holdup."

"Oh? Let's hear it."

Carolyne looked at Ginny. "You haven't heard this one, honey."

"Before I tell you about my experience, Wes, have you heard of—"

"Uncle Walter!" gasped Ginny. "You were in a stagecoach that was held up?"

"Yes, I was."

"When did this happen?"

"Almost exactly a year ago."

"Why haven't you told me about it before now?"

"It hadn't come to mind. Talking about Wes's experience made me think of it."

"Oh. Well, I'm sorry for interrupting, Uncle Walter."

He gave her a smile, then looked back at Wes. "I was going to ask if you've ever heard of the mysterious man called the Stranger?"

Wes eased back in his chair. "Oh, yes. Some kind of man, this John Stranger."

"I've heard about him, too," said Ginny. "They talk about him a lot in San Francisco."

"Good. Then you'll both know who I'm talking about as I tell the story. Like I said, it was almost exactly a year ago. I was traveling on a stage in Kansas between Junction City and Topeka. There were five passengers...all men. Just west of a little town called Paxico, a gang of outlaws came out of a dry riverbed and commanded the driver to stop."

"Were you scared, Uncle Walter?"

"Honey, I'd be lying if I said I wasn't. Anyway, the driver did what they told him. First the crew had to throw their guns to the ground, then the robbers made all of us get out of the stage and stand in line shoulder to shoulder. When they had relieved the guns from the two men who were carrying them, they made the driver and shotgunner stand with us and commenced to relieve us of our wallets, pocket watches, tiepins, and rings.

"When they had cleaned us out and were heading for their horses to ride away, all of a sudden this tall fella—he's taller than you, Wes—dressed all in black, appeared out of nowhere, got the drop on the robbers, and disarmed them."

"Black!" said Wes. "Yes, that's Stranger, all right. Except for his white shirt, everything else he wears is black...hat, boots, gun belt. He carries a bone-handled Colt .45 Peacemaker. And his horse is solid black."

"That's him," said Walter, chuckling. "Anyway, we got our stolen goods and money back. We helped this mysterious man tie up the gang and put them in their saddles. Before this man mounted up to take the robbers to the federal marshal's office in Topeka, the stage driver asked him his name. All he said was, 'Sir, people just call me Stranger.'"

Wes nodded. "Mm-hmm."

"Well, the driver pushed a little further and asked if he had a first name. Stranger grinned and said, 'You can call me John.' I've learned a whole lot more about him since that day. They say he's one rugged individual when it comes to handling outlaws, but he bends over to be kind and gentle to decent people."

"Uncle Walter," said Ginny, "I've heard that he's also a preacher. Have you heard that?"

"Yes. They say he's one of those hellfire and brimstone kind."

"I've heard that, too," said Wes.

Walter snapped his fingers. "Oh, yeah! And something else. Before Stranger rode away with the outlaws, he gave each of us a silver medallion."

"I've heard about those, too," said Wes. "Solid silver, exactly the size of a silver dollar."

"Right."

"I remember now," spoke up Ginny. "Somebody told me that each medallion has an inscription on it. Something from the Bible."

"That's right, honey. The same inscription is on every medallion."

"Walter, you ought to go get your medallion and show it to Ginny and Wes," put in Carolyne.

"Be right back," said Walter, pushing his chair back from the table.

Wes shook his head in wonderment. "Isn't this something? Walter has met John Stranger in person. I've heard so much about the man. He's helped so many people out of trouble. And I've heard he gives untold amounts of money to people in need."

Walter came back into the kitchen and held up the medallion for Ginny and Wes to see. It had a raised five-point star in the center, and inscribed around its circular edge were the words: THE STRANGER THAT SHALL COME FROM A FAR LAND—Deuteronomy 29:22.

"It's beautiful," said Ginny. "May I hold it, Uncle Walter?"

She examined the medallion closely, then smiled at Wes and said, "Would you like to see it?"

"Sure would."

After Wes looked at it, he handed it to Walter and said, "I wonder where Stranger gets the money to give to all these people?"

"Lots of people have wondered that," commented Carolyne. "We used to have neighbors to whom he gave ten thousand dollars when they lived in New Mexico. They talked a lot about him, expressing their appreciation for what he had done, and saying they wondered if he was some kind of millionaire.

They have since moved back to New Mexico."

"I heard about an elderly couple in Montana whose farmhouse had burned down," said Wes. "Stranger showed up one day, seemingly from out of nowhere, and gave them the money to rebuild. They were living in their barn at the time."

"That's really something," said Ginny. "I wonder what far country John Stranger comes from."

"You'll probably find that out when you learn where he gets all the money he gives away," said Walter.

Ginny chuckled. "Yes…and that will be never. But I'm sure glad to know there's somebody like him riding about this country helping people."

"This world could use more men like him," said Carolyne. "Well, tell you what. Wes, if you can stay longer, I want you and Ginny to have some time together. I'll do the dishes and clean up the kitchen."

Wes looked at Ginny. "I have to leave for Kansas City in time to be home by dark, which gives me another three hours or so. I was going to ask, Ginny, if you would like to go for a little ride with me? It's not very cold outside."

"Yes, I'd like that." Then she turned to Carolyne. "Are you sure it's all right, Auntie? I could help you with the cleanup and make the ride shorter."

"No, no. You two need some time to get acquainted. You go on. Have a nice time."

It was almost four o'clock when Wes and Ginny returned to the Hansen home. They had thoroughly enjoyed each other's company, and both were feeling a strong attraction to each other, but neither had voiced it. Wes helped Ginny out of the buggy and walked her to the front door of the house.

"Well," he said, hardly able to breathe for the nearness of her, "I'd better get going. Thank you so much for taking the ride with me."

She lit up with one of her captivating smiles. "Thank you for inviting me. And thank you for coming all this way to see me."

"You don't have to thank me for that." Wes looked into her expressive blue eyes. "The pleasure was all mine."

"Oh, not all yours," she corrected sweetly.

Wes took a deep breath. "I'd better get going. Ah…Ginny?"

"Yes?"

"May I come back and see you again sometime soon?"

"I would love it."

"All right. Don't be surprised if I'm back again before I head out on my next business trip next Monday."

Ginny giggled. "I'll try not to be surprised."

Wes untied the reins from the hitching post, then smiled at her and said, "Until next time…"

Ginny kept her eyes on him until he turned the corner at the end of the block. When she went inside, Walter was on his knees in the small vestibule, a hammer in his hand. He looked up. "Have a nice time?"

"Sure did. He's such a fine man." Cocking her head, she asked, "What are you doing?"

"Carpet's coming loose right here. I'm nailing it down."

"Oh. What's Auntie doing?"

"Washing clothes on the back porch."

"I'll go see if I can help."

When Ginny stepped out on the back porch, Carolyne was wringing out one of Walter's shirts. "Hello, sweetie. Have a nice ride?"

"Very nice. Here, let me help you wring out the rest of these clothes."

Carolyne studied her niece. "There's a glow in your eyes, Miss Grayson."

"Really?" Ginny picked up a shirt.

"Mm-hmm. It wasn't there before you and Wes left. Something happen on the ride?"

"Well, not exactly. I mean, nothing like a kiss or anything like that. It's just that...well, he's so special."

"Special?"

"Mm-hmm."

"I see. Could this be love?"

Ginny blushed. "Auntie, all I can say is that Wes Logan is a very charming young man."

Carolyne smiled but said no more.

As WES LOGAN DROVE TOWARD KANSAS CITY, his heart felt like it was on fire. Ginny Grayson was doing something to him that no other girl had ever done. Reflecting on the ride they took together, he thought how her every move and word thrilled him. He was positive he had fallen in love with her the first time he saw her.

Soon the uneven rooftops of Kansas City came into view. Wes's thoughts turned to Pierce Burns. Trepidation pumped in his veins. He had no money left with which to gamble and try to come up with the nine thousand dollars he owed the casino. He had two choices. He could either run or go to Burns and ask for more time to pay his debt.

When Wes entered his room at the boardinghouse, he began pacing the floor. Lieutenant Wesley Logan had fought many a fierce and bloody battle in the Civil War, but facing Pierce Burns seemed worse than facing the blazing guns of the Confederates on a smoky battlefield.

He suddenly stopped his pacing and looked at his reflection in the mirror above the dresser, saying aloud, "Wes, put the confrontation off one more day. Go see Ginny tomorrow and face Burns tomorrow night."

✦

At the same time Wes Logan was wrestling with his thoughts, Deputy Sheriff Bart DeWolfe, at the Cass County Jail in Harrisonville, stood outside the cell of Nate Roach, Tom Portell, and Lambert Thaxton. The gang members in the other cell were on their feet, staring at Lambert, who was writhing on the floor and clutching his midsection.

Lambert sucked air through gritted teeth as he drew up his knees and moaned. His face was a deep purple.

"Deputy, you gotta do somethin'!" gusted Dub Thaxton. "It's probably appendicitis! Take him to a doctor, quick! If that thing ruptures, he could die in minutes. Hurry!"

The deputy shook his head. "I can't take him to a doctor without Sheriff Landis's permission. I'll run and get the sheriff. We can bring the doctor with us on our way back."

"There might not be time!" wailed Dub. "It'll take too long to do all that. You've got to take him out of that cell and get him to the doctor fast!"

"I said I can't do that."

Dub's face was swollen with rage. "Take him now! If he dies, I'll hold you responsible!"

Lambert ejected a howl of pain that made DeWolfe wince and say, "All right."

Dub's beefy features relaxed.

The deputy took out his gun and cocked the hammer, and said to Roach and Portell, "Move back against the wall."

He watched them obey, then took the key ring off his belt and inserted it in the lock of the cell door and swung it open. As he moved to Lambert, both Roach and Portell glanced at Dub and grinned. Dub nodded his head.

DeWolfe leaned over the groaning Lambert and took hold

of his arm. "Come on. You'll have to walk. Let's go."

Lambert tried to get up.

As if on cue, Nate Roach said, "Want us to help him, Deputy?"

When DeWolfe glanced at the two men against the wall and told them to stay put, Lambert took advantage of that fraction of a second and kicked DeWolfe's legs out from under him.

Instantly, Roach and Portell were on top of DeWolfe. Portell wrested the gun from his hand, pointed it at the stunned deputy, and hissed, "You stay right there or I'll put a bullet in you!"

Bart DeWolfe watched in horror as Lambert leaped to his feet and took the key from the door and freed the rest of the gang.

As Portell eased the hammer down on DeWolfe's gun, Dub laughed and said, "Little brother, you should've been an actor. You did a great lob!"

"I did my best, big brother."

Motioning toward the cell where the deputy lay, Dub told Lambert to lock him in. The younger Thaxton swung the door shut and locked it, grinning at DeWolfe. "Not very smart, are yuh?"

The deputy gave him a look of loathing mixed with frustration.

Dub swung his gaze to Louis Wertz and Clarence Quint. "You guys want out?"

Wertz laughed. "Do you have to ask?"

"Just thought you might like it here," said Dub. "Let 'em out, Lambert."

Bart DeWolfe carried a .41 caliber derringer inside his boot in a special holster. It was his only hope of stopping the escape.

When Wertz and Quint were free, Dub said, "Our guns are out in the office. Let's go."

The last men out of the cell were the first to head for the office. The Thaxton brothers, Tom Portell, and Nate Roach brought up the rear. They were about to pass through the door when Lambert looked back at DeWolfe and said, "Hold it, Dub. I think this stupid deputy oughtta be shot."

"Why?"

"Because he's a stinkin' lawman, that's why."

"You know other lawmen will hound us like wolves after cottontails if we kill one of their own," said Dub. "Let's get outta here."

Suddenly, Lambert grabbed the revolver from Tom Portell's hand, snapped the hammer back, and fired at DeWolfe. The deputy jerked with the impact of the bullet and ejected a moan.

"C'mon, Lambert!" bawled Dub. "Let's go!"

Portell and Roach were already out the door, heading down the narrow corridor to the office. As Dub moved ahead of Lambert, Bart Dewolfe pulled up his pant leg, whipped out the derringer, and fired.

The bullet struck Lambert Thaxton in the back, dropping him in his tracks. Dub swore vehemently, picked up DeWolfe's revolver and shot him again. The deputy slumped down and stopped breathing.

Portell and Roach found Dub bending over his brother, feeling for a pulse.

"Stinkin' deputy shot him in the back," Dub said. "Had a derringer on him. Lambert's dead. No time to try to take the body. Let's move!"

Just before noon the next day, Carolyne Hansen and Ginny Grayson were preparing lunch when they heard Walter talking to someone in the front part of the house.

A moment later, as Ginny was putting plates and eating utensils on the kitchen table, Walter came in with a smile on his face and said, "Ginny, you'd better set another place. We've got a visitor again."

Both women looked up to see Wes Logan standing at the kitchen door.

"Wes!" Ginny's eyes were dancing. "Two days in a row! You said you'd be back before you leave for your next business trip, but I had no idea it would be this soon!"

"I...hope you don't mind."

"Mind? Of course not! Do we, Auntie Carolyne? Uncle Walter?"

"Not at all," said Carolyne, smiling. "Welcome back, Wes."

"Thank you, ma'am."

"We'll have lunch ready in just a couple minutes. If you men want to wash your hands, now would be an excellent time."

While both men were at the washbasin, Walter said, "Did you hear about the jailbreak, Wes?"

"No...what jailbreak?"

"The Thaxtons."

Wes dropped the towel he had just taken from the rack on the cupboard.

"Yeah," Walter said. "The news was all over town before bedtime last night. Somehow the Thaxton gang managed to get that young deputy, Bart DeWolfe, to open one of the cell doors. They overpowered him and escaped, taking two other prisoners with them. They locked Bart in one of the cells."

Wes frowned and bent to pick up the towel. "You said somehow the gang managed to get DeWolfe to open one of the cells. I take it he isn't able to talk?"

"He's dead. They shot him twice, apparently with his own gun. It was hard for Sheriff Landis to work out the sequence of it, but Bart always carried a derringer in his boot. He managed to get the derringer out and shoot Lambert Thaxton in the back. Lambert's body was found in the cell block right by the door."

Wes shook his head in disbelief. "So the Thaxton gang, minus Lambert, is on the loose."

Ginny stepped close and said, "Wes, I hope the gang won't come after you to get even."

Wes's mind flashed back to the moment just before he left the Cass County Jail. Dub Thaxton had gripped the cell bars and screamed at him. "I'll get you, Logan! You're as good as dead already! Do you hear me! You're dead!"

Wes handed the towel to Walter. "I hope they won't either, Ginny."

As they began eating lunch, Walter said, "I'm really sorry Bart DeWolfe had to die, but I'm glad he took Lambert Thaxton out."

Walter took a bite of his food, then said, "Carolyne, isn't there something in the Bible about someone who lives violently will die the same way?"

"Yes. It's been a long time since I read it, but it was Jesus who said something to the effect that those who take the sword will perish with the sword. I remember my Sunday school teacher—what was his name? Oh, yes! Mr. Blumenthal." She looked at Wes. "This was in Chanute, Kansas, where I was born and raised. I was about eleven or twelve at the time."

Wes nodded.

"Mr. Blumenthal read it to the class from the Bible. The subject came up because an outlaw had been hanged that week in Chanute for killing a man in a saloon brawl. The outlaw was wanted on several counts of murder in other parts of Kansas.

Mr. Blumenthal pointed out that the guilty man had lived a life of violence and that the long drop from the gallows platform to the end of the rope was a violent one. He had lived by the sword, so to speak, and he died by the sword."

"This seems to hold true so often," said Walter.

Carolyne nodded. "I recall that Mr. Blumenthal explained that 'taking the sword and perishing with the sword' is not referring to law officers who protect society with weapons, or soldiers who use weapons to defend their land from aggressors. He was talking about those who use violence to break the law and to hurt and kill innocent people."

"That has to be right," put in Ginny. "Certainly Jesus Christ would want innocent people and law-abiding citizens to be protected by law officers...even if they have to use weapons or a hanging rope to do it."

"Of course," said Carolyne. "I remember that a few months later, two gunslingers got into a quick-draw gunfight on Main Street. One was killed, of course. Mr. Blumenthal brought the same Scripture up again in class the next Sunday, pointing out that the man who was killed in the gunfight had chosen to live a life of violence. And what really brought the truth home, was that the very next week the victor in the gunfight was killed by another gunslinger in Wichita."

Walter took a sip of coffee. "So it was with Lambert Thaxton. If you live by the gun, chances are pretty strong that you'll die by the gun. Live a violent life...die a violent death."

"That's it," said Carolyne. "They go hand in hand."

Wes looked across the table at Ginny. "I've got a little time before I have to head back to Kansas City. How about us taking another ride?"

"Of course. As soon as I help Aunt Carolyne clean up after lunch."

"No need of that, honey," said Carolyne. "You two go enjoy yourselves. It won't take me long to clean up."

"But, I really should—"

"No, Ginny. Go on, now."

As Wes drove the buggy with Ginny at his side, they took a country road and drove among the farms that dotted the land. The trees were bare and the air still had a nip to it.

For a moment, Wes's thoughts drifted to the upcoming moment that night when he must face Pierce Burns and ask for more time to come up with the money to pay his debt. He quickly put his attention back on the beautiful young woman sitting beside him.

As the buggy rolled over the country roads, Ginny asked more questions about Wes's work, wanting to know how he happened to become a traveling hardware drummer and if he was happy with the job.

While giving answers that seemed to satisfy her, Wes felt like he was going to burst if he didn't tell Ginny how he felt about her. He was explaining how much he liked the job when he abruptly pulled the buggy off the road and parked it in a grove of trees.

Ginny looked around, then met his gaze. "Why are we stopping here?"

"Because I'm going to explode if I don't stop and tell you something."

"What?" she said, looking puzzled.

Wes took hold of her hand. "Ginny, you may think me an impetuous fool, but…I…Ginny, I'm falling in love with you. I know I am. I just had to tell you before I burst into a million pieces."

She sat motionless and stared at him.

He shook his head. "You think I'm a fool. I'm sorry, I just know what's going on inside my heart, and I—"

"Oh, no, Wes," she said, finally locating her voice. "I don't think that at all. I just didn't think it could happen this fast. But I'm falling in love with you, too."

"Really?"

"Really."

"Oh, Ginny, this makes me so happy! You are absolutely the girl of my dreams. Could I...could I kiss you?"

She smiled and nodded.

He gently took her in his arms and planted a tender kiss on her lips. They stared into each other's eyes for a long moment, then Wes said, "Oh, Ginny, you've made me the happiest man in the whole world!"

Tears misted her eyes. "And you've made me the happiest girl in the whole world."

He embraced her for a long moment, then said, "I hate to do it, but I have to take you home and head for Kansas City."

"All right," she said softly. "Will you be able to come see me again before you go out on your next trip?"

Wes thought of Pierce Burns and told himself he had to resolve the situation with the man that night. "Sure," he said. "Can't tell you which day, but I'll be back before it's time to leave again."

As they drove toward town, Wes said, "Ginny, I don't mean to be nosy, but something concerns me."

She slid her arm inside his and looked up at him. "I don't think you're nosy. What is it?"

"Well, you told me about the poverty you were facing in San Francisco, and I'm wondering if things are better for you now that you're living with your aunt and uncle."

Ginny was silent for a moment, then said, "Things are a little better, Wes. At least I have three good meals a day."

"I'm glad for that, but…"

"What?"

"I see that you're still wearing that old worn-out coat, and your shoes are in need of new soles."

"Uncle Walter said they will buy me some new shoes and clothes come spring, when they have more money. He does gardening for people in town."

"I see."

"I've been thinking that I should find some kind of employment to provide my own needs."

Soon they were back in town, and when Wes turned the buggy onto Grove Street, Ginny squeezed his arm and said, "I sure am glad we took this ride."

He looked into her deep blue eyes. "Me too. Now there won't be an explosion."

Ginny laughed. "I sure wouldn't want that to happen!"

Pierce Burns stood at his office window in the Silver Dollar Saloon, looking down at the darkening street. He watched the elderly lamplighter move along the boardwalk and touch fire to the lanterns spaced some forty feet apart.

The night was young and things were relatively quiet in the Silver Dollar. It was so quiet that Burns could even hear the heavy footsteps on the stairs, though his office door was closed.

When the knock came at the door, he called out, "That you, Sid?"

"Yeah, boss," came a deep-voiced reply.

"C'mon in."

The door opened and Sid Veatch's huge frame filled the

opening. He stepped inside and closed the door. "Millie said you wanted to see me, boss."

"Yeah. I've got a little job for you."

"Collection job?"

Burns's lips curved in a tight smile. "How'd you guess?"

"Well, about half the time when you want to see me in your office, there's somebody who needs squeezin'. Let me guess. Bruce Lyman?"

Burns chuckled. "No. Not yet. I gave him three days. It's only been two."

"Oh. Yeah. He's got one more day before we lean on him. Let's see…Jay Nethercott. He's overdue, isn't he?"

"Not anymore. He was so scared that he came to my house this afternoon and paid me there."

"Good. Well, then I guess the next in line would be Wesley Logan. He was due back this week, wasn't he?"

"Yeah. And my instincts tell me he should've been in here with the money by now. I want you to take Jocko and go to the boardinghouse where Logan lives. I want to know if he's back."

"Okay."

With grit in his voice Burns said, "If Logan's skipped out on me, you and Jocko are gonna track him down. He may be a big hero in the eyes of the public for foiling that stagecoach robbery, but he owes the Silver Dollar a big chunk of money. If he doesn't pay it immediately, he's a dead man."

"Can't blame you, boss."

"If you find Logan at home, you bring him here in a hurry. Welchers are lower than rattlesnakes as far as I'm concerned. And I hate rattlers."

"We'll go check on Logan right now, boss." Even as Veatch was speaking, there was a knock at the door. "Yeah?" Burns said loudly.

"It's Jocko, boss. Wes Logan is here to see you."

"Bring him in!"

The door opened and Wes Logan stepped into the office with Jocko Wade behind him. Wade was almost as big as Sid Veatch and looked meaner.

As Logan moved toward the desk, Burns said, "Close the door, Jocko. I want both of you boys to stay while Wes and I talk business."

The door clicked shut and the two men took a step closer to Logan. Burns said, "You ready to pay up?"

Wes Logan shifted from one foot to the other. "Mr. Burns, I've had a streak of bad luck. I...I need more time to pay you the nine thousand dollars I owe you."

"Well, how much of it do you have with you now?"

"I don't have any of it, sir," came the tremulous reply. Veatch and Wade exchanged glances. Pierce Burns's hawklike features went crimson. "Your streak of bad luck doesn't interest me, Logan!" His voice sounded like flint on steel.

"S-sir, if you would just give me a little more time, I know I can come up with the money—all nine thousand dollars."

"Nine thousand?" rasped Burns. "Your failure to pay me right now, as agreed, has just sent the interest in motion. The amount is now nine thousand five hundred!"

Wes swallowed hard. "Yes, sir." He could hear the heavy breathing of the two massive men behind him.

"Tell you what, Logan," said Burns, "I'm gonna give you until tomorrow night at this time to come in here and cross my palm with nine thousand five hundred dollars. If you don't do that, you'll have one more night to pay me. However, the amount will then be eleven thousand dollars. You got that?"

Wes's stomach lurched. Taking a deep shuddering breath, he said, "I'll do my best to come up with it, sir."

The casino owner's eyes were like blazing fire pits in his angular face. "You haven't done your best up till now?"

"Well, yes, but—"

"Then you do better than your best, Logan, or else! And don't try running! I'll send Sid and Jocko after you, and they'll find you. I'm mad now, but I'll be a lot madder if you try to disappear on me! Understand?"

"I understand, Mr. Burns. I'm not going to run out on you. I just need some more time."

"You've got two days."

Wes could feel the eyes of Burns's two toughs glowering at him from behind as he said, "I'll do it somehow, Mr. Burns."

"You'd better. Unless you like the idea of dying a slow, agonizing death and being put in a pine box six feet underground."

Wes Logan stepped onto the boardwalk and hurried down the street. When he reached the corner, he looked back and saw that both Sid and Jocko were watching him.

He rounded the corner and headed toward the boardinghouse. The night air was cold and drove its chill into his bones. His stomach was still churning, and his mind was filled with futility and sheer black despair.

Suddenly he was thinking that his best chance to come out of this alive was to head for Central or South America and hide in the jungles. Surely none of the toughs who were hired by the rich casino owners could find him in a grass hut hundreds of miles from civilization in a hot, humid, mosquito-infested jungle. Dub Thaxton wouldn't be able to find him either.

Just as suddenly he shook the thoughts from his mind. Even if somehow he could elude them, what kind of a life would it be, living out his days in a jungle? And more than that...now there was Ginny. There was no way he could run away and leave her.

There had to be a solution to this predicament.

Wes cursed himself for ever letting gambling get a hold of him. It wasn't the patrons of the casinos who got rich, it was the men who owned them.

Wes was walking so briskly that if he went any faster he would have to break into a run. The boardinghouse was now just two blocks away.

A carriage passed by, the candles in its headlights giving off a pale yellow glow. The driver looked his way and said, "Good evening, sir."

Wes mumbled a greeting but the carriage had already passed him.

Where was he going to get the kind of money he owed Pierce Burns by tomorrow night? Or a total of eleven thousand dollars in two nights?

"Rob a bank," he said aloud. "That's what I'll have to do. Put on a mask and rob one of the banks downtown."

He shook his head vigorously. "No, I can't do that. I'd get caught. I'd go to prison, and Ginny would be out of my life. I can't lose her now. But what am I going to do?"

He was only a half block from the boardinghouse now. Somehow by morning he had to have a solution or his life was over.

8

WHEN WES LOGAN ENTERED THE VESTIBULE of the boardinghouse, his landlord was talking to two men. "Ah, gentlemen, here he is now!" said the landlord when he turned to see who had come in.

Instantly, Wes thought of the day Wayne Mitchell and Ray Kramer from Wells Fargo came to see him with a five-hundred-dollar check in hand. His mind went to Pierce Burns, and he found himself wishing that whoever these two men were, they would have a check for ten thousand dollars to give him.

The landlord went back into his apartment, and the two men turned to face Wes.

"Mr. Logan," said the younger of the two, "my name is Thomas Howard, and this is my associate, John Smith. We read in the newspapers about you single-handedly thwarting the Thaxton gang's attempted robbery of the Wells Fargo stagecoach south of Harrisonville a couple weeks ago. We have a business proposition to discuss with you."

Wes glanced from one man to the other. "Has this to do with my being in the hardware business?"

Thomas Howard nodded to his colleague, who said, "It's totally different from the hardware business, Mr. Logan, but we believe you would be a real asset to our organization. We're prepared to make you an offer to join us." Smith looked around the vestibule and down the hall. "Could we talk to you in your room?"

Wes's first thought was that Dub Thaxton was fulfilling his threat and had sent two of his friends to kill him. But his instincts, which had been sharply honed when he was a combat officer, told him this wasn't the case. Thaxton would want to exact his revenge personally. "Sure," Wes said. "Come on in."

Wes took the men's hats and coats and hung them in his closet. He noted that John Smith's hair was thinning out on top, though the man was only in his midtwenties. He indicated where they should sit then moved a hardback chair into a facing position and sat down. "You were saying, Mr. Smith, that you and Mr. Howard have an offer prepared, wanting me to join your organization."

"Yes. If you accept our offer, you stand to make a great deal of money. We did some checking with the home office of the Cushman Hardware Company in San Francisco, Mr. Logan, and without bringing your name up, we simply asked what the general salary is for their drummers. Believe me, the kind of money you can make with our organization will make your present income look like peanuts."

"So, what exactly would I be doing, gentlemen? What is your business?"

John Smith chuckled. "Before we tell you that, let me say that we were both very much impressed with the newspaper stories written by Neal Golan. We thought your precision movements in thwarting the Thaxton gang were superb. It showed what you're made of."

"I'm sure," put in Howard, "that your military experience developed this kind of expertise when it comes to guns and danger."

Wes shrugged. "No doubt it had a lot to do with it."

"Tell me," said Howard, leaning toward him, "would you have actually blown Lambert's head off if the other gang members had resisted?"

Wes felt a bit off balance at the question, especially when he noted the gleam of anticipation in the man's eyes as he waited for an answer. Glancing at Smith, Wes saw the same eager gleam in his eyes. *Who are these men?*

Thomas Howard studied Wes and said, "Well? Would you have done what you threatened, Mr. Logan? Would you have blown Lambert's head off?"

"The answer to your question, Mr. Howard, is that I absolutely would have pulled the trigger of the derringer if the other gang members had resisted. Seeing as how the derringer is .47 caliber, I assure you Lambert would have been minus his head if I had pulled the trigger."

Smith and Howard eyed each other, then Smith said, "Good! We need a man like you in our organization. If you'll join us, it'll pay handsomely, Logan. We guarantee it."

"Right," said Howard, whose keen eyes reminded Wes of a predator. "Our organization is only four years old, but if the business keeps doing as well as it has since we started…you, Mr. Logan, could pocket somewhere between forty and fifty thousand dollars in the next twelve months."

Wes Logan could hardly believe his ears. If he could present proof to Pierce Burns that he had this kind of money coming, Burns could very well be persuaded to give him some time to pay off the debt without adding any more large lumps of usury. "You interest me very much, gentlemen. Now will you tell me the name of your organization, and what it does?"

Smith and Howard exchanged sly smiles.

Howard looked Wes straight in the eye and said, "Our

organization's name is the James-Younger gang. My real name is Jesse James, Mr. Logan, and this is my friend and associate, Cole Younger."

Wes's brain was awhirl. He had begun to think the two men were into something illegal, but until Jesse James revealed it to him, he had no idea to whom he was talking. His heart was in his throat. He had just been invited to join the most infamous gang of robbers in the country!

Taking advantage of Logan's stunned silence, Cole Younger said, "We need a man like you, Logan. You would be a genuine asset to the gang."

"Right," said Jesse. "And you would get rich while filling a real need."

Wes wiped a nervous hand over his eyes. "Fellas, this sounds real good, but I must tell you up front that I have a couple of personal problems that could keep me from taking you up on your offer."

"Maybe there's a solution to your problems, Wes," said Jesse.

"Can I call you Wes?" Cole Younger asked.

"Sure."

"Tell us about your problems."

"Well…first of all, I have some gambling debts at three different casinos, and if they aren't paid in a very short time, there will be hired killers on my trail."

"Give us names, facts, and figures, Wes," Jesse said.

Wes told them of his debts to Dolph Boswick, Jack Wall, and Pierce Burns. He explained that he must have the full amounts for Boswick and Wall on his next business trip to their towns. He then explained about his conversation with Burns earlier that very night…and the terms the owner of the Silver Dollar Casino had laid down.

Again, Cole and Jesse exchanged glances.

Cole looked at Wes. "So what you need by tomorrow is nine thousand five hundred dollars to pay Burns in full."

"Yeah. As I just told you, if I go another day before paying him, it'll be eleven thousand dollars. If that amount isn't paid by two nights from now, Burns will have me killed."

Cole turned to Jesse. "How about you and me steppin' out into the hall for a brief conversation?"

Jesse rose to his feet.

"Be right back, Wes," said Cole.

As he waited, Wes pressed fingertips to his closed eyelids and tried to still the thoughts whirling around in his head.

When the door opened, Wes looked up at the outlaw leaders. They were smiling.

"Wes," said Jesse, "Cole and I have discussed your situation. We've agreed that if you will join the gang, we'll advance you the money to pay off all of your gambling debts. We'll take a reasonable amount from your share of each job until we've been repaid...with no interest."

Wes Logan felt a tremendous feeling of relief. This was the one and only way out of his predicament and his imminent departure from this world.

His thoughts went to Ginny. He couldn't tell her he had joined up with the James-Younger gang. She would have to think he was still traveling as a hardware drummer. By making the kind of money Cole and Jesse had mentioned, he would soon be rich, even with portions of the gambling debt money taken from his share of the loot for the next few months. When he had put aside a sufficient amount, he could bow out of the gang, marry Ginny, take her somewhere far from Missouri, and start a new life with plenty of money.

Wes ran his gaze over their faces and said, "Fellas, this is more than I ever dreamed of."

"Is the financial deal we've offered good enough?" Jesse asked.

"It most certainly is!" Thinking again of Ginny, Wes said, "I need to ask you something."

"Sure," said Jesse.

"Will there be time off between jobs? You know, for handling things that might take a day or so?"

Cole laughed. "Sure! An outlaw's life isn't all plannin' and doin' holdups! We take in enough money that we can afford to have some pleasure time!"

"Before we ask for a commitment from you, Wes," said Jesse, "what's the second problem you said could prevent you from taking us up on our offer?"

"Somebody else is after me."

"Who's that?" said Cole.

"Dub Thaxton. When he and his gang were put in the jail at Harrisonville, he said he would escape before they could hang him, and he'd kill me. I guess you probably heard that the gang—minus Lambert—escaped from the jail before the federal marshals could transport them to Kansas City for trial."

"Yeah," said Jesse, "we know all about Lambert getting shot and killed by the deputy…and that Dub and the rest of his bunch are on the loose."

"Dub wouldn't think of tryin' to come after you if you belong to our gang," Cole said. "They're our rivals when it comes to who, when, and where we rob, but he wouldn't be fool enough to come after one of our men. It would mean his own funeral."

"So how about it?" said Jesse. "You gonna join us?"

A slow smiled spread over Wes Logan's face. "Seems like the smart thing to do. By accepting your offer I become an outlaw…which is something I never dreamed I'd do. But it's either that or be hunted down and killed by whichever casino owner gets to me first. I'd rather be a live outlaw than a dead hardware drummer."

"So you're in?" said Cole.

"I'm in."

Jesse extended his hand. "Welcome to the gang."

"Make that two welcomes!" said Cole, shaking Wes's hand.

Jesse rubbed his palms together. "Now, let's get down to this money thing. Wes, we know what you need before tomorrow night. When do you need the rest of the money?"

"The next day. I'll ride to Nevada, pay off Dolph Boswick, then I'll ride on to Joplin and pay off Jack Wall. As soon as that's done, I'll head back to wherever you fellas and the gang are hiding."

"Sounds good to me," said Jesse.

Cole glanced around the room for moment. "Wes, do you have a piece of paper? I need to draw you a map so you can find us."

As he handed Wes the map to the Younger farm, he said, "We'll have the money ready in the mornin'. From here it'll take you a little over an hour to ride to the farm. Be there at ten o'clock. We'll give you the money and you can pay off Pierce Burns tomorrow, then head for Nevada the next mornin'."

"I'll be there."

"Good," said Jesse. A serious look came over his features as he said, "Just one thing to say at this point. I figure you should be able to ride to Nevada and Joplin and take care of your business in three days."

Wes nodded.

"If you should fail to return to us by that time, that would put you in more trouble than you're facing right now. Understand?"

Wesley Logan nodded. "Jesse, I assure you, I want to be a part of the gang. I appreciate what you're doing for me, and I'm eager to make the kind of money you spoke about earlier. I'll deal straight with you."

"And I believe you. We're looking forward to having you with us."

As Wes took their hats and coats out of the closet, Jesse said, "I guess you know our background. We've both worn Rebel uniforms, and we both fought for Quantrill. Does that bother you...you being an ex-Union officer?"

"Not in the least," said Wes. "The war's over. Let's make ourselves a good living."

That night, Wes contemplated his future with Ginny. Just before falling asleep, he thought of how he would be able to provide her with the best of everything.

The next morning, Wes walked to a stable a short distance from the boardinghouse and rented a horse, then rode southeast toward Lee's Summit.

As he galloped the horse down the road, he savored the feel of the moment. At that same time yesterday morning he had been weighed down by the load of his gambling debts and the threats on his life. Now the load had been lifted, thanks to one little act of what people thought was courage when he put the derringer under Lambert Thaxton's chin. Actually, it had been more an act of desperation. Wes would always be grateful to Jesse James and Cole Younger.

Ted Pack and Gene Vader were standing behind two large oak trees, looking up the road, when they saw a lone rider trotting his horse toward them. Pack raised binoculars to his eyes and turned the focus wheel. "It's him all right, Gene. Tall, slender... and wearin' the hat and coat exactly like Jesse and Cole described."

"All right. Guess we can get back to our work now."

As Wes Logan trotted past the oak tree, unaware that he was under scrutiny, he pulled out Cole's map and checked it again. There was the Younger farm, coming up exactly as Cole had shown on the map.

When he rode onto the lane leading to the house, he saw a few men working near the barn. Then he saw Jesse and Cole come out the front door.

The gang leaders welcomed him and called the rest of the men together to meet their newest member.

After introductions, Cole said, "All of you guys can go back to your chores. Jesse and I need to talk to Wes for a while."

As they stepped into the parlor of the old farmhouse, Jesse said, "Last night we didn't explain the structure of the gang. Right now there are nine men in Cole's gang, seven in mine, plus one woman. You know about Belle, I assume?"

Wes grinned. "I read the papers. I was wondering where Belle and her husband are."

"They're shopping in Lee's Summit right now. Should be back soon. Anyway, since I'm still one man short, Cole and I agreed that you'd be in my gang."

"Suits me," said Wes.

"Cole! Jesse!" came Clell Miller's voice from the front porch. "Jim and Belle are back."

"Is Belle really as tough as the newspapers make her out to be?" Wes asked.

"Tougher," said Cole. "You don't want to get on her wrong side."

When the wagon drew up, Jesse stepped out on the porch. "Go ahead and pull around back, Jim. Holler at some of the boys and tell them I said to come and carry in the groceries. Our new man is here."

A few minutes later, Jim Reed shook Wes's hand and said, "We're mighty glad to have you, Wes. That was some doin's when you gave Lambert his surprise and put the whole gang on hold."

"Sure was," said Belle, extending her hand. She had a strong grip. "Welcome aboard, Wes. We're glad to have you."

Wes had heard that Belle lacked some feminine qualities and had been cheated in the beauty department. He could see for himself that the rumors had not been understated.

"Well," said Belle, "I'll head for the kitchen and start puttin' stuff away."

"I'll help you." Jim followed her as she moved toward the rear of the house.

As soon as they left the room, Cole opened the drawer of an old desk and pulled out four envelopes and held them toward Wes. "Three of these are marked with the names of the casino owners. They hold the amounts you said you owed them. The fourth envelope has your name on it."

Wes's brow furrowed. "I don't understand."

"You need to buy yourself a good horse, bridle, and saddle. We figured you didn't have any of your own."

"That's right. I rented the horse I rode here."

"There's also enough money to buy yourself a new revolver and gun belt," said Jesse. "Are you still carrying your derringer?"

"Sure am. Right here in my coat pocket."

"Well, carrying a derringer as a spare weapon is a good idea. Cole and I do that, too. But you need a side arm."

Cole looked him in the eye. "You do know how to use a revolver?"

"Of course. I still have my service revolver, holster, and belt at home."

"Well, go ahead and get yourself new ones."

"And something else," said Jesse. "Since you're now a member of the gang…forget gambling, okay?"

Wes's face flushed and he grinned sheepishly. "I already have. I'll never gamble again."

"Good."

Running his eyes over their faces, Wes said, "Thank you for doing this for me. I could never tell you how much I appreciate it. And I'll pay you back the extra money, too."

"No, you won't," said Cole. "That money is a gift for joinin' the gang."

Wes shook his head in amazement. "You two are something else."

With that, Cole and Jesse walked the new man out to his horse. Wes swung into the saddle and said, "See you in three days."

"We'll look forward to it," said Jesse.

As Wes rode off the Younger farm and headed for Kansas City, he told himself he would have time tomorrow as he rode south to stop and see Ginny for a few minutes.

It was early afternoon when Pierce Burns heard male voices outside his office, along with the sound of footsteps coming up the stairs.

The expected knock on the door came with Sid Veatch's voice telling him that Wes Logan was there to see him.

When Burns saw Logan's face, he knew he had the money…all of it.

Drawing up to the desk with Sid at his side, Wes pulled the

fat envelope from his coat pocket and said, "I took a chance that you might be here at this time of day, Mr. Burns. I have nine thousand five hundred dollars here to pay my debt in full, and I wanted to put it in your hands as soon as possible."

A thin smile broke across Burns's face. He stood up and took the envelope. "You're a resourceful guy, Logan. I'd like to ask how you came up with it so quickly, but I won't. I'm just happy to have the money and to know that I can take you off my blacklist."

Wes chuckled hollowly and placed the envelope in Burns's hand. "I'm glad to be off your blacklist, too. Believe me."

Burns laid the envelope on the desk and extended his hand. As Wes met his grip, he said, "You are now free to gamble at my tables again, Logan. And quite welcome to do so, I might add."

Wes looked down at the envelope, than back at Burns and said, "Aren't you going to count it?"

"Later. You've earned my trust."

Giving Sid Veatch a sidelong glance, Wes said, "I'd feel better, Mr. Burns, if you would count it before I go."

Burns looked at him as if he had never been in such a situation before, then nodded. "All right. I'll count it. Sit down."

While Logan and Veatch looked on, the casino owner counted the money aloud. When he was done, it was exactly to the dollar. Setting his steady gaze on Wes, he said, "All here. Your debt is paid in full. As I said, you're now welcome to gamble at the Silver Dollar anytime you wish."

Wes thanked him and left the office, escorted by the huge Sid Veatch. When he untied his new horse from the hitching rail, he looked at Veatch and said, "Take care, Sid."

With that, he swung into the saddle and rode away. As he trotted down the dusty street, he mumbled, "You'll never see me again, Pierce Burns."

From there, Wes rode to the Western Union office in downtown Kansas City and wired the Cushman Hardware Company office in San Francisco, telling them he was no longer working for them. He had found other employment.

Ginny Grayson was hanging up laundry behind the Hansen house when she saw Wes Logan ride around the corner of the house. She dropped the wet clothes back in the basket and wiped her hands on the apron.

As Wes's feet touched ground, he opened his arms and said, "Hello, loveliest of all ladies."

"Flatterer." Ginny entered his embrace. They kissed several times, then Ginny said, "It's wonderful to see you again, darling."

Wes closed his eyes. "'Darling'…that sounds good." He kissed her again. When their lips parted, he looked into her eyes and said, "I love you, Ginny. I love you very, very much."

"And I love you just as much," she said softly. Easing back, she took note of the light in his eyes. "Has something good happened?"

"It sure has! The most beautiful and wonderful woman in the world has fallen in love with me!"

He held her close for a few moments, then said, "Ginny, I can only stay a few minutes. I have to keep moving. I have to start my route again tomorrow, so I have to ride back to town and get ready."

"And you'll be gone how long?"

"Well…close to two weeks."

"I'll miss you terribly."

"I'll miss you terribly, too." He took her in his arms and kissed her good-bye, then mounted the horse. Looking down at her, he said, "Do you like my new horse?"

"Well, yes! When did you buy him...her...it?"

Wes laughed. "It's a him. Just this morning. This way, when I'm home, I won't have to rent a horse to come and see you...and I can come more often."

"Wonderful!"

"I'll be here as soon as I can," he said. "Don't forget that I love you."

"How could I forget that?"

As he trotted away, she called after him, "Be careful, Wes! No more stage holdups!"

Ginny went back to her work. As she was hanging up the wet wash, she felt a tingle run through her body. Not only did she have the love of a very special man, but one day he would ask her to marry him.

She thought about life with Wes Logan as her husband. She had no idea what kind of income a hardware drummer brought in, but she figured it must be pretty good.

9

ON THE THIRD DAY AFTER JESSE JAMES and Cole Younger gave Wes Logan the money for his gambling debts, they were walking from the barn toward the house. Some of the gang members were still working inside and around the barn.

The Missouri sun dipped into a long-fingered bank of clouds low on the western horizon.

Cole glanced at the sunset and said, "It'll be dark soon, Jesse. You don't suppose—"

"No," cut in Jesse. "He'll be here. Wes isn't gonna take off on us. He'll—"

"Look there!" said Cole, pointing up the road.

Wes was trotting his horse toward them and waved.

"What did I tell you, Cole?" said a smiling Jesse. "I knew he'd be back just like he said."

"I guess I'm a worrywart," Cole said with a chuckle.

Wes reined in at the porch. "Howdy, fellas."

"Welcome back," said Jesse.

"Glad to see you," said Cole. "Get everything taken care of?"

"Sure did. I'm ready to ride with the gang."

"We're ready, too," said Jesse. "We've got some robberies planned out of Missouri. We're trying to let things cool down in this state before we pull some more jobs here."

"I'm sure you know what you're doing," said Wes. "After four years, you still haven't gotten caught. That tells me you know how to handle the business. How long will we be gone?"

"Close to three weeks, I'd say," Jesse replied.

Wes nodded, thinking of Ginny. He would have to get a message to her.

Cole eyed the Colt .45 on Wes's hip. "Hey, that's a nice gun!"

"Yeah. Some real good friends of mine bought it for me. Gun belt and holster are pretty nice, too."

"Tell you what," said Jesse. "How about you giving us a little demonstration tomorrow? I'd like to see how well you handle it."

"Sure. Be glad to."

They heard a cry from the barn and turned to see one of the gang members lying on the ground below the open door of the hayloft.

Three gang members—Bill Whelan, John Younger, and Duane Gard—ran from the back side of the barn, while Sly Chapman and Charlie Pitts bolted from the door on the ground floor.

They gathered around gang member Ed Loomis, who was unconscious. While John Younger and Bill Whelan carried him to the house and the others followed, Duane Gard stayed with Wes and showed him where to hang his bridle and saddle. When the horse was in the corral, they hurried toward the house.

Belle Reed was kneeling beside Loomis, who lay on a couch in the parlor. She was bathing his face in cold water as the rest of the men stood around.

"How bad is it, Belle?" asked Gard.

"He's comin' around now," she said without looking up.

It took Loomis another few minutes to fully regain consciousness. His eyes were glassy, but he assured Belle he wasn't hurt seriously. He was a bit dizzy, but his mind was clear enough that he could tell them he had slipped and fallen out the open door of the hayloft. Fortunately he had been able to break his fall with his hands but had still hit his head on the ground.

While the gang was eating supper, Jesse explained to Wes that they were planning four bank robberies, two train robberies, and at least two stage holdups in the next few weeks. These would be in Texas, Kansas, and Iowa. If things worked out as planned, they would be back to the Younger farm in about twenty-one days. They would leave day after tomorrow for the Texas panhandle.

Belle looked across the table at Ed Loomis, who now had a severe headache. "What about you, Ed? You gonna feel like goin' with us?"

Loomis touched fingertips to his brow. "I'll let you know tomorrow. Maybe I'll be all right by then. If so, then I'll sure be able to ride the next day."

"Well, if you're not up to it, Ed," said Cole, "we'll understand. You took quite a blow, fallin' that far. You'll get your cut the same as if you went with us."

Loomis, who was fairly new to the gang, looked surprised. "I wouldn't expect to take a share of the money if I'm not there to do my part."

"Hey, pal," said Cole, "I doubt if you took that dive from the hayloft on purpose. We take care of our own. If you ain't up to ridin' this long ol' trip, you'll get your share anyway."

Jesse looked across the table at Wes and said, "Cole and I will let you give that little demonstration first thing in the morning, okay?"

"Sure. Whatever you say."

✦

The next morning, Ed Loomis still had a severe headache and was experiencing a great deal of dizziness. He left the table during breakfast and went back to bed.

Immediately after breakfast, the men went about their different chores while Cole and Jesse took Wes Logan out behind the barn and let him show them his skill with a handgun. Both gang leaders were impressed with his accuracy.

Wes told them he needed to ride into Kansas City to take care of some business before they left.

He went directly to the Western Union office and sent Ginny a telegram, saying some things had come up and he wouldn't be back for at least three weeks, but he would come see her as soon as possible after his return.

The gang rode out the next day without Ed Loomis.

Dub Thaxton and his men rode up to the boardinghouse where Wes Logan had lived. Thaxton dismounted and said, "You boys wait here."

The bearded outlaw went inside and knocked on the door marked Landlord.

A middle-aged man opened the door. "May I help you, sir? Needing a room?"

"Ah…no. I'm lookin' for an old friend of mine. Wes Logan. Does he still live here?"

"No, sir. He moved out four days ago."

"Oh. Can you tell me where he moved? We were in the war together, and I was just passin' through. Wanted to see him."

"I have no idea where he went. All I know is he up and quit his job and left the same day."

"Did he have any friends you might know? Somebody who visited him a lot, and you picked up their names?"

"No, sir. None. Sorry, but I really can't help you."

Dub nodded. "Okay. Thanks."

Upon returning to his men, Dub said, "Nothin'. It's like the dirty rat has disappeared off the face of the earth. The landlord said he quit his job four days ago and took off. That jibes with what the hardware company's telegram said."

"Looks like you ain't gonna get to have your revenge on him, Dub," said Frank Baldwin.

Dub swung an angry fist through the air and swore. "Guess all I can do is hope to run into him somewhere. If I ever do, he's a dead man."

Nineteen days after the James-Younger gang had ridden out on their robbery spree, Ed Loomis was sitting on the front porch late in the afternoon and saw a cloud of dust that indicated riders approaching.

When the riders drew closer, Loomis recognized Jesse James and Cole Younger in the lead. He left his chair and stepped to the porch railing. By counting the riders, he knew that two were missing. When they got closer, Ed searched their faces and by the process of elimination he soon realized Bill Whelan and Duane Gard were the missing men.

As the weary, dust-covered gang rode up, they paused at the porch and set their eyes on Ed Loomis. Cole Younger asked how he was feeling.

"I'm fine. The headaches have finally disappeared." With furrowed brow, he said, "Bill and Duane?"

Cole sighed. "Both of 'em got shot durin' the train robbery we pulled outside of Amarillo. There were some tough-minded passengers on the train who decided to give us some resistance. One man sort of took over as leader." Hipping around in the saddle, he glanced at Belle, then back to Loomis. "At least Belle was able to put a bullet in the leader. Hit him dead-center in the heart."

"Good for you," Ed said, turning his gaze to Belle.

She smiled and swung from the saddle, then looked up at her husband. "Jim, if you'll take care of my horse, I'll head for the kitchen. Gotta feed this bunch before they die of hunger."

"Sure, babe."

"You've heard the bad news, Ed," said Jesse, "but we've got good news, too. We did real well on this trip. You're gonna be happy with your share."

"Sounds great, Jesse, but I still don't feel like I deserve it since I didn't go with you."

"We've already been over that." To the others Jesse said, "Let's put the horses away, fellas. Then Cole and I can sit down and divide up the loot."

Before Belle had supper ready, Jesse and Cole had the money counted. They put aside their own shares, then gave each man his cut.

When Wes Logan was given his share—minus a substantial payment on the advance he had received earlier—he still had over fifteen thousand dollars in his hands.

During supper, Ed Loomis looked around at the others and said, "I sure wish I'd been able to go with all of you. Of course I wouldn't have enjoyed seein' Bill and Duane go down…but I'd have enjoyed the rest of it."

Cole smacked his lips and wiped his mouth with the back of his hand. "Tell you what, Ed…there's one thing I wish you could've seen. In Centerville, Iowa, Wes Logan here saved my life while we were robbin' the Centerville Bank."

Ed swung his gaze to Wes, who was obviously embarrassed.

Cole gave the details, pouring accolades on Wes. He reached over and patted Wes's shoulder. "Yes, sir, Wes, in my eyes you're a hero!"

"Just doing what I should have done, Cole. That bank officer pulled the gun out of his drawer and was aiming it right at you."

Belle took up the story. "That ain't all. When we waylaid a stagecoach about halfway between Lawrence and Ottawa, over in Kansas, we were linin' the passengers up after I pulled my gun on 'em inside the coach and made 'em get out. Suddenly these two riders came along and tried to get the drop on us. Wes reacted faster'n a bolt of lightnin'…shot 'em both outta their saddles and ended that threat in about three seconds."

Loomis grinned as he ran his gaze between Cole and Jesse. "You fellas need to be plenty glad you talked this hardware man into joinin' the gang."

"That we are," said Jesse.

"Especially me," said Cole. "Just think how awful it would be if I'd been killed and my three brothers got into a power struggle about who would be boss of the Younger bunch!"

Later that night, when it was time for everyone head for bed, except those who would remain on guard, Jim Reed moved up to Wes Logan's side just as Wes was about to join the men heading for the barn. The gang was large enough now that some of the men had to sleep in the hayloft.

"Wes," he said in a low tone, "I just want to say how glad I am you joined the gang."

"Thanks, Jim."

Elbowing him playfully, Jim half whispered, "If you keep it up, you'll soon be givin' Belle a run for her money on who's doin' the most killin' in the gang."

While the other gang members around Wes Logan were snoring and enjoying sound sleep, he lay awake, staring into the darkness. Through some small holes in the barn roof, he could see stars twinkling in the black sky.

He thought about Jim Reed's words. He hadn't joined the gang because he had a thirst for killing people. He had killed plenty of men on battlefields, which was his duty as a soldier. He had also killed the three men on this trip because they presented a threat to his comrades in the gang.

His reason for joining the gang, he told himself, was for the money. He was in a tight spot, and becoming a member of the gang had taken care of that problem. Not only that, but now he was in a position to get rich. If he had to shoot someone now and then, so be it. Wesley Logan was going to become a wealthy man. He would marry sweet Ginny, take her far away, and the two of them would live like royalty for the rest of their lives.

His mind went again to the three men he had killed. Suddenly he thought of the conversation that day in the Hansen home when Carolyne told of the Scripture used by her Sunday school teacher concerning those who would perish by the sword. He recalled Walter's words: "If you live by the gun, chances are pretty strong that you'll die by the gun. Live a violent life…die a violent death."

Wes shrugged off Walter's words and thought about the money he had in his pocket. Even after the deduction for the portion he owed Cole and Jesse, he had more money for three weeks of riding with the gang than he would have made in three years as a hardware drummer. He rolled onto his side and thought about how good it was to be on the road to riches and to be free of debt to the casinos.

Again, Ginny came to mind. With so much money in his pocket, he wanted to buy her a nice present.

It was early afternoon when Ginny Grayson and her aunt were sitting in the front porch swing, enjoying the touch of warmth in the air. Spring had come, and soon the trees and flowers would be blooming.

Both women saw the rider at the same time.

"Oh, it's Wes!" Ginny exclaimed as she dashed off the porch.

Carolyne rose to her feet but stayed where she was.

Wes slid from the saddle and gathered the lovely redhead into his arms. Looking into her eyes, he said, "I've sure missed you."

"And I've missed you."

They kissed, then Wes looked up at Carolyne and his face tinted.

"What are you embarrassed about, darling?" Ginny asked.

"Well…I…ah…"

Ginny giggled. "It's all right, darling. I've told Auntie Carolyne and Uncle Walter about us."

They were close enough for Carolyne to hear what they were saying. Smiling, she said, "That she has, Wes, and her Uncle Walter and I give you our blessing. We're very happy for you."

"Thank you, ma'am."

"Can you stay and eat supper?"

Wes grinned. "I was hoping you'd ask. Yes, ma'am."

While he tied the reins to the hitching post, Carolyne said, "I know you two want to be alone. I have things to do in the house anyway. Walter's helping a neighbor, but I expect him back any time. When he comes home, Ginny, tell him I need him in the house. You two need some time together."

When Carolyne turned and entered the house, Wes guided Ginny up the steps and seated her in the swing. "You sit still, little lady, while I get something out of my saddlebag."

He returned to her carrying a small, beautifully wrapped package.

"Oh, Wes, you shouldn't have gone and—"

"Oh, yes, I should have! This is because I love you."

He sat down beside her and watched her unwrap it. When she took out the little box and lifted the lid, her mouth fell open. "Oh, Wes! A cameo pin! It's beautiful."

Smiling, he said, "You really like it?"

"Oh, yes! It's so dainty!" She hurriedly pinned the cameo on her worn calico dress and said, "Don't go away! I've just got to show this to Auntie Carolyne."

While Ginny was gone, Walter came down the street and turned into the yard. He smiled when he saw Wes and said, "Hello! Glad to see you back."

Walter stepped up on the porch. "So, your wire said you'd be running longer this time because of some unexpected things that came up. Everything all right?"

"Oh, sure. Just fine. I—"

"Walter," came Carolyne's voice as she came out to the porch. "Look what Wes bought for Ginny! Show him, honey."

Ginny proudly displayed the cameo pin to her uncle. When Walter had commented on its beauty, he turned to Wes and said, "I appreciate your doing this for Ginny. Carolyne and I don't have the money to provide these kinds of things for her."

Wes smiled. "Walter, you and Carolyne are doing a great deal for Ginny. You have provided a home for her, which she desperately needs."

Walter put an arm around his niece's shoulder and smiled at her. "We're very happy to have her in our home."

"And I'm very happy to be here, Uncle Walter. You and Auntie Carolyne have been so good to me."

Carolyne stepped up beside her niece. "We wish we could do a lot more, sweetie. But I'll tell you this much, no other aunt and uncle love their niece more than we love ours."

Ginny kissed her aunt's cheek. "Thank you." In her mind, she told herself that the expensive cameo pin was an indication that when she became Mrs. Wesley Logan, her days of poverty would be over.

The next morning, Jesse James told Cole Younger and the rest of the gang that he was going to St. Joseph to see his girlfriend. He would be back late that night.

It was about one o'clock in the afternoon when Jesse rode into St. Joseph and trotted his horse to the business section. Reaching the heart of downtown, he hauled up in front of Westerman's Department Store and dismounted, then wrapped the reins around the hitching rail.

Two silver-haired men paused on the boardwalk and spoke to him. Jesse returned the greeting. As he rounded the backside of his horse, a man called to him from a wagon passing by. Jesse smiled and called out, "Hello, Ralph! Nice to see you."

The friendliness of some of St. Joseph's citizens gave the outlaw leader a warm feeling. Because Jesse was known as some kind of Robin Hood who often gave money to poor folks, many of the common people liked him and would never consider turning him over to the law.

When he stepped onto the boardwalk, he paused to allow three couples to pass by, then entered the store. Henry Westerman, the proprietor, looked past a female customer he was waiting on and said, "Well, look who's here. Hello, Mr. Howard."

When the woman took her package and left, Jesse stepped up to the counter. "Nice to see you, Henry."

Westerman shook the outlaw's hand. "You, too, Jesse. It's been a while. I see from the papers that you and Cole have been busy in other states."

"Mm-hmm. We have."

"What can I do for you?"

"I've been gone for a while, and I'm on my way to see Zee. Thought I'd buy her some nice perfume."

"Oh. Well, come over here to the cosmetics counter and let's see what might interest you."

It took Jesse only a moment to pick out the most expensive perfume.

Westerman wrapped it in pretty paper for him, and when Jesse paid, he added ten dollars.

Westerman smiled. "This is why you have so many friends, Jesse, you're so generous."

"I try to be. See you later."

As Jesse headed for the door, Westerman said, "Don't make it so long next time."

Jesse looked back and smiled. He was still looking back when he stepped onto the boardwalk and ran into a tall, muscular man in black who was passing by.

"I'm sorry, sir," Jesse said. "I didn't see you."

"It's all right," said the man, who towered over Jesse by at least six inches.

While Jesse was noting the low-slung, bone-handled Colt .45 Peacemaker on the tall man's hip, the man was studying Jesse's face. Squinting, he said, "Don't I know you?"

People on the boardwalk recognized Jesse and paused to look on as he replied, "I don't think we've ever met. My name is Thomas Howard."

The rugged-looking, square-jawed man said, "Somehow the name 'Howard' doesn't seem to go with your face. Seems to me your name is more like James. Jesse James."

Jesse placed his package on a bench in front of the store.

The people gawked wide-eyed and rushed to get out of the way as Jesse moved his hand over the handle of his revolver. He regarded the man with wary eyes. "I don't see a badge. You can't be a lawman."

"I'm not a lawman, but I'm on the side of the law…and Jesse Woodson James, the son of Reverend Robert and Zerelda James, is on the wrong side of the law. I must take you to the Buchanan County sheriff down the street."

Jesse's features hardened as he backed up a few steps, his hand hovering over his gun. "You'll have to out-gun me first, mister!" he hissed.

"Jesse!" came a male voice from the crowd. "Don't pull that gun! You can't outdraw him! Don't you know who he is?"

Jesse shook his head as he kept his eyes on the tall man who had a pair of twin jagged scars on his right cheek.

"He's John Stranger!"

Jesse's face lost color. "Is it so? Are you Stranger?"

"Yep. Now, I want you to very slowly reach down, take the gun out of its holster, and hand it to me butt first. I'm taking you to Sheriff Todd."

Jesse's pale face sagged as he carefully slid his gun from the holster and handed it to Stranger as ordered.

Suddenly there was a shuffling of feet on the boardwalk, and a young man with a deputy's badge on his chest burst on the scene, having threaded his way through the crowd. "Sheriff Todd is out of town, Mr. Stranger. I'm Deputy Royce Caldwell. I'll be glad to put this dirty killer behind bars. Sheriff Todd will be back in a couple of hours."

Somebody in the crowd shouted, "Hey! Let's get a reporter from the paper, quick! We're gonna have Jesse James in our jail!"

A young man took off running down the street, saying he would bring a reporter. Caldwell cuffed Jesse's hands behind his back while the crowd looked on. "Jesse," he said, "your days of robbing and killing are over."

Stranger extended the gun to Caldwell. "This is Jesse's revolver, Deputy. I've got to keep moving."

Caldwell looked at him quizzically as he took the gun. "Sir, you caught and disarmed the most famous outlaw in this country! Aren't you going to stick around? I'm sure the reporter will want to interview you."

"That's really not necessary," said Stranger. "And I must be going. I have a very important appointment in Kansas City, and I must head that way right now."

As the crowd watched John Stranger ride away, the young man who had run to fetch a reporter came back out of breath, saying that Harold Atkins, the number one reporter for the *St. Joseph Tribune* would come to the jail in about twenty minutes.

Caldwell thanked him, then tucked Jesse's gun under his belt. "Let's go."

Caldwell ushered James down the street toward the sheriff's office and jail. The crowd was breaking up, and people were scattering. Two men hurried away, darting between buildings, whispering to each other.

Both Caldwell and James heard the people talking excitedly about how John Stranger had intimidated Jesse James and took his gun away from him.

As soon as Caldwell guided Jesse inside the sheriff's office, two men hastened in behind them. Before the deputy could turn around, a gun barrel came down on Caldwell's head, dropping him to the floor, unconscious.

10

ZEE MIMMS LIVED ALONE in a small house on the west side of St. Joseph. She earned her living by making women's dresses, men's shirts, and baby clothes.

Darkness had fallen, but she was still sewing on a dress at the table in her small sewing room when she heard a light tap on the window. Frowning, she shoved back the chair and went to the window. Without pulling the shade back, she called, "Who is it?"

"It's me, honey. Jesse."

This time she parted the shade from the window's edge. She could barely make him out in the pale light of the quarter moon. Shaking her head, she said, "Sweetheart, why didn't you come to the front door? I'll meet you there."

"No, no! The back door! Let me in the back door!"

Zee let him in. "Jesse, what—?"

His kiss silenced her question.

When they parted, Jesse said, "I have to be extra careful, honey. The sheriff's after me like a bloodhound."

"Our sheriff?"

"Yes. Has he been here?"

"Why, no. What's happened?"

"Sit down. I'll tell you."

Zee listened intently as Jesse told her about the John Stranger incident in town when he had gone to the department store to buy perfume for her. While the sheriff was taking him to the jail, two of his old Civil War pals, who were also James-Younger sympathizers, coldcocked the deputy. Jesse had taken his gun from under the deputy's belt and run for the woods east of town. After dark, his two friends brought him his horse, and now here he was.

Zee embraced him and laid her head against his chest. "Oh, Jesse, I'll be glad when you can just be Thomas Howard and leave the outlaw life behind. I'm thankful you didn't draw against that John Stranger. I've read that some experts say he's the fastest man alive on the draw."

"Yeah. I've heard the same thing. That's why I didn't try it."

They held each other for a long moment, then Jesse said, "Zee, I'm sorry about the perfume. My mind was on being handcuffed and taken to jail. I didn't think about it till I was running for the woods."

"It's all right, Jesse. It's the thought that counts."

It wasn't long before Jesse kissed her good-bye and said he would he back whenever they returned to Missouri after more jobs in other states.

When he arrived back at the Younger farm and told the gang what had happened, everyone grew sober at the mention of John Stranger. Finally, Wes Logan broke the silence, saying he was glad the two friends had freed Jesse from the deputy.

With each job they pulled, Wes Logan proved himself more valuable to the James-Younger gang. Little by little he became especially close to Jim and Belle Reed. Though he had told the entire gang he had a girl in Harrisonville, named Ginny Grayson, he shared with the Reeds that he was putting money aside so that one day he could marry Ginny and give her a life of luxury, the opposite of what she had known since she was born. Wes and Jim found they had much in common when it came to their goals in life.

During the next several months, Wes romanced Ginny when the gang took time off between robbery sprees, letting her continue to believe that his absences were due to his drummer's job.

Whenever Wes was out and about, he kept an eye out for Dub Thaxton, even though Cole and Jesse had told him there was nothing to worry about.

By the time winter came in late 1870, several of the gang members had become casualties during the robberies, and new men were being added to take their places.

At the beginning of the year, the winter weather was so severe that it prevented the gang from pulling all the robberies they had planned. This cut into their financial goals, but it did give Jesse some time to spend with Zee. Not so for Wes Logan, who had to keep Ginny thinking that he was traveling on his sales routes. However, what time they did spend together brought the two of them closer together.

Spring came, bringing its warmer weather, and rain instead of snow. Cole and Jesse made plans to travel into Kansas, Nebraska, and Iowa on a long string of bank robberies and told the gang they would stay at it for several weeks to make up for lost time during the winter. They would also hit a train or two and a few stagecoaches. The gang would leave the Younger farm on Thursday, March 23.

When Wes visited Ginny on Wednesday, March 22, he told her his drummer's job was going to keep him away longer than usual on the upcoming trip, and he couldn't tell her exactly when he would be back. But he would see her as soon as possible.

On Friday morning, March 24, Ginny Grayson helped her aunt finish up what housework had to be done, then put on a light wrap and donned a small hat. "Well, Auntie Carolyne, I'd better be going. My appointment with Mr. Strann is at nine-thirty. I don't want to be late."

Carolyne smiled. "We wouldn't want that, would we? What did Wes say when you told him you were applying for a clerk's job at Harrisonville's general store?"

"I didn't tell him."

"Oh? Why not?"

"Because if I don't get the job, Wes won't know that I even tried, and I won't have to be embarrassed. From what Mr. Strann said when we talked for those few minutes on Tuesday, the job is practically mine already. If for some reason it doesn't work out though, Wes will never know the difference. If it does, then it will be a nice surprise for him."

"Honey," said Carolyne as she walked with her niece to the front door, "I don't mean to be nosy, but I care so much about you. Will you tell me something?"

"Sure." Ginny adjusted her hat. "What do you want to know?"

"Has Wes so much as mentioned marriage to you yet?"

Ginny giggled. "Oh, yes. He brought it up some time ago. We've discussed it quite a bit."

"So he does want to marry you?"

"He sure does."

"Please don't misunderstand me," said Carolyne. "You

know Uncle Walter and I will keep you as long as you want to stay with us."

"I know that," Ginny said softly. "But what you want to know is…have we talked about a date?"

"Mm-hmm."

"No, we haven't. Wes said he wants to improve his financial status to a greater degree before he takes me as his wife. And I appreciate that, Auntie. Since he wants to provide for me even more than sufficiently, I'm willing to wait."

Carolyne opened the door and kissed Ginny's cheek. "I'll be waiting for you to come home with the good news. I'm just sure Ward Strann knows a good worker when he sees one."

Ginny patted her hand. "Well, if I do get the job, I'll give some of what I make to you and Uncle Walter to help with the grocery bills and some of the other extra expenses you have with me living here."

"Now, honey, that's not necessary. When we took you in, we did it because we love you and wanted to help you."

"I know. And I appreciate it more than I can ever tell you. But I want to earn some money and help pay my way here, because I love you and Uncle Walter. Now I must hurry or I'll be late."

On the following Monday, middle-aged Ward Strann was waiting at the front door of his general store an hour before opening time. He smiled when he saw Ginny through the window. "Welcome!" he said, unlocking the door. "You're not nervous about your first day on the job, are you?"

She stepped inside and gave him a shy smile. "Mr. Strann, I have to be honest. Yes, I am."

Strann closed the door and locked it, pocketing the skeleton key. "Well, there's no reason to be. You're a bright young lady, and as my wife told you Friday, she'll be right here at your side until she feels you're ready to do the clerking by yourself. This will leave me free to carry on as usual."

At that moment, Lucinda Strann came from the back room. "Well, good morning, Ginny! Are you excited about your first day?"

"Very excited, Mrs. Strann, but as I just told Mr. Strann, I'm a bit nervous too."

Lucinda hugged her, then held her at arm's length. "I know you'll do fine."

"Ginny," said Ward, "I explained to you on Friday that we're vulnerable to robbers because we have money in our cash drawer during business hours. We've been robbed six times in the seventeen years we've been operating the store."

"Yes, sir."

"Do you still want the job?"

"Yes, sir."

Ward smiled. "Plucky little gal, aren't you?"

"Not really, sir. Just short on money. I really need the job."

"Well, I'm glad you want the job. You're going to do fine."

The store owner showed his new trainee where he kept a loaded Colt .45 on a shelf under the counter. When he asked if she had ever handled a revolver, she shook her head. Ward said he hoped she would never have to use it, but it was necessary that she know how.

Removing the cartridges, he showed her how to use both thumbs to cock the hammer, and how to squeeze the trigger after aiming the muzzle where she meant for the bullet to go.

Ginny was a bit shaky as she held the gun, but within a few minutes she satisfied both Stranns that she could use it if she had to. Ward loaded it again and laid it on the shelf beneath the counter, within easy reach.

Lucinda began teaching Ginny the basics and showed her how to wait on customers, tally their bills, and make change. As soon as the store opened, she would show Ginny how to load the grocery sacks. Ginny asked a few questions, and soon it was time to unlock the front door and begin the day's business. As soon as Ward Strann turned the key in the lock and opened the door, several customers filed in.

By the time Friday came, Ginny was handling her job as if she had done it for years. Lucinda told her when she came to work that morning that the training sessions were over. She planned to go back to being a housewife. Now it would be up to Ward and Ginny to handle the store.

It was just after four o'clock that afternoon when Ginny finished adding up a woman's bill and told her the amount. There were a few customers moving along the aisles in the store, picking up items from the shelves.

Ginny took the woman's money, made change from the cash drawer, then said, "I'll have to get some more paper sacks from the shelf down here."

As Ginny knelt on the floor, Ward completed tallying a man's bill and said, "That'll be twelve dollars and forty-seven cents, Mr. Weckbaugh."

The man handed Ward a twenty-dollar bill. Just as Ginny reached toward the back of the shelf for a stack of paper bags bound with string, she heard Ward slide the cash drawer open.

Suddenly, a gruff male voice cut the air: "Hold it right there, mister!" Even as he spoke, Ginny could hear him snap back the hammer of a gun. The voice came again: "Put all the money in this bag!"

Ward's voice shook as he said, "Go easy with that gun. I'll do as you say."

"You don't, and I'll blow your brains out! The rest of you people play like statues!" His voice thickened. "Anybody moves, this man dies!"

Ginny's heart pounded. Abruptly, it struck her that the robber wasn't aware of her presence behind the counter. He had to be standing back far enough that he couldn't see her.

"Hurry up!" snapped the robber.

Ginny's eyes went to the revolver that lay well within her reach. Could she do it?

Ward's trembling fingers were having a hard time grasping all the money in the drawer. The paper bills kept slipping through his fingers.

"I said hurry up!" barked the robber. "Or I'll shoot you and fill the bag myself!"

When several bills floated toward the floor, the robber swore at Ward and rasped, "Pick 'em up!"

Ginny closed her fingers around the butt of the revolver. It seemed to adhere itself to her hand.

The robber shouted at Ward again, giving Ginny the perfect moment to ear the hammer back with both thumbs.

When Ward bent down to pick up the fallen bills with trembling fingers, Ginny sprang up suddenly and lined the muzzle of the Colt .45 on the bridge of the robber's nose and cried out shakily, "Now you play statue, mister!"

On Tuesday, April 4, the James-Younger gang was holed up in an abandoned barn just outside Abilene, Kansas. They were set to stop a Denver-bound train on its seventeen-mile stretch between Abilene and Salina. Jim Reed had learned that the train was carrying several thousand dollars in cash from one of the banks in Kansas City.

While the gang waited for Clell Miller and John Younger to return from Abilene, Jesse and Cole filled in the newer gang members on the duties they would perform during tomorrow's train robbery.

The sound of galloping hooves met their ears and Frank James hurried to the barn door and announced that Clell and John were back. All eyes went to the pair when they entered the barn.

"Everything's on schedule, fellas," said Miller. "The train will pull out of Abilene as usual at seven-fifteen tomorrow mornin'."

"Good!" said Jesse. "This haul should help make up a whole lot for the times we were snowbound last winter."

Wes Logan chuckled. "I could use some making up for last winter!"

"That's a good way to put it, Wes!" Belle Reed said.

John Younger moved toward Wes with a rolled-up newspaper in his hand. "Got somethin' for you."

"What's this?"

"*Abilene Times.* Clell and I saw this in a newsstand at the depot."

"You did tell us your girl's name is Ginny Grayson, didn't you?" Clell said.

"Yeah."

"And she lives in Harrisonville?"

"Yeah."

"Well, your little gal got herself written up in the paper! She put a gun on a lone robber at the Harrisonville General Store last Friday, and the guy's sittin' in the Harrisonville jail, waitin' for his trial."

Frowning, Wes said, "How could she have done that? Ginny doesn't carry a gun."

"Read it for yourself. Sounds like that little gal has some spunk!"

On Wednesday, April 26, Ginny Grayson walked up the steps of the Hansen front porch after a busy day at the general store. Just as she opened the door, she heard a buggy pull into the driveway and saw Wes Logan pulling rein.

"Hello, beautiful!" he called, smiling from ear to ear.

"Hello, yourself."

Lines penciled themselves across her normally flawless brow when she saw him take a cane in hand and ease slowly to the ground. As he limped toward her, she watched him favor his left leg. "Wes, what happened?"

"I'll tell you after I get a big hug and kiss," he said, pausing at the bottom of the steps.

Ginny descended to his level and met his lips with her own.

"Come in," she said. "Can you stay for supper?"

"I sure can! After being away from you for so long, I've got to feast my eyes on you…feel the touch of your hand. Could we go for a ride after supper, so we can be alone?"

"Won't have to. My aunt and uncle are in Overland Park, Kansas, visiting friends. They won't be home for a few days."

"Well, good. We'll just be together right here."

"Come in. You can tell me what happened to your leg while I prepare supper."

When Wes was seated at the kitchen table after starting a fire in the cookstove for Ginny, she looked over her shoulder and said, "Okay. Tell me what happened."

"Well, the stage I was on between St. Louis and Columbia,

three weeks ago today, got held up by robbers. There was a shoot-out, and I got hit in my left thigh. The bullet went all the way through but it didn't hit the bone. They took me to a doctor in Columbia. He cleaned out the wound and sewed it up. Said I was not to walk on it for at least two weeks, and then only with a cane."

She pulled her lips into a thin line. "So it's going to be all right? You'll be able to walk on it in time? Without a limp?"

"Sure will. Would have been real bad if the slug had shattered bone."

"That's for sure."

"I had to stay in Columbia for a couple of weeks so the doctor could keep a check on the wound...make sure it was healing all right."

Ginny frowned. "Don't they have a Western Union office in Columbia?"

"I...I didn't want to worry you. And besides, I had told you it would be a few weeks before you'd see me again. So I figured it would be best to just come on and see you as soon as I got back. I had to stay at my boardinghouse in Kansas City for a couple days. My company had some new hardware samples on a train. I had to be there to pick them up."

Ginny was about to speak when Wes blurted, "Say, little gal, I read about you in the *Columbia Free Press*. Shocked me good. For one thing...I wasn't aware you were employed at the Harrisonville General Store. And for another thing—"

"I didn't have the job when you left, Wes," she said defensively. "How could I have told you?"

"Okay. But the other thing, sweetie, I didn't know you had the grit to put a gun on a robber. The article told in detail how you hid on the floor behind the counter and pulled a gun on the guy. Remind me to walk carefully around you. I'd hate to be a robber and have you put a gun on me!"

Ginny set her dark blue eyes on him and held him in her steady gaze. "You'd hate to be a robber, huh?"

Wes chuckled. "Yeah. And have you to face. I saw another paper a week or so later and read that the guy has gone to prison for twenty years."

"That's right. They put robbers in prison, Wes."

Wesley Logan was suddenly uncomfortable under Ginny's hard stare. Blinking, he said, "Honey, is something wrong? You don't seem quite like yourself."

Ginny laid down the paring knife and the potato she was peeling. Taking a step toward the table, she fixed him with eyes like pinpoints and said, "I thought you loved me."

It was Wes's turn to frown. "Ginny, I do love you. What's wrong here?"

"What's wrong here is your lying tongue," she said flatly. "If you love me, why don't you tell me the truth? Why have you been deceiving me for so long about your job?"

Wes's face turned suddenly pale. "What are you talking about? I haven't been deceiving—"

"Quit lying, Wes!" She hurried out of the kitchen.

"Ginny! Wait a minute! Where are you going?"

Wes was working his way out of the chair when Ginny returned, holding a folded newspaper. "Sit down!" she said, a cutting edge to her voice.

Wes eased back onto the chair.

She jammed the newspaper in his hand, eyes flashing. "Here! Read it like I did. Right there on the second page. It tells about a train robbery that took place between Abilene and Salina, Kansas, on April 5! It was the Jesse James–Cole Younger gang!"

"Well, honey, so it was. What has that got to do with me?"

Wes had managed to press an innocent look on his face.

"Well, before you read it, let me tell you what it says. Aboard the train—unknown to the gang—were four federal marshals who were escorting a large amount of cash from a bank in Kansas City to a new bank in Denver."

"So?"

"So there was a big shoot-out. Some passengers helped the marshals. Two of the newest men in the gang were shot dead, and two others wounded before the gang could get away, taking both of their wounded men with them. One of the federal men was killed, as well as two of the passengers who jumped in to help the marshals."

Brow furrowed, he said, "I'm sorry. But what has this to do with me?"

Ginny held his gaze for a few seconds, then said, "One of those wounded gang members was a certain Wesley Logan who used to be a drummer for the Cushman Hardware Company of San Francisco."

"Wh-what?"

Shaking the page in front of him, she pointed to the line that held his name. "Right there!"

"But...but—"

"But what? It says right there that aboard the train was a man named Cletus Joiner who used to own a hardware store in Jefferson City, Missouri. In an interview with the reporter who covered the robbery story, Joiner told him that he recognized one of the gang members as Wesley Logan, who once was a hardware drummer, and he told him that he saw Logan get shot in the left leg. But Logan was carried away by the gang as they fled the scene, carrying several thousand dollars of money they had taken from the train."

Wes swallowed hard.

Looking down at his bad leg, Ginny said, "Want to change your stagecoach robbery story?"

Wes Logan was speechless. While he was trying to find his voice, Ginny said, "My aunt and uncle read the story. They told me I have to break up with you."

He forced his eyes to meet hers.

Ginny's gaze was unflinching. "Why did you deceive me?"

Wes shook his head and ran splayed fingers through his thick mop of hair. "Ginny, I…I'm s-sorry. I—"

"Were you lying all those times you said you loved me?"

"No. I wasn't lying. I do love you. With all my heart."

"Then please explain how you could live a lie before me…how you could deceive me like you did. And tell me why you became an outlaw."

Wes set pain-filled eyes on her. "Do you still have any love for me at all?"

Ginny's lips quivered. "Yes, I still love you as much as ever." She thumbed tears from her cheeks. "I can't understand if you love someone how you could be so deceitful."

He reached out and took hold of her hand. "You want an explanation. May I give it?"

Ginny looked back at the stove. The fire Wes had built was dwindling. She hadn't gotten far enough to have anything cooking on the stove. Turning back to him, she said, "Let me hear it."

"Please sit down."

She eased onto the chair closest to his and let him hold her hand.

"It actually goes back to before I joined the James-Younger gang, Ginny."

She nodded.

Fumbling for words, Wes came clean with her about his

gambling debts and explained how Jesse James and Cole Younger came to him with an invitation to join the gang after they read in the papers about how he thwarted the Thaxton robbery. He told her about Jesse and Cole paying his gambling debts in exchange for his membership in the gang.

Wes told her he had been able to put aside almost forty thousand dollars since joining the gang, even with portions of each of his shares being held back by Jesse and Cole for his debt to them. Just after the train robbery, when he was shot, Cole and Jesse had taken out the final payment from his share. He explained that his plan had been to get one hundred fifty thousand dollars set aside, then quit the gang and marry her. They would relocate someplace far away and begin their new life together. They would be happy and wealthy for the rest of their lives.

"So you see, darlin'," said Wes, "it was my plan for our future that caused me to live a lie before you. I wanted to give you so much more than I could on a drummer's salary. And besides, without the money from Cole and Jesse to pay off the casinos, I'd have been hunted down and killed for welching on those debts. I...I was afraid if you knew I had joined up with Cole and Jesse, you would want me out of your life."

Wes paused, then said, "Now I have to know if that's what you want. If you want me out of your life."

Ginny sat in silence, thinking about what she had just heard. After several minutes, Wes squeezed her hand. "Well?"

She looked into his searching eyes and swallowed with difficulty, then said, "Wes, there's a heavy strain of bitterness inside me for having to live poor all my life. I've read about rich people and their lives of luxury, and I wanted it so bad for myself. I don't like the outlaw part of it, but the prospect of wealth is very appealing."

Wes's face brightened. "Then you'll still marry me? I mean…when I've met my goal of one hundred fifty thousand dollars in my pocket?"

More tears surfaced in Ginny's eyes as she said, "Yes."

"Oh, sweetheart!" he breathed, kissing her soundly.

Looking at him with concern etched on her lovely features, Ginny said, "Darling, there is a problem though. If I don't break up with you, I will be put out of this house."

"All right. Then come with me."

"Come with you?"

"Sure. Jesse and Cole will make room for you at the Younger farm where the gang stays most of the time."

"But would they want a woman there?"

"There's already one woman in the gang."

"Oh. That's right. I forgot about Belle Reed. I've read about her in the papers. She and her husband are both in the gang."

"Right. In fact, it was Belle who took care of my leg. She's the one who sewed it up and tended it."

Ginny's eyes widened. "Then you haven't had a doctor look at it?"

"No."

"But there could be something seriously wrong and—"

"Honey, Belle's really good with gunshot wounds. She's patched up a lot of them. I didn't dare show up at a doctor's office or a clinic. They'd have had the law on me. I'll be fine. Really."

Ginny looked into his eyes. "All right. If you say so. I'm glad you had Belle to take care of your wound."

"Yeah. Me too."

"I remember reading how Belle often rides the stagecoaches as a passenger in order to hold them in check when the gang pulls the stage over. And that she dresses like a man when the gang holds up banks and trains. She must be some tough gal."

Wes grinned. "Mm-hmm. Tough and homely as a mud fence."

"Really?"

"Really."

There was a moment of silence, then Wes said, "Since your aunt and uncle will want you out of the house when they learn that you're still going to marry me, shouldn't you be gone when they get back?"

Tears filled Ginny's eyes and spilled down her cheeks. "I hate to break their hearts. They've been so good to me. But I want to be with you."

"I'm sorry this will have to hurt them, honey, but I guess it'll just have to be."

Ginny nodded. She wrapped her arms around his neck. "You promise that when you've got the money, we'll get married and leave for some faraway place?"

"I promise."

"Oh, Wes! It will be so wonderful to be rich!"

Neither of them felt hungry. Instead Ginny packed her things and Wes loaded them in the buggy. Then she left a note for her aunt and uncle, telling them she loved Wes so much that she couldn't separate from him. She thanked them for what they had done for her and told them she loved them.

They drove to the general store and Wes waited in the buggy while Ginny went upstairs to the apartment where the Stranns lived and told them she was quitting her job because she was leaving town immediately.

11

ON THE WAY TO THE YOUNGER FARM, Wes told Ginny about Jesse and Cole and all the other gang members, and gave her details on how the gang operated.

When Ginny realized Wes was expecting her to be a part of the gang, just like Belle Reed, a squeamish feeling washed over her. "Wes," she said, her voice quivering, "when I said I'd come with you, I wasn't aware that you were counting on me becoming an actual gang member. I...I couldn't do it."

"Sure you can. You should have heard all of them when they read in the paper about you handling that robber at the store. They think you have spunk."

"I was just doing what I could to help Mr. Strann. I couldn't be a robber and take money from people at gunpoint."

"Well, if I bring you to the hideout and tell Jesse and Cole you want to stay there, they'll expect you to do your part. Just look at it this way: By being a part of the gang, you'll be helping the two of us build our nest egg so we can live like royalty for the rest of our lives. If you could help Mr. Strann by using a gun, why can't you help the future Mr. and Mrs. Wesley Logan by using one?"

Ginny thought on it. "Well, if you put it that way, what can I say? But, Wes..."

"Mm-hmm?"

"All I know about guns is what Mr. Strann showed me. I've never even fired one."

Wes chuckled. "Don't worry about that. I'm sure Belle will be glad to teach you."

When they arrived at the Younger farm, Jesse and Cole were a bit upset that Wes would bring his girl to the hideout until he told them the whole story. Ginny was warmly welcomed by the gang leaders and everyone else, especially Belle, who was delighted to have another woman in the gang.

Cole and Jesse told Ginny that Belle would work with her and show her the ropes. Then Cole told her there was a small bedroom at the top of the stairs that would be hers. He went to a chest of drawers and took out a gun belt that held a Colt .45 in its holster. Smiling, he handed it to her, and said, "Wes can punch a hole in the belt so it'll fit you."

Ginny looked at the gun. "Mr. Younger, I know I used one of these to keep that man from robbing the store, but I…well, I've never even fired one before."

Cole laughed. "Belle can give you some lessons. That'll be no problem. I still like the way you handled that guy. I have no doubt you'll be a real asset to the gang. You'll be in Jesse's half of the gang, since Wes is."

Ginny looked at the gun again, then at Wes. "I don't want to shoot anyone."

Jesse stepped up and frowned at Ginny, then swung his gaze to Wes and said, "I need to talk to you alone."

Belle stepped close to Ginny as Jesse and Wes left the room. Patting her shoulder, she said, "Don't worry, honey. You'll only have to shoot people who resist bein' robbed. After a while, you'll get where it doesn't bother you."

Jesse and Wes faced each other on the front porch of the farm-house.

"She's a spunky gal, Wes. She proved that when she put the gun on that robber. But you'll have to convince her she'll have to carry her weight in the robberies, even if it means she has to put a bullet in somebody. If not, she'll have to go. We can't have someone around who won't use a gun when necessary."

"I'll take care of it," said Wes. "Let me have a talk with her."

The two men entered the house, and Wes limped toward Ginny. Smiling, he said, "Honey, let's you and me have a little talk."

When they were alone on the front porch, he said, "Ginny, with the two of us pooling our money, it won't take long to reach our money goal. We'll be able to marry and live like a king and queen even sooner than I had originally planned. But you'll have to go along with Cole and Jesse's wishes and let Belle train you to use the gun."

Ginny's voice trembled. "But Wes, I can't kill anyone."

He pulled her close and said, "Honey, I promise. You'll never have to shoot anyone."

She studied his eyes. "How can you be so sure?"

"Because I'll stay close to you. If anyone needs shooting, I'll take care of them."

"All right. I just hope it isn't too long before we can leave the outlaw trail for a life of wealth and ease."

"We will, sweetheart. We will."

The next morning, Belle took Ginny into the woods and gave her a three-hour lesson in the use of the Colt .45. Belle was pleased at how quickly Ginny caught on, and told her they would have another lesson the next day so Ginny could work on her accuracy.

On Ginny's part, she was amazed at how tough and hard Belle really was.

When Belle had trained Ginny for a week, the teacher was pleased with the accuracy of her student and reported it to Jesse and Cole. Both men were happy to hear it. A meeting was called, and the gang leaders officially welcomed Ginny into the fold.

Cole and Jesse told the group about a new series of robberies they had planned. The first one was a stagecoach carrying a heavily loaded cash box from the Shawnee County Bank in Topeka, Kansas, to the Osage County Bank in Osage on Tuesday, May 30. They wanted both Belle and Ginny to be on the stage as passengers. They would carry .32 caliber pistols in their purses.

When the meeting was over, Ginny took Wes aside. She pointed out that if she was inside a stagecoach with a gun in her purse, Wes would not be there to handle the situation if she was forced to shoot a passenger. Wes assured her that if anybody had to be shot, Belle would do it.

On May 30, a nervous Ginny Grayson climbed aboard the designated stagecoach in Topeka with Belle Reed and four male passengers.

Though Ginny was shaky, she took courage in the fact that Belle was experienced at what they were doing.

When the gang arrived back at the Younger farm that evening, Cole and Jesse gathered them in the parlor while Bob Younger carried the metal cash box to a table and Charlie Pitts placed a canvas bag beside it.

Jesse ran his gaze over their faces, then smiled at Ginny, saying, "We're all proud of our newest member. Belle says you did a great job inside the coach, helping her disarm those four men and hold them at gunpoint while the rest of us relieved the crew of the cash box. If you gals will get supper going, Cole and I will count the loot and we'll each get our share after we eat."

When supper was over and the kitchen cleaned up, Cole and Jesse handed out the shares to the gang members. When Ginny found that she was holding ten thousand dollars in her hands, she marveled at how easily it had become hers. She had never seen that much money in her entire life.

While Cole was commending everyone for a job well done, Ginny smiled at Wes, who sat beside her. They were twenty thousand dollars closer to the time when they could light out to establish their new life far away from Missouri—their rich new life.

As time moved on, Ginny was trained further by Belle. Soon she was dressing like a man as they held up banks and trains.

In mid-June, the gang held up the Bank of Falls City in Falls City, Nebraska. Ginny was inside the bank with Wes at her side. He had laid aside his cane, and though he walked with a slight limp, he could ride his horse with little discomfort.

Wes and Ginny were holding guns on the customers while Jesse and Frank were at the tellers' windows. At the same time, Cole and Bob Younger were holding guns on one of the bank officers at the vault while he stuffed money in a bag.

Belle and Jim Reed kept two bank officers and a frightened secretary at gunpoint, while two other gang members stood at the door to commandeer unsuspecting customers who entered the bank. The rest of the gang was outside, keeping their eyes open for the approach of lawmen.

When all the money had been stuffed in the bags, the robbers began to back toward the door, holding their guns on employees and customers. Pausing at the door, Jesse said loudly, "All of you listen to me! I'm Jesse James, so you know I mean business! As soon as we get mounted up outside, we're gonna be blasting the front of this bank with bullets, including the door and the windows. So I'd say you'd better get on the floor in a hurry when we go out this door!"

As they headed out, Belle saw one of the bank officers reach in his desk and pull out a revolver. She swung around and fired her gun before he could bring his into play. The roar of the shot echoed off the walls as the man peeled out of his chair and hit the floor. Gunsmoke lifted in a cloud toward the ceiling as the robbers hurried out the door and headed for their horses.

That night, at a camp spot in a ravine, Belle and Ginny were bathing alone in a nearby river.

"How did you like your cut of today's robbery, sweetie?" Belle asked.

Ginny set dull eyes on her but didn't reply.

"Hey, you deaf?" pressed Belle. "I said how did you like the money you made today?"

"It was all right."

"Okay, so it wasn't as big as most bank jobs you've heard us talk about. You still got a nice chunk."

Ginny said no more.

Belle looked at her with squinted eyes. "Oh. Now I know what you're upset about. I shot that fool bank officer. Right?"

Ginny looked her in the eye. "Yes."

"Hey, I had no choice. The guy was gonna open fire on us." When Ginny did not respond, Belle said, "Well, wasn't he?"

"I guess so."

"What do you mean, you guess so?"

Ginny brought her hands out of the water and ran wet palms over her face. "I just—"

"You think he was pullin' that gun to play games?"

"No."

"Then if I hadn't plugged him, he might've shot you or Wes. How about that?"

"Of course I don't want Wes to be shot, or any of us. It's just that—"

"What?"

"Well, there's a place in the Bible that says if you take up the sword you will die by the sword. Or as my Uncle Walter once put it...live by the gun; die by the gun."

"What are you gettin' at? Are you sayin' if we use guns to make our livin', we'll die by gettin' shot?"

"That's what the Bible says."

Belle laughed. "Ho-ho! The Bible! Honey, forget it. That Bible is only a bunch of fairy tales. It's nonsense. Forget that Bible stuff. That's for fanatical imbeciles."

As the weeks passed, Ginny and Wes continued working with the gang, putting aside as much of their share of the loot as they could. Some money was spent on dresses for Ginny, which she only wore when riding a stagecoach with Belle. She dreamed of the day when she could wear nice dresses for better purposes.

On September 30, in Denver, Colorado, Dottie Carroll stood at the kitchen window and watched her two children playing with neighbor children in the backyard. James and Molly Kate made friends easily and had brought pride to their mother when she saw how they made the children in the new family next door feel welcome on the very first day they moved in.

Turning from the window, Dottie placed the steaming teakettle on a cool part of the cookstove, looked affectionately at her friend Sarah Kelton and said, "It seems so strange that you and Les don't live next door anymore."

Sarah sipped her hot tea, then replied, "We like Colorado Springs, and Les is glad to have the new job…but we sure miss you, Dr. Matt, and the kids. It was so nice having the chief administrator of Mile High Hospital living right next door. And I not only miss the tea times you and I used to have together, but I miss those little visits from James and Molly Kate."

Dottie sat down at the table, picked up her own cup of steaming tea, and took a sip. "Well, at least I'm glad Les had to come to Denver on business today, so you and I could have some time together."

The sound of happy children filtered in from the backyard. Dottie toyed with her cup, then took another sip.

"Dottie, dear. I've known you long enough to sense when something's bothering you. You're trying not to let on, but I know you're carrying some kind of load. Can you talk to me about it?"

Tears welled up in Dottie's sky blue eyes. "Sarah, it's Breanna."

"Breanna? What about her?"

"You know she still does some visiting nurse work, even though she and John are married."

"Yes."

"Well, she went to Redstone, Colorado, a few weeks ago to

help the town physician, Dr. McClay Lowry, until his new permanent nurse could get there from back East."

"Redstone. That's in the Rockies, but on the west side of the Continental Divide, isn't it?"

"Yes."

"So what's wrong?"

"John and Breanna have exchanged a few telegrams since she went over there, just to keep up with each other."

Sarah smiled. "The chief United States marshal is pretty hard to keep up with."

"That's for sure. Anyway, a wire came to John a few days ago from Redstone's town marshal, Mike Halloran. He told John that Breanna had disappeared."

"What? Disappeared?"

"Yes. Halloran said it was evident she had been abducted." Dottie brushed a few stray honey blond strands from her forehead. "What makes it so frightening is that there has been a psychopathic killer on the loose in and around Redstone. He has murdered several people."

"Oh, how terrible! No wonder you're upset, honey."

"John left for Redstone immediately but no one has heard from him since."

"Oh, dear."

Dottie burst into tears. "Sarah, I'm afraid Breanna's been murdered, and maybe John, too!"

Sarah got up and leaned over Dottie, putting an arm around her. "Now, honey, you've got to get hold of yourself. It may not be that at all. Both Breanna and John are in the Lord's hands. You've got to trust Him to take care of them."

Sarah continued to speak soothingly. Finally, Dottie stopped weeping and looked up at her friend with swollen eyes. "Today is Breanna's birthday. She was supposed to be home two days ago. I had a big party planned for her…"

"You poor, poor dear. This has to be awful for you. I assume Dr. Matt is at the hospital?"

"Yes. He usually takes Saturdays off, but he had to go in this morning. He said he'd be back about one o'clock."

Sarah took hold of Dottie's hand. "Honey, I know you and Dr. Matt have already put a lot of prayer into this situation, but I'd like for us to pray right now."

Dottie smiled faintly. "Yes, we have, Sarah. But let's you and I talk to Jesus about it together."

When both women had prayed, Sarah said, "Since John wasn't told that Breanna's body was found, there's good reason to believe that she's still alive. We've got to hang on and—"

The front door opened and Matt Carroll's voice rang through the hall: "Dottie! Where are you?"

"In the kitchen, honey!"

The tall, handsome physician appeared in the kitchen doorway with a wide smile on his lips. "Honey! Breanna's alive!"

"Oh, praise the Lord! How—where—"

Matt pulled a yellow envelope from the inside pocket of his suit coat. "This telegram is from her!"

Dottie's eyes were misty. "Well, tell me! What does she say?"

Matt smiled at their former neighbor. "Hello, Sarah. Nice to see you." Then he turned to Dottie. "She says she's been through a harrowing experience but she's unharmed. John is with her. The Western Union messenger brought this to me at the hospital. Breanna says that she and John will be home on Monday. She'll fill us in on all that happened when they see us. John's preaching at Redstone's church tomorrow."

Dottie broke into tears of relief, thanking the Lord that both John and Breanna were all right. Matt held her in his arms while she wept.

After a few minutes, Dottie said, "Matt, we need to spread the news to Pastor Bayless and our friends all over town."

"I'll take care of that immediately. I'll go to the parsonage first. If the pastor isn't terribly busy, I'm sure he'll help me spread the word."

"I'll plan a belated birthday party for Breanna on Tuesday night," Dottie said. "And right now I'm calling the children in to tell them the good news about their aunt!"

The big engine chugged heavily, sending huge puffs of black smoke skyward as it pulled the passenger train over Vail Pass in the Colorado Rockies. It was Monday, October 2. In coach number two, John Brockman held his wife's hand as they talked over the entire episode she had experienced while chained in a mountain cabin by Redstone's psychopathic killer, and how marvelously the Lord had delivered her from certain death.

When they had exhausted the subject, Breanna squeezed John's hand and said, "Darling, you told me before I left Denver for Redstone that you had something big planned as a birthday present. I'd sure like to know what it is. I mean...my birthday is past now, but my curiosity is killing me."

John chuckled. "It's not past tense, even though Saturday was your birthday. Actually, Dottie and I had something worked out, and it's still planned."

"Oh. You mean it was for my birthday, but the actual thing planned wasn't to take place till later?"

"That's it."

"Well, smarty, let's hear it."

John was about to tell her when suddenly, across the aisle, a middle-aged man began choking and gagging.

John stood up to let Breanna pass by him. She hurriedly crossed the aisle and addressed the man's wife. "Ma'am, I'm a nurse. May I help him?"

"Oh, please do! He was eating a sandwich I had packed in my hand luggage, and a bite lodged in his throat!"

"John, help me get him in the aisle on his knees, head bent forward."

When John had the man positioned as Breanna directed, she bent over him and cupped his chin in one hand, then pounded him on the back. It took only seconds for the food to dislodge, and when Breanna heard it come up, she reached into his mouth and pulled it out.

The man sucked in a big gulp of air, coughed several times, then began breathing normally. John hoisted him to his feet as Breanna said, "Are you all right, sir?"

"Yes, ma'am. You saved my life."

The man's wife wrapped her arms around him and looked at Breanna through her tears, saying, "Oh, thank you! Thank you!"

"You're quite welcome, ma'am."

Obviously relieved to be breathing normally, the man said, "I'd like to pay you, ma'am. Nurses get paid for their services."

"Not this time. I'm just glad I was able to help you."

"How can I ever thank you sufficiently?" he asked.

"It's thanks enough just to see you breathing."

"What's your name, dear?" asked the man's wife.

"I'm Breanna Brockman." She reached for John's hand and said, "This is my husband, John."

The man slapped his forehead. "Oh! Please forgive me, sir, I should be thanking you, too."

"No need. I was just obeying my wife's orders. I'm quite used to doing what she tells me."

Breanna elbowed his ribs, giving him a mock scowl, and the couple laughed.

Abruptly, the front door of the coach swung open, and a man who had run for help came in with the conductor on his heels. They quickly saw that all was well, and the couple told the conductor what John and Breanna had done.

When the conductor was gone, John gestured toward the empty seat in front of his and Breanna's, which faced backward. "Please come and sit down so we can talk."

The man and wife were pleased at the invitation, and when all four were seated, John said, "You know our names, but we don't know yours."

"I'm Lloyd Desmond, and this is my wife, Cora. We live in Grand Junction and are on our way to visit relatives in Cheyenne City. We—" Lloyd's gaze fell on John's badge. "Oh! You're a chief United States marshal!"

John nodded. "That's right."

"Out of which office?"

"I'm in charge of the Denver office."

Lloyd's eyes widened. "Wait a minute! Sure. I know who you are." He turned to his wife. "Cora, you remember this man! He cleaned up a gang of hoodlums in North Platte when we lived there. And he preached at our church. Remember?"

Core's eyes widened. "You...you're John Stranger!"

Lloyd frowned. "But your wife said your last name is Brockman."

"It is. I simply went by Stranger for many years, for various reasons. When I became chief U.S. marshal in Denver a few months ago, I let my real last name be known."

"I thought you looked familiar when we first got on the train, but I couldn't place you. Well, Mr. Stranger...uh...Chief Brockman, it sure is good to see you again."

"I remember the sermon you preached that day, Chief Brockman," said Cora.

"Well, you're ahead of me," John said with a chuckle.

"It was about when the dear Lord Jesus was on the cross, and how he saved that dying repentant thief. You told how both thieves had the same opportunity to be saved. One opened his heart to Jesus and the other rejected Him."

Lloyd moved forward on the seat and looked at John with admiring eyes. "And you closed off the sermon by saying the two thieves were no more than twelve feet apart, but in eternity they would be worlds apart because the repentant thief would be in heaven and the thief who rejected Jesus would be in hell. I'll never forget it."

"Me either," said Cora. "And I'll never forget when you gave the invitation at the end of the sermon. You told the crowd that those who were saved and those who were unsaved in the building were at that moment only a few feet apart. But those who refused to come to the Saviour that day and died without Him would be in hell and those who were saved would be in heaven—worlds apart forever, just like the two thieves."

"Yes, sir, Chief Brockman," said Lloyd, "that was powerful! And as I recall, we had several people come to the Lord that day."

"Yes, we did," said John. "And with your help just now, I do recall preaching that sermon that day."

The Brockmans and the Desmonds talked for a while, then Lloyd explained that Cora had not been feeling well of late. She needed to take some medicine and then settle down for a nap. They thanked the Brockmans once more for saving Lloyd's life, then returned to their seats.

12

WHEN THE DESMONDS HAD RETURNED to their seats, Breanna looked at her husband and said, "I've never heard you preach that sermon, darling. It sounds like a good one."

"Has to be. It's about Jesus."

Breanna squeezed his arm. "Of course. But when John Brockman preaches about Jesus, it is especially good."

John sat next to the window now. "You're so kind," he said, looking into her dark blue eyes.

"It's more than kindness, darling. I just know good preaching when I hear it. And when my husband preaches, it's always good."

He smiled at her, then looked out the window. The train was winding its way below the towering peaks, along the edge of a vast canyon. He spotted a trail among the pines that seemed to run all the way up to the sky. To the left of the trail was a lofty promontory that would offer a majestic view of the deep canyon's walls and crags.

John felt Breanna's hand slide into his, and as he turned to look at her, she leaned toward him gently and kissed him on the cheek. The touch of her lips was very soft, almost like a touch of breeze sliding past.

Grinning, he said, "Mm-mm! Thank you!"

"You're welcome," she said with a giggle. "All right, mighty Chief Brockman, let's get back to the plan you and my sister made for my birthday present."

"All right. Let's test your memory. I have never met any of these relatives of yours we'll be talking about, but with that much of a hint, what is next Saturday?"

"Mmm…October 7."

"Yes. Anything else?"

Breanna thought a moment. "Ah…no. I can't think of anything."

"I'll give you another hint. Frank and Eloise Baylor of Emporia, Kansas."

"Oh! It's Uncle Frank and Aunt Eloise's anniversary!"

"Good! We've got your thinking wheels in motion. Now, which anniversary is it?"

Breanna's fingertips went to her forehead. "Why, it's their fiftieth!"

"Excellent! Now here's the story. Your cousin Diane Baylor Kirby sent a letter to me at the office about six weeks ago. Before you went to Redstone."

"Diane! I haven't seen her since the day she married Dale Kirby five…almost six years ago. Of course we've kept in touch by mail. Anyway, go ahead, darling."

"Well, Diane wrote to me because what she had planned was a surprise for you."

"Okay."

"I might add that she also wrote to Dottie and Matt at the same time. Diane is planning a big fiftieth anniversary celebration for her parents at their home in Emporia on Saturday. Her letters were to invite the Carrolls and us for this momentous occasion. But she also wanted me to make it a surprise birthday present to you that we would attend."

Breanna's eyes lit up. "This is wonderful, darling! You mean it's all set that we're going?"

"All set. I didn't change a thing when you came up missing at Redstone. I was trusting the Lord to let me find you alive and well and able to make the trip to Emporia."

"Oh, it'll be so good to see my relatives again! And to be with Uncle Frank and Aunt Eloise on their fiftieth anniversary! Darling, this is a wonderful birthday present. And just think, Dottie and Matt will be there, too."

"Dottie will. But not Matt."

"Oh?" Disappointment showed on her face. "Why not?"

"The American Medical Association is meeting in Denver next weekend, and as you know, Dr. Matthew Carroll is the local host."

"Mmm. I forgot about the AMA meeting. That's too bad. Like you, Matt hasn't met any of our relatives."

"I wish he could go with us," said John, "but at least yours truly will get to meet all of them."

"Praise the Lord! I'm especially eager for you to meet Uncle Frank. I've told you that as Papa's only brother, he's almost a duplicate. When you meet Uncle Frank, it will almost be like meeting Papa."

"I'm looking forward to it, honey. Of course, I'm looking forward to meeting both of your parents in heaven."

"That'll be a wonderful day. I still miss them so much, John."

She hugged his neck and planted a warm kiss on his lips in spite of the audience in the coach. "Thank you, darling. It's the best birthday present you could have given me!"

John pulled her close. "Well, I've got some more birthday presents for you at home."

✦

When the train pulled into Denver's Union Station, John directed Breanna's attention to the crowded platform and to four familiar faces eagerly scanning the train windows.

As soon as the Brockmans descended to the depot platform, Dottie Carroll rushed to Breanna and wrapped her arms around her, weeping as she murmured thanks to the Lord that her sister was alive and unharmed. After a lengthy hug, Matt and the children embraced Breanna and welcomed her home.

When the hugging and kissing were over, James and Molly Kate stayed on either side of Aunt Breanna and held her hands as everyone walked to the parking lot.

While they walked to the buggy, Dottie told Breanna about the birthday party at the Carroll house the next night. Breanna thanked her, then told her that John had given her the details about the trip to Emporia.

Matt suddenly announced that he and Dottie were taking them all to supper at Denver's Westerner Hotel before they took them home.

John agreed that would be fine, but he and Breanna were treating all of them to supper. No matter what Matt said, John stayed firm until Matt agreed that supper would be on the Brockmans.

While they were enjoying their meal, Dottie said, "I can't wait any longer to hear about your ordeal in Redstone, Breanna. Do you mind telling us about it now?"

"Of course not."

Breanna told how shocked she was to learn there was a killer on the loose in and around Redstone, who had already murdered two people just before she arrived. She had barely started working for Dr. McClay Lowry when the killer struck again. As the days passed, more people were killed. "Then one night I was abducted from my room at the boardinghouse. The killer managed to gag and blindfold me without letting me see his face. He tied me up and put me in a wagon—the longest ride I think I've ever endured. I could tell we were going up into the mountains because of the angle of the climb. And I could hear water nearby.

"When he finally stopped the wagon, he took me inside a cabin and chained me to a post. I never saw his face, and he disguised his voice when he talked to me. That's what made me think it must be someone I knew in town. He said he was going to kill me on my birthday. That's when I knew for sure it was someone from town, because I'd mentioned it to a few people when I was talking about getting home in time to celebrate with all of you."

Breanna went on to explain that during her captivity, she was left alone all day until the killer came each evening to taunt her. In her loneliness and fear, the Lord had brought Hebrews 11:1 to mind—that faith is the evidence of things not seen. She clung to that verse, believing that even though she could see no way to live through the ordeal, the Lord would spare her life and let her live on to serve Him and be the wife that John needed. Even as the salvation of her soul had come by faith when she was a girl, so her life was spared by faith, in spite of the insane killer's threat and intent.

"What a testimony!" said Matt. "Praise God for His magnificent Word!"

Dottie leaned toward her sister and said in a low voice, "Honey, tell us who the killer turned out to be and how the Lord delivered you."

Tears pooled in Breanna's eyes as she told how God had protected her by letting a vicious cougar attack and kill the man on the morning of her birthday, just before he entered the cabin to murder her. John and Marshal Mike Halloran had learned who the killer was, and they showed up at the cabin just as the cougar was ripping and tearing at the man.

James and Molly Kate had stopped eating, their wide eyes fixed on Breanna as Dottie said, "Tell us, Breanna. Who was the killer?"

She closed her eyes for a moment, then looked at her sister and said, "The killer was Dr. McClay Lowry."

Matt's head bobbed in disbelief as Dottie gasped and said, "Dr. Lowry! Did you say Dr. Lowry?"

"Yes. He turned out to be a classic example of a psychopathic killer. He even murdered his own wife."

Dottie shook her head in utter disbelief. "Dr. Lowry," she muttered, looking at her plate. Then lifting her eyes once again to her sister, she said, "Thank God for His hand on you, honey."

"Amen," said Matt.

"Amen," echoed James.

"Yeah, amen," said Molly Kate. "I'm sure glad I still have my Aunt Breanna!"

On Tuesday morning, Breanna stayed home to rest up from her ordeal in Redstone. Ordinarily she would have gone back to work at her sponsoring physician's office, or at Mile High Hospital, but John had said he wanted her to rest until they made the trip to Emporia and returned to Denver. Then she could go back to work for Dr. Lyle Goodwin or the hospital.

Breanna gladly went along with his wishes.

After breakfast, she walked with John to the barn and corral. He had to be at the office early to catch up on paperwork.

When they were yet some fifty yards from the corral, Breanna's big black stallion spotted her. His ears went up and he bobbed his head as he trotted up to the pole fence, whinnying a greeting.

"Aw, there's Mommy's big boy," she said, hurrying ahead of John. Breanna stood on her tiptoes and wrapped her arms around the stallion's neck. "Did Mommy's big boy miss her? I love you, Chance!"

The horse nickered his own message to her, pressing his muzzle against her neck.

Suddenly, John's big black gelding, Ebony, came around the back corner of the barn and whinnied, then galloped up to the fence. He pressed close to Chance, nickering in like manner.

"Look at that, John," said Breanna. "This big boy missed me, too!" Ebony nickered again, pressing even tighter against Chance.

"I think Ebony wants a hug, too, honey."

Breanna laughed and let go of Chance. When she hugged Ebony's neck. Chance snorted and bobbed his head, then shook it.

John laughed. "It's quite obvious, Mrs. Brockman, that you actually own both horses."

"No, I don't, darling. They own me!"

John moved toward the corral gate. "Well, you can make Chance happy again, 'cause I've got to saddle up Ebony and head for work."

Breanna caressed Chance's long face and talked baby talk to him while John bridled and saddled Ebony. When he led his horse outside the corral, Breanna rubbed Chance's ears and said, "Mommy will ride you good in a day or two, sweetheart."

Chance whinnied his objection as John led Ebony toward the house with Breanna by his side.

As they walked slowly, John said, "Honey, I haven't even told you about our travel schedule on Thursday."

"All right. I'm listening with great anticipation."

"Well, you, Dottie, and I will leave here Thursday morning on the six o'clock train to Cheyenne City. We'll have about an hour's layover there. Then we'll take the Kansas City–bound train as far as Topeka. We'll stay the night in Topeka at the Sunflower Hotel. At eight-thirty Friday morning, we'll take the Wells Fargo stage that runs all the way to Wichita, but we'll get off when it makes its stop at Emporia."

Breanna gripped John's muscular arm. "I'm so excited I can hardly stand it!"

"Happy belated birthday, sweetheart," he said as they reached the back of the house. He folded her in his arms and kissed her.

From the corral came a shrill whinny. John looked at Chance and said loudly, "Eat your heart out, big boy! She may be your mommy, but she's my wife!"

Chance whinnied again, stomping a hoof.

Breanna laughed and called to the horse, "It's all right! You and I can have our moments when you-know-who has gone to work!"

John took Breanna in his arms and kissed her again, then mounted up and rode away, saying he would see her that evening.

The belated birthday party was held at the Carroll home that night. In addition to the Carroll family, Pastor Robert Bayless and his wife, Kathy, were there, along with many friends, including Dr. Lyle Goodwin and his wife, Martha; Sheriff Curt Langan, his wife, Stefanie, and their adopted children;

Stefanie's mother, who was also head nurse at Mile High Hospital, Mary Donelson; and ex-Chief U.S. Marshal Solomon Duvall.

Dottie asked Breanna to tell the guests about her experience with Redstone's psychopathic killer and how the Lord had so wonderfully answered all their prayers in sparing her life. By the time she finished her story, everyone was praising the Lord. Then Pastor Bayless led them in prayer and thanked the Lord for the way He had kept His hand on Breanna. By the time Bayless said his amen, tears were flowing freely.

When Breanna had opened all her presents, Dottie came from the kitchen carrying a birthday cake with candles lit.

On Monday, October 2—the same day John and Breanna Brockman rode the train over the Rockies to Denver—Deputy U.S. Marshals Rick Dowd and Ike Lynch rode into Olathe, Kansas, to buy Rick Dowd a new pair of boots. He'd torn the heel off his left boot when he slipped on a rock while watering the horses at a creek.

Dowd and Lynch were on their way south to Hillsdale, where they would pick up a prisoner to transport him back to Leavenworth.

They slowly rode past the Johnson County Bank and stopped a half block farther in front of the Olathe Boot and Saddle Company.

Just east of Olathe, the James-Younger gang sat their horses in a thick wooded area. Jesse and Cole faced the rest of the gang. Jesse put his gaze on the two newest gang members, Lefty Carson and Dan Simmons, and said, "Since this is the first bank job you've done with us, you'll stay outside and keep a lookout for the approach of any badge toters. Remember, if you see any coming your way, one of you hurry into the bank and let us know. You'll have Belle and Ginny out there with you. They know what to do in case something out of the ordinary happens."

Carson and Simmons looked at the two women who were dressed as men. They had tucked their hair up under their hats and wore their gun belts low on their hips. Leather gloves disguised their hands. Earlier that day, when the two men had first seen the women in their masculine getups, Carson had commented to Simmons that Belle was so homely and rough-looking she could easily pass for a man. But the lovely Ginny wasn't fooling anybody.

"All of you know your places," spoke up Cole. "This ain't the biggest bank we ever hit, but it oughtta be a decent haul. Any questions?"

Cole ran his gaze over their faces, giving them a few seconds to respond. When silence prevailed, he said, "Okay. Let's go add some money to our coffers."

Belle Reed and Lefty Carson trotted out of the thick stand of trees; Ginny Grayson and Dan Simmons followed. When Cole and Jesse saw them nearing the outskirts of Olathe, they dispatched three more men, and when they were on their way, two more trotted out. Soon the whole gang was strung out as they headed into the town two and three at a time.

Twenty minutes later, Belle and Ginny remounted their horses when they caught sight of the gang members inside the bank making their way to the door. Carson and Simmons swung into their saddles.

Suddenly Jesse James and Cole Younger burst out of the door, followed by the others. Jesse shouted, "Better get out of the way, folks! There's gonna be gunfire real quick!"

People were scrambling for cover as the rest of the gang

vaulted into their saddles and Jesse opened fire on the front door and windows of the bank—his usual method of operation.

Just as Jesse was peppering the bank with bullets, Deputies Rick Dowd and Ike Lynch came out of the boot store.

"The bank's being robbed!" cried Lynch, whipping out his gun.

The deputies ran toward the action. At the same time, the town marshal and two of his deputies charged out of the marshal's office, pulling guns from leather. Together, the five lawmen ran headlong up the middle of the street and started firing at the robbers.

Olathe's Main Street seemed to explode with gunfire as the sharp reports slammed against buildings. Cole shouted the order to ride south out of town.

As the group ran toward their mounts, the horses' dancing hooves lifted cloudy banners of dust and ricocheting bullets whipped up a weird whining sound.

"Let's go!" shouted Cole above the din.

Suddenly a bullet struck Lefty Carson's horse in the head, and it collapsed beneath him. Lefty fell to the street, a bit stunned, then scrambled to his feet.

Ginny Grayson was closest to him. She holstered her gun and leaned from the saddle, shouting, "Take my hand! Get up behind me! Hurry!"

Belle, who was next to Ginny, grinned to herself when she saw one of her bullets drop the town marshal.

As Lefty stumbled toward her, Ginny felt the hot breath of a bullet on her right cheek as it whizzed by and struck the front of the bank, showering splinters on the boardwalk.

All of a sudden, Lefty stiffened and fell. He rolled over, gasping, and Ginny saw a blood-ringed bullet hole in his shirt at the left shoulder. At the same instant, Dan Simmons fell from his dancing horse and hit the dust. He had been hit in the head.

"C'mon!" shouted Jesse. "Let's get out of here!"

"Wait!" cried Ginny. "Lefty's down! We've got to take him with us!"

"No time for that!" bellowed Cole. "Let's go!"

Wes fired at one of the town's deputies, who was dashing from the cover of one wagon to another. A small group of townsmen had joined the lawmen.

Wes moved his horse closer to Ginny's. "Let's go, honey!"

"Now!" Cole added.

Lefty cried out, "Help me, Cole! Help me! Don't leave me here!"

Ignoring him, Cole blared, "Go! Everybody! Go!"

The other gang members started bolting, whipping their horses for speed.

Ginny started to get off her horse, her attention on Lefty, whose shirt was getting soaked with blood.

"Ginny!" shouted Cole. "Stay on that horse! Get outta here!"

"But Lefty's hurt! I'm going to help him!"

Wes pushed his horse close to Ginny and glared at her with hot eyes. "Stay in that saddle and ride! Now!"

She saw the look in Wes's eyes and heard Belle swearing at her, telling her to go.

Guns were still blazing as the James-Younger gang—minus a dead Dan Simmons and a wounded Lefty Carson—galloped out of Olathe southward, holding their tightly packed money bags.

The sounds of Lefty's cries followed them as they thundered down the wide street. Ginny took one look back and tears misted her eyes.

When the dust settled in Olathe, Lefty Carson lay in the street, gripping his wounded shoulder as people gathered around him. His gun lay inches from his fingers. Someone kicked it out of reach.

Lefty saw Dan Simmons lying dead a few feet from him. The voices of the people shouting excitedly told him the gang had killed the town marshal, one of his deputies, and a woman bank customer who had taken a bullet through the window.

When the gang crossed back into Missouri, they stopped at a creek to give the horses a moment to rest and take a drink.

Ginny wept as she held her horse's reins. Wes stood close to her and said in a level tone, "Ginny, you have to understand that we had no choice but to leave him there."

"No, I don't understand!" Her cutting tone was finely honed on a whetstone of anger and betrayal. "He's one of us! Would it have been the same if it had been me lying there, wounded and bleeding? Huh? Would it?"

A tightness crept up between Wes's shoulder blades. "Ginny, I—"

"Yes, it would," cut in Cole Younger, moving up to them. "That's part of this business, Ginny. We all understand that. I thought you did."

"No, I didn't," she said curtly. "I know we're bad, but are we less than human?"

Cole put steady eyes on Wes and said, "You'd best make her understand." Then he walked away.

Wes lowered his voice and took hold of Ginny's hand. "Can't you see we didn't have a choice? If we had taken the time to pick up Lefty and put him on one of our horses, more of us would have been shot."

Ginny stared at him silently.

Belle was standing near. "He's right, Ginny," she said. "We all take the risk of gettin' shot in this business. It goes with the territory. Certainly you can see that. Lefty took a bullet. He was willin' to risk it to make big money, and he lost. Even as Dan Simmons lost. Life's tough in this business."

Tears filled Ginny's eyes. "But Lefty was still alive, Belle. I'm sorry Dan got shot, but at least he was dead. Nothing more could be done for him. But Lefty is alive, and he's in the hands of the law. They'll probably hang him just for being part of the gang, even if they have no proof that he's killed anyone."

"Time to ride," said Jesse James. "Wes, you work on her. Let's go."

Ginny was still visibly upset as they rode north. Wes tried to reason with her. After a while, Ginny began to grow calm and told Wes she understood. She didn't like it, but she understood.

When they reached the Younger farm, Belle and Ginny cooked supper as usual. After supper, the gang gathered in the parlor. Jesse and Cole stood before them and began talking about the next jobs and the big train robbery planned for the next afternoon.

With both gang leaders talking intermittently, they went over the plan to get their hands on the biggest gold shipment they had ever had the opportunity to steal. It had been in the works for several days, and this one was going to make them rich.

Jesse told them how they would improvise to cover for Lefty and Dan. Then Cole explained one more time that they would build a barricade on the tracks at the west end of the trestle where it crossed the Kansas River three miles east of the little town of Lecompton. They must have it in place by four-thirty, for the Kansas City–bound train from Cheyenne City would reach the trestle at approximately five o'clock.

When all the details had been covered for the third or fourth time, Jesse rubbed his hands together, saying they would all be rich as royalty when they rode away with the gold.

13

AT OLATHE, FEDERAL DEPUTY MARSHALS Dowd and Lynch watched Dr. Saul Trevick and Eve Claremore, his nurse, take Lefty Carson into the surgical room.

When the door closed, Lynch said, "Since the doc says he can have Carson patched up in an hour, I think we'd best take him on to the Kansas City office today and let Chief Cofer question him."

"I agree," said Dowd. "Why don't you stay here in case it's more serious than the doc thinks. I'll send a wire to the marshal in Hillsdale and tell him we'll come back tomorrow for the prisoner going to Leavenworth. Then I'll rent a wagon. There's no way Carson's gonna be able to ride a horse. We can bring the wagon back on our way to Hillsdale."

"Sounds good," said Lynch.

Some twenty minutes later, Nurse Claremore came out. "Deputy Lynch, Dr. Trevick sent me to tell you the slug only chipped a little bone. The prisoner will be able to travel as far as Kansas City with no problem. Doctor says he really shouldn't try to ride a horse, though."

"My partner and I figured as much, ma'am, so he went after a wagon and team to rent right now."

"Fine. We should be finished in about forty minutes."

A short time later, Rick Dowd reentered the clinic and found three patients waiting to see the doctor. Ike Lynch looked up and said, "The nurse said the wound is no worse than the doctor figured. Get a wagon?"

"Yep. And sent the wire."

"Good. Might as well sit down."

"Also," said Dowd, "I took both of our horses to the hostler. He'll keep them overnight without charge. That way, we can both ride in the wagon. We'll put Carson in the back."

"Fine with me," said Lynch.

It was nearly noon when a sullen Lefty Carson was hoisted into the bed of the wagon. His left arm was in a sling and his face was a sickly gray.

Ike Lynch climbed onto the seat and picked up the reins.

Dowd looked at the prisoner. "Make yourself comfortable. We're taking you to our chief in Kansas City. He'll have some real important questions to ask you."

Carson had not spoken a word to the lawmen since they had picked him up and taken him to the clinic. He didn't speak now.

Dowd closed the tailgate of the wagon, latched it, and set steady eyes on the outlaw. "You don't have to say anything to us, but you'd better be ready to loosen that tongue when you're facing Chief Cofer."

Carson narrowed his eyelids. "I don't have to say nothin' to nobody," he grunted through clenched teeth.

Dowd grinned wryly. "No, you don't. But the less you cooperate, the longer your sentence will be. Of course, if you choose to be totally obstinate, the jury might just decide to vote to hang you, since you've been riding with the bloody

James-Younger gang, whether there's evidence you're a murderer or not."

Carson swallowed hard and sniffed mulishly. He laid his free hand on his wounded shoulder and flicked a glance at Dowd.

"Anyway, Lefty," said the deputy, "you've got a little while to think about it while we drive you to the federal building in Kansas City." He started toward the right side of the wagon, then paused. "Sure was thoughtful of Jesse and Cole and the rest of them to just leave you to go to prison or the gallows. Nice bunch you chose to run with."

When Dowd climbed up and settled on the seat, he said, "Well, let's hit the road, Deputy U.S. Marshal Lynch. Our friend here is eager to talk to Chief Cofer."

As the wagon headed north out of Olathe, Lefty Carson's thoughts went to the subject raised by Deputy Dowd. Lefty had already been having evil thoughts about the gang for their cowardly desertion of him in the midst of blazing guns and flying bullets. The only person who showed any concern for him was Ginny Grayson.

Lefty had kept his hard-shell attitude because it was the outlaw thing to do, but Dowd's words echoed through his head. He relived that wild moment when he lay on the ground, bleeding, and Jesse's voice came above the roar of the gunfire, telling the gang they needed to go. He could still hear Ginny's anxious words as she told him Lefty was down and they needed to take him with them. Cole's voice had cut through the din, saying there was no time for that.

Lefty had soft thoughts toward Ginny as he recalled that she'd started to get off her horse to help him but was stopped by Cole.

He could still hear her arguing with Cole and Wes, and

Belle swearing at her, telling her to get going.

Lefty felt a molten rage come to life inside him. Over and over he heard Cole and Jesse's heartless words, and Wes and Belle telling Ginny to ride. Stung raw by the memory of it, he decided they needed to pay for what they'd done to him, and pay dearly.

As the wagon bumped along the road, Carson twisted about so he could see the two lawmen in the seat. "Deputy Dowd?"

Rick leaned back some, his eyes on his prisoner.

"I've been thinkin' about what you said. The gang really did do me dirty. I'll be glad to talk to your chief. I have some information that'll be music to his ears."

Dowd and Lynch exchanged grins, then Dowd looked down at Carson and said, "Now you're showing some good sense, fella."

It was nearly four o'clock when Chief U.S. Marshal Layton Cofer, a man in his midsixties, with a thick head of silver hair, ran his gaze over Deputies Lynch and Dowd, then looked on the prisoner and said, "All right, Lefty, let's hear it."

Carson adjusted the sling on his left arm and leaned closer to the chief's desk. "If I give you this information, will they go easier on me in court?"

"If I learn the information is valid, I most certainly will see about that," said Cofer.

"Well, I ain't gonna sit here and lie, sir. Those low-down hunks of human vermin deserted me. I hope you catch every one of 'em. But if you do, I want to give you some information about the desertion so's you'll go easier on one particular gang member."

"We'll see about that later," said Cofer. "Let's hear it."

Lefty's jaw squared as he said, "There's a big gold shipment comin' outta Denver tomorrow on Union Pacific. It'll be put on the Kansas City–bound train at Cheyenne City in the mornin'…meant for the Kansas City Bank and Trust Company."

Cofer's mouth fell open and his eyes widened. "That shipment is top secret! How did James and Younger learn of it?"

"I don't know that."

Cofer's face reddened. "Don't give me that! I want to know James and Younger's source of information and I want to know it right now!"

"I'm sorry, sir. I'm telling you the truth. I've only been runnin' with the gang for a few weeks. I don't know how Jesse and Cole usually did things, but when they brought up this gold shipment and their plan to rob the train, they didn't volunteer—in my hearin', anyhow—where they learned of it."

Cofer leaned back in his chair. "All right. I'll have to take your word for it. Tell me when and where this train robbery is to take place."

"Well, accordin' to what Cole and Jesse said, they're plannin' to build a barricade on the tracks at the west end of the bridge that crosses the Kansas River a couple miles east of Lecompton. The train's supposed to reach that spot about five o'clock tomorrow afternoon. That's where and when. I can't tell you any more than that."

"That's enough," said Cofer. Then he said to his two deputies, "We'll put together a team right away. The marshal in Hillsdale will have to hang on to his prisoner another day. I want you two on the team that's going to bring an end to the James-Younger gang."

"We wouldn't miss this opportunity for the world, sir," said Lynch.

Rick Dowd grinned. "Just think of it, Ike. Us and the rest of the men Chief Cofer puts on the team will go down in history as the lawmen who put the James-Younger gang's necks in the noose!"

Cofer chuckled. "In the meantime, let's lock up Lefty over at the jail. We've got to go talk to the powers that be at Kansas City Bank and Trust and do a little adjusting of that gold shipment."

The Kansas City Bank and Trust Company had closed its doors for the day's business when Chief Cofer and his deputies arrived, but they were able to get the attention of the secretary nearest the front door. When she learned from Chief Cofer that it was imperative they talk to Edmund Harris, the vice president in charge of receiving gold shipments, they were ushered immediately into Harris's office.

The vice president and the chief U.S. marshal were well acquainted. After shaking hands, Cofer introduced Dowd and Lynch. An additional chair was placed in front of Harris's desk, and when all were comfortably seated, Harris said, "Now, what is this important information Miss Wellman said you need to talk to me about, Chief?"

Cofer laid a foundation by having Dowd and Lynch tell about the bank robbery that morning in Olathe, and how they had picked up Lefty Carson, a wounded member of the James-Younger gang.

Cofer then proceeded to tell Harris the details of the planned robbery to relieve the Union Pacific train of the gold being shipped from Denver.

A bit pale of face, Harris said, "Chief, this is earthshaking news. From what you just told me, it has to mean there's someone on the inside who's friendly to the gang and no doubt is being well paid for providing the information."

"That's what I think," said Cofer. "The main thing now is to stop the gold from being put on that train in Denver tomorrow morning, let alone keeping it from being loaded on the train in Cheyenne City. You're the man to handle it and that's why we're here."

Harris nodded solemnly. "Exactly. But I must have the gold shipped as soon as possible. We're handling it for a large precious metals distributing company. They're one of our largest accounts. They're set to sell it to jewelry manufacturers over a four-state area, and they're all expecting to have the gold in their hands within the next few days."

"I understand," said Cofer. "But since there's someone on the inside leaking information, we need to put some thought to when and how we actually ship the gold."

"You're right. And I'll let you help me. Let's go to the railroad station right now, before Roger Wheaton leaves his office. He's the Union Pacific vice president in charge of the gold shipments we get from out West."

Before Cofer and Harris left the office for the depot, Cofer told the deputies to go home and get some rest. They were to report to his office at eight o'clock in the morning. He would put several more men on the team, and they would get their instructions by nine and be on their way to the trestle with a big surprise for the James-Younger gang.

Shortly thereafter, Harris and Cofer were seated in the office of Roger Wheaton at the depot. With Wheaton was his young assistant, Gordon Naylor.

When Harris told them the story, Wheaton said with a suddenly dry mouth, "Gentlemen, this astounds me. It's inconceivable that those outlaws could find out about the gold being on tomorrow's train."

"Well, they did," said Cofer. "And I must ask you to wire your people in Denver and tell them not to put the gold on that train to Cheyenne City."

"Of course," said Wheaton. Then he said to his assistant, "Gordon, you will take care of it."

"Most certainly, sir," said Naylor, getting up from his chair.

Lifting a hand, Harris said, "Wait a minute. There's something else."

Harris looked at Wheaton and said, "Roger, I want you to delay the shipment only until Wednesday. But I want to play it safe just in case something unforeseen happens and Chief Cofer's men should not apprehend the gang. I want the gold taken off the train when it stops in Topeka. Disguise it as some other kind of cargo. I'll explain more about this in a moment.

"I want the gold put on a specially prepared Wells Fargo stagecoach to fool the gang if they are still at large and in contact with whoever has fed them the information about the gold shipment. This means that only your most trusted people can know about it. Understood?"

"Of course," said Wheaton. Then he said to Naylor, "Gordon, make sure this information only goes to those directly responsible."

"Yes, sir," said Naylor. He looked at Harris. "One question, sir."

"Yes?"

"You said you want the stagecoach specially prepared. Exactly what do you mean?"

"Have the Wells Fargo people build a false bottom underneath the coach floor. If it's five inches deep, it'll look to be just a part of the stage, but it'll be sufficient to hold the gold. Tell them to bill the bank, in care of me, for the cost."

"All right, sir."

"Chief Cofer and I discussed this on the way over here," Harris said. "There's a Wells Fargo stage out of Topeka to Wichita on Monday, Wednesday, and Friday mornings. We want the gold on that stage on Friday. One of the stops is Emporia. Chief Cofer will arrange to have the gold taken off the stage at Emporia by an army unit out of Fort Scott. They will carry it to my bank here in Kansas City.

"We figure that if the James-Younger gang is somehow still functional by then, they won't be able to track the gold no matter what, since Gordon will be keeping all of this a secret except for those most trusted railroad employees who have to know about it."

"You gentlemen have it well planned," Wheaton said. "Gordon, you can go now. Make these arrangements and report back to me at my home."

"I will, sir."

"And Gordon…"

"Yes, sir?"

"Make sure you only give this information to those you trust; impress upon them the importance of total secrecy."

"I'll take care of it, sir."

When Gordon Naylor was gone, Wheaton said, "I'll come to the bank first thing in the morning, Edmund, and let you know how Gordon has fared with Wells Fargo on this." Then he added to Cofer, "I'll come to your office after I've been to the bank, Chief, and advise you too."

"No need for that," said Cofer. "I'll be at Edmund's office by eight o'clock so we can both hear it from you at the same time. That way, if there is some problem or difficulty that needs working out, we can handle it together."

✦

That evening at the Younger farm, Ginny Grayson and Wes Logan were taking a moonlight walk. As they strolled leisurely, holding hands, Ginny was unusually quiet. Looking down at her, Wes said, "Honey, is something bothering you?"

She stared straight ahead. "I guess you could say that."

Wes planted his feet, bringing them to a stop. "Come on, now. What is it?"

Ginny shook her head. "Maybe it's best that I keep it to myself."

"Hey, sweetheart. We shouldn't keep secrets from each other."

She looked up at him with narrowed eyes and a frown on her forehead.

"Well, I know I kept some secrets from you, but I explained it all."

"Mm-hmm. I don't really think you could call this a secret. It's just that—"

"That what?"

"Well…"

"Come on. Out with it. Did I do something wrong?"

"Yes, you did."

"When?"

"In Olathe, when I was wanting to help Lefty escape with us. Cole snapped at me, and I understand that he wanted me to go at that instant." A pained look etched itself on Ginny's face. "But you snapped at me, too. Quite sharply. It stung me, Wes."

"Oh. Well, I guess I was just concerned that we get out of there. We were in a pretty dangerous position."

Ginny bit her lower lip. "I didn't know you had it in you to

196

snap at me like that…to speak to me in that harsh tone."

Wes pulled her to him and looked down into her tear-filmed eyes. "I'm sorry, honey. It was a tense moment. I really didn't mean to be harsh."

She laid her head against his chest. "See what I meant? I should have kept it to myself."

"Oh, no. It's best that you told me how you felt. I'll be very careful never to snap at you again. I love you."

"I love you, too."

He held her a long moment, then said, "Am I forgiven?"

Easing back to look into his eyes, she smiled faintly and said, "You're forgiven."

Wes grinned. "Whew! I'm glad for that. I couldn't stand it if you wouldn't forgive me."

She gave him her hand and they continued walking.

After a few silent seconds, Wes said, "I was thinking earlier, Ginny…"

"Mm-hmm?"

"Cole and Jesse told us how much gold is going to be on that train tomorrow. I did a little figuring in my head, and with our combined shares it will be enough to put us over the goal we set for ourselves."

"Really? I hadn't bothered to try to total it up."

"Well, I added it up three times. We'll have over one hundred fifty thousand dollars."

Moonlight danced in Ginny's suddenly wide eyes. "Oh, Wes! It's wonderful! You mean, once the gold is in our hands, we can pull out of the gang, get married, and head to faraway places?"

"That's exactly what I mean! We'll turn the gold into cash when we're in some safe place."

"Oh, I'm so glad! I—"

"What?"

"Well, today in Olathe when the shooting started, a bullet whizzed past my cheek. Another inch—even a fraction of an inch closer—and I'd have been killed. I'm glad this outlaw life of ours is almost over."

"It is," said Wes, leaning down to kiss her lips lightly. "We're about to begin our brand-new life."

"Oh yes! Our brand-new very rich life!"

When Wes and Ginny returned to the farmhouse, they settled down in the parlor to join the gang in talking about the big train robbery.

A lone rider trotted his horse cautiously into the farmyard.

Sly Chapman and Jim Reed were that night's sentries. They stood behind huge cottonwood trees some twenty yards from the front of the house.

Working the levers of their carbines, they peered around the cottonwoods and waited for the rider to draw nearer. When he was close enough, both of them emerged from the shadows, and Chapman said, "Hold it right there, mister!"

The rider's face was an alabaster mask in the moonlight as he pulled rein and said, "Fellas, my name is Gordie Naylor. I'm a longtime friend of Cole Younger and also a friend of Jesse James. I need to see them."

"Gordie Naylor," repeated Reed. "This better be important. They're about to hit the sack."

"It is very important," Naylor assured him.

"All right. You stay here with Mr. Chapman. I'll be right back."

Jim walked briskly to the house and mounted the porch steps to tap on the door. When it opened, he was looking at Frank James.

"We've got a lone rider out here who says he needs to see Cole and Jesse right now. Says it's very important. Name's Gordie Naylor."

By this time, the low rumble of voices inside the parlor had dwindled to nothing.

"What is it, Frank?" came Jesse's voice.

"Jim says there's a rider out here who wants to talk to you and Cole. Name's Gordie Naylor."

"Bring him in here!" Cole said loudly.

When Naylor was ushered into the parlor, he set serious eyes on Cole and Jesse and said, "Do you want to talk privately, or does it matter now?"

Cole said, "I assume this is about—?"

"Yes. There's been a change. That's why I came here without an invitation."

"Somethin's wrong?" said Cole, brow furrowed.

"Not really. Just a change you have to know about."

Cole and Jesse huddled close, whispering to each other. When they finished, Cole turned back and said, "We'll talk right here in front of the bunch. Before we do, I want everybody in here. Frank, since you're right there by the door, will you tell Jim and Sly to come in?"

When the sentries entered, Jim went to the chair where Belle sat, and stood behind her.

Cole motioned to Naylor and said, "C'mere, Gordie."

Cole put an arm around the man's shoulder and said to the rest of the gang, "My brothers and Jesse know this man, but the rest of you don't. This is Gordie Naylor, assistant to one of the vice presidents of Union Pacific Railroad. Gordie used to live on a neighborin' farm about half a mile east of here. Us Younger boys and Gordie grew up together...went to school together. We're pals. Right, Gordie?"

Naylor smiled. "Right, Cole."

"The reason we could plan to rob the train tomorrow with all that gold on it is because Gordie—as a trusted employee of

Union Pacific—is the one who gave us the information. Jesse and I paid him handsomely for the information. Right, Jesse?"

"That's correct."

"We didn't tell any of you how we got the information about the gold shipment," said Cole. "And probably wouldn't have. But since Gordie's here, we want all of you to know that he's a mighty good friend of the gang. Without him, we wouldn't be gettin' filthy rich off this gold robbery."

"Then hooray for Gordie!" spoke up Clell Miller.

There was a chorus of voices speaking their agreement.

"You won't remember all these names, Gordie," said Cole, "but I want you to hear 'em, anyhow."

When Cole had pointed out each face, along with the name, Naylor was surprised to see two women. He had heard much about Belle Reed but didn't know the gang now had another female member.

Chairs were placed so the gang leaders and Naylor could sit down facing the others.

"Okay, Gordie," said Cole. "What's this change you came to tell us about?"

Naylor had everybody's rapt attention as he told them about Lefty Carson giving the authorities the information about the gang's plan to rob the Cheyenne City–Kansas City train of its gold shipment.

"I shoulda shot him before we left the scene!" growled Cole.

"One of us should have," said Jesse. "Low-down traitor. I hope they hang him. Go on, Gordie."

Naylor went on to explain that Edmund Harris of Kansas City Bank and Trust, and Chief U.S. Marshal Layton Cofer had come to the office at the railroad station and told Roger Wheaton and himself that they had to change plans for the gold shipment because the James-Younger gang had found out about it.

Naylor laughed. "Wheaton was very upset because he knew someone within the Union Pacific offices was feeding the information to you."

"Gordie," Jesse said, "how many people employed by Union Pacific know about the gold shipment?"

Naylor thought on it a moment, counting silently on his fingers. "There'd be sixteen. Seventeen, with me. That's office people here and in Denver and Cheyenne City. The men who do the loading and unloading of the baggage cars don't know anything in advance."

"Mm-hmm," said Jesse. "Well, seventeen is enough to spread the suspicion around so you won't be in any danger, I'd say."

"That's going to narrow considerably with what I'm about to tell you."

Naylor went on to explain that Harris had Wheaton delay the gold shipment until Wednesday. It would be on the same trains out of Denver and Cheyenne City. When the train arrived in Topeka Wednesday evening, the gold would be taken off and the train would go on to Kansas City without it. This would take the gold off the train before it reached the trestle.

As further insurance, in case something went wrong and the gang wasn't apprehended at the trestle Tuesday afternoon, the gold would be transferred to a specially equipped Wells Fargo stagecoach under cover of darkness. It would be under heavy guard during the night and leave Topeka on Friday morning, making its regular run to Wichita.

Jim Younger laughed. "Well, we ain't gonna get apprehended, 'cause we won't be there!"

There was a round of laughter.

"At the present time," said Naylor, "the stage is being worked on inside the Wells Fargo barn in Topeka. It's being rigged with a special compartment under the floor, which is undetectable from normal angles. When the stage stops in Emporia, there will be an army unit out of Fort Scott to meet it. The soldiers will load the gold into an army wagon and deliver it to Edmund Harris at Kansas City Bank and Trust. The way I see it, Cole, Jesse, is you'll need to stop the stage before it reaches Emporia."

"I was thinkin' the same thing," said Cole.

"Me too," put in Jesse. "That would be the safest way to do it. Gordie, we really appreciate your riding all the way out here to let us know about the change in plans."

"Yes, sir," said Cole. "You're a real pal. If we showed up at that trestle tomorrow, there'd no doubt be a battalion of federal marshals there to greet us."

"I'd like to see the look on their ugly faces when we don't show up!" said Belle, chuckling.

Naylor looked at Cole and Jesse. "This is where the list of suspects will narrow. I have to keep the new plan a secret except to four other people in the Union Pacific offices. When you boys stop that stage south of Topeka and take the gold, my boss is going to really put the pressure on to find out who in the company has given the information to the James-Younger gang."

"You knew it was risky to begin with, Gordie," said Cole. "But Jesse and I paid you well. Right?"

Naylor stood up. "You sure did, Cole. The generous amount you paid me covers even the new risk. Well, I'd better get home."

Cole pulled a wad of bills out of his pocket, peeled off a sizable amount, and slapped them into Naylor's hand. "Gordie, thanks again. Here's a little bonus for your extra risk."

Naylor thanked him, and Cole and Jesse followed him to his horse. They watched as he rode away and was soon swallowed by the night.

14

THE DUB THAXTON GANG WERE HIDING OUT at an old farmhouse a few miles east of Kansas City after pulling off a series of robberies in Nebraska and Iowa. They had added another gang member to take Lambert's place—a tough, brutal outlaw named Earl Kopatch.

Ernie Mills yawned and looked around at the other men sitting on the front porch. Night sounds filled the air and a full moon bathed the surroundings in a soft glow.

"Hey, guys," Ernie said, "it must be past midnight. I think I'll drag this tired body to bed."

Nate Roach struck a match on the porch railing and held his pocket watch up to the flame. "You're right, Ernie. Its twenty-one minutes after twelve. Guess we'd better hit the sack."

"One nice thing about our business, boys," came the husky voice of Dub Thaxton, "we ain't got no place to report in for work in the mornin'. Monday just left us, and accordin' to Nate's watch, it's been Tuesday for twenty-one minutes. If we wanna sleep till the crack o' noon, so what?"

Everybody laughed.

Earl Kopatch was still laughing when he turned his eyes toward the shadowed face of his boss and said, "Dub, I tell yuh. I'm plenty glad you invited me to join the gang after your brother got killed. I've picked up more money since I joined you than I made in the previous four years."

"Well, I'm glad you're happy about it, Earl, 'cause we're all plenty glad to have you. You've shown us many a time that you c'n carry your weight when we're robbin' and stealin' money. Why, just the other day, I was thinkin'—"

Thaxton's words were cut off by the sound of galloping hooves.

Instantly, every man was on his feet, gun in hand.

"Keep calm, boys," said Dub, holding his own cocked weapon. "Could be somebody friendly or somebody just passin' by."

The rider turned onto the place.

"Well, he ain't passin' by," said Ray Dodd. "But for his sake, he'd better be friendly."

The rider slowed his horse to a walk about forty yards from the house and called out, "Dub! You there on the porch?"

"Yeah, I'm one of 'em," Thaxton replied. "Sounds like Gordie Naylor."

"You're right, it's Gordie! I figured I'd have to talk a guard into wakin' you up."

"We're stayin' up a little late, Gordie. Just got back from Nebraska. Come on in."

As Naylor drew up and dismounted, Dub said, "Fellas, I'd like all of yuh to meet Gordie Naylor. He's a big shot with Union Pacific in Kansas City."

When Naylor reached the top of the porch steps, Thaxton extended his hand and said to his men, "Gordie and I go back about a hundred years. Well, that might be stretchin' it a bit, but we been friends for a long time. He's done me and Lambert many a favor and shown himself to be a friend. Ran onto him a while back on Twenty-fifth Street in Kansas City...just after

Lambert was killed. Since he's my friend, I told him where we were hidin' out and invited him to come and see me sometime. So what brings yuh out here at this time o' night, ol' pal?"

"Two hundred thousand dollars worth of gold. There's a shipment comin' out of Denver, and it's all yours if you're willing to hold up a stage to get it."

This had everyone's instant and complete attention. Suddenly Ernie Mills was no longer sleepy.

"Well, let's go in the house and sit down where we can see each other," said Thaxton.

As Gordon Naylor followed the tall, thick-bodied gang leader, he smiled to himself. *With the fee I charge Dub, and the money Cole Younger has already paid me, I can hightail it for California to start a new life.*

When the lanterns were lit and everyone was seated, Dub said, "I know even though you're a big-shot railroad man, you still don't make real big money. How much will you take to give me this information about the gold?"

"Well, I figured since we're friends, Dub, I'd ask for 5 percent."

"Five percent. Ten thousand?"

"That's it." Gordie grinned. "In advance, of course."

"You're sure we'll be able to get our hands on it?"

"Without a doubt."

"Okay. The ten thousand is yours." Dub turned to Frank Baldwin. "Go get ten thousand for my friend Gordie."

Baldwin was back in short order and laid the money in Dub's hand.

"You wanna count it?" Dub said with a grin.

"Course not. I trust Frank because he's one of your men."

"Good. The money's yours if I like the setup."

↑

Later, as Gordon Naylor rode away from the old farmhouse, his pockets were stuffed with money. He chuckled to himself, envisioning how it would turn out when both gangs showed up to rob the stage somewhere south of Topeka.

On Wednesday morning, October 4, just an hour after Chief U.S. Marshal John Brockman left home for work, Breanna looked through a parlor window and saw the retired chief U.S. marshal, Solomon Duvall, riding up to the house.

As she moved toward the front door, an unwelcome thought passed through her mind. Since retiring, Solomon had always filled in for John at the office when he had to leave town.

The silver-haired widower smiled as he topped the porch steps and the door swung open. "Mornin', Breanna."

"Good morning, Solomon," she said, returning the smile. "I'd like to think you just came by to see me, but I have this strange feeling that John has had to leave town and you're here as acting chief U.S. marshal to tell me about it."

Duvall chuckled. "What is it about you females, anyway? Seems like the Lord gave you an inside track on figurin' males out. My mother had it and my wife had it."

"So where's my husband gone, and how long till he gets back?"

"Well, I can tell you where he's going, but I'm not exactly sure when he'll be back. There was a telegram waiting for him when he got to the office this morning. It was from Chief U.S. Marshal Layton Cofer in Kansas City."

"Yes. I met him once when I was with John on a trip to

Washington, D.C. He came to the depot and spent about an hour with us between trains."

"Well, John sent for me after reading the telegram. From what he said when I got there, it actually came late last night but wasn't delivered to the office until just before he got there this morning. He said to tell you he's really sorry he won't be able to go with you and Dottie to Emporia, but duty calls."

"Mm-hmm. We talked about it when he took the appointment from President Grant and pinned on the badge. I knew there would be times like this."

Duvall explained the situation concerning the gold shipment. Chief Cofer's wire requested that John put as many federal deputy marshals on the train as possible to protect the gold in case the gang tried again. "But the Denver U.S. marshal's office is already shorthanded, so John assigned the only three deputies he had available and went along with them to make the fourth man to guard the gold."

He explained that the four men were now on the Denver train headed for Cheyenne City, where they would board the Kansas City–bound train.

"It was a rush thing, Breanna. In order to get John and his deputies on the train with the gold, they had to hold the train for a half hour. It'll still reach Cheyenne City in time to get them and the gold on the train to Kansas City."

"I see," said Breanna. "So John won't be headed home until he and his men have safely escorted the gold to its destination in Kansas City?"

"That's right. And that destination is the Kansas City Bank and Trust Company."

Breanna rubbed her forehead. "Did John say anything about trying to come to Emporia from Kansas City for the anniversary celebration?"

"He said he'd like to, but he has no idea exactly how long he might be tied-up. So he said to tell you if he doesn't make it, it's because he just couldn't. If that's the case, he wants you to tell your family he's sorry he didn't get to come."

Disappointment showed on Breanna's lovely features. "I'll explain it so they understand."

"I hear Matt won't be able to go either because of the medical convention this weekend."

"That's right. Looks like it will be just sis and me."

"Well, I hope you have a good time, Breanna."

She released a weak smile. "I'm sure we will. It just won't be the same without our husbands."

"It's too bad. I know you both would like to show your husbands off to your relatives."

"Some other time, I guess. Solomon?"

"Yes'm?"

"Would you mind stopping by the Carroll house when you get back to town? Tell Dottie about John not going?"

"Be glad to."

"Thank you. And thanks for letting me know the situation."

"My pleasure, Breanna. Well, I'd better get going. They'll need me at the office, I'm sure."

It was ten o'clock on Wednesday morning when Deputy Wayne Peters entered the office of Chief U.S. Marshal Layton Cofer. He was carrying a yellow envelope.

"That from Chief Brockman?" Cofer asked.

"Yes, sir." Peters handed the envelope to his boss.

"Sure hope it's good news." A smile broke over Cofer's face as he read the lines.

"He must have put some deputies on the train with the gold," surmised the deputy.

"Not as many as I would like. Only four of them. John's shorthanded, according to what he says here. But I feel a whole lot better because Chief John Brockman himself is one of the four men."

"Great!" said Peters. "From what I know about him, his presence is like having an army!"

"You've got that right," said Cofer.

The deputy rubbed the back of his neck. "Ah…Chief?"

"Mm-hmm?"

"Do you suppose you should have told Chief Brockman about the plan to take the gold off the train at Topeka and transfer it to the stagecoach?"

Cofer snapped his fingers. "I probably should have. I was just trying to keep the telegram as brief as possible." He shrugged. "Oh, well. The railroad people will have to tell him sometime before the train reaches Topeka. He probably already knows it by now. It'll be all right."

On Thursday morning, October 5, Matt Carroll pulled his buggy into the parking lot at Denver's Union Station. The sun was barely topping the eastern horizon.

He hopped out of the buggy and hurried around to the other side to help Breanna and Dottie alight.

The women carried their overnight bags while the doctor carried their two heavy suitcases. As they headed for the terminal building, Matt hefted the suitcases a bit higher than normal and said, "You'd think you girls were going to be gone a month with all the stuff you must've crammed in these!"

Dottie playfully punched his arm. "Matthew Carroll, you

know it takes a lot more luggage for a woman to travel than a man. We like to wear something different every day. You men can travel light because the only thing you ever change are your long johns!"

Breanna laughed. "Yes, and sometimes you go a long time before you even do that!"

"Forget I said anything," Matt said, shaking his head.

The Cheyenne City–bound train had been in the depot all night, but the boiler in the engine was already hot, and steam was hissing from its sides.

Matt checked the suitcases with the baggage man and escorted the women aboard the train. When he had put their overnight bags in the rack, the bell on the engine began to clang and they heard the conductor's voice outside the coach calling for everyone to board.

Matt leaned past Dottie and kissed Breanna's cheek. "Sis, I'm sorry John couldn't go along, but maybe he'll show up at Emporia in time for the festivities."

"I hope so. I sure wish you could come too."

"So do I, but as John would put it, duty calls."

The doctor kissed his wife tenderly on the lips and reminded her that he loved her and would miss her; then he left the coach.

Moments later, the engine's whistle cut through the air, steam hissed from its bowels, the wheels spun on the steel tracks throwing out sparks, and the train began rolling. Dottie and Breanna waved to Matt and soon were out of sight.

On Friday morning, October 6, Dottie and Breanna sat side by side in the buggy carrying them from the Sunflower Hotel to Topeka's Wells Fargo office.

"I miss Matt and the children already," said Dottie. "This is the first time I've ever been away from them for more than a few hours."

"Well, even though John and I have been apart so much since we married, I never get used to it. I miss him terribly each time we're apart."

"Wait till you have children to miss, honey. That'll be real hard. Believe me."

"When the Lord gives me children, Dottie, I won't be doing this traveling nurse business anymore."

"Of course not. That would be impossible. You certainly couldn't take a baby with you."

Breanna smiled to herself, thinking, *That might be happening sooner than you imagine, sweet sister.*

"Here's the Wells Fargo office, ladies," said the driver, swinging the buggy up close to the stagecoach that was being loaded.

The driver hopped out and helped Breanna down, saying, "I'll take your overnight bag and check it along with the others, ma'am."

"I'd rather keep it, sir. I'm a nurse, and I keep my medical bag in here."

"Oh, certainly. I understand."

The driver stepped up to Dottie's side of the buggy. "Would you like to keep your overnight bag too, ma'am?"

"No. You can give it to the stagecoach crew to put in the boot or in the rack along with our suitcases."

The driver helped Dottie down, then busied himself with their luggage.

When the driver was paid, the sisters entered the Wells Fargo office to purchase their tickets. There were two well-dressed men standing near the counter, both putting money into their wallets.

The agent smiled at Dottie and Breanna. "May I help you, ladies?"

While the agent was making out their tickets, he said to the men, "Gentlemen, these two ladies will be riding on the stage with you. As far as Emporia, that is. This lady with the parasol is Mrs. Dorothy Carroll. And this lady is Mrs. Breanna Brockman." He flicked a glance between them and commented, "You look so much alike, you have to be sisters."

"We are, sir," said Breanna.

The agent smiled. "Ladies, the gentleman in the gray suit is Mr. Will Hoffman, and the gentlemen in the blue suit is Mr. Darold Marley."

Hoffman and Marley greeted them with a partial bow, and Dottie and Breanna made a slight curtsy.

"Will and I are from Wichita," said Marley. "We're partners in the Hoffman-Marley Clothing Company. We have clothing stores in four southern Kansas towns. Our home office is in Wichita."

"How nice," said Dottie. "And you have families?'

"We do," said Marley. "Will and his wife have a son and daughter who are both married. And he has one grandchild. My wife and I have three daughters—two are married. No grandchildren yet. I assume both of you are married?"

"Yes," Breanna said. "My husband, John, is the chief United States marshal over the western district of the country. His office is in Denver."

"I see," said Hoffman, eyebrows arched. "Chief U.S. marshal. I'm impressed." Then he said to Dottie, "And your husband? What does he do?"

"Matt is a medical doctor, Mr. Hoffman. He's chief administrator of Mile High Hospital in Denver."

"A medical doctor. Well, at least you can get sick for nothing."

Dottie chuckled. "Well, yes. That I can."

"Any children, ladies?" asked Marley.

"I have two," said Dottie. "A boy and a girl. Breanna doesn't have any children yet."

Breanna smiled at her.

"She's a certified medical nurse," Dottie added.

"A certified medical nurse," echoed Darold Marley. "Looks like medicine kind of runs in the family."

"You might say that," Breanna said.

Will Hoffman ran his gaze over the faces of both women. "Pardon me, ladies. You told the agent that you're sisters, but I just have to ask…are you not-quite-identical twin sisters?"

Dottie laughed, twirling the parasol on her shoulder. "This isn't the first time we've been asked that question, Mr. Hoffman. No. We're not twins. One of us is two years older than the other, and I'm not going to tell you which one."

Both men laughed, and Marley said, "We wouldn't expect you to, ma'am."

While Dottie and Breanna were inside the Wells Fargo office, Dub Thaxton and Earl Kopatch rode in and pulled up to the hitching rail across the street. As they dismounted, they eyed the team, the stagecoach, and the two men who were loading luggage onto the rack.

Thaxton had told Kopatch that since they were going to rob the stage, he wanted to see how many passengers would be on it and whether they were men or women.

They crossed the wide, dusty street and casually moved up to the feed and supply store next door to the Wells Fargo office. They leaned against the front of the store where they could hear anything that was said in the space between the stagecoach and the front door of the office.

Dub studied the coach and said, "You sure can't tell they have a secret compartment under the floor where the gold is stashed, can you?"

"Nope," Earl agreed. "They did a good job on it." He chuckled evilly. "But we know it's there, don't we?"

"Sure do," said Dub. "Thanks to my friend, Gordie Naylor."

Inside the Wells Fargo office, Dottie and Breanna put their change and ticket stubs in their purses.

"Breanna," said Dottie, "I'm going to the powder room."

"I'll go on outside," Breanna told her.

Breanna picked up her overnight bag and headed toward the door. Both Hoffman and Marley moved in front of her, offering to carry the bag.

"It's really not very heavy, gentlemen, I—"

"Nonetheless," said Darold Marley, taking it from her, "I'll carry it for you."

Breanna flashed him a smile. "Thank you."

As she and the two men moved outside, they were unaware of Dub Thaxton and Earl Kopatch watching them. As they moved toward the stagecoach at a leisurely pace, Will Hoffman said, "Mrs. Brockman, since you're a certified medical nurse, do you always carry your medical bag with you?"

"Oh yes. Never know when I might need it. The medical bag is inside the bag Mr. Marley is carrying."

Thaxton and Kopatch watched Breanna and the two men draw up to the coach and heard Breanna tell the shotgunner and driver why she needed the overnight bag close at hand.

Thaxton leaned close to Kopatch and whispered. "So

they've got a nurse ridin' this one."

Kopatch chortled. "Yeah! And ain't she a beauty? Maybe after we unload all that heavy gold from the secret compartment in the floor, we'll need her to rub some salve on our sore arms!"

At that instant, the Fargo agent came out of the office and move up to the stage. The driver and shotgunner were checking the harness.

Will Hoffman looked at the agent and said, "Is it just the four of us? Or will there be more passengers?"

"Well, besides Mrs. Brockman and Mrs. Carroll, there are two more ladies booked on the stage. They should be arriving any minute."

"Okay," Thaxton said to his cohort. "We can go now."

They crossed the street and mounted their horses. Kopatch turned back to look at Breanna. "That nurse is really good-lookin'. I'd almost welcome bein' sick just to have her takin' care of me!"

"Yeah. Havin' her around would make gettin' sick worth it."

They touched spurs to their horses' sides and rode out of town.

While Breanna chatted with the two businessmen, a buggy pulled up and two young women alighted, wearing fancy dresses. They both carried large purses and lifted overnight bags out of the buggy. The driver grinned at them and drove away.

The agent hurried to greet them and took their overnight bags, handing them over to the shotgunner. He turned back to the women. "Come on inside, ladies. I'll get your tickets for you."

As the women started to follow the agent, Breanna noticed

that the pretty one, who had long auburn hair, was looking at her as if she recognized her. When their eyes met, the lovely girl looked away and hurried to catch up to her traveling companion.

Just as the two young women stepped up on the porch, Dottie came out the door. She stopped and exclaimed, "Ginny! Is that you?"

Ginny Grayson's eyelids fluttered, and her face tinted.

Breanna observed with interest when Ginny looked back at her and said, "Dottie, I thought that lady was you!"

Dottie laughed. "She's my sister." She motioned to Breanna. "Honey, come here. I have someone I want you to meet."

Belle was looking on nervously as Breanna moved toward them.

"Breanna, I want you to meet Ginny Grayson—" She paused, looked down at Ginny's left hand, and seeing no ring, said, "It's still Grayson, I assume?"

"Yes," said Ginny. "I'm not married yet."

Dottied looked at her sister. "This is Ginny Grayson, Breanna. I knew Ginny and her parents in San Francisco. I was with her when her father died." Then she said to Ginny, "Your mother…"

"She died, too."

"Oh, I'm so sorry. Well, Ginny, I want you to meet my sister, Breanna Brockman."

When they had greeted each other, Ginny turned to her partner and introduced her as Maybelle Shirley. She told Maybelle that Dottie had been a good friend to her as she was growing up and often slipped money to her to help buy groceries for the Grayson family.

"Ladies," the Fargo agent said, "I hate to butt in, but we've got to get the tickets taken care of so we can get the stage on the road."

Dottie and Breanna remained outside while Belle and Ginny went into the office with the agent.

As soon as they had their tickets, Ginny took Belle by the arm and led her to a far corner of the station. "Belle, I can't put a gun on Dottie! We're friends. Very good friends. She's done so much for me."

Belle's unpleasant features went rock hard. She scowled and said, "You have to, girlie! Cole and Jesse expect you to do your job! You'll be in deep trouble if you don't!"

Ginny felt sick to her stomach as she and Belle moved outside. Breanna and Dottie were already inside the coach.

Ginny covered her feelings and forced a smile when Will Hoffman offered his hand to assist her into the stagecoach.

When everyone was seated, the two men introduced themselves to Belle and Ginny. A few seconds later the crew stepped up to the windows on the right side of the coach. The driver said, "Folks, we'd like you to know who's up top. This handsome young man next to me is your shotgunner, Bert Hughes. And I'm your driver, Zack Lee."

The passengers all murmured greetings, then the driver and shotgunner climbed up to the box. Zack Lee put the team in motion and the stage headed south out of town, leaving a cloud of dust.

15

DUB THAXTON AND EARL KOPATCH rode to a spot about ten miles south of Topeka and trotted their horses off the road into a large wooded area where the rest of the gang waited.

The two newest members, Cade Sheridan and Mel Fixx, saw them first and called to the others that Dub and Earl were back.

"So what's the story, Dub?" Ray Dodd asked.

Dub hitched at his gun belt. "The stage has two men on it and four women."

Everybody laughed, and Cade Sheridan was the first to speak their sentiments: "Hey, that's great, Dub! With only two men aboard, other than the driver and shotgunner, we won't have any trouble takin' the gold off the stage."

"For sure," spoke up Tom Portell. "Women never resist durin' a robbery. They're always too scared."

"And if those two men on that stage even look like they're gonna give us a hard time, we'll gun 'em down," put in Earl Kopatch.

A little more than half a mile northward, the James-Younger gang was hiding in the deep shade of another wooded area.

Keeping their voices somewhat hushed, they talked about the haul they were going to make that day. Excitement was high, for they all knew this would be the most lucrative single robbery they had ever pulled.

While the other men were carrying on, Wes Logan smiled to himself. This would be the robbery that freed Ginny and him from the outlaw trail. Soon they would be long gone and never have to rob anyone again.

Above the rumble of low-toned voices came the pounding of hooves and the rattle of a buggy. They turned to see the horse and buggy weaving amongst the trees toward them.

Bob Younger drew rein and slowed down. "Well, guys, Belle and Ginny are on the stage by now. As far as I could tell the stage was leavin' on time. The crew had luggage loaded in the rack."

"Good," said Jesse. "I like for things to happen as planned."

Jim Reed laughed heartily. "I'd sure like to be on one of them stages when Belle and Ginny whip out their guns and tell the poor unsuspectin' passengers they're about to be robbed!"

Jesse was still laughing as he said, "Yeah! Me too! Must be quite a shock when two innocent-looking females suddenly put a gun on you!"

"I tell you, Belle's a genius," said Reed. "An absolute genius."

"That's for sure," agreed Jesse. "If you aren't careful, Jim, she'll be gettin' a bigger cut than you!"

Cole Younger turned to brother Bob. "I assume the girls picked out a landmark out there on the road so they know exactly when to pull their guns."

"Sure did," said Bob, grinning gleefully. "It's that bridge up the road a couple hundred yards from here. They'll have the passengers well covered by the time we spring outta the brush."

✦

As the stagecoach rolled down the road, nettling daggers of dread pierced Ginny Grayson's thoughts. How was she going to put a gun on Dottie? She could feel the pressure of Belle's eyes on her as she said, "Dottie, I still think about Jerrod a lot, and his awful death in the fire."

The memory of her first husband's death was still a bitter one for Dottie. "I think a lot about it, too," she replied. "But when he made the rescue attempt, thinking that the life-sized doll was Molly Kate, in a sense he died a hero."

Breanna set her eyes on Ginny. "That's the way everyone in the family tries to look at it. Jerrod Harper died a hero."

Ginny glanced out her window, her stomach in a knot as she looked for the bridge. As soon as it came into view she would have to pull her gun.

She turned back to Dottie. "I was happy for you when you married Dr. Carroll. Of course I hated to see you leave San Francisco when Dr. Carroll took that position as chief administrator at Mile High Hospital. Is he still there?"

"Sure is. He loves his job. Breanna works at the hospital a lot when she's not traveling and doing her visiting nurse jobs."

Ginny felt Belle's eyes on her again as she flicked a glance at Breanna and said, "I didn't realize you were a nurse. Are you a C.M.N.?"

Breanna smiled at her and nodded.

Turning her gaze back to Dottie, Ginny said, "And how about James and Molly Kate? How are they doing?"

"Growing like weeds. Especially James. He's stringing out a lot. I think he's going to be a tall one."

"I'd sure love to see them."

"Well, maybe you can come to Denver and visit us sometime.

We have two guest rooms in our house. You'd sure be welcome."

Ginny pressed a smile on her lips and said, "I'll just do that." As the words came from her mouth, she flicked a glance at Belle and felt the sting of her smoldering eyes.

Ginny quickly returned her gaze to the sisters. "So where are you going, Dottie?"

"We're headed for Emporia. We have an aunt and uncle there who are having their fiftieth wedding anniversary."

"Oh, how nice. I'm sure they'll be thrilled to see you."

"I'm curious about you being in Kansas," said Dottie. "Are you living in this state now?"

As Belle listened intently, Ginny lied, saying, "Yes, I am. Maybelle and I live on neighboring farms near El Dorado. That's down near Wichita."

"Yes, we know. Breanna and I are from Kansas. Born and raised here...near Topeka."

"Oh, yes. Now I remember. You used to talk a lot about Kansas. And, of course, that's why you have relatives here."

"That's it. So you two live on neighboring farms?"

"Mm-hmm. The Shirleys are good friends with my aunt and uncle. I've been living with them since shortly after Mom died. It didn't take long for Maybelle and me to become friends. We've been in Topeka visiting some relatives of hers."

Ginny casually glanced out the window and judged they were now about a mile from the bridge.

Belle twisted a bit on the seat so she could look Breanna in the eye, and said, "We know what your sister's husband does, Mrs. Brockman. What about your husband?"

Breanna smiled. "John is the chief United States marshal of the Western District. His office is in Denver."

Belle felt her heart turn to lead, and she was suddenly aware of her fingernails digging half-moons into her palms. It took effort to paint a smile on her lips, but she did, murmuring, "That's nice."

The James-Younger gang sat their horses in a stand of trees. Bob Younger waited tensely in his buggy, ready to pull in front of the stagecoach when it reached the ambush spot. At the moment, the gang was completely out of sight from the road in the deep shadows of the oaks, willows, and cottonwoods.

Suddenly, Rufe Orvick, a recent addition to the Younger half of the gang, announced, "Here comes the stage!"

Belle stared out the window as the stage bobbed and weaved along the dusty road. When she saw the bridge coming up, she slipped her hand inside her purse and closed her fingers around the butt of the .36 caliber pistol, easing back the hammer.

She turned her face to Ginny, who was already looking at her, and gave a tiny nod.

Ginny's lips compressed as she slid her hand inside her purse. Her heart thundered in her chest and the knot in her stomach tightened.

The stage rolled onto the bridge, and when it dropped off seconds later, a tense Ginny Grayson watched Belle's hand. When Belle brought out the cocked pistol, Ginny did the same.

The four passengers' faces registered shock when they found themselves looking into the threatening black muzzles. Belle spoke in a subdued voice so the crew up in the box couldn't hear her. "Sit still and keep your mouths shut! This stage is bein' robbed by the Jesse James–Cole Younger gang, and if you wanna live, you do as you're told!"

Dottie and Breanna stared wordlessly at Ginny as she held the gun steady. She averted her eyes from theirs.

Belle set dangerous eyes on the two men and said, "Okay, fellas, if you're wearin' shoulder holsters, I want you to reach in very careful-like and take out your guns. Make a fast move and you're dead."

"I'm not wearing a gun," said Hoffman, his face void of color. "And neither is Darold."

Belle's gaze flicked to Marley. "That so?"

"Yes."

A scowl etched itself on Belle's homely face. "Open your coats and show me!"

When they obeyed, and Belle saw no holsters, she was satisfied. "Okay. Sit still and don't move. Jesse and Cole and the boys will be along any second."

Up in the box, Zack Lee and Bert Hughes stiffened as a buggy suddenly pulled out in front of them. The team was already coming to a stop as Lee pulled back on the reins. "We've got us a holdup, Bert," Lee said.

Abruptly, the coach was surrounded by more than a dozen mean-looking riders, each one wielding a gun.

One of the riders drew up and snarled at the driver and shotgunner. "Throw those guns down! I'm Jesse James, and you know what'll happen if you try anything funny!"

Cole Younger jerked open the stagecoach door and shouted, "Passengers outside! Line up! I'm Cole Younger, and you know what'll happen if you don't do as I say! A lot of people didn't, and a lot of people are six feet under!"

While the passengers were filing out, with Dottie giving Ginny a look of consternation, the crew's guns plopped to the soft earth.

"All right, you two," said Jesse, keeping his gun lined on

driver and shotgunner, "throw the cash box down!"

"We ain't carryin' one on this trip," said Zack Lee. "You can come up and look for yourself."

"I'll take your word for it," said Jesse. "You two stand up on the seat and keep your hands in the air."

Lee and Hughes obeyed and were shocked to hear Jesse James command four of the gang members to rip the bottom off the coach and get the gold.

They were equally shocked when Cole spoke to two of their female passengers and said, "Belle, Ginny, you did good. I assume you took the guns off these two dudes."

"They didn't have any," said Belle, flashing a smile at her husband as he headed for the coach, carrying a crowbar. Frank James, Clell Miller, and Arch Clements were with him, carrying hammers.

The rest of the gang made a partial circle around the coach while Belle and Ginny held the passengers at gunpoint. Cole told Sly Chapman to relieve the two male passengers of their wallets.

While this was being done, Wes Logan stepped up to Ginny, only then noticing that she was quite upset about something. "What's bothering you?" he asked.

Ginny's eyes darted to Dottie. "I'll tell you later."

Wes moved on and joined the rest of the gang as they carried gold bars to Bob Younger's buggy, loading them on the floor and in the space behind the seat.

"I'd never have guessed all that gold was beneath our feet," Will Hoffman said.

"Me either," said Marley.

There were tears in Dottie's eyes as she looked at Ginny and said with a tremor in her voice, "How can you be a part of this?"

Ginny would not meet her probing gaze.

"Ginny," pressed Dottie, "what's happened to you? What made you go bad?"

Still the pretty redhead remained silent. Her stomach felt like some kind of beast was trying to claw its way out.

"Ginny," said Dottie, wiping tears from her cheeks, "talk to me. I've always been your friend, haven't I?"

"You shut up, blondie!" Belle said. "That's enough! Leave her alone! It's none of your business why she joined the gang. One more word outta you and I'll mess up that pretty face of yours!"

Breanna's temper caught fire. She glared at Belle and said, "You leave my sister alone, Belle Reed! If you had the least modicum of human compassion, you'd know it's a terrible shock to see Ginny holding a gun on her!"

Belle stomped up to Breanna and fixed her with hateful eyes. "I'm tellin' you just once to shut your trap, nursie! One more word outta you and I'll pound that pretty face of yours so hard, even that badge-totin' husband of yours won't know you!"

A scarlet stain spread across Breanna's cheeks and she felt her blood reach the boiling point. But she knew of Belle Reed's reputation for violence and pressed her lips into a thin line but didn't say anything more.

Jesse James was still holding his gun on the driver and shot-gunner when he moved toward Belle and said, "What's all the fuss about?"

"Aw, we got this gal here who knew Ginny out in San Francisco. This one," she added, pointing the gun at Dottie. "And as you can plainly see, this other one is her sister. She's got a smart mouth and some starch in her backbone. I was just warnin' her to shut her trap before I rearrange her pretty face."

Though he was keeping his attention on Lee and Hughes, Jesse flicked a quick glance at Breanna, and said, "It's best not to rile Belle, lady. Better button your lip good and leave it that way."

"I don't like her anyway, Jesse," said Belle. "Her husband's a lawman."

"I guess that's plenty reason enough not to like her," chuckled Jesse. Then to Breanna he said, "Like I said, Mrs. Lawman, button your lip and leave it that way."

When Jesse walked away, Ginny met Dottie's gaze with a look that said, *I'm sorry.*

Down the road, in their chosen thicket, the Thaxton gang waited. Two of the gang, Cade Sheridan and J. R. Killian, were at the edge of the brush, watching for the stage to show up.

Dub Thaxton sat in the shade with his back against a tree, talking to his men sitting on the ground around him in a half circle.

Their conversation was interrupted when Cade Sheridan called out, "We got a problem, Dub! Better get up here!"

Thaxton scrambled to his feet. "Whattaya mean?"

"The stage just showed up, and we were about to alert you when this buggy pulls out in front of it. Now it's surrounded by a whole bunch of men!"

When Thaxton reached the edge of the road and looked northward, he released a string of profanity.

"Somebody else is holdin' up the stage!" said Nate Roach.

"Must be fourteen or fifteen of 'em, Dub," said Killian. "Who do you suppose they are?"

Dub squinted and studied the scene. "I can't be sure, but I have a hunch it's James and Younger and their bunch! I'm pretty sure I'm lookin' at Cole's gray roan and Jesse's black and white piebald. Hard to mistake 'em. How many other gangs would just happen to have that rare combination?"

"I see your point," said Killian. "It's gotta be them."

"How would they know about the gold, Dub?" asked Mel Fixx.

White spots appeared on Thaxton's cheeks, contrasting with the black fire in his eyes. "I don't know, but they're takin' the gold off right now and puttin' it in that buggy! C'mon! We'll get that gold yet!"

"How we gonna do it, Dub?" asked Frank Baldwin. "We're outnumbered."

"We'll pull a surprise on 'em right now!" hissed Thaxton, heading for his horse. "C'mon! There's nine of us. With the element of surprise on our side, we can cut enough of 'em down so's we can take the gold."

The last of the gold bars were being placed in Bob Younger's buggy. Cole was ecstatic as he stepped up beside Jesse and said, "We've done it, ol' pal! We've done it! We're filthy rich! I've never seen so much gold all in one place!"

"Yeah!" said Jesse. "Just think, Cole, Zee and I can get married now! I can really set her up good."

Jesse's words caused Wes and Ginny to steal a glance at each other.

When Ginny saw Wes's smile, she tried to smile back, but it wouldn't come. There was too much turmoil inside her. She kept thinking of all the things Dottie had done for her and her parents during the years they lived in San Francisco. She owed Dottie so much, and now she was holding a gun on her.

Cole eyed Jesse with speculation. "You, ah…ain't figurin' on retirin' from our line of work, are you? I mean, just because you're gonna ride away from here a very rich man?"

Jesse laughed. "Hey, pal! Of course not! I'll marry Zee and set her up good, but ol' Jesse James and his big brother, Frank, still want to get a whole lot richer. Right, Frank?"

"Right, Jesse," Frank said with a chuckle.

Cole nodded. "Good. We keep this up, we'll all be millionaires many times over. Then we can retire."

A chorus of voices spoke their agreement.

Wes glanced at Ginny again. They wouldn't be around when the gang members became millionaires. The one hundred fifty thousand dollars plus would be enough for their retirement.

Jesse looked up at Zack Lee and Bert Hughes. "All right, you guys, we're leaving. You stay right up there till we're completely out of sight. Got that?"

"Yeah," said Lee.

"Mr. James," spoke up Will Hoffman.

Jesse's head whipped around. "Yeah?"

"Your men took our wallets. We both have important papers in them that mean nothing to you. Could we have them back, minus the money?"

Jesse looked around at Sly Chapman. "Sly, give 'em their wallets...minus the money, of course."

Suddenly Belle Reed's voice split the air. "Cole! Jesse! There's somebody creepin' up on us over there in the woods!"

Instantly, gunfire exploded from the dense trees and brush at the side of the road, making the place sound like a battlefield. Bullets were flying, and horses were neighing with fright, fighting their bits.

Sly Chapman buckled as a slug hit him in the midsection. He went down, dropping both wallets, and collapsing on top of them.

Belle and Ginny fell to their knees. Belle was screaming at Ginny to fire at the attackers, but Ginny was petrified with fright and unable to raise her gun.

Breanna grabbed Dottie and pulled her under the stagecoach, telling her to lie flat.

The James-Younger gang's saddle horses darted across the road and gathered in a meadow of tall grass a short distance from the road. Bob Younger's horse was rearing and pounding earth with its front hooves. Bending low, Bob guided the horse across the road near the spot where the saddle horses had gathered.

Some of the men of the James-Younger gang were taking refuge behind the stage as they returned fire, while others went to their bellies. From beneath the stage, Breanna saw both Will Hoffman and Darold Marley go down with bullets ripping into them as they were bent over Sly Chapman, trying to retrieve their wallets.

Seconds later, Zack Lee struck the ground in a lifeless heap. Right behind him, was his shotgunner, who had taken two of the Thaxton gang's bullets.

Jesse was firing at the attackers from the back end of the stagecoach, and while reloading his gun, he caught a glimpse of Dub Thaxton darting from one tree to another. Whipping his head around, he saw Cole on his belly in a low spot, blasting away. "Cole!" he shouted, "It's the Thaxton gang! I just saw Dub!"

"That dirty— How did he find out about the gold?"

"Who knows? We gotta take 'em out!"

Cole lined his gun on one of the Thaxton men and dropped the hammer. The man went down in a heap. "That's one less!" he shouted.

Wes Logan was firing at the attackers from a spot a few

yards further from the stagecoach. He heard the conversation between the gang leaders and felt his blood heat up when Jesse mentioned Dub Thaxton.

While reloading, he looked beyond Cole to Jesse and called out, "Where'd you see Thaxton?"

"He's over here to my right behind a tree!"

The roar of guns and clouds of blue-white smoke filled the air as Wes rose to his feet, bent low, and dashed past the nervous stagecoach team, then dived into tall grass at the side of the road.

From where she knelt beside the stagecoach, Ginny saw Wes change places. When he disappeared in the tall grass, she began to weep.

Belle fired two shots, then growled at Ginny, "What're you bawlin' about? Put that gun to use!"

"We're all going to be killed!" sobbed Ginny.

"We will if everybody acts like you! Do what I tell you and put that gun to use!"

Ginny wiped tears from her eyes and thumbed the hammer back on her pistol. When she found a target, she fired. The bullet missed but made the man flatten himself on the ground.

Wes parted the grass and caught a glimpse of Dub's homely face. To get a clear shot, he raised up, took a quick bead, and fired. Thaxton saw him in time to duck out of the way. Wes's bullet chewed bark where his head had been a split second before.

"Logan, I'm gonna kill you!" Thaxton roared.

Suddenly from the other side of the tree, the big gang leader came on the run, firing at Wes.

16

DUB THAXTON'S COLT .45 spit fire as he charged Wes Logan in a fit of blind rage, cursing him. Dub's bullets chewed terra firma just behind Wes as he took aim and dropped the hammer of his gun.

Thaxton let out a deep grunt when the slug hit him in the chest. His legs gave way and he dropped to the ground some twenty yards from where Wes lay.

Wes raised up and saw Dub making an attempt to get up, his gun still in hand.

Wes drew a bead on him, but before he could squeeze the trigger, there was a sudden shower of hot lead hissing around him. He dropped flat and began crawling back toward the stagecoach.

Cade Sheridan was standing behind a tree, firing at the James-Younger gang, when he saw Dub Thaxton go down. He noted that Earl Kopatch, Ernie Mills, and Mel Fixx were unleashing a barrage of lead toward the man who had just shot Dub. When the man disappeared in the grass, they put their attention back on the rest of the James-Younger bunch.

Bullets were flying like angry hornets, but Cade Sheridan

still went after Dub, who was now sprawled on the ground face down. When he reached his boss, he saw that he was still breathing. He grabbed Dub by the shirt collar and dragged the bulky man behind a large oak tree.

Dub looked up through glassy eyes as Cade ripped opened his shirt and said, "Let's see how bad you're hit."

The battle raged on. Though Thaxton's bunch had been whittled down, those who could still fight continued to pepper the other gang with bullets. Another ten minutes made it clear they were no match for Jesse, Cole, and their men.

Cade Sheridan stayed close to Dub, firing as fast as he could. When the hammer of his smoking gun snapped hollowly on an empty cartridge, he rolled onto his side to reload. He ran his gaze over the area, looking to see how many men they had left. He could see Nate Roach lying dead off to his left, and J. R. Killian was down, gripping his rib cage while blood flowed between his fingers.

He called to Ernie Mills and Earl Kopatch who were on his left. "Hey, guys! Nate's dead. Dub's wounded. J. R.'s wounded. Who's that firin' over there on the other side of you?"

"It's Mel," replied Kopatch. "Ray and Frank are dead. We'd better take Dub and J. R. and get outta here!"

When gunfire from the woods suddenly ceased, Arch Clements turned to Jesse and said, "They're leavin'. Shall we chase 'em?"

Jesse didn't answer right away but looked to Cole, who was hurrying toward them.

Ginny's sobbing filled the silence. She was on her knees, her head bent toward the ground. Belle was sitting close by, holding a blood-soaked bandanna against the left side of her head and looking at Ginny in disgust.

"Let 'em go," Cole said. "We shot up most of 'em. Main thing is, we've still got the gold. Bob's got it in the buggy across the road. I saw Wes drop Thaxton, but somehow amid all the shootin', one of their men was able to drag him outta sight. What's our own damage?"

While Jesse and Cole began checking their ranks to see who was hurt or dead, Wes put his arm around Ginny and knelt beside her, trying to calm her down. Dottie and Breanna crawled out from under the stagecoach just as Jim Reed dashed up and knelt by Belle.

"What is it, darlin'?" he said. "You're bleedin' bad!"

"Bullet nicked my ear." She ran her gaze to Breanna. "Hey, nursie. C'mere. I've been hit."

Dottie joined Wes and Ginny while Breanna moved toward Belle and bent over her, saying, "Move the bandanna, would you? Let me take a look at it."

When Belle took away the cloth, blood began running down the side of her face.

"It's bad, honey," said Jim.

Breanna turned to Belle's husband. "My medical bag is in my overnight bag in the box on the stage. Would you get it for me, please?"

"Sure. How bad is the wound?"

"I can take care of it. Please. I need the medical bag."

Breanna pressed the bandanna on the wound and said, "Belle, ears tend to bleed profusely when they're cut. It'll take me a while to get it under control. I'll have to take a couple of stitches."

Cole and Jesse were headed toward Breanna when they saw Jim Reed about to climb up to the box of the stagecoach.

"What's wrong here, Jim?" asked Jesse.

"Belle's been shot. Bullet nicked her ear. Lucky we've got a nurse. I'm gettin' her medical bag for her." As he began to climb, Jim said, "How's it look for the rest of us?"

"Sly's dead," said Cole. "My brother Jim's got a slug in his chest, and Rufe's got a slug in his belly. We were just comin' to get the nurse. Charlie and John are with Jim and Rufe."

Jesse looked around at the bodies on the ground. "The driver and shotgunner are both dead, as well as those two passengers who wanted their wallets back. They got hit pretty quick after the shooting started."

Reed backed down to the ground, overnight bag in hand, and said, "Belle's really bleedin' bad." Even as he spoke, he hurried away with Cole and Jesse on his heels.

Bob Younger was pulling the buggy across the road with Clell Miller walking beside it. Suddenly Clell pointed up the road northward and called out, "Jesse! Cole! Somebody's comin'!"

A wagon was rolling along at a leisurely pace, throwing up small clouds of dust. A man was at the reins and a woman sat beside him.

"What do we do?" asked Frank James, looking to his brother and Cole Younger.

"Just relax," said Jesse. "Cole and I will take care of the farmers."

By the time the wagon drew near, Breanna was working steadily on Belle's wounded ear. Ginny had stopped crying and was listening to Dottie as she spoke to her in soothing tones.

The farmer pulled rein when he saw the stagecoach with people huddled close by and bodies lying on the ground.

Cole and Jesse moved up to the wagon as it rolled to a halt.

"Howdy," said the farmer, who appeared to be in his late sixties. "What happened here?"

"Stagecoach got robbed," said Cole. "We came along just as

the robbers were takin' people's money. There was enough of us to give 'em a tussle. Most of 'em got away though. We have a nurse who was ridin' the stage. She's tendin' to the wounded as she can get to 'em."

"Oh, this is awful!" said the farmer's wife. "Look, Arthur. There are four dead men over there."

"I see 'em, dearie." Then to Jesse and Cole, "Anythin' we can do?"

"Not really," said Jesse, "but we thank you."

"So the robbers got away, eh?"

"Most of 'em, like I said. Some are dead over there in the woods. You ever hear of the Dub Thaxton gang?"

"Oh, yeah."

"That's who we had to fight off."

The farmer's bushy eyebrows arched. "Really? The Thaxton gang. Hear that, Maude? Well, you fellas can be mighty thankful it wasn't the James-Younger gang you encountered. You'd all be dead. Them guys are real killers."

"Real killers, huh?" said Cole.

"Yep. Tough as nails, and plenty good with their guns. 'Specially that there woman who rides with 'em. That Belle Reed. Hear tell she can lick a man in a fistfight and outshoot him in a quickdraw."

"That so?" said Cole, glancing toward Belle. He caught Jim Reed's eye and grinned.

"You're sure there's nothin' we can do?" said the farmer. "You folks are welcome to come to our house. We're 'bout eleven miles on down the road. Be more comfortable for gettin' your wounded folks fixed up."

"Much obliged," said Cole, "but we'll be fine. Thanks."

The farmer nodded, snapped the reins, and the wagon rattled on down the road.

✦

Cade Sheridan had managed to get Dub Thaxton in the saddle and was sitting behind him, struggling to keep the gang leader's huge bulk from falling. Dub was doubled over and breathing hard, telling Sheridan to hurry up and find him a place to lie down.

Earl Kopatch rode double behind J. R. Killian, who was clutching his right side and moaning.

Fixx and Mills led the riderless horses behind their mounts.

They had gone about two miles south of the spot of the shoot-out when Ernie Mills said, "Guys, how about over there?" He pointed to an old barn about a half mile across a field in a large stand of trees. There was no visible road leading to it.

"I don't know," said Earl. "I don't see a house."

"Looks like a heap of black rubble just to the left of those two big willows," spoke up Mel. "House must've burned down. Place looks deserted."

"Well, leastwise, we wouldn't have anybody botherin' us," said Ernie. "Barn looks like the roof is still intact."

"Let's do it," said Kopatch.

When they drew up to the old barn, they saw that the house indeed had burned down. The only thing recognizable was the blackened rock structure of the fireplace. The barn looked to be in decent shape, though the other outbuildings were weatherworn and dilapidated.

J. R. Killian passed out when he was taken from the saddle. Earl Kopatch and Mel Fixx carried him inside the barn, followed by Cade Sheridan and Ernie Mills, who were carrying Dub.

The two wounded men were laid on a thick bed of old straw in a horse stall. The place smelled musty and old, and the straw had a foul-smelling odor.

While Cade and Ernie worked on Dub, Cade said, "I don't think we ought to give up on that gold."

Gritting his teeth, Thaxton spoke through lips that barely moved. "Whatcha talkin' about? Them dirty rats'll be gone with that gold in no time flat."

"I don't think so. We wounded some of their men. They've got to take 'em someplace, and because they're wounded, it can't be very far."

"You might be right," said Dub.

"I'd like to sneak back and follow 'em. That okay with you?"

"I suppose," said Dub, a grimace of pain contorting his face. "But even if yuh spot 'em holin' up somewhere, what c'n yuh do?"

Cade's mouth curved in a confident grin. "I'll take Ernie, Earl, and Mel with me. We'll find a way to steal the gold."

Dub almost smiled, and a glint appeared in his pain-filled eyes. "Y'know, if there's anybody c'n pull it off, it's you four guys. Go ahead, Cade. Check it out. In the meantime, these boys c'n work on me and J. R."

The bodies of the stagecoach crew and the two passengers who had been killed, along with Sly Chapman, were dragged into the woods and laid in a ditch. When that was done, the bodies of the three dead Thaxton men were dumped in the ditch with them.

While this was going on, Jim Reed remained close to Belle, watching Breanna stitch the ear.

Cole Younger left the spot where his brother and Rufe Orvick lay, and looked at Breanna with worried eyes. "Lady, aren't you about done here?"

"Close," she said, flicking him a glance. "You did tell me to finish on her before I started on your brother and the other one, didn't you?"

"Yeah, but I didn't think it would take you so long to patch up an ear. Jim and Rufe's wounds could be fatal."

"Give me five minutes and I'll be done here," said Breanna. "I do wish, however, that you would take them to the nearest doctor. Their chances of living would be much improved if they had a nice clean room with a nice clean bed for each of them…and some nice clean water."

"No doctors. They have a way of gettin' the law on you when you ain't lookin'."

"She's right about them needing a clean place with water," said Jesse. "Let's take them to a farmhouse somewhere nearby where she can work on them properly. I'd have taken that old farmer up on his offer, but eleven miles is too far. We need to find something closer."

"Yeah, but it still might be too far to the nearest farm," said Cole. "It'll take time to get there. Maybe time that Jim and Rufe can't spare."

"Cole," said John Younger, who stood over his wounded brother, "there's a farmhouse back up the road about half a mile."

"That's plenty close," said Jesse. "Let's take them there."

Cole nodded. "Okay, let's do it." Looking at Breanna, he said, "You done?"

Breanna had a bandage on Belle's ear and was holding a roll of gauze ready to wrap a strip around her head. "Almost."

"That can wait. We gotta get Jim and Rufe to that farmhouse in a hurry so you can go to work on 'em."

Breanna frowned. "But this will only take—"

"No argument, lady! Let's go!" He turned to the others. "Load Jim and Rufe in Bob's buggy, fellas." Then he turned to Jim Reed. "You want to take Belle on your horse with you?"

"Sure."

"We'd best take the stagecoach and hide it in that barn, Cole," said Jesse. "If we leave it here, the law may come snooping around the area."

"Right. We can hide Bob's buggy and our horses in there too."

"As long as we're taking the stage," said Jesse, "let's lay Jim and Rufe on the seats. They'll be more comfortable than in the buggy."

"Good idea. Let's move out."

Young widow Clara Dunne was in her kitchen when she heard a knock at the front door. Eight-year-old Larry was in the hall just outside the kitchen. "I'll get it, Mama!" he said, and ran toward the front of the house.

Before Larry could get there, his little sister, Laura, had the door open. A stocky man of medium height, dressed in suit and tie, smiled at the little girl as he removed his hat and said, "Hello, Laura. Remember me?"

"Sure," said the six-year-old, who had her two upper front teeth missing. "You're our new pastor. And your name is Pastor Richard Skiver. You preached to us last Sunday."

"Right, honey," he said, stepping aside a bit and reaching behind him to draw his wife into view. "And this is Rosie— Mrs. Skiver."

"Uh-huh. I saw her Sunday, too. She's pretty."

"Why, thank you, Laura," said the lovely pastor's wife.

"Hello, Larry," said the preacher as the boy drew up. "Do you remember us?"

"Sure do. Those were good sermons you preached Sunday. I liked the one Sunday night especially...'bout Pontius Pilate on the day he died, wishin' he'd treated Jesus right and had gotten saved."

"And I liked Sunday morning's sermon best," said Clara,

drawing up behind her children. "You did such a marvelous job describing the pearly white city. Hello, Mrs. Skiver. Please, come inside."

As the Skivers stepped inside, the pastor said, "Mrs. Dunne, we're making calls on all the families who come to the church so we can get acquainted. Could you spare us a few minutes?"

"Of course. Larry, run out to the barn and tell Uncle Ben that Pastor and Mrs. Skiver are here."

As Larry darted toward the back of the house, Clara said, "Come into the parlor and sit down."

When they were seated, the pastor said, "We've read what records there are in the church about our families, and we understand you are a widow, Mrs. Dunne."

"Yes. Dave died last winter in January...of pneumonia."

"I'm so sorry."

"Thank you. It has been difficult, but the Lord has been good. He has given each of us a great measure of grace to accept Dave's death, and of course, we have the sweet peace of knowing we will be reunited with him in heaven."

"It's wonderful to know, isn't it?" said Rosie.

"The records show that your children are both saved, Mrs. Dunne," said the preacher. "Laura received Christ as her Saviour this June and was baptized the next Sunday."

Clara nodded and smiled at her daughter.

"And Larry was saved and baptized in August of 1869."

"That's right."

"And Ben Tyler is your brother and has been a member of the church since last March."

"That's right," said Clara. "Ben was saved when he was ten years old. He's twenty-four now...four years younger than I. We were both saved on the same Sunday in our family's church in St. Louis. Mother and Dad had been saved some three weeks before that. It took Ben and me a little while for the gospel to come clear after our parents were saved. When Ben came here in March, he transferred his membership to our church."

The pastor nodded. "One of the deacons told me that Ben sold his farm outside of St. Louis shortly after your husband died, so that he could come here and take care of you and the children."

Clara smiled. "Yes. He had quite a farm there. He would have made a good living. But bless his heart, he sold it and came here because he loves us so much. He's running this farm magnificently. We had the best crop ever this year. My brother is a wonderful man, Pastor. He works so hard and is so unselfish and caring. He's one in a mill—"

"Here's Uncle Ben!" announced Larry as he preceded the tall, lanky man into the parlor.

Skiver got up from his chair as Ben reached out to clasp his hand. "Hello, Pastor Skiver! So good to see you! And Mrs. Skiver, it's nice to see you again. That was great preaching on Sunday, pastor. I love the way you so eloquently lift up and magnify the Lord Jesus."

The pastor thanked him, then explained to Ben the reason for their visit. He followed that by commending Ben for the sacrifice he had made to come and care for his sister and her children.

Ben smiled. "Pastor, I don't think of it as a sacrifice. Clara and these precious children needed me. The Lord doesn't make mistakes. He took Dave for a divine reason, so it was in His divine will that I sell my farm and come here. It's a tremendous joy to help Clara run this farm."

"Help?" said Clara, laughing. "What do you mean, little brother? Except for some chores that Larry does, you're doing it all!"

"Well, whatever…but I'm enjoying every minute of it."

"I appreciate your good attitude, Ben," said the preacher, "but let me also say that the Lord has a special blessing in store for you. Such a deed does not go unnoticed by the God of heaven. In Hebrews 6:10, He says, 'God is not unrighteous to forget your work and labour of love, which ye have shewed toward his name, in that ye have ministered to the saints, and do minister.' What you're doing here, Ben, is a work of love for these dear ones of yours. Yes, sir, you've got a special blessing coming."

The Skivers talked with Clara, Ben, and the children for a few more minutes, then Clara offered them coffee. When the coffee had been consumed, the Skivers spoke their appreciation for the kind welcome and said they had to be going.

At the door, the preacher turned and said, "As your new pastor, I want you to know that I consider myself on call anytime…day or night. If there's ever anything I can do for you, please let me know."

"We'll do that, Pastor," said Ben. "And please come back sometime for another visit."

"Yes, please do," said Clara.

"Thank you," said Skiver. "We will. See all of you on Sunday."

When the Skiver buggy reached the end of the lane and turned onto the road, they waved, and the Dunnes and Ben Tyler waved back.

"Well, I've got to get back to my work at the barn," said Ben.

"Can I come and help you, Uncle Ben?" Larry asked.

The tall, slender man ruffled the boy's hair. "Seems like I recall that your mother had some household work for you."

"Well…I was supposed to clean out the pantry and straighten the stuff on the shelves."

"Did you get it done?"

"Uh…not quite."

Ben chuckled. "Then I'd say you'd better finish it, then come on to the barn. I'll put you to work out there when I know your work is done in here."

"Okay, Uncle Ben. I'll get right on it, 'cause workin' at the barn is more fun than doin' housework."

An hour later, Clara took bread out of the oven. Laura was "helping" her by cleaning up the cupboard. Larry had swept the pantry and was working at putting everything neatly in its proper place on the shelves when they heard the front door open and heavy steps moving down the hall.

Larry started toward the hall door, but Clara said, "No, son. I'll see who it is."

She crossed the kitchen to the hallway as the heavy footsteps came closer. She stiffened when she came face-to-face with four rough-looking men who held guns in their hands. The first two men were a contrast. The taller one was blond, the other one was dark-headed, but both looked mean. The dark-headed one had a droopy handlebar mustache.

"What do you want?" she asked, her voice coming out on a trembling note.

"The house," came the quick reply of the blond man with pale blue eyes. "We're takin' over."

"This is my house," Clara said, "and whoever you are, you're not welcome!"

The dark-haired man moved toward her, raised his gun as if to strike her, and hissed, "Shut up! Welcome or not, we're movin' in."

Clara took two steps back and ejected a shrill scream. "Get out of here, I said! Get out!"

The blond man matched her steps and punched her in the

mouth. Clara saw a shower of stars and fell to the floor.

The children were now at the kitchen door, and both screamed when they saw their mother on the floor with blood bubbling at the corners of her mouth.

Ben Tyler was tightening a hinge screw at the front door of the barn when he heard Clara's scream. He dropped the screwdriver and plunged out the door but found himself facing a mean-looking band of men with guns drawn. He heard the children scream and a tingling sensation slithered down his spine.

"What do you want?" he demanded.

"We're taking the place over," said the youthful, slender man who stood closest to him. "We're going to put this stage-coach, the buggy, and all our horses in your barn."

Until that instant, Ben had not noticed the vehicles and other horses that stood behind the motley group. "Who are you?"

The same slender man replied, "I'm Jesse James. Ever heard of me?"

Ben's blood ran cold. "Yes, I've heard of you."

"Good. Then you know it'll be fatal if you give us trouble. Your wife and children's screams are only indications that my pal Cole Younger and some of our boys have met them and explained that they're taking over. You planning on giving us trouble?"

Ben felt rage begin to simmer in him and rise up like liquid fire, but he fought it down. He must keep cool and go along with whatever the James-Younger gang wanted. "I won't give you trouble as long as my sister—not my wife—and my niece and nephew are left unharmed."

"Good," said Jesse. "Now, let's get these animals and the

stage and buggy inside the barn before some nosy lawman comes along."

As one of the gang members swung the barn door wide, Ben said, "Why are you wanting to hole up here?"

"We've got three wounded gang members being carried inside the house right now, mister. What's your name?"

"Ben Tyler."

"One of them is a woman. We've got a nurse with us. She was traveling on the stagecoach before we stopped it. And we need a nice place for her to work. Understand?"

"I understand."

"We'll be staying until the wounded ones are able to travel. You have a problem with that?"

Ben's angular jaw squared. "Yes, and you would too if you were in my boots. But I promise not to give you any trouble if my sister and those two children are left unharmed."

Jesse moved closer, having to tilt his head back to look Ben in the eye. "We could just shoot you down in cold blood right here, Ben. But I'll give you another chance. We won't harm the woman and the brats if they don't force us to. But don't you 'if' me anymore. Got it?"

Ben met Jesse's hard glare with his own unflinching gaze. "Yeah. I got it. Question..."

"What?"

"Is the wounded woman in your gang Belle Reed?"

"Yeah. What of it?"

"Last I knew, she was still running with you. I figured it had to be her."

"It's her, but she'll be all right. Belle's tough."

17

CLARA DUNNE LED COLE YOUNGER and the other gang members carrying the wounded men—Rufe Orvick and Jim Younger—to the two closest bedrooms from the parlor.

Belle held her gun trained on Dottie, Breanna, and the children as they waited in the parlor. She glanced toward Ginny sitting on a couch and staring vacantly at the floor, then turned back to her captives.

When Jim and Rufe had been placed on beds across the hall from each other, Cole came back to the parlor with Clara, leaving the others to watch over the wounded men.

"Mr. Younger, how long are you planning to stay here?" Clara asked.

"Till Jim and Rufe are able to travel...however long that takes."

As they entered the parlor, the front door opened and the rest of the gang came in with Jesse nudging Ben Tyler in front of him.

When the children saw their uncle, they ran to him and wrapped their arms around his waist, asking him to make the bad men go away.

Ben reached out to pull Clara into his protective embrace while he held the children close with his other arm and said,

"Don't worry, Larry and Laura, the Lord will take care of us. He's looking down at us right now. Jesus loves us, and He won't let these people hurt us."

Dottie and Breanna glanced at each other when they heard Ben's words, then Breanna went to Belle and said, "You can put the gun away now. The boys are back. Why don't you let me wrap the gauze around your head to protect the bandage on your ear. Then I can go tend to Jim and Rufe."

Belle gave her a dirty look, slid the gun into her holster, and sat down on a straight-backed chair by the nearest window. Breanna opened her medical bag and went to work.

"Hurry it up, lady," Cole said. "Jim and Rufe are both losin' blood."

"It'll only take a minute or two," Breanna replied. While wrapping the strip of gauze around Belle's head, she looked at Ben, who was still holding Clara and the children, and said, "You're right, Mr. Tyler. Jesus is looking down at you right now, and He will take care of you."

Clara's weeping stopped and the children looked up at Ben as he ran his gaze from Dottie to Breanna. "Sounds like you know Him."

"Yes. Dottie and I are born-again, blood-washed, heaven-bound children of God."

"Well, praise God!" Ben's gaze ran to Ginny, who was sitting quietly on the couch with Wes standing beside her.

"It's good to have you ladies here," Clara said a bit shakily. "I can tell you're sisters."

"Yes, we are," Dottie said.

Ben flicked another glance at Ginny, then smiled at Breanna and Dottie. "Well, you're our sisters in the Lord. And—"

"Shut up!" snapped Jesse James. "Cut out all this Bible stuff; I don't want to hear it."

247

Frank James swore, using Jesus' name, and said, "No more of it, y'hear? We don't like all this gooey Christian talk."

Breanna bristled at hearing the name of her Lord used profanely and shot Frank James a fiery look.

He lowered his eyelids in a contemptuous manner, saying in a level tone, "You got a problem, lady?"

"You used my Lord's name in vain, and I don't like it." Every eye in the room was on Frank and Breanna.

Clara squeezed her brother's hand, admiring Breanna's spunk.

"Oh, yeah? And I don't care that you don't like it."

"It's none of your business, nursie!" said Jesse, moving up beside his brother. "Keep your mouth shut!"

Breanna raked both of their faces with blazing eyes. "You two ought to be ashamed of yourselves! Your father, Robert James, was a Baptist preacher. He believed God's Word and preached it until the day he died. He preached the gospel of Jesus Christ and preached the Bible straight from the shoulder."

The James brothers glared at Breanna, their faces beet red.

"And then there's your poor mother," Breanna said. "My heart goes out to that dear, godly woman, who died only recently, bearing the shame of what her two sons turned out to be. Both of you have rejected the Lord Jesus Christ, whom your father preached as the only way to heaven."

Frank's eyes looked wild as he said, "How do you know so much about our family?"

"I get around."

Jesse moved close to her, his hands clenched into fists at his side. "Well, you just shut up, do you hear me? What Frank and I do is none of your business!"

"It's my business when someone takes my Lord's name in vain, Mr. Jesse James…and it's God's business too. And if you and Frank don't repent and turn to Jesus for salvation, you'll face Him lost and condemned at the white throne judgment!"

Jesse swore and slapped Breanna with a stinging blow. "Shut up about this Jesus stuff, woman!"

Ben stiffened and made a move in Jesse's direction. Suddenly, Cole Younger stepped in front of him and eared back the hammer of his gun, aiming it at Ben's face. "Just hold it right there!"

"Tough bunch you've got here," Ben said. "Takes a real man to slap a woman."

Jesse's head whipped around.

"Let it go, Jesse," said Cole. "My brother and Rufe need nursie's help without any more interruptions." He turned to Ben. "Go back to your sister."

Ben was breathing hard as he backed away and put his arm around Clara.

"Hurry up, nursie," said Cole. "Get that gauze around Belle's head and go take care of Jim and Rufe."

Breanna finished her task and said, "Belle, do you realize you came within an inch of being killed when that bullet nicked your ear?"

Belle looked at her coldly but didn't reply.

While Breanna was tying a knot in the gauze, Jesse moved close. "What's your name, nursie?"

"Breanna Brockman."

"Where you from, Breanna Brockman?"

"Denver."

"Denver," echoed Cole, rubbing his chin. "Brockman... Brockman. Are you related to the big-shot U.S. marshal in Denver? John Brockman?"

"Chief United States Marshal John Brockman is my husband."

Clell Miller spoke up. "Isn't he the guy they used to call the Stranger?"

Breanna nodded. "That's him."

"Jesse's got it in for your husband, nursie," said Frank. "He took Jesse's gun away from him one day in St. Joseph a few years ago. Turned him over to Deputy Sheriff Royce Caldwell. If it hadn't been for a couple of Jesse's friends jumping the deputy, they'd have hanged him…all because of your husband."

Jesse's breathing was labored as be hissed, "I oughtta kill you, nursie, because of what your husband did to me!"

Dottie bounded across the room, shouting, "You leave my sister alone! She hasn't done anything to you!"

"Get back to where you were, lady," Cole said, pointing a stiff finger. He turned back to Jesse. "Back off. It ain't Mrs. Brockman's fault what her husband did. We've got to treat her good. She's all we have to take care of Jim and Rufe."

Jesse wiped a hand over his mouth and turned away, mumbling something to Frank.

To Cole, Breanna said, "I need you to come with me as I examine the wounded men. You'll have to make the decision which one I start on. It could take a while, and I can't be responsible for what happens to the man who has to wait."

"Let's go," said Cole.

"I'm going, too," spoke up Jesse.

When Breanna and the two gang leaders were out of the room, Jim Reed sat down beside Belle and took her hand. "Hurt much, honey?"

"Some. But I can handle it."

Ben spoke words of reassurance to Clara and the children, then looked across the room at the lovely redhead who was still sitting quietly and staring at the floor. He wondered why she needed the man called "Wes" to guard her, for he hadn't moved from her side.

Ben's heart went out to the girl who looked so frightened.

250

Moving across the room, he flicked a glance at Wes Logan, then knelt down in front of Ginny and said, "Ma'am, please don't be afraid. Everything's going to be all right. The gang will be leaving when the wounded men are able to travel. When they're gone, I'll take you and the nurse and her sister to the nearest Wells Fargo station. Then you can be on your way to wherever you were going."

Wes threw back his head and laughed. "What do you think, farmer? You think Ginny's a passenger?"

Ben blinked as he looked up at him. "Well, isn't she?"

"Ginny's part of the gang. She helped Belle set up the holdup from inside the coach."

Ginny finally looked up. When she met Ben's gaze, he said, "Little lady, you don't look like an outlaw."

"Mind your own business, plowboy!" snapped Wes. "She is an outlaw, and what's more, she and I are engaged. You leave her alone!"

Breanna had finished looking over Rufe Orvick's wound and was now in the bedroom where Jim Younger lay in a half-conscious state. She turned to Cole and Jesse. "They're both about the same. Bad shape. Rufe is definitely bleeding internally with that slug in his stomach."

Jim Younger ran his tongue over dry lips and tried to focus on Breanna as she said to Cole, "Your brother, Mr. Younger, is losing blood too. Bad thing about him is the slug is dangerously close to his heart. I'm not a surgeon, but I've worked with many of them on gunshot wounds like these. I'll do my best. Which one do I begin with?"

"Cole," said Jim, looking up at him with pleading eyes, "don't let me die. Please, Cole. Don't let me die."

"You get busy on Jim right now," Cole said levelly.

Breanna opened her medical bag. "I thought that would be your decision. Can't blame you. Blood is thicker than water."

Jim rolled his eyes to Breanna. "Please....don't let me die."

"I'll do my best," she assured him.

"You'd better," warned Jesse.

Breanna flicked him a look of annoyance.

Cole's voice grew sharp as he said, "You wouldn't let him die on purpose because he's an outlaw, would you?"

Breanna fixed him with steady eyes and said evenly, "Mr. Younger, I took an oath as a certified medical nurse to do all that is in my power to relieve human suffering and to save human lives. Though I am in total disagreement with the way Jim and all you other outlaws live, I will do my best to save his life. And the same with Rufe if he's still alive when I've done what I can here."

"You'd better not let my brother die. I mean it."

"I remind you...I'm not a doctor. You mustn't expect me to be as proficient as a surgeon."

"You said you've worked with surgeons on gunshot wounds like this one."

"Yes."

"Have you performed surgery on wounds like this by yourself?"

"Several times, yes."

"And?"

"Well, about half of the men who had serious gunshot wounds to the chest or stomach died in spite of what I could do for them."

A wintry look shuttled across Cole's narrowed eyes. "Then my brother better be in the half that lived when you're done here. If Jim dies, Mrs. Brockman, you die. Understand?"

Breanna closed her eyes momentarily, then said, "You're being unreasonable, but yes, I understand."

"You like livin'…Jim likes livin'. Jim lives…you live."

"I'll need some assistance in order to do the surgery."

"What kind of assistance?"

"I prefer feminine assistance. I'll need someone to help me directly in the wound, someone to hand me my instruments, and someone to keep us supplied with hot water."

"Well, Belle ain't up to helpin', so if you need three, it'll have to be your sister, Clara, and our girl, Ginny."

"I'm sure about Dottie and Clara," Breanna said. "You might have to talk to Ginny. Last time I got a glimpse of her, she wasn't looking so good."

"Be right back," Cole replied. "C'mon, Jesse. She won't need us in here."

When Cole and Jesse were gone, Breanna used scissors to cut away the upper front part of Jim's shirt. When she began cleaning around the wound with wood alcohol, she said, "Now, Jim, the surgery will have to be done without anesthetic. I have no ether and no chloroform. You're going to be in a great deal of pain."

"I'm hurtin' right now."

"It's nothing to what you're going to feel when I probe for that slug. Just thought I'd warn you."

There was a white ring of fear around Jim's mouth as he said, "Please don't let me die, ma'am."

"Like I said, I'll do my best."

As Breanna completed sterilizing the area where she would be working, the women entered the room. Breanna noticed that some of the men—including Jesse and Cole—stood in the hall.

Breanna chose Dottie to work directly with her on the

wound to keep Jim from losing too much blood. Clara would be at her side to give her instruments, and Ginny would come and go with the hot water.

Breanna hurriedly gave instructions to each woman, telling them what she required of them.

Just before Breanna began probing for the slug, Belle Reed entered the room and sat down on a straight-backed chair. Breanna frowned and said, "There are enough people in this room already."

"Don't let it fret you, nursie. Cole decided he wants me in here to keep an eye on what's goin' on. He wants the job done right."

"How much do you know about surgery?" Breanna asked.

"Well...not much."

"So what are you going to be looking for?"

"I dunno. Just shut up and get on with it."

Wes Logan eased up to the door. "Mrs. Brockman, if you need anything during the surgery—outside of what Ginny will be doing—please let me know."

Breanna nodded, then began digging for the slug in Jim's chest.

Jim gritted his teeth and began to squirm.

"Sorry," said Breanna, "but there's no other way to do this. Dottie, see if you can hold his shoulders down."

As Breanna probed again, Jim jerked and let out a high-pitched wail. Dottie pushed down as hard as she could, trying to hold him still.

"Hey!" Belle said. "Go easy on him! Do you have to hurt him like that?"

Without turning around, Breanna said, "Yes, I do. There's no way to get the slug out without digging for it. If I don't get it out, it's a toss-up which will kill him first...loss of blood or lead poisoning."

"Well, go easy! You're hurtin' him bad."

"Don't blame me for his hurting," Breanna retorted. "If he hadn't been robbing the stagecoach, he wouldn't have a bullet in him."

"Good for you, sis," Dottie whispered.

When Breanna pushed the metal probe deeper, Jim ejected a wild howl. His body jerked and he passed out.

Ginny, who was at the foot of the bed, covered her mouth in dread.

Breanna looked at her. "He didn't die, he just passed out." She pointed to the rise and fall of his chest. "See? He's still breathing."

"Well, at least he's not feelin' it now," Belle said. "Hurry up before he comes out of it."

"Don't tell me how to do my job," said Breanna.

Cole Younger appeared at the door, trying to see past Breanna and get a glimpse of his brother. "He's quit hollerin'. Is he all right?"

"He passed out, Cole," said Ginny. "It's best this way."

As Breanna continued her work, all three of her helpers did their jobs well. When the slug was finally out, Belle leaned closer to observe Breanna's skillful hands as she worked quickly, with Dottie's help, to tie off the bleeders. Clara looked on, praying in her heart that Jim would live through the ordeal. She couldn't stand the thought that Breanna would have to die just because Jim did.

When Breanna had successfully stopped the bleeding, she repaired the damage to the flesh as much as she could and began stitching him up.

"Is he gonna make it?" pressed Belle.

"I believe he will. He was plenty close to dying there for a few minutes." She let her words hover in the air a few seconds, then said, "I want to remind you, Belle, how close you came to being killed when that bullet nicked your ear. It was actually just about as close to your skull as this slug was to Jim's heart. You came as close to dying as he did."

"Well, I didn't die, nursie. The slug didn't split my skull. It only nicked my ear."

"Mm-hmm. How about the next time bullets fly when you're pulling a robbery? What if there's a bullet with your name on it?"

Belle adjusted her position on the chair but remained silent.

"Let me tell you what the Lord Jesus Christ said, Belle. It's found in the twenty-sixth chapter of Matthew. He said, 'They that take the sword shall perish with the sword.'"

Ginny's head snapped up at Breanna's quotation of Matthew 26:52 and she began listening intently.

Breanna paused in her stitching work to glance at Belle. "The same thing that Jesus said about the sword would apply to the gun. If you continue this outlaw life, Belle, you'll probably die by the gun. You came plenty close today."

Belle stared at Breanna, anger showing in her eyes.

Ginny's thoughts went to the day in Olathe when she felt the hot breath of the bullet on her right cheek. An inch closer.... She swallowed hard. Her uncle's words reverberated through her mind: *Live by the gun, die by the gun.*

Cole appeared at the door and said, "No need to hurry, Mrs. Brockman. Rufe just died."

Breanna set her eyes on Belle and gave her a look that said, *Rufe lived by the gun. See what happened to him?* Then she turned to look at Cole and said, "I'm sorry."

He nodded silently. "How about Jim?"

"I'm not a doctor, but I believe he will make it."

"Good. Then you'll make it, too."

"Let me remind you, I had to cut awfully close to Jim's heart in order to remove the slug. If I caused damage of which I'm not aware, he could still die."

Cole frowned. "Well, if he does, you die, too. We won't need you anymore."

With that, Cole turned away from the door to find himself facing Ben Tyler.

"Cole," said Ben, "I'm sure Mrs. Brockman did the best she could. She's not a doctor. You're expecting too much of her. And you have no right to threaten her like that."

Before Cole could react, Wes Logan moved up to Ben and rasped, "You've got no business talking to Cole like that, plowboy!"

"And he's got no business threatening that dear lady's life! She's done her very best to keep Jim alive!"

Wes swore as he whipped out his gun and cracked Ben across the mouth with the barrel. The impact knocked Ben to the floor.

As he made an attempt to rise, Cole pulled his gun and pointed the muzzle at his head, saying, "Cool off, dirt farmer!"

Ben pulled a bandanna from his hip pocket and pressed it to his mouth. His voice quivered with fury as he said, "There's no reason Mrs. Brockman should have to die if Jim dies. Haven't you outlaws got any sound reasoning at all?"

Wes raised his gun. "You want more, is that it?"

Ben's eyes showed no fear.

Wes was about to strike him again when he saw Ginny standing at the foot of Jim's bed, staring at him with shock and disgust.

He pulled his eyes away from her and looked at Ben. "You'd best learn to control your tongue, plowboy." With that, he turned and walked away.

Cole moved into the bedroom doorway and said, "Nursie, it still stands. Jim dies…you die!"

When Breanna saw Dottie's lips quiver and tears mist her eyes, she whispered, "Don't worry, honey. The Lord will take care of me."

Ginny murmured that she would be back in a few minutes then hurried out the door. She pressed through the gang members who filled the hallway and saw Wes going out the front door. Hastening her pace, she reached the door after he had closed it. When the door opened again, he turned to see who it was.

"Ginny, you'd better get back in there and help that nurse."

She fixed him with steady eyes. "There was no reason for you to hit Mr. Tyler like that. What's gotten into you? I've never seen you like this before!"

"I don't have to account to you! Back off, Ginny! That insolent farmer had it coming!"

Ginny took a backward step, her head bobbing. "How… how can you speak to me so harshly, Wesley Logan? I'm only trying to understand why you would act that way. Ben was only defending Mrs. Brockman as a real man and a gentleman would. Why should she die if Cole's brother dies? Like Ben said, there's no sound reasoning to it."

"Oh, it's Ben, now, is it? You must be liking the way he looks at you."

"What? He hasn't been looking at me."

"Oh, no? Don't tell me you haven't noticed it."

"Well, I haven't! It's something you're imagining. Back to the reason I came out here. Why did you hit Ben—Mr. Tyler—with your gun? Can't Cole fight his own battles?"

Wes took a deep breath and ran a palm over his eyes. "Look, the robbery didn't go off as planned because of Thaxton and his bunch showing up. We don't have our share of the gold yet. I've got to keep things good between Cole and Jesse and us in case we have more unexpected problems. I want everything to be right for you and me, so we can have the future we've been dreaming about. So I stuck up for Cole to keep his confidence."

"But you didn't have to hit Ben Tyler with your gun! Something's gotten into you, Wes! I've never heard you swear before! You've never spoken so harshly to me, either."

"Get off my back, Ginny! I don't have to give an account to you for everything I do…or the way I do it!"

Ginny looked at him for a few seconds then turned and went back inside the house.

18

THE SUN WAS SINKING LOW in a partly cloudy sky when Cade Sheridan rode up to the old barn. The big door swung open and Earl Kopatch said, "Find 'em?"

"Sure did. How're Dub and J. R. doin'?"

"We got the bleedin' stopped for now, but they're not in good shape. I ain't no doctor, but I'd say J. R.'s the worst off. They really need some professional medical attention."

"Dub awake?'

"Yeah. J. R.'s either sleepin' or passed out, I don't know which."

"Let's go in. I'll explain to Dub what I found, and the rest of you boys can hear it, too."

Mills and Fixx were seated on the floor of the horse stall next to Dub as Kopatch and Sheridan came in. Cade knelt down by Dub and said, "They're holed up at a farm 'bout a half mile north of where we jumped 'em. Sign at the front gate says its the Dunne Farm. I'm sure they've got their wounded men inside the farmhouse and, no doubt, they've got that nurse we saw at the stage station takin' care of 'em."

Dub nodded. "Makes sense. The Dunne family must be prisoners."

"Just about have to be," said Cade, "unless the gang killed

'em. Earl told me your bleedin' stopped. And J. R.'s. I was thinking while I was ridin' back here that we'd oughtta find a way to grab that nurse and bring her here to take care of you and J. R. Whattaya think?"

Dub's eyes took on a bit of light. "That's a good idea. I been thinkin' about sendin' you boys out to kidnap a doctor. Think you could grab the nurse?"

"I'd sure like to try. I'll take Earl with me, since he's the only one other than you who's seen her. She's gotta come outside now and then. We'll have to use a little ingenuity maybe, but I think it can be done."

"What about the gold?" Dub asked.

"Well, the stagecoach is gone from that spot in the road. I figure they've got it and the buggy they were usin' inside the barn. It's a big barn. And they must have all their horses in there, too. The gold's probably in the buggy or maybe in the stage."

"You don't suppose they carried it into the house?" Kopatch asked.

"I thought at first they might've. They were all inside the house as far as I could tell, at least for quite a while. Dub, you know that Wes Logan dude who shot you?"

"Yeah…" The mention of Logan's name filled Dub's eyes with a mixture of hatred and contempt.

"Well, about an hour before I left to come back here, Logan came out onto the front porch of the farmhouse by himself; then this redheaded gal came out. A real looker. I was too far away to hear what they were sayin', but they were havin' some kind of argument. Pretty soon, she went back into the house. Seemed quite upset. Logan stayed out there by himself for quite a spell, then a bunch of the gang came out—seven or eight of 'em, anyway—and went to the barn. They stayed inside except for a couple of 'em who went to the privy behind the house. Then they went back to the barn and nobody came out again before I left. I rode away askin' myself why they'd stay in the barn like that unless they've got the gold out there and are makin' sure it stays well guarded."

"Well, if that's the case," said Dub, "how are you ever gonna get your hands on it?"

Sheridan scratched behind his ear. "It ain't gonna be easy, but I believe these three guys and I can figure out a way to do it. Since your friend Gordie Naylor told you there was $200,000 worth of gold on that stage, it's well worth goin' after."

"Gordie," Dub said. "I've been wonderin' how the James-Youngers found out the gold was on that stage. You don't sup-pose—?"

"Wouldn't be the first time somebody got double-crossed, Dub," said Kopatch. "You paid that guy a pretty nice fee for the information. I wonder if James and Younger paid him a nice fee too."

"Sorta smells like it," said Dub. "When I get well, I'm havin' me a little talk with Gordie."

Cade laughed. "Unless the James boys get to him first."

"Well, we'll worry about Gordie later. Right now, we've got two more important things to handle. Most important is to get that nurse here. Next is to get our hands on the gold."

Sheridan stood up and glanced toward the west windows in the barn. "Tell you what, Dub. The sun's just now startin' to drop below the horizon, but there'll be enough light left for me and Earl to go back and watch the house for a while. Maybe that little nurse will decide to take a walk outside. If so, Earl can spot her."

Dub turned to Kopatch. "Do you think you remember what she looks like?"

Kopatch grinned. "Don't worry, Dub. I remember what she looks like, all right. What a beauty! I'll know her when I see her."

"There were two women hidin' behind the stage when we were havin' our shootout," said Mills. "One of 'em was shootin' at us. Anybody see what they looked like?"

"I could tell those were women," said Fixx, "but there was too much smoke to be able to see what they looked like. I never did see the nurse or the other woman."

"Well, the one that was shootin' had to have been ol' Belle Reed," grunted Thaxton. "She rides them stages to get the drop on the passengers, you know."

"C'mon, Earl," said Cade. "Let's go see if the nurse shows up outside the house. We just might be able to grab her."

When Sheridan and Kopatch came within two hundred yards of the Dunne place, they took a path across a field and left their horses in a thick stand of trees. They crept close to the back of the house and watched the back door and porch. There was some traffic between the house and privy, and the house and barn, but all were men. No women came outside.

Darkness had fallen when Sheridan and Kopatch returned to the barn where their gang was hiding. The only light in the place was from a single lantern hanging on a nail above the horse stall where Dub and J. R. lay.

J. R. was conscious but not enough to talk.

"How'd it go?" Dub asked.

"We'll go back tomorrow," Cade said. "That nurse is bound to come outta the house in the mornin'. We'll be close enough to grab her if she does. If there's somebody with her, we'll conk 'em on the head, grab the nurse, and hightail it outta there."

"Yeah," said Kopatch, "and while we're waitin' to grab her, we'll be workin' on a plan to grab the gold a little later."

When darkness had fallen, Clara Dunne, with the help of Dottie and Ginny, cooked supper for everybody. Breanna was given her meal in the room where Jim Younger lay. He was still unconscious, and she refused to leave him in case he should get worse.

The outlaws silently endured it when Ben Tyler led in prayer, thanking the Lord for the food.

During the meal, Ginny sat by Belle Reed and avoided eye contact with Wes Logan, who sat near the table, balancing his plate on his lap. Try as he might, Wes could not get Ginny to look his way.

When supper was over and the women were doing the dishes, Wes came into the kitchen and drew up beside Ginny, who was drying dishes. She kept her eyes averted.

He leaned around her and finally made eye contact. "How about a little moonlight walk?"

Ginny turned her head and laid a dry dish on the cupboard next to the others she had placed there. "There's lots of work here yet. We fed a big crew."

"I'm willing to wait. How about it?"

She gave him a weary look. "I'm tired."

"Just a little walk?"

"It will be late by the time I'm finished here."

Placing his hand in front of her with thumb and forefinger only a half-inch apart, Wes said, "A teensy-weensy walk?"

Dottie and Clara watched the exchange of words, but when Ginny glanced at them they looked away.

"Please?" said Wes.

Ginny sighed. "Oh, all right. Come back in a half hour."

Ginny was quiet as they walked along the lane leading to the road. The moonlight cast long shadows from the tall cottonwoods lining the lane.

Wes finally broke the silence. "Are we going to talk at all?"

She gave him a testy stare. "Do you have something to say?"

"Well, yes."

"Then say it."

"What you want is an apology, right?"

"I want more than that. I want an explanation. And if I can accept that, I want a promise that such a horrible thing will never happen again."

Wes looked down at her a bit surprised. "Horrible? I did something horrible?"

"Yes. I saw a side of you I hadn't seen before and I didn't like it."

"Okay, okay. I'm sorry. You have my apology. I shouldn't have acted that way toward you. I'm not ordinarily short-tempered. Please forgive me."

"There's something I don't understand and I need an explanation."

"What don't you understand?"

"If you love me as you say you do, how could you be so brusque toward me? You were like a different person, Wes."

"Ginny, look…it was the strain of the whole situation that caused me to act that way. I'm nervous about that gold. Wells Fargo is going to report the missing stagecoach to the law. This will bring federal marshals into the area. They'll search every barn in a radius of twenty miles. Maybe more. If Jesse and Cole don't get us and the gold out of here shortly, we're in trouble. We'll go to prison and the gold will go back to its owners. The dream you and I have shared will be gone, and our lives will be ruined."

Ginny was silent as they slowly walked on.

Looking down at her, Wes said, "Well, don't you have something to say?"

"Yes." She looked up to meet his gaze. "I want out of this outlaw business."

"We're planning that, honey. We've just got to—"

"I mean now."

"Why? We still have a good chance—"

"Do you know what the Bible says about living a life of violence like we do?"

"The Bible? What do you mean?"

Ginny explained to him about the Scripture Breanna had brought up to Belle about taking up the sword and perishing by it.

Now Wes was silent.

Looking up at him again, Ginny said, "I'm afraid to go on being an outlaw and carrying a gun. I want out."

"Ginny, we'll be out shortly. You can't just quit all of a sudden."

"Can't I?"

"No. You've got to stick it out so we both get our share."

"I don't care about that anymore. I'm scared to death. My uncle once said, 'Live by the gun, die by the gun.' Wes, we've not only taken sides against the law, but we've taken sides against God. This is a dangerous thing to do. I'm scared. Really scared."

Wes cast a smoldering look at her. "That's enough of this religious talk, Ginny. I don't want to hear any more about it. When we—I mean the gang and us—get away from here with the gold, you and I will get our share. Then we'll sneak out that very night and be gone. By the time Cole and Jesse know we're missing, we'll be so far away they'll never find us."

Ginny was silent.

Wes stopped and took hold of her arm, turning her toward him. "Now look. I want to know something."

"What?"

"Have you changed your mind?"

"About what?"

"About us!"

She pulled her arm from his grip and looked toward the house. "I want to go back."

He grabbed her arm again, this time pinching down tight. "I want an answer, Ginny!"

"You're hurting me, Wes. Let go."

"I want to hear it! Have you changed your mind about me?"

She jerked her arm free and started toward the house. "We'll talk about it later."

Wes lunged after her and pulled her back. "We'll talk about it right now!"

"You're hurting me!"

He stubbornly held his grip and said, "Do you love me or not?"

His harsh treatment caused a flicker of fear to rise within Ginny, and with it the thought that she had never loved him. She had only been infatuated with him, and now even that was gone.

What would he do if she told him the truth? "Yes, I still love you, Wes."

"And you still want the life together that we planned?"

"Yes," she lied again.

"That's better," he said, releasing his hold on her arm.

She started to rub the painful spot, but he quickly wrapped his arms around her and planted a hard kiss on her lips. Ginny was afraid to show how he repelled her, so she kissed him with the same warmth as before.

When they entered the house, they found that part of the gang was sleeping in the barn to guard the gold, while those in the house were preparing places to sleep.

Since Jim Younger was in Clara Dunne's room, and Rufe Orvick's body had been taken to the barn, Clara announced that she and her children would sleep in Ben's room, which had a second bed.

Before anyone said anything, Jesse looked pointedly at Ben and told him he would spend the night on the parlor floor where the other gang members could keep an eye on him.

"Breanna," Cole said, " I want you to stay by Jim's side all night and keep an eye on him."

Ginny spoke up. "Cole…Breanna—I mean, Mrs. Brockman—is very tired. She's worn out from the surgery and other work she did today. Just look at her. I'll stay up and watch Jim. She can sleep in Laura's room. I'll awaken her if Jim needs her."

"Tell you what, Ginny," Dottie said. "Let's do it in shifts. You take whichever half of the night you want, and I'll take the other. That way, you'll get some sleep, too."

"Let's make it a threesome," Clara said. "I'll take a shift, too. Splitting the night three ways will make it so nobody has to miss a lot of sleep."

Ben spoke up. "Clara, Larry and Laura are frightened with all of this going on. You go ahead and sleep with them in my room; I'll take the third part of the night shift."

Ginny Grayson had taken a liking to Ben Tyler. He was such a kind and gentle man. She smiled at him and said, "Mr.

Tyler, it's very kind of you to take your sister's place. I agree those poor children need their mother's presence so they can sleep."

Suddenly, Wes Logan stepped in front of Tyler and said curtly, "Ginny's not taking a shift. You can split the night with Dottie."

"Wait a minute!" Ginny protested. "I want to do my part."

"You'll do as I say! I don't want you taking a shift." Pointing at Ben with his chin, he said, "This guy already has eyes for you, and while I'm sleeping he's liable to sneak into Jim's room to see you."

Ben bristled. "What are you talking about? I don't—"

"You shut up, plowboy! I'm not blind!"

"Wes, you're imagining things!" Ginny said.

"Hah! I've seen him looking at you lots of times, and don't tell me you haven't noticed it too! I don't want him anywhere near you." As he spoke, Wes set piercing eyes on Ben. "You keep your eyes to yourself, you hear me?"

"Wes, cool down," Jesse said. "We don't need this kind of—"

Ben went eye to eye with Wes. "I have not looked at Miss Grayson in an improper way. It's like she said...you're imagining things."

"I know what I've seen," Wes retorted, "and I want no more of it. Keep your eyes to yourself!"

"It's all in your mind. I won't say that I haven't noticed Miss Grayson's beauty and charm. But I have not looked at her wrongfully. And while we're talking about her, I'll say that I think deep down inside, she's not an outlaw."

"Haven't looked at her wrongfully, eh?" breathed Wes. "You're a liar!" As he ejected the last three words, he swung a fist toward Ben's jaw.

In one smooth move, Ben sidestepped the blow and seized

Wes's wrist, bending his arm back sharply.

Wes howled, trying to free himself, but the harder he tried, the more pressure Ben put on.

Jesse stepped in. "Wes, I told you to cool down." Then to Ben, "Let go of him."

"I'll let go because you and your bunch have the guns," clipped Ben. "But you keep him in line. I don't like his accusations."

Wes took a step back, wincing, and gave Ben a venomous look.

"That's enough, Wes," Jesse said, stepping between them. "We don't need any trouble while we're here. We've got enough problems to think about as it is."

Wes nodded. "There won't be any trouble, Jesse, as long as this dirt farmer stays away from Ginny."

"What do you mean?" Ben said, scowling. "I haven't tried to be alone with her."

Cole moved up close. "You'd better not, either. Ginny is Wes's girl."

Wes took Ginny's arm. "You're going to sleep right over here on the couch, and I'm going to sleep on the floor beside you. You'll not be splitting a shift with Dottie and that hick farmer."

"All right, Wes. I'll do what you say."

"There's no reason I can't share a third of the night with you two," Breanna said, looking at her sister and Ben.

"Honey," said Dottie, "Ginny's right. You look awfully tired, and you're quite pale. Ben and I will handle it. You get yourself a good night's sleep."

"All of you listen to me," Cole said in a loud voice. "I'll have one man awake on shifts right here in the parlor all night. If any of you need to go out to the privy, the man who's on duty at the time will escort you out there. Don't even think of trying to run for help. If any one of you comes up missin', we'll kill the rest because of your foolishness. Got it?"

"We understand," Ben said.

Breanna spoke to Ben and Dottie. "I still say I'm taking a shift. And Dottie knows better than to argue with me. I'll take the first shift. You two work out number two and three."

Dottie sighed and looked at Ben. "She's more stubborn than any ol' mule you ever saw. Which shift do you want?"

"Ladies choose first," he replied.

"All right. I'll take the second shift."

"I'll wake you for it, Dottie," said Breanna. "Where will you be sleeping?"

"Over there on the other couch." She turned to Ben. "I'll wake you for the third shift. Where will you be sleeping?"

Ben gestured toward a spot on the floor close to the hall. "Right over there."

When Breanna entered the room where Jim Younger lay, she found him asleep. There was a Bible on a small table next to the dresser. She picked it up and sat down on the chair beside the bed and began reading. After a few minutes, she found her weary mind going dull. She closed the Bible and rubbed her eyes.

Seconds later, she heard the children talking to their mother as the three of them came down the hall. Clara paused at the door and looked in. "Breanna, I really do wish you had chosen to sleep the whole night. You do look awfully tired and peaked."

"I'll be fine, Clara." Looking past her, Breanna said, "Good night Laura. Good night, Larry."

Only seconds later, Breanna heard Jim and Belle Reed's voices as they came from the parlor. Belle told Jim to go on, she would be there in a little while.

Belle stepped into the bedroom, eyeing the sleeping Younger brother. "I ain't sleepy," she said, "so I'll spend some time in here. How's he doin'?"

"Sleeping peacefully," Breanna said in a low voice.

Belle pulled a chair up to the bed and sat down, making a slight adjustment of the gauze strip around her head. "Nursie, you'd better keep Jim alive."

Breanna rubbed her weary eyes. "Belle, I would do my best to keep this man alive, even without Cole's threat. I'm a nurse. My life's work is to make sick people well and to save lives."

"Well, let me give you some examples of people Cole has threatened to kill…and did."

When Belle finally ran out of stories, Breanna said, "Let me explain something to you."

"What's that?"

"I have no desire to die, but neither am I afraid of death."

"Aw c'mon, dearie, everybody's afraid to die. None of us knows for sure what lies beyond our last breath. If anything."

"I know."

Belle laughed. "Oh, sure you do."

"That's right. I know that as a born-again child of God, I am one of His sheep. Jesus is the great Shepherd. In Psalm 23:4, David said, 'Yea, though I walk through the valley of the shadow of death, I will fear no evil: for thou art with me.' The reason David wouldn't be afraid was because the dear Shepherd would be there to take him through the valley when he took his last breath. It's wonderful to know, Belle, that when I close my eyes in death, I'll open them in eternal life. And the first face I see will be that of the Shepherd.

"My wonderful Lord Jesus went to the cross of Calvary to provide a way for a sinner like me to be saved and to have all my sins washed away in His precious blood."

Belle sat staring at Breanna but remained silent.

"How about you, Belle? What will you see after you take your last breath? Where will you be?"

Belle cleared her throat. "Don't ask me that kind of stuff, Breanna. It's always been my belief that when a person dies, he or she goes out of existence. There ain't no heaven, and there ain't no hell."

"Wrong. Jesus Christ came into this world to demonstrate that death is not the end. He died on the cross, didn't He?"

"So I've heard."

"You think it's untrue?"

"Naw. History tells about Him dyin'."

"Yes, but even more important, God's Word—the Bible— tells about Him dying. And it not only tells of His death on the cross, but it tells that He came out of the grave three days later. He came back from the dead, even as He had said He would."

Belle shook her head. "Yeah, but all you have is the Bible to say He came back from the dead. History doesn't mention it."

"Oh, but it does. Many times. But even if it didn't, since God said it in His Word, that's enough. And the same Bible tells that there is a heaven where believers in Christ go when they die, and a burning hell where nonbelievers go."

"I don't believe that Bible stuff, Breanna. It's all a bunch of fairy tales."

"May I remind you of what Jesus said about taking the sword and perishing with the sword? How about the gang members who were in on the stage robbery and are now dead? Sly Chapman and Rufe Orvick?"

Belle chuckled hollowly. "Nursie, I don't believe that 'takin' the sword and perishin' with the sword' stuff, either. I live by the gun, but I don't intend to die by the gun. That's plain nonsense."

There were tears in Breanna's eyes as she picked up the Bible and said, "Belle, if Rufe and Sly hadn't been living by the gun...if they hadn't been there on the road to rob the stage today, they would still be alive right now. Tell me I'm wrong."

Belle swallowed hard but didn't reply.

Opening the Bible, Breanna said, "I want to read to you about God's only begotten Son. I want you to hear how He went to the cross so He could provide you a way to have your sins forgiven and to miss hell. I remind you once more how very close you came to being killed today. God spared your life to give you another chance to be saved and miss hell."

Belle jumped to her feet and swore at Breanna. "I don't want to hear it!" She stomped out of the room and down the hall.

Seconds later, Breanna heard a door slam shut.

19

THE SLAM OF THE DOOR caused Jim Younger to stir. He rolled his head and moaned, then opened glassy eyes. When he saw Breanna's face, he rasped out the word "Thirsty."

Breanna tended to his need, happy to get some water down him. When he had sipped all he wanted, she set the cup down and said, "How's the pain, Jim?"

"Not too bad." He spoke with a slight slur to his speech. "You're a good nurse. Thank you for savin'…savin' my life."

Breanna started to reply but remained silent when Jim drifted back to sleep. In a whisper she said, "Thank You, Lord. He seems to be doing better."

She eased back on the chair and thought of John, longing for him. She sat in silence, listening to people breathing steadily as they slept in other parts of the house.

About an hour had passed when Jim stirred again and woke up enough to take some more water. When Jim was asleep again, Breanna decided to change the bandage on his wound.

When that was done, she eased back in the chair again and talked to the Lord. She prayed that He would keep any harm from coming to Ben, Clara, and the children. She prayed for Ginny, whom she believed was not the hardened outlaw the others were, asking the Lord for an opportunity to talk to

Ginny about salvation. She also asked God to deliver Dottie and herself from the hands of the gang.

It was about ten minutes to one when Breanna heard soft footsteps in the hall and Dottie came in.

"I was going to come and wake you up in a few more minutes," said Breanna. "You didn't have to come quite yet."

"I was already awake. Figured I could give you an extra few minutes to sleep."

Breanna stood up and hugged her. "You're the sweetest sister anybody ever had."

Dottie chuckled. "You only say that because it's true."

Breanna kissed her cheek and said, "Jim's been awake twice. I gave him water both times. And I just changed his bandage. The wound is looking all right. If he wakes up, give him some more water. And if anything out of the ordinary happens, you come and get me fast, okay?"

"Sure will."

"All right. I'll go take the spot where you were sleeping. Come to think of it…where were you sleeping?"

"Ben brought in a cot from somewhere. It's in the parlor by the front window."

"All right. See you in the morning."

As Breanna turned toward the door, a queasiness washed over her. She stopped and used the dresser to steady herself.

Dottie took hold of her shoulders. "Honey, are you all right?"

The queasiness was easing. Nodding, Breanna said, "I'm just tired. I'll be all right."

"You want me to walk you to the cot?"

"No. I'll be fine."

Dottie shook her head as she sat down on the chair. "Lord, Breanna doesn't look good. Please take care of whatever is wrong." She glanced at the Bible on the table and picked it up. She had only read a couple of pages when her eyes started to grow heavy. Laying the Bible down, she yawned and said, "Lord, help me to stay awake."

Her attention went to the sleeping outlaw. She studied his rather handsome face, wondering why a man would choose such a foolish way of life.

Suddenly there were soft footsteps in the hall, and Dottie was surprised to see Ginny come in. Smiling, she said, "Why aren't you asleep?"

Ginny sat down where Belle had sat. "I just can't sleep, so I thought I'd come and see how Jim is."

Ginny's presence served to lift the heaviness from Dottie's eyes. "Won't Wes be angry if he wakes up and finds you gone?"

"I doubt that he'll wake up till morning, but to tell you the truth, I don't care if he does get angry. He's acting like a child." She looked at the sleeping outlaw. "How's he doing?"

"He's resting comfortably, as you can see. Breanna said he woke up twice and took water. So that's a good sign."

"Mm-hmm. Actually, Dottie, my concern is not so much for Jim but for your sister. I want him to live so Breanna will be allowed to live."

Dottie nodded. "I've put a lot of prayer to this, Ginny. I'm trusting the Lord to spare Breanna's life, and I'm confident He will."

Ginny sighed. "It must be wonderful to have that kind of faith."

"It is. And it's a gift from God."

Ginny nodded silently.

There were a few seconds of silence, then Dottie said, "Ginny, you're not like the rest of the gang. Especially not like Belle. How did you get to running with them?"

Ginny's head dropped, and she stared at the floor.

"Don't want to talk about it?"

"I'd rather not."

"All right. I won't pry. But I'd like to ask you something."

"Mm-hmm?"

"Many times when the gang pulls a robbery, bullets fly, don't they?"

"Yes."

"There were a lot of bullets flying today, weren't there?"

Ginny thought again of the day in Olathe when the bullet barely missed her head. "Yes. A lot."

"Let's say you had been killed today, as Sly and Rufe were. Where would you be right now?"

Ginny's head dropped again, and as before, she only stared silently at the floor.

"There's only heaven or hell, Ginny. Which would it be?"

"I...I don't know. Probably hell, because I'm an outlaw."

"People don't go to hell for being outlaws, Ginny, though God doesn't approve of outlawry, of course. According to Scripture, people go to hell because they refuse to repent of their sin and put their faith in the Lord Jesus Christ. God's only begotten Son is the one and only way of salvation."

Picking up the Bible, Dottie said, "I want to show you something."

Ginny's head came up as Dottie opened the Bible and began flipping pages.

When she found the spot she wanted, Dottie handed the Bible to Ginny. "Read this to me, Ginny. Right there. John 3:17 and 18."

Ginny took the Bible with trembling hands and read aloud: "For God sent not his Son into the world to condemn the world; but that the world through him might be saved. He that believeth on him is not condemned: but he that believeth not is condemned already, because he hath not believed in the name of the only begotten Son of God."

"Keep that page in front off you, honey," said Dottie, "and listen as I quote what Jesus said in Mark 1:15: 'Repent ye, and believe the gospel.' To repent is to change your mind about the direction you're going, turn completely around, and go in the opposite direction. In other words, when a person realizes he is lost and needs to be saved, he or she must repent—turn from the road that leads to hell—and turn to the Lord Jesus Christ, acknowledging their sin against Him and asking Him to save them.

"Jesus said that when you repent, you must also believe the gospel. The Bible calls it the gospel of Jesus Christ because it's all about Him and what He did so He could provide salvation to those who will believe on Him. The apostle Paul said the gospel is 'how that Christ died for our sins according to the Scriptures; and that he was buried, and that he rose again the third day according to the Scriptures.' When He did that, Ginny, He did it for all sinners, including you and me. The sinner who is willing to repent and believe that Jesus died for him on the cross and came back from the grave is forgiven of his sins and is given eternal life. Now, look at John 3:17 again. It says Jesus was not sent to condemn the world, right?"

"Yes."

"And the reason is that according to verse 18, every unbeliever is condemned already. That's why I said earlier that people don't go to hell because they are outlaws. They go to hell because they refuse to believe on Jesus to save them. Outlaws are condemned already, but so are lawmen, bankers, doctors, and housewives. All sinners are condemned already, according to verse 18, because they have not believed in the name of the only begotten Son of God for salvation. It is the unbelief that condemns the sinner. But when that sinner is willing to believe on the Christ of the gospel, salvation is his.

"I quoted the gospel to you a moment ago, Ginny. And if you will recall, there is only one person in the gospel—Jesus Christ. And there is no church or religious system in the gospel. And there are no religious rites or ceremonies in the gospel. Salvation is found only in the Lord Jesus. Look at verse 17 again. 'That the world through him might be saved.' Just Jesus.

"When a person believes that and repents, calling on Jesus to save him, the condemnation is removed. See what it says there in verse 18? 'He that believeth on him is not condemned.'"

Ginny nodded.

"Do you believe that what you just read and what I quoted is true?"

"Well, I...ah...I don't know a lot about it, but it makes sense to me."

"But do you believe it?"

"Well...yes. I do."

"Are you willing to repent and put your faith in Jesus to save you?"

Ginny looked shaken. "I...I'll have to think about it a little, Dottie."

"Honey, don't let the little while become a big while. You need to settle this before you die, and you don't know when that might happen."

Ginny closed her eyes and drew a deep breath. "I just need to go over it in my mind. I need some time to do that."

"Can I show you something else in the Bible that's related to it?"

"Mm-hmm. I guess so."

Dottie glanced at Jim Younger, saw him sleeping soundly, then took the Bible and flipped its pages once more. When she had Proverbs 31 in front of her, she looked Ginny in the eye. "I said a while ago that you're not like Belle or the rest of the gang, even though you are one of them. Are you proud that you're an outlaw?"

Ginny's face flushed. "No. I'm not."

"Good. Since God created you, made you female, and you're now a young woman…shouldn't you want to be the kind of woman God meant for you to be?"

Ginny nodded slightly.

"I want to show you what a woman is supposed to be in the eyes of God," Dottie said, placing the open Bible in Ginny's hands once again. "Here in Proverbs 31. Start with verse 10, and read it to me, all the way to the last verse. Verse 31. As you'll see, the passage is all about what God wants in a woman."

Ginny read the passage, pausing at times to let the words sink in. When she had finished, Dottie said, "All right, honey, now I want you to read verses 10 and 30 to me again."

Ginny nodded. "Who can find a virtuous woman? for her price is far above rubies." Her eyes swept across the page and down, settling on verse 30. "Favour is deceitful, and beauty is vain: but a woman that feareth the LORD, she shall be praised."

"Good. Now, look again at verse 10. God says the virtuous woman is so valuable that her price is what?"

"Far above rubies."

"Mm-hmm. And you know that rubies are so precious their value is very high."

"Yes."

"Now, let's think about the word *virtuous,* for this passage is all about that virtuous woman whose price is far above rubies. The word speaks of a woman's morals, but it also takes in strength, energy, activity, and industry in the proper direction, which is explained in the passage. In verse 30, we are told that the virtuous woman is one who fears the Lord, and it says she shall be praised. According to verse 28, her husband and children have already praised her, so the praise in verse 30 would be praise that comes from God, Himself. Are you following me, Ginny?"

"Yes."

"All right. The fear of the Lord—the utmost reverence for His power and holiness, and hatred for sin, mingled with love, adoration, and respect for Him—only abides in the woman who has been saved. This fear of the Lord is a wellspring of life that makes a woman the kind of wife and mother God wants her to be."

Dottie saw that Ginny's hands were trembling. "Are you satisfied that living the outlaw life will make you the kind of wife and mother God wants you to be?"

Tears formed in Ginny's eyes. She started to speak, but suddenly Wes Logan was in the room, scowling. "Ginny, what are you doing in here?"

Looking up at him, she thumbed away the tears that were about to spill and said, "I couldn't sleep, so I came in to see how Jim was doing. Dottie and I got to talking."

Wes's eyes fell on the open Bible. His scowl deepened. "So what're you crying about?"

Ginny sniffed. "You wouldn't understand."

"Well come on. I want you back on that couch."

As Ginny was rising from the chair, Dottie said, "Honey, please think on the things we've talked about."

Wes looked at the Bible again, then with a stern look in his eyes, said to Dottie, "Exactly what have you been talking about?"

Dottie met his gaze with an unflinching look of her own. "We've been talking about being saved…about how the Lord Jesus Christ died on the cross of Calvary to save sinners."

"Well, lady, you leave Ginny alone about this religious stuff."

"We haven't discussed religion," Dottie countered. "We've talked about knowing God and being acceptable to Him. This is salvation, not religion."

Wes grabbed Ginny's hand and dragged her down the hall.

"Dear Lord," Dottie whispered, "the seed has been sown in Ginny's heart. Please water it and draw her to Yourself."

When they entered the parlor, which was dimly lit by a low-burning lantern, Ginny saw that Frank James was now the guard on duty. Bob Younger had been there when she left to check on Jim.

Wes pulled her up close to him and kissed her, then eased her down to a sitting position on the couch. Letting go of her hand, he said, "Now, go to sleep."

"Night, Ginny," said Frank.

She nodded. "Good night, Frank."

Soon Wes was snoring as he lay on the floor by the couch. Ginny still found sleep elusive. As the sounds of Wes and others sleeping filled the air, she wrestled with the things Dottie had shown her in the Bible and had said to her—about salvation, heaven, hell, and how she looked in the eyes of God as a woman.

Ginny Grayson wanted to go to heaven when she left this world, and there stirred within her the desire to have her price far above rubies in the eyes of God while she was still on earth.

✢

It was shortly before dawn when Breanna awakened and was overwhelmed with nausea. Gripping her stomach, she rolled off the cot and stood to her feet. She noticed that Dottie was now asleep on the floor where Ben Tyler had bedded down before he took his shift in Jim Younger's room.

Frank James came off his chair and said in a low tone, "Where you going?"

Breanna clutched her midsection. "I need to go to the privy."

"All right. I'll escort you out there."

When Breanna went inside the privy, Frank glanced eastward and saw a faint hint of light on the horizon. His attention was brought to Breanna when he heard gagging sounds and retching.

When Breanna came out, she was wiping her mouth with a hankie.

"Something you ate for supper, you suppose?" said Frank.

Breanna shrugged but didn't reply.

When they entered the parlor, Dottie was sitting up on the cot. "Breanna, what's wrong?"

"I'll tell you later, honey. You get back to sleep."

While dawn was breaking on the eastern horizon, Earl Kopatch and Cade Sheridan were bellying down in a field close by the Dunne farm. They had a clear view of the backyard and back porch of the house, as well as a view of the front side of the barn.

They saw men milling about in front of the barn and agreed that the gold must be there. They turned their attention

284

on the house in hopes the nurse would soon put in an appearance.

While breakfast was being devoured by the gang members who had stayed in the house, Breanna was in Jim Younger's room, tending to her patient by giving him hot tea.

Dottie came in. "Breanna, Clara's wanting to know if you feel up to eating."

"Not really."

"But you've got to keep up your strength."

"I just don't think I could keep anything down."

Dottie glanced at Jim, whose mouth was open to take in the tea. "How about some tea, honey? Looks like Jim's holding his down."

"All right. I'll try some tea."

"And maybe a biscuit?"

Breanna sighed. "Well, I'll try a bite or two."

"When are you going to tell me what's wrong, honey?"

Breanna managed a wan smile. "How about now? Jim's just taken his last teaspoon of tea. Let's talk in the room across the hall."

When they were in the other bedroom and the door was closed, Dottie said, "All right, sis. I'm listening."

"Well, it's quite simple, dear. My problem is one that you went through twice."

Dottie's eyes widened. "Breanna! You're...you're—"

"Yes. And I'm sure John won't care whether it's a boy or a girl. He's equally fascinated with your Molly Kate and James."

"You mean John doesn't know?"

"No. I wasn't sure when I left home. I had a strong suspicion, of course, but I didn't want to tell him I was going to have a baby, then find out it really wasn't so. I'm sure now."

Dottie wrapped her arms around Breanna. "Oh, honey, we've got to get out of here. You need to be home so you can rest properly, and—"

"I want to get away too, Dottie, but we'll have to let the Lord work it out. I'll be fine except for the morning sickness."

"So you want this kept a secret?"

"Mm-hmm. John won't mind that I told you first—under these circumstances, especially—but I want him to be the next to know."

"My mouth is sealed."

"Thank you. Of course, some of the others might figure it out when I make regular trips every morning to the privy, looking pale, but I'll let that take care of itself. Now, I guess I'd better try to put down that tea and maybe a biscuit."

When Breanna arrived in the kitchen, the gang members who had slept in the barn were at the breakfast table, and the others were at the barn.

Clara looked at Breanna. "Are you all right?"

"I'm fine. I think, though, I'll just try a cup of hot tea and one biscuit."

Belle Reed was seated at the table. Patting the empty chair next to her, she said, "Siddown, nursie. Where's your sister?"

"She's staying with Jim while I have some breakfast."

Clara came with a cup of steaming tea and a biscuit on a small plate. "There you go, Breanna. Let me know if you want more."

"Thank you. I will."

When Clara was gone, Belle said, "So how's Jim doin'?"

"His pulse it getting stronger, and his color is better. He was able to take some hot tea a few minutes ago."

"Good. You think this means he's gonna make it?"

"Yes, I do. Of course, complications could set in, but I believe he's over the hump."

"Good. Cole's out at the barn, but I think he'd like to hear this good news. He was comin' in to see Jim and ask you about him a little later, but I think I'd better go tell him."

Breanna had eaten half the biscuit—which was all she wanted—when Cole came in with Bob and John at his side. Belle hurried ahead of them to Breanna. "They want to see Jim and talk to you at the same time."

When they reached the room, Breanna said, "Dottie, the Younger brothers want to see Jim. I'll take it from here."

"All right. Did you have your tea and biscuit?"

"Yes." Breanna's eyes were drawn to a pile of blood-soaked bedding on the floor. "Dottie, I was going to change the bedding."

Picking it up, Dottie said, "Clara told me she wanted to wash Jim's bedding, along with the bedding that Rufe bled on, so I figured I'd go ahead and change it while Jim was awake and able to shift from one side of the bed to the other for me."

As Dottie hurried from the room, the Younger brothers moved up to the bed and looked down at Jim, who was sleeping.

"So Belle says you think Jim's gonna pull through," said Cole.

"I believe so."

"Tell us about it."

Dottie appeared in the kitchen just as the rest of the gang members were leaving the table and filing out the back door.

"Oh, yes, the bedding," said Clara. "I have the other bedding on the back porch with the rest of my wash. You don't really need to help me, Dottie."

"I'll be glad to unless I'm needed more here in the kitchen."

"I'll handle these dishes," said Ginny. "You help Clara."

Dottie nodded, then paused. "Have you been thinking about our talk, Ginny?"

"Yes."

"Good. See you later."

On the back porch, Dottie found that Clara already had hot water in one galvanized tub and cold water in another. On a shelf were a couple of bottles of lye soap.

Earl Kopatch and Cade Sheridan lay on their bellies, watching the house closely.

"Been a slug o' men come and go, Cade, but only that one woman who's been gettin' ready to do her wash. She's gotta be the farmer's wife."

"Yep, I'd say so. What's got me puzzled is how come them other women ain't showed up. Especially that nurse. She's gotta be in th— Hey, look! There she is! That's her, Cade. The nurse!"

"You're sure that's her?"

"Of course. I got a good look at her yesterday at the stage office. Who could forget a good-lookin' little blond like that? It's her, all right."

"Aha! Looks like she's gonna help the farmer's wife do the washin'."

"We gotta grab her."

"We'll have to do it just right. It'll be perfect if the farmer's wife leaves her alone for even a few minutes."

"Put your head down! Somebody's comin' from the barn."

✦

As Clara and Dottie were dropping the wash into the galvanized tub of hot water, they both looked up and saw Red Cassidy, one of the gang's newest members, coming from the barn.

"Wonder what Red wants," mumbled Clara.

"Who knows? Maybe he wants to help us with the wash."

Clara snorted. "Sure."

When Cassidy drew up to the porch, he said, "Jesse didn't think it was too good, you ladies bein' out here by yourselves, so he sent me to keep an eye on you."

"You really think we could do something to hurt you big tough outlaws?" said Clara.

"Jesse doesn't trust you, that's all I know." Red had the hair to match his name. "Don't let me stop you. Go ahead and do your wash."

When the wash was rinsed and wrung out, Clara said, "Okay, Dottie, time to hang them up."

At that moment, the back door opened and Ginny said, "Clara, Larry and Laura were playing at the pantry and they spilled flour on their clothes. They need you right now."

Clara looked at Dottie. "I'll be back as soon as I can."

"Don't worry about it. You take care of the children. I'll hang up the wash."

Red Cassidy followed Dottie as she carried a heavy basket of wet wash to the clothesline, then said, "Lady, I just thought of somethin' I gotta talk to Jesse about. I'll be back in a few minutes."

Dottie sent him a dull look. "Go ahead."

"Don't get any ideas of runnin' for it when I go inside that barn. Cole will kill your sister for sure if you take off. Understand?"

Dottie gave him another bland look. "I'm not going any-where."

Ten minutes later, Red Cassidy left the barn and headed for the clothesline. When he didn't see Dottie, he looked for her on the back porch. She was nowhere to be seen.

When he came near the clothesline, he saw a wet sheet par-tially pinned to the line, swinging in the breeze. The basket of wash was still on the ground. Looking toward the privy, he dashed to it, but when he yanked the door open, it was unoc-cupied.

From there he darted into the house. Clara was cleaning flour off her children's clothes with a wet cloth.

Red hurried in, looking around. "That Dottie woman come in here?"

"No," said Belle. "She's out there hangin' up the wash."

"No, she ain't. She's done took off."

Belle hurried toward Jim's bedroom, crying loudly, "Cole! We got a problem! Cole!"

DOTTIE CARROLL FOUND HERSELF ABOARD a galloping horse and held in the tight grip of Cade Sheridan, who rode behind her. There was a gag tied over her mouth, and her hands were bound to the pommel. Earl Kopatch rode next to them.

Dottie was terrified. Who were these men, and what were they planning to do with her?

Soon they left the road and galloped across a field. She observed the blackened ruins of what had once been a farmhouse. As they began to slow the horses, she realized they were taking her to the old weatherworn barn.

She whined when Sheridan untied her hands from the pommel and grunted, "If you pull that gag off and try to scream for help, I'll have to coldcock you. Don't fight me, and you'll be all right. The gag stays on until I take it off. Got it?"

She made another whining sound and nodded.

Sheridan dragged her through the barn door and toward a horse stall where two men lay in the straw and two others were standing over them. She quickly saw that the two men in the straw were wounded. The smaller man was breathing with effort, obviously asleep or unconscious. The big man was eyeing her.

"We did it, Dub!" Cade said. "Here's the nurse who was on the stage."

Dottie's head came around, and she looked at him askance, her thoughts jumbling in her head. *Nurse? He thinks I'm Breanna! How did they know there was a nurse on board the stagecoach? Did he say Dub? Oh, dear Lord in heaven…this is the Thaxton gang! Help me, Lord! Help me!*

"You did good," said Dub. "Take the gag off her and let her go to work."

"J. R.'s passed out," Ernie Mills said. "The pain got so bad he couldn't stand it."

Mel Fixx spoke up. "Seems to me she oughtta work on you first, Dub. After all, you're the head of this outfit."

"Yeah," said Dub. "Work on me first, lady."

Dottie's heart banged against her ribs. She knew a little about gunshot wounds, being married to a physician and surgeon, but she didn't know enough to do Dub Thaxton any good.

"We had to grab her while she was hangin' up wash behind the farmhouse," Cade said, removing the gag from Dottie's mouth. "There was no way we could get inside and grab her medical bag. But we figured, bein' a nurse, she could still do you and J. R. more good than we can."

Dub's pain-filled eyes watched Dottie's face. "C'mon, little nursie, fix me up. I'm bleedin' pretty bad."

Dottie thought of Breanna. *Would Cole Younger really kill her if he thinks I've run away? No, Cole still needs Breanna to care for Jim.* Fearing the Thaxton men were desperate enough to go back to the Dunne farm and try to abduct Breanna, Dottie told herself she would let them believe she was the nurse. Breanna might be in more danger here than she was at the Dunne farm.

One question picked at her mind. *How did the Thaxton gang know there was a nurse aboard the stagecoach?*

Dottie knelt down beside Dub Thaxton and said, "I'll try not to hurt you, but I've got to examine the wound."

"Do what you have to," said Dub, stiffening a little as she opened his shirt and took away the blood-soaked bandannas the men had pressed against the wound to stay the flow of blood.

While Dottie probed about the gaping hole with her fingertips, Dub said, "S'pose we oughtta know your name, little nurse."

"Dorothy. My friends call me Dottie."

Cade Sheridan knelt beside her. "Well, since you're here to save the lives of our boss, and our friend J. R., we most certainly are your friends. So we'll call you Dottie."

Earl Kopatch moved close enough to touch his knee to her back. "So tell us, Dottie, how bad is Dub's wound? Will you be able to get the slug out of his chest?"

Though Dottie was not medically trained, all she had to do was take one look at Dub's wound to know the slug was very deep and the flow of blood coming from the ragged hole in his chest meant he would die soon.

She closed the shirt over the wound and looked up at Kopatch. "I need to talk to you men about how I'm going to go after the slug, since I have no forceps. I want Dub to rest quietly. Could we talk somewhere?"

"Sure," said Sheridan. "Over there by the milkin' stanchions."

"Be back in a minute," Dottie told Dub.

The four men followed Dottie to the row of stanchions where the farmer had once milked his cows.

Turning to face them, she kept her voice just above a whisper. "I hate to tell you this, but your boss is going to die. At best, the only thing you could supply me to probe for that slug and take it out would be a knife. Like the one on your belt." She pointed to the knife in a leather sheath on Mel Fixx's waist.

"You're welcome to borrow it," said Mel.

Dottie shook her head. "It wouldn't work. If I try to take out the slug, the shock of it will kill him. Even if I had forceps it would be too much. He's lost a lot of blood."

"Hey, guys!" came Dub's voice.

"Yeah, Dub?" Ernie Mills called out.

"I think J. R. just died. It doesn't look like he's breathin'. Send Dottie to check on him."

Dottie hurried to the spot where J. R. Killian lay in the stall. Under Dub's watchful eye, Dottie pressed fingers against the side of J. R's neck. When she could get no pulse, she took hold of his wrist. Again, there was no sign of life. She held her cupped hand close to his sagging mouth. There was no breath.

Sighing, she turned to Dub. "You're right." She looked toward the other four and called out, "Your friend J. R. is dead."

Dub coughed, which made him cry out from the pain it lanced through his wound. Dottie moved to him, opening the shirt again.

Cade Sheridan whispered to his companions, "From what the nurse is tellin' us, it won't be long till Dub goes too. I think we need to go after that gold. Whattaya think?"

"That's the whole reason we jumped the James-Youngers," said Kopatch. "At least we oughtta find a way to get our hands on it."

"I agree," said Mills.

Sheridan nodded. "Okay. Since Dub's a goner, let's leave the nurse with him to keep him as comfortable as possible and we'll try to get into the barn at that farm. Let's grab as much of the gold as we can and hightail outta here. Let me handle it with Dub, okay?"

The other three agreed, and Cade headed toward the stall.

Kneeling beside Dub, Dottie said, "I explained to your men that the slug is embedded very deep in your chest. I have no delicate surgical instrument with which to attempt removing it. And even if I did, the shock of the probing could kill you. I'm not skilled at removing slugs. You need a doctor."

Hunkering down next to Dottie, Cade said, "Dub, we've been talkin'. Dottie told us how bad it is for you. We decided we'd find a doctor and bring him here. With his medical bag, of course."

Dub coughed again. Blood appeared at the corners of his mouth. He wiped the blood away with a shaky hand. "Get that doctor here fast."

"Since we don't know where the closest doctor is," said Cade, "two of us will go one way, and two the other. We'll probably end up with two doctors, but that's better than none."

Leaving their dying leader and Dottie, the gang saddled up and rode away.

At the Dunne farm, it was a somber bunch that waited in the parlor. Belle and Jim Reed sat on one of the couches, while Ben Tyler sat on the other couch with Laura on his lap. Young Larry was sitting next to him with his mother on the other side.

Ginny looked grim as she sat on a straight-backed chair with Wes Logan standing beside her. The rest of the gang was at the barn, except for Jesse, Cole, and Red Cassidy, who were on a mission.

Breanna had stayed in Clara's room with Jim Younger.

"I know Dottie wouldn't have run to get help," said Clara.

"She knows that would put her sister in danger, and the rest of us, for that matter. As much as we all want out of this situation, she wouldn't risk it."

"That's right," said Ben. "She had to have been taken away by force. But who would do that? And why?"

"I think Cole and Jesse will be able to shed some light on those questions when they come in," said Belle. "I agree. Dottie wouldn't have left here on her own."

Footsteps were heard on the porch just before Frank James pulled the door open to let in Jesse, Cole, and Red.

"She was abducted, all right," Jesse announced. "We found boot prints at the clothesline. It was two men. Apparently they carried Dottie to their horses back in the woods. We found the hoof marks and followed them to the road. It was impossible to tell which direction they rode."

"We also found the spot where the men were lyin' in the grass, waitin'," said Cole. "I told Jesse and Red I have a feelin' Dottie was taken by members of the Thaxton gang. It's the only thing that makes sense to me. I think they're stayin' around close, plannin' to get their hands on the gold."

"I agree it makes sense," Jim Reed said. "Sure they would still like to have the gold! But why grab Dottie? They don't even know who she is."

Breanna stepped further into the room and said, "Maybe they plan to use Dottie as a hostage and demand that you turn the gold over to them."

Jesse shook his head. "Naw. They're outlaws. They know we wouldn't give them the gold in exchange for the life of a woman who means nothing to us."

Breanna shot him an icy look.

"Right, Jesse," put in Frank. "They didn't grab her to use as a hostage."

"Then there's only one other reason that would make sense," said Breanna. "We know some of the Thaxton gang were wounded...even their leader. Some of the wounded may have died by now, but those who are still alive need medical attention. Somehow they found out there was a nurse aboard the stage. Maybe they even had a description of me. But they mistook Dottie for me and abducted her."

"I think you're right, Breanna," said Ben. "They thought they were grabbing the nurse."

"And if that's the case," said Breanna, "when they figure out that Dottie isn't a nurse, they sure aren't going to bring her back. They'll—" Her voice broke. "They'll kill her."

Clara went to Breanna and wrapped her arms around her. "I know it looks bad, honey, but Dottie's in God's hands. He will take care of her."

Ginny left her chair and joined them, gripping Breanna's shoulder. "Clara's right, Breanna. God will take care of your sister."

"Come back over here and sit down," Wes ordered Ginny.

Belle spoke up as Ginny headed back to the chair. "Hey, girl...don't get religious on us. You've been comin' along good as one of us. You get religion it'll ruin you."

"Nice speech, Belle," said Logan.

Jesse turned to Cole and said, "Tell you what. Since it's pretty plain that what's left of the Thaxton gang is hanging around to find a way to get their hands on our gold, I think it would be best to remove it from the premises."

"And put it where?"

"Well, if you and your men are in agreement to get it out of here, how about me and my men taking the gold back to the Younger farm? I know you want to stay here until Jim's able to travel. As soon as he's well enough, you and your men can come and meet us at your place. We'll divide up the gold then."

Cole looked at the floor as he contemplated Jesse's suggestion. He nodded and said, "Good idea. I wouldn't do this if it was someone else, but you know I trust you, Jesse...and Frank...and the rest of your boys. If we've figured the Thaxton bunch correctly, they'll be makin' an attempt to grab the gold. I think you guys should wait till about an hour before dawn to pull out. Still be dark for your departure, but you'd soon have light for the rest of the trip."

"I was thinking the same thing, Cole," Jesse said. "We'll pull out at four o'clock in the morning."

Breanna stepped closer to Cole and flicked a glance at Jesse. "You two should find out where the Thaxton gang is hiding and go rescue Dottie before they find out she's not a nurse."

"Your sister is on her own," Cole said. "What happens to her is her problem."

Breanna fought the rise of panic as she retorted, "But it's your fault this happened to her! If you hadn't robbed the stage we were on and brought us here, Dottie wouldn't be in the hands of those vile men!"

"I'll say it again, lady. She's on her own. We ain't gonna waste our time lookin' for her."

"Then let me go."

"Absolutely not. You're stayin' here so you can look after Jim. And lady, if you should sneak off the place to look for her, we'll kill Ben, Clara, and her children."

Cole's words terrified Laura, who was still seated on her uncle's lap. She wrapped her arms around Ben's neck and cried, "Uncle Ben, don't let those bad men kill us! Please!"

At that point, Larry began to cry.

Clara rushed to her children and laid hands on both of

them, whispering words of comfort and encouragement.

"Haven't you got any heart at all?" Ben said, his eyes full of contempt. "You shouldn't frighten these children!"

Cole whipped out his gun and pointed it at him. "Shut up or I'll blow you full of holes right in front of 'em!"

Laura screamed and Larry howled in terror.

Breanna stepped up to Cole, eyes flashing. "What kind of man are you? Those children never did anything to you!"

"You shut up, too! Get on back there with my brother!"

Breanna's features lost what little color they had. "How can you expect me to just ignore my sister's plight? She's in danger."

"Well, you'll have to ignore it, lady, unless you want people to die because you left this farm to hunt for her."

Ginny, who had been silent for several minutes jumped up from her chair and stepped up to Cole. "If you and these other outlaws were real men, you would go find Dottie and bring her back!"

"Whose side are you on, girl?" Jesse said.

She pivoted to look at him. "Is it wrong for me to care about Dottie? After all, she's a human being!"

Jesse's eyes were like ice as he said, "Ginny, I don't want to hear any more from you. Dottie's on her own...we don't have time to worry about her. We've got our own problems."

She threw up her hands in frustration. "Yeah? Well, what if it was Zee? Huh? What would you do then, Jesse? You'd go rescue her, wouldn't you? Well, Dottie's life and welfare are just as important to her husband as Zee's are to you!"

"Now, look. I told you—"

Ginny cut him off. "The whole bunch of you are spineless cowards, that's what you are! You've no sense of chivalry at all! Because of you, Dottie is now at the mercy of those Thaxton beasts, and nobody in this bunch even cares!"

Wes grabbed Ginny's hand. "That's enough, Ginny. Come sit down. You're irritating Cole and Jesse."

She jerked her hand free, her eyes blazing. "I'm not irritating just Cole and Jesse, am I? I'm irritating you, too! You're as spineless and uncaring as they are!"

Wes grasped her hand again, bearing down hard. "I said sit down."

Ben Tyler stiffened at such treatment of a woman, but Clara, who was sitting beside him with her children, gave a slight shake of her head. He nodded and remained silent.

Ginny looked Wes up and down as she said, "If you had any decency, you would talk the rest of these outlaws into going with you. You'd find where the Thaxton bunch are hiding and you'd rescue Dottie!"

Wes gritted his teeth and ground out his words. "I agree with Cole. The Carroll woman is on her own."

Ginny's voice was low and trembling as she said, "You're as low as the rest of them."

"Shut up!" Wes shouted, slapping her across the mouth.

Ben's entire body tensed. His smoldering gaze silently tracked Logan's movements as he led Ginny toward a chair.

Breanna went to Ginny's side and put an arm around her. "Wes, her mouth is bleeding. You cut her lip."

Logan looked down at Ginny's mouth but his face didn't change expression.

"Here," said Breanna, tugging at the hand still in Wes's grip. "I'll take her to the kitchen table so I can work on her."

Wes suddenly let go of Ginny's hand and said, "Take her."

Breanna guided Ginny toward the parlor door. When they moved into the hall, Breanna stopped and looked back at Wes, saying levelly, "It takes a big, brave man to slap a woman around."

Logan stared at her silently.

"You and I are through, Wesley Logan!" Ginny said. "I've lost all respect for you. What I thought was love in my heart, I now know was only infatuation. And you've killed even that."

"Wait a minute!" gusted Logan. "You can't mean that! We're going to have a talk."

"No talk," Ginny said flatly. "Stay away from me. We have nothing to discuss. We're through."

Logan moved through the doorway and shoved Breanna out of the way. He grabbed Ginny's arm. "We're going outside and talk right now!"

"Let go of me! You're hurting me!"

Before anyone could stop him, Ben Tyler was across the room and standing in front of Logan, shouting, "Let go of her!"

Wes glanced back through the door at Jesse, but he only moved his head slowly back and forth and said, "The boys and I don't get involved when it comes to a man and his woman, Wes. But I'd suggest you don't cause a ruckus here. These people have treated us decent. Including Ben."

Wes shot Ben a threatening look and said, "You stay out of it. Me and my woman need to go outside and have a private talk."

Ginny wiped blood from her lip. "I'm not your woman, Wes. And the real man in this place is Ben Tyler. He's a good, hardworking man with character, integrity, and the right kind of attitude toward women. He gave up his own farm to come here and run this farm for his widowed sister and her children. Besides that, Ben is a Christian, and I admire him for that."

Wes glared at Ben. "You stole Ginny's affections from me!"

"You're wrong, Wes!" Ginny said. "Ben has made no move toward me at all. He didn't steal what I felt for you. You destroyed that yourself! In spite of the fact that I'm an outlaw, Ben has been kind to me and a perfect gentleman. That's more than you've been."

Wes ejected a vile curse and whipped out his gun. "I'm gonna kill you, Tyler!"

Ben took a step away from Ginny, his eyes fixed on the angry man.

"Wes," Jesse said calmly, "put the gun away."

Logan ignored Jesse and snapped the hammer back, growling the words, "You had no right to steal Ginny from me!" Even as he spoke, he tightened his hold on the gun and his finger pressed tight against the trigger.

In a flash, Ginny cried, "No!" and leaped in front of Ben. The gun roared at the same moment.

Ginny's body jerked from the impact of the bullet and she slumped to the floor.

Suddenly the front door burst open and Clell Miller came in, shouting breathlessly, "Jesse! Cole! Some of the Thaxton gang are sneakin' up behind the barn!"

Already they could hear gunfire.

"Everybody to the barn!" Cole shouted. "You, too, Wes!"

Wes Logan stood like a statue over Ginny with the smoking gun in his hand. Then he blinked as if he had just awakened from a nightmare, glanced at Ginny once more, then dashed out the door on the heels of Cole and Jesse.

"Put her on the bed in your room, Ben," said Breanna. "I'll get my medical bag."

Ginny was still conscious as Ben gently picked her up and carried her toward his room.

Rapid gunfire reverberated across the grounds to the house.

Belle paused at the bedroom door and watched Ben place Ginny on the bed. Breanna rushed past her, medical bag in hand. "Thank you, Ben. I'll need some hot water."

"I'll get it," came Clara's voice from the hallway.

Leaving Laura and Larry to stand beside Belle, Clara hurried away.

Ben watched Breanna as she examined the spot on Ginny's left side where the bullet had struck her. Taking scissors from her bag, Breanna began cutting the dress away from the wound.

"Do I need to leave the room?" Ben asked.

"No...the wound is just below the waist, in her hip."

Ben kept his gaze on Ginny's face. Her eyes were closed, and she was clenching her teeth. Sweat beads covered her forehead.

When Breanna laid the blood-stained scissors aside, Ben looked at her and said, "How bad is it?"

"The slug is lodged in her hip, but it's not very deep. Didn't hit the bone. Praise God for that. I can have it out in a matter of minutes. She'll be fine."

When Ginny opened her eyes Breanna said, "Honey, I don't have any anesthetic. There's going to be some extreme pain when I remove the slug."

Ginny swallowed hard. "It's...all...right, Breanna. At least Ben...didn't get...shot."

Ben leaned close and looked into her pain-filled eyes. "Ginny, I don't know how to thank you for what you did. You took the bullet meant for me. It probably would have killed me, since Wes was aiming for my midsection. I'm sorry you've got to go through the pain, but I'm glad you'll be all right."

"The...pain will...be worth it, Ben," she said, wincing. "Your life was...well worth...saving."

Tears filmed Ben's eyes but words failed him.

When Clara came back with the pail of hot water, Breanna

enlisted her help. Ben stepped into the hall and held the children close while Breanna went to work. Belle looked on from her place at the door.

The gunfire at the barn was becoming sporadic by the time Breanna had the slug out and had stitched up the wound. It had taken only a matter of minutes.

While bandaging the wound, Breanna said, "You're a good patient. I'm proud of you."

Ginny managed a weak smile.

"And I'm also proud of you for taking that bullet to save Ben. That was a very unselfish and brave thing to—"

"The gunfire's stopped," Belle blurted out.

Clara nodded. "Whatever happened up there, it sounds like it's all over."

Belle pulled back the sheer curtain and looked out the window.

"What's it look like?" Ben asked.

Belle studied the scene. "It's all over. Some of the boys are headin' for the house. Well, at least it's Cole, Jesse, Frank, and my husband. The others are movin' around up there, and—"

"And what?" said Breanna.

"Couple of 'em are carryin' a man inside the barn. I guess he must be dead. If he was wounded, they'd bring him down here for Breanna to work on."

Clara moved up beside Belle and peered through the window. "Can you tell who it is? The dead man, I mean."

Belle squinted. "I...oh..." She looked down at Ginny, then peered through the window again. "It looks like Wes Logan."

21

CLARA DUNNE WATCHED INTENTLY as the lifeless form was carried into the darkness of the barn. "It's Wes. The shirt of the dead man is the one Wes was wearing. And...look. That's Wes's hat that Arch Clements just picked up and took inside."

Ginny Grayson looked at Breanna, then at Ben, who had come inside the room once more. She closed her eyes and swallowed hard, then looked at Ben again, who was now standing beside the bed.

Belle left the window and went to the bedroom door as the sounds of the men entering the house met their ears. She stepped into the hall. "We're all in here, fellas."

As the four men drew near, Belle said, "Looks like you must've wiped 'em out."

"We did," Cole said. "There were only four of 'em, but they put up a good fight. We lost one."

"Yeah," said Belle. "Looked to us like it was Wes."

"Yep. Took a bullet in his heart. Killed him instantly."

The four outlaws crowded around the bedroom door, peering in. Cole flicked a glance at Ginny and said to Breanna. "How's she doin'?"

"The slug was in her hip. Not deep. Didn't hit the bone. She'll limp for a while, but she'll be fine."

Cole nodded, then looked back at Ginny. "I guess you heard what I just told Belle."

She nodded solemnly.

"So what about the rest of the Thaxtons?" Belle asked.

Jesse answered. "We have no way of knowing where the rest of them are hiding out or how many are left. Can't be very many. Cole and I assume Dub's still alive and sent those four men to steal the gold."

Breanna put pleading eyes on Jesse, then Cole. "I'm asking you to please search for the Thaxton hideout and bring my sister back to me."

Jesse shook his head. "We don't have time to go scouting all over the area, trying to find your sister. Besides, she's not our responsibility."

Breanna brushed a stray lock of hair from her forehead. "You know, Jesse, a little while ago when Wes was showing signs of violence, you told him not to start a ruckus because Clara and Ben had treated the gang decently."

"Yeah?"

"I really thought you might have a small decent streak yourself. But now I know I was wrong."

A cocky look came over Jesse's face and he said, "The reason I'm a successful outlaw leader is because I let all the decency drain out of me when I formed my gang."

"Well, I'm sorry for you."

Jesse chuckled humorlessly and shrugged. "I'm happy."

"You won't be when you face God."

From where she lay, Ginny Grayson had a full view of Jesse's face. She watched as the arrogant man swallowed hard and looked away from Breanna.

Ginny spoke up in a weak voice. "Jesse, Wes learned how wrong he was, didn't he?"

"Wrong about what?"

"Wes laughed when I brought up to him what the Lord Jesus said in the Bible: 'They that take the sword shall perish with the sword.' He didn't believe it was true that to live by the gun is to die by the gun. But it happened anyway."

Jesse flicked a glance at his brother and Cole, then looked back at Ginny. "That was just coincidence."

"Yeah," put in Belle. "That's all it was. Right, Jim?"

"Sure. That Bible stuff is ridiculous."

"That's what I told her," said Belle. "I'm livin' by the gun, but I'm plannin' to die in bed of old age."

The four men laughed.

"Me too," said Jesse. "There's no bullet ever gonna have my name on it." He turned to Cole. "I need to talk to you."

"Let's go outside," said Cole and walked away with Jesse on his heels.

Belle hurried to catch up with Jim and slipped her arm around his waist.

"It's time for Ginny to get some rest," Breanna said. "We can look in on her later. I've got to go across the hall and see how Jim Younger's doing."

Ben leaned over and squeezed Ginny's hand. "See you later. You do as Breanna says and rest."

Clara picked up the pail of water, looked down at Ginny, and said, "I'll never be able to express how I feel, Ginny. You saved my brother's life."

Ginny smiled and gave a slight nod.

Breanna began gathering her medical instruments and folding them in a towel when she said, "Honey, please rest."

Ginny nodded.

"And if you need me at any time, just call out. All right?"

Ginny nodded again.

Breanna paused. "I know it was all over between you and Wes, but are you hurting in your heart?"

"Not like you might think, Breanna. I'm sorry he was killed, of course. But what bothers me the most is that Wes died without the Lord. He went to the same place I would have gone if I'd been killed by his bullet."

Breanna angled her head to one side, her brow crinkling. "Ginny, dear, I was going to talk to you about that very thing when you were feeling better."

Ginny's voice was unsteady and her hands shook slightly. "Please, Breanna. Help me. I want to be saved."

Breanna laid the towel down. "How much do you know about it?"

"Enough to know I'm lost. I'd be in hell right now if that bullet had taken my life. You see, Dottie talked to me last night during her shift with Jim. I couldn't sleep, so I came in to talk with her. Dottie used the Bible to show me about being saved, and she showed me from Proverbs chapter 31 about being a virtuous woman before God."

"Well, that's wonderful. But you didn't open your heart to Jesus?"

"No. Dottie tried to get me to, but I told her I wanted to think about it. Well, I have. And I want to be saved. I want to be a woman whose price is far above rubies. I can rest later. Will you help me now?'

"I most certainly will!" Breanna picked up the Bible from the dresser and pulled up a chair to the bed.

"I'm so sorry Dottie was abducted by the Thaxton gang, Breanna. I hope she's all right."

"She has to be. I'm trusting the Lord to protect her from harm and bring her back safely. I'm human, so I have my moments when fear tries to take over in my mind about it, but

I know my God is able to protect Dottie in spite of the circumstances."

Looking at the Bible in Breanna's hands, Ginny said, "Would you read the chapter in Proverbs to me first? I want to hear it again."

"Certainly."

When Breanna had finished reading, Ginny was wiping tears. "Oh, I do so want to be like that," she said, sniffling.

Breanna patted her hand. "You will be, sweetie. Now let me read some passages to you from the New Testament."

When Breanna had given Ginny several verses concerning the new birth, forgiveness of sins, and redemption, explaining them thoroughly, she turned to Romans 10:13 to "draw the net."

Ginny repeated in a half whisper what she had heard. "Whosoever shall call upon the name of the Lord shall be saved." Tears streamed down her cheeks. "I'm ready, Breanna. I want to call on the Lord to save me. I want to be the kind of woman who, in God's sight, has a price far above rubies."

When Ginny had called on the Lord Jesus to save her, Breanna prayed aloud, asking the Lord to keep His hand on her and guide every step of her life, now that she was His child.

"Breanna," Ginny said, "when Dottie lived in San Francisco she tried to tell me about Jesus. She tried to tell my parents, too, but we wouldn't listen. Mama and Papa both taught me that the Bible wasn't true, and though they loved Dottie, they told me I wasn't to listen to her when she talked to me about Jesus. I'm so glad I listened this time."

"So am I, honey," said Breanna, rising to her feet. She pushed the chair back against the wall, then leaned over the bed and planted a kiss on Ginny's cheek. "You take yourself a nap. I'll see you later."

A wide smile spread across Ginny's face. "It's so wonderful to know I'm going to heaven!"

Breanna headed for the door. "That it is, sweetie. We'll talk more about your new salvation later. Right now, you go to sleep."

Ginny was still smiling when the door closed. "Thank You, Lord Jesus," she breathed, closing her eyes. "Thank You for saving a sinner like me."

At the same time Breanna was dealing with Ginny Grayson about salvation, Chief U.S. Marshal John Brockman was sitting in the U.S. marshal's office in Topeka. Because Kansas was in the Western district, U.S. Marshal Clayton Saunders was under John's command.

Shortly after John had boarded the train in Cheyenne City with his three deputies and they were riding in the baggage coach with the gold, the conductor had come in saying there had been a change in plans. He explained that because of anticipated trouble with the James-Younger gang, the gold would be taken off the train that day when it stopped at Topeka, instead of going on to Kansas City as originally scheduled. The gold would be disguised as another kind of cargo and placed on the regular stage to Wichita the next morning. It would be hidden beneath the floor of the stage in a specially built secret compartment.

If the gang struck, it would probably happen between Topeka and Kansas City. In order to implement further precautions, the gold would be taken off the stage when it reached Emporia by a U.S. Army unit out of Fort Scott, Kansas. The soldiers would load the gold into an army wagon and carry it over back roads to vice president Edmund Harris at Kansas City Bank and Trust Company.

When John heard this and realized the gold was on the stage Breanna and Dottie would be taking to Emporia, he told his deputies they could take the next train west through Topeka and go home. He was going to surprise his wife and sister-in-law by showing up to ride the stage with them.

When they went to watch the transfer of the gold from the train to a freight wagon that would carry it to the Wells Fargo office and the specially built stagecoach, Saunders shared that he was having some internal problems in the Topeka office and needed his supervisor's help. John agreed to cancel his plans to surprise Breanna and Dottie.

It had taken almost two days for John to help Saunders iron out the problems. By then, John knew the anniversary celebration in Emporia would be about over. He bought himself a return ticket to Denver.

"Well, sir," Marshal Saunders said, "I sure am glad you were here to help me get these difficulties taken care of. It's about time to head for the depot. Don't want you to miss your train."

John rose to his feet.

Suddenly there was a knock at the office door, accompanied by a male voice calling out, "Telegram, sir!" The young deputy who worked the desk in the outer office handed Saunders the telegram and quickly left the room.

The marshal ripped open the envelope and glanced at the yellow paper. "It's from Captain Trevor Warrick, sir. He's the man in charge of the army unit that picked up the gold at Emporia."

John watched the expression on Saunders's face change as he read the message. "What's the matter?"

Saunders's face was grim as he said, "Sir, something terrible has happened. The stage that was carrying the gold has disappeared."

"What? My wife and sister-in-law were booked on that stage! What do you mean…disappeared?"

"Captain Warrick says the stage never arrived at Emporia. A farmer reported seeing the stage a few miles north of Osage City, but no one has seen it since. Town Marshal Bruce Thornton in Osage has been alerted by the army that the stage disappeared somewhere near there, and they have him keeping an eye out for it. Troops from Fort Scott are headed that way to do a thorough search."

John hurriedly put his hat on and turned toward the door. "I've got to send a telegram of my own. Is the Western Union office still where it was two years ago?"

"Yes, sir. Right on Main Street, next door to Wiley's General Store."

"I'll let you know what I'm doing once I get an answer back from my wire."

Minutes later, Brockman entered the Western Union office. He sent a telegram to Frank and Eloise Baylor, asking if Dottie and Breanna had arrived. He paced the floor until the reply came about forty minutes later. The Baylors' wire advised him that Breanna and Dottie had not arrived. Their stage never came in. The Wells Fargo people told them it had disappeared and they had army units out of Fort Scott coming to search for it.

Brockman wired Marshal Bruce Thornton in Osage City, explaining that his wife and sister-in-law were on the missing stage and that he would be riding there as fast as possible.

At the Dunne farm, Jesse James and Cole Younger entered the parlor after a private talk outside. Cole looked toward Belle Reed, who was listening to Frank James and her husband as they made plans about their share of the gold.

"Belle," he said, "would you go tell Breanna I want to talk to her?"

"Sure," she headed for the parlor door.

"Where are Ben, Clara, and the brats?" Cole asked.

Belle looked over her shoulder. "They're in the kitchen."

"Tell 'em I want 'em in here."

"Will do."

"New plan since we had the shoot-out with Thaxton's boys?" Frank asked.

Jesse nodded. "Yeah. We need to get all of us out of here."

"What about Jim and Ginny?"

"That's what I want to talk to the nurse about," Cole said.

Footsteps sounded in the hall. When Belle and Breanna entered the parlor, Belle said, "The others are coming."

Breanna set her gaze on Cole. "Belle says you want to talk to me."

"Yeah. I want to know if Jim can travel."

Breanna frowned. "Well, he's coming along even better than I expected, but there's no way he can ride a horse."

Ben and Clara and the children entered the room.

"Siddown," said Cole. "We're talkin' about our departure, and I figure you need to know what's happenin'."

Cole turned back to Breanna. "I wasn't plannin' on Jim ridin' his horse."

"You had Bob's buggy in mind?"

"Yeah."

"Jim would have to lie down. As I recall, Bob's buggy isn't wide enough for that. I wouldn't advise it. I'll be honest with you—the sooner all of you are gone, the better. But if you try to take Jim in the buggy, he's going to have problems."

Cole scratched his head. "All right, how about if we take

Clara's wagon and team, and one of her mattresses? Put Jim on the mattress in the bed of the wagon?"

"That would be a lot better," Breanna said, "but in his condition, he shouldn't travel even that way for at least a week."

"But if he had the mattress, it'd cushion him good enough, wouldn't it?"

"Well, whoever drives the wagon will have to take it easy. Hard bumps, even lying on a mattress, could start him bleeding internally."

Cole nodded. "And how about Ginny? Could she ride on the mattress?"

Breanna sighed. "At this stage in her recovery process, it would be risky."

"I'm gonna go talk to Jim about this," said Cole. Then to Jesse he said, "Would you go out and tell the guys at the barn to come in? I want everybody in on this."

Cole looked at Breanna "Let's have Ginny in here too. I want her to know what's goin' on."

"She's sleeping," Breanna said. "I gave her a sedative with salicylic acid in it to help relieve her pain."

"Then wake her up! We gotta make plans, and she has to be in on it."

Ben Tyler stood up and moved toward the door. "I'll carry her in here and put her on the couch, Breanna."

"All right. Let's go."

Breanna gently awakened Ginny and told her that Cole and Jesse were planning to take the whole gang and leave, and wanted her in on the discussion.

A bit groggy, Ginny nodded.

Ben leaned over her. "I'll carry you, Ginny, if it's all right."

She rubbed her eyes and smiled slightly. "Of course. Thank you."

The rest of the gang was filing into the parlor as Ben gently placed Ginny on one of the couches. He sat on the arm of the couch, looking down at her.

"You go ahead and tell everybody, Cole," said Jesse.

Cole announced that the whole gang would be leaving at dawn. They were taking Clara's wagon and team to transport Jim.

Looking at Ginny, Cole said, "I asked Breanna about you ridin' on the mattress too, Ginny."

"You won't have to worry about me, Cole. I'm not going."

"Not goin'?"

"That's what I said."

"Why not?"

"Because I wouldn't fit in the gang anymore."

"Just because Wes is dead? You broke it off with him anyway."

"That has nothing to do with it. But I'm out of the gang."

Jesse's features flushed a deep red. "Ginny, you've got a big share of the gold coming. But if you bow out now, you won't get a piece of it!"

"I don't want stolen gold," she said flatly.

Jesse took a step closer to the couch where Ginny lay. "I don't understand this, girl! What's happened in your brain, anyhow?"

"It's not my brain that's affected, Jesse. It's my heart."

Jesse and Cole eyed each other, puzzled looks on their faces.

Fixing her with a harsh stare, Cole snapped, "What're you talkin' about?"

"I'm talking about the fact that I now have Jesus in my heart, and my old life is gone. I have a new life. My outlaw days are over."

The entire room was silent as a tomb.

Taking advantage of it, Ginny gave her testimony, telling

everyone how Dottie had shown her from the Bible about being saved and being the virtuous woman of Proverbs 31. She went on to tell them that Breanna had led her to the Lord a little while ago, and she was now going to aim her life to be priced far above rubies in the eyes of God, like the woman described in Proverbs.

The gang members sat in stunned silence.

Ginny took a deep, shuddering breath, and with tears streaming down her cheeks, she said, "I know I must face the law for the crimes I've committed while riding with the gang, but I'm trusting the Lord to work His will in my life."

Belle stared at Ginny, eyes bulging. "You're out of your mind! You've become another one of these crazy religious fanatics!"

"I'm not a religious fanatic, Belle! I'm a born-again child of God!"

"Amen!" said Ben, popping his hands together. "Praise the Lord! You did the right thing, Ginny!"

Jesse and Frank stole a furtive glance at each other. This was the same thing their father had preached until his death, and their mother had wept many tears when she saw her sons rejecting the truth over the years and finally becoming outlaws.

Neither James brother said anything, but they both knew what the other was thinking. The rest of the gang sat in silence.

Cole turned to Jesse and said, "This throws a new light on things. You and I need to have a private talk outside."

"Yeah," said Jesse. "The rest of you sit tight. We'll be back shortly."

The two gang leaders walked toward the lane leading to the road.

"I know what you're thinking, Cole."

"Tell me what I'm thinkin'."

"If we leave Ginny behind, she can tell the law the location of our hideout at Lee's Summit. And even though she hasn't been to the one at Smithville, the law will find it once she tells them its vicinity. Right?"

"You got it. Havin' this change in her, she's no good to us anymore. We could force her to go or kill her and dump her body somewhere."

"Yeah. We could. But I don't think you want to kill her any more than I do. She did us a good job, and it was really Wes who messed things up by treating her so bad."

Cole nodded as they drew up to the side of the lane. "I like Ginny. As you said, she did us a good job. I don't want to hurt her, much less kill her. But you're right; we don't dare leave her here to tell the law the location of our hideouts."

"I'm thinking, Cole, that it's probably time we find us a new hideout, anyway. You know we've been nervous about the law or the army finding us at either place. With the kind of money we're going to have when we sell the gold, it won't be a drop in the bucket to buy us some remote farm somewhere and let the law and the army look their eyes out for us."

"You're right. Let's do it."

When Cole and Jesse returned to the parlor, Cole said, "Ginny, you're right. You wouldn't fit with us anymore. We appreciate the good job you did us, and because of that, we're gonna leave you here to do what you want with your life."

"Thank you, Cole, Jesse. I was afraid you'd force me to go with you."

Jesse said, "We discussed the fact that you can tell the law the location of our two hideouts. But we're never going back to either one of them. We're going to find a new place, so you'd be wasting your breath if you told the badge-toters we can be found at the Younger farm or at the farm near Smithville."

✦

That evening after supper, the outlaws looked on while Ben led the small group of Christians in prayer as they gathered around Ginny on the couch. Ben thanked the Lord for drawing Ginny to Himself, and asked Him to bring Dottie back to them unharmed. As he continued to pray, he said, "Lord, my heart is heavy for these people in the gang. They need Jesus, but their hearts seem so hard. I pray that You will help them see that Jesus died for them on the cross, as He did for all sinners, and—"

"That's enough!" butted in Belle Reed. "Ain't none of us gonna be sucked into becomin' fanatics like you! So cut the saintly gibberish!"

"Right!" spoke up Frank James. "Leave us alone! Jesse and I had enough of that Bible stuff to do us a lifetime. We sure don't need any more of it. And the rest of this gang don't want any of it either!"

That night, after lights out, Breanna prayed once more for Dottie's safe return and thanked God that the outlaws were going to leave Ginny with Ben and Clara.

22

JUST BEFORE DAWN, BREANNA BROCKMAN emerged from the privy, wiping her mouth with a soft cloth. She stood swaying for a moment, bracing a hand against the side of the small wooden structure.

When the residual waves of nausea left her, she headed back toward the house. Charlie Pitts and Jim Reed were loading the mattress in the back of Clara's wagon by lantern light. The rest of the gang members were leading their saddled and bridled horses toward the house.

Clara Dunne and her children stood on the back porch, wearing light jackets, for the October air was cool. Clara was unhappy about losing her wagon and team, but the joy she felt from getting rid of the outlaws surpassed the loss.

Ben had carried Ginny to the back porch and now stood beside her as she sat wrapped in a blanket.

Breanna returned to the porch, and Clara laid a hand on her shoulder. "You feel better, honey?"

Breanna's face was pale as she nodded.

Presently, Jim Reed and Charlie Pitts emerged from the house, carrying Jim Younger, who was wrapped in a blanket. Bob and John Younger hopped into the bed and helped place their brother on the mattress.

As the eastern sky glowed with light, giving the promise of sunrise, the stars winked out one by one as if reluctant to give way to the day. The rolling hills and vast sweep of fields awaited the amber benediction of the sun.

Cole Younger tied his horse to the back of the wagon and climbed up onto the seat.

"All right," Jesse said, "let's all mount up!" He turned and looked at Ben. "We'll leave you with the stagecoach and the dead men. Take good care of them."

"Yeah," responded Ben, giving him a dull glance.

Breanna was leaning over Ginny, checking on her, as Belle stepped up on the porch and said, "Ginny, I want to say one more time what a fool you are to follow this religious stuff."

"You go your way, Belle, and I'll go God's."

Belle laughed. "What stupidity! And let me tell you again, Miss Fanatic, I'll keep on livin' by the gun...but I'll die in bed of old age."

When Ginny didn't reply, Belle gave her a malicious grin, wheeled about, and left the porch. She looked back once as she drew up to her horse, then mounted and rode away beside her husband.

The small group on the porch waited in silence as they watched the buggy and riders move down the lane toward the road. When they reached the road and turned east, Clara put her hands to her mouth, breathing exultantly through her fingers.

When they vanished from sight, Ben shouted, "Praise the Lord!"

"Amen!" said Breanna.

Ben motioned for all to gather around Ginny's chair. "Come. Let's give thanks to the Lord." When the amen was said, a golden tide of light was spreading across the land, giving promise of a better day.

Turning to Breanna, Ben said, "I'll saddle my horse right now and ride to Osage City. I've gotten to know the town marshal, Bruce Thornton, quite well. He can call for federal help to go after the gang and to help me search for Dottie."

"I appreciate it. Dottie can't be very far away."

"We'll find her, Breanna. I know we will. And she'll be all right."

"Yes...the Lord has given me peace in my heart about it."

"Me too," spoke up Ginny. "I don't know much about all of this yet, but I prayed for Dottie last night before I went to sleep, and something came over me that said it's going to be all right."

Clara looked toward the east. "Oh, I'm so glad they're gone!"

Suddenly little Laura gulped a sob and cried out, "I'm afraid they'll come back, Mommy! I don't want those bad men to come back!"

Clara put an arm around each of her children and pulled them close to her, telling them the bad men were gone for good.

"But they hate us!" Larry said. "Maybe they'll come back and kill us like that Cole man said!"

Ben knelt down in front of the children, taking their hands in his. "Listen to me. The bad men are gone for good. They won't be back."

Laura sucked in a shuddering breath. "You promise they won't come back, Uncle Ben? Promise?"

"Yes, honey. I promise."

His words were all the children needed. Their tears quickly dried up, but Clara still held them close as Ben rose to his feet.

"Before you go, Ben," said Breanna, "would you carry Ginny back to her bed? She needs to rest."

"Of course. Be my pleasure."

There was a sparkle in Ginny's eyes that Clara and Breanna had never seen before as Ben leaned down and picked her up, cradling her in his arms.

"Ginny, you're light as a feather," he said.

She chuckled lightly. "No, I'm not. It just seems that way because you're so strong, Ben."

Clara and Breanna looked at each other and exchanged smiles.

The morning sun was bright against the dirty windows of the old dilapidated barn, and streamers of yellow light poured through cracks in the walls.

Dub Thaxton's body was quaking and sweat beaded his pale brow. Blood was trickling from his month, and Dottie used his bandanna to wipe it off his chin.

She thought back to yesterday when she had talked to Dub about his eternal destiny. He was at death's door, and even though he was an outlaw and a killer, she wanted him to be saved. She told him how Jesus loved him and how He died on Calvary's cross to provide Dub the one and only way to miss hell. She quoted many salvation verses and explained about repentance toward God and faith in Jesus Christ, but Dub had stubbornly rejected Jesus, saying he had lived all of his life without Him and didn't need Him now.

As Dottie wiped more blood from his chin, Dub coughed and choked on it, gasping for breath. Suddenly terror filled his eyes. "Help me!" he said hoarsely, reaching out a trembling hand and grasping her sleeve. "Help me! I don't wanna go to hell!"

"I told you yesterday how to be saved, Dub. All you have to do—"

Dub Thaxton suddenly stiffened, made a strangling sound, and went limp. His eyes remained open in a wild and vacant stare.

Dottie shook her head as she forced the eyelids closed and covered his face with his hat. "Too late now, Dub."

She went outside, mounted Dub's horse, and trotted across the field. When she reached the road, she put the horse to a gallop and headed for Osage City.

Ben Tyler pushed his bay gelding as fast as he could go. He caught the attention of people along Main Street as he rode into Osage City at a full gallop. At one corner he had to veer the horse around a wagon pulling onto Main and then skidded the horse to a halt in front of the marshal's office. As he dismounted, his attention was drawn to Dottie Carroll, who was coming out the door with a tall man in black. There was a badge on his chest.

Dottie spotted him. "Ben! I'm so glad to see you!"

"Dottie! Are you all right?"

"I'm fine," she said, smiling. "How's Breanna?"

"She's fine, too."

"Praise the Lord!" said the man in black.

"Oh! I'm sorry. Ben Tyler, this is John Brockman, Breanna's husband."

As they clasped hands, John said, "Dottie's told me a lot about you, Ben. Marshal Thornton certainly speaks highly of you."

Ben grinned. "And you have a wonderful wife, Chief. Breanna's an excellent nurse."

"That she is. You're sure she's all right?"

"Yes, sir. The outlaws are gone. They took the gold and left at dawn this morning. I've come to tell Marshal Thornton so he can contact the proper authorities."

"You'd better let Marshal Thornton know quickly," said John. "He's about to go to the Western Union office and send a wire to the army, asking them to come and help him free all of you at the farm."

"I'll do that. But since he hasn't come outside yet...Dottie, how did you get away from the Thaxtons?"

"Dub's four men left yesterday to find a doctor. They never came back. Dub died this morning, so I took his horse and rode here to tell the marshal about the James-Younger gang holding all of you captive."

"I see. Then those men had to be the four who tried to steal the gold from our barn under Cole and Jesse's noses. There was a shoot-out. All four of Thaxton's men were killed. One of Jesse's men was killed, too."

"Hmm. Then it looks like the Thaxton four wanted the gold more than they wanted to find a doctor for Dub."

"I'd say so."

"Which of Jesse's men was killed?"

"Wes Logan."

"Oh! It was Wes? How did Ginny take it?"

"She handled it well. You'll be glad to know that she refused to go with the gang."

Dottie's face lit up. "Oh, wonderful!"

"I have something more to tell you about Ginny, but first I'd better go in and let the marshal know about the gang."

The door opened and Marshal Bruce Thornton came out, obviously in a hurry. He stopped in his tracks. "Ben! Mrs. Carroll just told me about— How did you get away?"

"You'll have to change what you were going to say in the telegram to the army, Marshal. Let's go in and I'll explain it."

When they were all seated in the office, Ben told Thornton the story, closing off with the news that the James-Younger gang had gone east from the farm, no doubt heading for the Missouri border.

"I'll wire the army so they can get on their trail," the marshal said.

"Good. I hope they catch them. The stagecoach and its team are still in Clara's barn, Marshal. Will you notify Wells Fargo so they can come and get them?"

"Sure will."

Thornton followed John, Ben, and Dottie outside, then hurried off to send the wire.

John looked at his sister-in-law and said, "We'd better send a wire of our own. We need to let your aunt and uncle know that you and Breanna are all right."

As they walked toward the Western Union office less than a block away, Dottie said, "I want to hear about Ginny. You said you had something to tell me, Ben."

"I sure do. She's your sister now."

"She's my wh—? Ben! Are you telling me she…?"

"Uh-huh."

Dottie stopped, which brought both men to a halt. Tears filmed her eyes. "Ben, tell me about it!"

John stood by and listened as Ben explained that because of Dottie's witness to Ginny, Breanna had the joy of leading her to the Lord.

Dottie was weeping so hard she could hardly talk. "Oh, praise the Lord!" she squeaked. "Praise the Lord! All those years in San Francisco I tried to witness to Ginny and her parents, but they wouldn't listen. I'm so thankful she opened her heart to Jesus! And this is why she wouldn't go on with the gang!"

"There's more. I'll tell you after you and Chief Brockman send your telegram."

The trio met up with Marshal Thornton in the Western

Union office. He had sent his message and was now waiting for a reply from Fort Scott.

John sent the wire to Frank and Eloise Baylor, then they bid Marshal Thornton good-bye and headed back up the street toward their horses.

"All right, Ben," said Dottie. "You said there's more. I'm listening."

John grinned. "Me too."

"Even before she got saved, Ginny saved my life."

"How's that?" Dottie asked.

Ben told her of Wes Logan's anger toward him and how Wes had pulled his gun, intending to shoot him. A split second before the gun fired, Ginny jumped in front of him and took the bullet. He explained that Breanna had removed the slug from Ginny's hip and that she would be fine when the wound healed.

"What a wonderful girl, Ben! Such courage and unselfishness."

"The English language doesn't have words to describe her, Dottie," he said, a quiver in his voice. "I've never met anyone like her. She's...well, she's—" He slapped his palm against his thigh. "See what I mean? There aren't any words. She's just too wonderful to describe!"

John laughed. "Dottie, I think our friend, Mr. Tyler, has been bitten by the love bug."

Ben shook his head. "Is it that obvious?"

"Quite."

"Very quite!" said Dottie, laughing.

Dottie Carroll, Ben Tyler, and John Brockman rode out of Osage City, heading for the Dunne farm. They rode at a leisurely pace so they could talk, and Ben told them how Ginny had given her testimony to the James-Younger bunch.

"Dottie, she told them how you talked to her about being saved and showed her in Proverbs 31 about the virtuous woman in God's eyes…and then how Breanna led her to the Lord."

Dottie rode between Ben and John and wiped tears from her face with a hankie. Ben looked past her at the tall lawman. "Chief Brockman, I need your help concerning Ginny."

"Whatever it is," Brockman said, "if it's humanly possible, consider it done."

"I appreciate that, sir. By now you know that Ginny Grayson was a part of the James-Younger gang."

"Yes."

"The reason she joined them was to be with this Wes Logan who was killed yesterday in the shoot-out at Clara's barn. She thought she was in love with him. But Ginny began to see what Logan really was. He was treating her pretty bad. She had enough of it and flat out told him right in front of a bunch of us that she realized she hadn't actually been in love with him at all. It was just infatuation. And she told Logan that by the way he had treated her, he had even killed that. She told him they were through. Even if she hadn't gotten saved, sir, she would've left the gang."

"Sounds like it," John said.

"Yesterday morning I was talking to Jesse James, Chief. Just the two of us. He was talking about Ginny, saying what a good job she had done in helping Belle Reed when they rode as passengers on the stagecoaches. While talking about it, he told me that Ginny had not shot one person since she started riding with the gang, though she carried a gun and took part in all the robberies."

"Mm-hmm," nodded John.

"Well, sir, when Ginny gave her testimony to the gang, she said she knew she must face the law, but she was trusting the Lord to work His will in her life. What I need to know is, as a chief U.S. marshal, is there anything you can do to help her? She knows she deserves to go to prison, and I realize the law will put her there unless someone within the judicial system sees that she got caught up in something over her head."

John Brockman thought on it as they continued to trot down the road. Dottie looked at Ben and silently mouthed, *He will help, believe me.*

"Tell you what, Ben. Since Ginny so boldly refused to go on with the gang, undoubtedly knowing there could have been a serious reprisal for so doing, and because she purposely took the bullet to save your life, knowing it could kill her, and because she has become a child of God with a whole new potential in her life, I will use my influence with the judicial system to get her a full pardon."

"Thank you, sir. Thank you. I guarantee you'll never be sorry."

"And I double guarantee it," said Dottie, pulling out her hankie again.

Soon the Dunne place came into view. Moments later, when they left the road and trotted their horses up the lane toward the house, they saw Breanna, Clara, and the children sitting on wooden chairs, wearing light wraps. In their midst, sitting in an overstuffed chair and wrapped in a blanket, was Ginny.

John's line of sight fixed itself on Breanna as she bounded off the porch and ran toward him.

Ben and Dottie kept going as John slid from his saddle and took his wife into his strong embrace.

When Ben and Dottie reached the house, Ben helped her from her horse, then dashed up the porch steps and knelt down in front of Ginny. He took both of her hands in his and said, "I have wonderful news!"

Her eyes were dancing. "What is it?"

Making a half turn, Ben looked back at John and Breanna.

"That man—Breanna's husband—is Chief United States Marshal John Brockman!"

"I sort of figured that's who he was," Ginny said.

Ben started to blurt out the news, then said, "No! I'll let Chief Brockman tell you."

When John and Breanna reached the porch, Breanna left John's side and wrapped her arms around her sister. "Oh, Dottie!" she said breathlessly. "I'm so glad you're all right! I prayed so hard!"

"Thank you, sweetie. I'll tell you all about it later."

"I want to hear every word!"

Dottie pressed her lips close to her sister's ear. "Have you told John about the baby?"

"No," Breanna whispered back. "I haven't had a chance."

"Do it soon."

"I will."

Breanna proudly introduced John to Clara and the children. She then led him by the hand to Ginny, who was taken a bit off balance when the tall, handsome man clicked his heels and planted a gentlemanly kiss on her hand.

"Miss Grayson," he said, "I commend you for being willing to sacrifice yourself to save Ben's life. This tells me what kind of a young lady you are. And let me say how happy I am to learn that you have become a child of God."

Blushing, Ginny said, "Thank you, sir."

Ben's face was alive with joy. "Tell her the good news, Chief."

John knelt down to look Ginny in the eye. "Ben has told me all about you riding with the James-Younger gang and why. I'm talking about Wes Logan."

"Yes, sir," she said, dropping her eyes to her lap.

Breanna laid a hand on Ginny's shoulder. The young

woman looked up and felt the warmth of Breanna's assuring smile.

"Miss Grayson. Ben tells me that in riding with the gang and taking part in the robberies, you never shot anyone. Is this so?"

"Yes, sir. I never shot anyone."

"Good. Then let me say it this way. Because of the fine character you have displayed by saving Ben's life at the risk of your own, and the courage you showed to boldly tell Jesse James and Cole Younger that you would no longer be a part of the gang, I'm going to see that you get a full pardon."

Tears welled up in Ginny's eyes and her lips trembled.

"While you're here recovering from your wound, I will ride to Topeka and talk to federal Judge Stephen Gentry. He and I have known each other for a long time. He trusts what I tell him."

Ginny blinked at her tears. "Yes, sir."

"I can tell you right now that you will get the full pardon. You won't even have to be arrested and stand before the judge."

This time, Ginny burst into sobs.

Ben dropped to his knees and took her in his arms.

While she clung to Ben and wept, Clara said, "Well, praise the Lord! This is good news!"

Breanna raised up on her tiptoes and brushed John's ear with her lips, whispering, "Darling, I have some good news too. But I only want to share it with you at the moment. Could we take a little walk?"

He looked into the eyes he loved so much and said, "M'lady, I'd love to take a walk with you."

23

BREANNA HELD ON TO JOHN'S ARM as they strolled across a field. "I feel so bad that Dottie and I didn't make it to Uncle Frank and Aunt Eloise's anniversary celebration. They must be worried sick."

"I'm sure they were, sweetheart, but they aren't now. I sent a wire to them before Dottie, Ben, and I left Osage City."

"Oh, thank you! That relieves my mind."

Breanna's heart was in her throat as they walked further. She didn't know how to start.

"Okay," John said, "what's the good news for my ears only?"

Breanna swallowed hard. "Well…" She tugged at his arm. "Can we go over there and sit down on that fallen tree?"

"Sure."

When they were sitting, Breanna said, "If you were to have one wish, but only one, what would it be?"

John laughed. "Come on, now, darlin'. That could cover a wide field. Couldn't you narrow it a little?"

"All right. If you could have one wish, and only one—about us—what would it be?"

The tall man chuckled. "I'd wish…well—"

"C'mon. What?"

John scrubbed a hand over his mouth, his fingers smoothing his mustache. "You really mean it? What would it be?"

"Yes.

"About you and me?"

"Mm-hmm."

"I don't want to hurt your feelings."

"John, you aren't going to hurt my feelings. Come on. What is it?"

He looked her square in the eye. "I'd wish for a son or a daughter."

Breanna laid her head against his shoulder. "That's really it?"

Cupping his hand behind her neck, he said, "I've hurt your feelings."

She pulled back and flashed a delighted smile. "Well, Daddy, that's exactly what you're going to get...a son or a daughter!"

John's heart lurched and his face seemed to drain of color. "You're kidding me."

Breanna reached up and touched his cheek. "I'm not kidding you. You're going to have a son or a daughter in about seven months."

John leaped to his feet and gripped her shoulders. "Breanna Baylor Brockman...it's really true?"

"Yes," she said, choking on the word.

He looked toward heaven and shouted, "Oh, thank You, Lord! Thank You! I'm going to have a—I mean, Breanna's going to have a baby! Hallelujah! Glory to God! Whoopee!"

Breanna smiled through her tears as he sat down beside her and laid his hand over hers. "Well, darling," she said, "you're going to get your wish. I'm sure glad it wasn't something else."

His throat filled with emotion as he wrapped his arms

around her and kissed her soundly, then said, "When it comes to us, there could be no greater wish."

Ben and Ginny were alone on the back porch after Clara and the children went in the house to give them some time together.

Ben leaned close and said, "Ginny, what will you want to do when you're healed up and can travel? Where will you go?"

"The first thing I want to do is go back to my aunt and uncle and ask their forgiveness."

"I'll be glad to take you there," he said.

"Thank you, Ben."

"But where will you live? Back with them?"

"I…I don't know. I'm sure they will forgive me, but they might not want me living in their house anymore."

Ben swallowed hard. "Ah…Ginny?"

"Mm-hmm?"

"I…well, I've got to tell you something."

"Yes?"

"I'm falling in love with you. I…I want to court you."

Ginny's eyes widened. "Oh, Ben! Really?"

"Really."

She put her hand over her heart. "I have to tell you—"

"What?"

"I'm falling in love with you, too. I want you to court me."

Ben's hands trembled as he took hold of hers. "The preacher was right. He was right!"

"What do you mean, Ben?"

"We have a new pastor. He was here just the other day. He told me that because I was willing to sell my farm and come here to take care of Clara and the children, God had a special blessing for me."

Ginny tilted her head and frowned. "I don't understand."

"Oh, Ginny, don't you see? If I hadn't come here I would never have met you! You're my special blessing, Ginny! You!"

They embraced, and while they held each other, Ginny said, "I'm glad you look at me as a special blessing."

"That's exactly what you are, and you always will be." Ben eased back to look at her. "I can't court you unless you live close by."

"That's true."

"I know." Suddenly Ben saw Clara standing at the door. "Oh, sis, come here."

"Ben, I'm sorry," she said. "I didn't mean to eavesdrop. I heard your excited voices and I came to make sure everything was all right."

"It's more than all right, sis. Ginny and I—"

"I know. I heard."

"Good! What I want to know, sis…would it be all right if Ginny lived here with you and the children for…well, for a while?"

"Of course, but—"

"I know, it wouldn't be proper for me to live here in your house if Ginny was living here. So I'll tell you what."

"What?"

"You know the Maxwell house down the road? It's for rent. I can live there and still take care of the farm for you. It's only a couple of miles."

Tears were flowing down Ginny's cheeks as she searched his eyes and said, "Ben, are you sure?"

"I'm positive."

She looked up at Clara. "Are you sure?"

"Honey, I'd love to have you! Just think! We've got a wonderful church. You can get baptized and really begin to grow.

Our new pastor is a great preacher. You'll like him. His wife is sweet. The people of the church will love you."

A serious expression came over Ginny's face. "Then, if I live with you, I'll do my share of work around the house and in the yard. I'll wash and iron and help you cook and—"

Clara interrupted her with a laugh. "Hey, leave me a little something to do!"

"Then you'll stay?" Ben said, squeezing her hand.

"Of course."

"Wonderful! As soon as you can travel, I'll take you to see your aunt and uncle."

"Well!" said Clara. "I'm going to go in and tell Larry and Laura that we have a new permanent houseguest!"

"Sis…" said Ben.

"Yes?"

"I…well, why don't you tell them Ginny will be staying here for…well, a while?"

Clara giggled like a little girl. "All right. I'll tell them we have a new permanent houseguest for a while!" With that, she hurried into the house.

Ben knelt in front of Ginny again and said, "Darlin', in my eyes you have already reached it."

"Reached what?" she asked, joyful tears forming in her eyes.

He leaned close and kissed her cheek. "Your price is already far above rubies!"

EPILOGUE

JIM REED LIVED BY THE GUN and died by the gun. He was shot and killed in August 1874, by bounty hunter John T. Morris, who collected a handsome amount for his deed.

On June 5, 1880, Reed's widow, Belle, married outlaw Sam Starr and continued her life as "Bandit Queen," Belle Starr. Belle lived by the gun and saw her gun-toting husband, Sam, shot down and killed by an old enemy named Frank West on December 17, 1886.

Belle continued to live by the gun and made many enemies in her outlaw career. She died by the gun on Sunday, February 3, 1889, while riding alone on horseback. An unknown assailant shot her from the saddle. As she lay in the road she apparently tried to raise herself up, but a second shotgun blast struck her in the face and killed her. The killer was never identified.

John Younger lived by the gun. He was shot dead by Pinkerton detective Louis Lull and a lawman named Ed Daniels on March 17, 1874.

Jim Younger, who lived by the gun and carried the scars to prove it, finally came to the place where life seemed empty and hopeless. On October 18, 1902, he shot himself in the right temple and died instantly.

Jesse James continued to live by the gun as the years passed. His gang was pulling more and more train robberies and infuriating the railroads, who finally joined together and offered a ten-thousand-dollar reward for Jesse's capture or death, emphasizing that they would prefer the latter. The temptation of such an amount was too much for brothers Bob and Charlie Ford, who were fairly new members of the James gang.

On Monday morning, April 3, 1882, the Ford brothers rode up to the white frame house on the hill in St. Joseph, Missouri, where Jesse, his wife, and two children were living. Jesse invited them into the parlor. Zee and the children were in the kitchen. The three outlaws sat down to talk. The Ford brothers had already agreed that Bob would be the one to shoot Jesse. It would be Charlie's job to get Jesse's attention away from Bob. As it turned out, Charlie didn't have to do a thing. Jesse looked up on the wall at his prized photograph of General Thomas J. "Stonewall" Jackson and noticed that it was hanging crookedly. He stood on a straight-backed chair to adjust the frame, and while his back was toward the Ford brothers, Bob shot him in the head, killing him instantly.

In 1884, Charlie Ford heard rumors being circulated in the outlaw world that Frank James had vowed revenge on him and his brother. The thought of a life of looking over his shoulder was more than he could bear. Charlie put a gun to his head and committed suicide.

Bob Ford had found fame in killing the country's most notorious outlaw, and until early 1892, he worked in carnivals and Wild West shows doing a melodrama called "How I Killed Jesse James." In mid-1892, Bob left the carnival and Wild West circuit and opened a saloon. A few days later, Bob was shot dead by a drunken gunman in the employ of a competitive saloon.